DOUGLAS FORD

The Bloody Bucket

VISSARIA COUNTY
DISPATCHES

First published by Vissaria County Dispatches 2026

This novel is entirely a work of fiction. The names, characters and incidents portrayed in it are the work of the author's imagination. Any resemblance to actual persons, living or dead, events or localities is entirely coincidental.

Douglas Ford asserts the moral right to be identified as the author of this work.

No generative AI was used to create the text or cover art of this publication, nor the logo for Vissaria County Dispatches. Logo design by Jeff Darwin.

First edition

ISBN: 979-8-9895731-7-2

Editing by Lisa Lee Tone
Cover art by Jeff Darwin

This book was professionally typeset on Reedsy.
Find out more at reedsy.com

Contents

Advance Praise for The Bloody Bucket

"Douglas Ford's *The Bloody Bucket* is a potent blend of history, hauntings, twisted horns, and ancient evil in a dark academia tale that is steeped in Florida unease and stained with blood. Full of stories inside stories, of goats and crows, possession and poetry, sacrifices and open wounds, *The Bloody Bucket* is a masterpiece of the occult and deeply, deeply disturbing. Expect to see this one on all the award lists."**—Lee Murray, five-time Bram Stoker Award®-winning author of *Grotesque: Monster Stories***

"Where do you find inspiration for a deeply terrifying haunt? Sometimes it's there in the history of the land right under your feet, in the tangled web of stories passed down for generations. Steeped in the lush and sometimes dangerous landscape of Florida, *The Bloody Bucket* is a chilling reminder that while we may try to forget the past, it's never all that far away. Ford skillfully weaves history, folklore, and just the right bit of the terrifying occult into a mesmerizing tale that will resonate long after you close the cover."**—Jennifer McMahon, author of *My Darling Girl***

"Douglas Ford is a Floridian witch doctor, the anti-Carl Hiassen, a swampland shaman capable of imbuing every page with the humidity and kudzu and blood of the Alligator State and exposing its scaly underbelly. *The Bloody Bucket* overflows with the brackish beauty of a writer besotted by an unplumbed region and regaling the rest of us with its exquisite literary spillover." **— Clay McLeod Chapman, author of *Wake Up and Open Your Eyes***

"Ford has concocted the perfect cocktail: mixing one part Gothic, one part slasher, and one part Florida folklore. *The Bloody Bucket* will intoxicate you but it will not leave you hungover. Instead, you will want to return to its pages to imbibe again and again."—**Elaine Pascale, author of *The Solstice***

"Ford delicately weaves a web of myth, folklore, and the supernatural, expertly exploring both personal and collective trauma. I've not read a better story about Florida. This book is truly special."—**Robbie Dorman, author of *Words of Christ in Red* and *Underneath***

"Reading *The Bloody Bucket* is like sleepwalking into the dark and tangled cypress swamps of Old Florida and succumbing to a fever dream, where the bloody heart of a long-dead beast echoes like a war drum, stirring up spirits, monsters, and devils, whose dark histories and terrible secrets are woven into a rich tapestry of folklore. This is Douglas Ford at his absolute best, a tangled web of haunted history steeped in blood, grief, guilt, and terror. Destined to be one of the year's best horror novels."—**Derik Cavignano, award-winning author of *The Art of Dying* and *The Burying Point***

"A delicious dark blend of fiction: Dark Academia, dark history, dark folklore, a touch of *Hell House LLC*, a dash of *Sinners*. This is the kind of horror novel a student of horror writes for those us who love horror. "—**Mark Matthews, author of *To Those Willing to Drown***

"Beginning with an omen and building on mystery and dread, *The Bloody Bucket* by Douglas Ford is a cache for horror fans, academia veterans, and literature buffs alike. The hopes and anxieties of the protagonist, Nat, will endear her to readers while worry for her brings them to the edge of their seats. What waits for her on the marshy edge of a small Florida campus? Well, that's for Ford to know and the rest of us to find out." —**Rebecca Cuthbert, author of *The Hauntings Back Home* and *Six O'Clock House & Other Strange Tales***

For Jerlin, with all my love and devotion.

Also, for librarians everywhere,
but especially in Florida.

Keep up the good fight.

"The gods are dying . . . Somewhere in space there are floating unheard-of corpses."
—Jean Ray

I

Part One

"Every midnight open the box and let the beasts out."
—Zora Neale Hurston

One

The call came soon after the crow fell from the sky, fried dead by electrical current.

Erik saw the whole thing happen, leaving him in a confused mixture of horror, awe, and sadness. When he found me, I could see each emotion lighting up his pupils like passing billboards, each blink like a destination getting closer and closer. I imagined the voice of some unseen announcer: *Come see the sizzling crow lying on its back! Up ahead soon—see the shock recorded in the crow's black eyes! Not too late to witness the zapped crow's dying breath!* He led me outside to where the branches of a pine tree grew perilously close to a power line. Underneath those branches, I saw it, the crow on its back, just like Erik described. Other crows circled overhead, expressing their grief and anger in loud caws.

The word for a group of crows came to mind: a *murder.*

"You said a long time ago it couldn't electrocute them," Erik said. He meant the power line, its proximity to the tree branches a perpetual source of concern. We crouched over the fallen bird, and he gazed up at the sky as if the poor thing's comrades might hear the implication in his statement—that we somehow bore responsibility for this death.

My eyes followed his, and I felt the accusation of the crows circling overhead. I pointed toward the branches of the pine, now vacated of all avian life. "You see how they're avoiding those branches?"

Erik followed my finger and nodded. "Do they think the tree did it?"

"Maybe. But do you know what I think really happened?"

He shook his head.

"I think the bird accidently created a connection. An electrical one. See how close the branch is to the power line?"

Erik studied their proximity and nodded. "I kept asking you if it was dangerous, and you said no."

"It's not—except I think the bird touched both the branch and the wire at the same time. If it just landed on one or the other, it would've been fine. But it probably touched them both at once. Maybe when it landed."

"Zap," said Erik.

"Yeah. Zap."

"I bet he never saw it coming," said Erik, and I wished he hadn't said that, because immediately, a different kind of connection formed in my brain. *Like stepping off a curb in front of a speeding car.* I pushed the association away as quickly as I could. As quickly as I walked past mirrors because I often didn't like what I saw in reflecting glass. *Shut it away*, I told myself.

"But you said you saw the whole thing. Maybe it happened differently."

Still looking at the dead bird, Erik said, "I heard a sound like hissing and saw him fall. What should we do with him? Is it safe to touch him? Because of the electricity, I mean."

At the age of thirteen, my brother possessed an intelligence that continually impressed me. At his age, I used to pick up objects all the time without any thought at all, including a few dead things. I smiled at him. He thought ahead. He'd never step off a curb . . .

Shut it away.

"I don't know. Probably? Let's be on the safe side." I pointed toward the garage, still not cleaned out since we lost our father, leaving the house and an unpaid mortgage in my name. "Let's grab some gloves and an old box."

"We can bury him?"

"Sure."

My phone chose that moment to ring. Normally, I ignored numbers I didn't recognize, but a premonition told me to answer. The bird's death by electricity left a strange energy in the air. My mother would have reminded us to beware strange omens and not accept unexpected calls when birds fall from the heavens. But she was dead. I took a few steps away and answered.

"Hello?" Overhead, the air churned with the wings of the dead crow's friends.

"Natacha Miller?"

I didn't answer, knowing that someone using my full name usually wanted an overdue payment. From the sky came an angry squawk that chided me for not having better sense.

Then, as if offended by silence, the voice amended my name, using the one that I preferred.

"Nat?"

"Yeah, speaking." Instinctively, I wandered away from the tree and the power line. I looked back and saw Erik had gone looking for the gloves and the box.

"This doesn't sound like Nat. This might be a hustle. No one hustles Dick Fowler."

Hearing that name summoned memories of a ruffled tweed jacket and gin I could smell through the receiver. I held the phone away as if to keep it from overpowering me. I remembered Fowler all too well. "It's Nat, all right. I met you at SOFA," I said, using the acronym of an academic organization called *Scholars of Fantastic Art.* I no longer belonged to SOFA or went to their annual conference, where academics, both employed and unemployed, met to share papers on works of fantasy and horror literature. Once upon a time, I finished my master's degree with a plan to forge onward toward earning a PhD. I met Fowler at one of those conferences, where I became a little too acquainted with his gin-soaked breath. Probably not as well acquainted as he wanted.

On the phone, Fowler said, "I remember you with an accent. A delightful one. Like wind in the Caribbean. A tasty cocktail under a palm tree."

My finger hovered over the button that would have ended the call, wondering how anyone, much less an academic with even the barest knowledge of post-colonialism, could come up with something so blatantly offensive. "Seriously? You didn't just say that to me. Who calls someone out of the blue and says something like that?" Never mind that my voice sounded nothing like that. "I'm hanging up now."

"No, wait, don't go. *Now* I recognize your voice. I guess I remember you sounding different. Besides, I meant it as a compliment. That's what I teach my students when they write persuasive essays. Strategic use of flattery."

"It wasn't flattering at all. I'd say you failed in dramatic fashion," I said. "How did you even get my number?"

"You gave it to me. Quite the networker you were, as I recall. Full of energy and enthusiasm. We talked about you hoped to find a faculty gig near home someday. That's how we got to talking. You said you'd give anything to teach at a college like mine. *Anything*. That is, once you got the PhD. That ever happen?"

"No, just the master's degree."

"You ever get a job?"

"I work at the Shell Factory," I said, referring to my job at a local tourist attraction where vacationers shopped for knickknacks.

"They make shells in factories now? What a brave new world. When I was growing up, they were free. You just had to go to the beach. Look, I'm on the hunt for someone to do some teaching." He went on to describe a vacancy he needed to fill at a regional state college, and classes started soon—within weeks, in fact. I let him talk, but I already planned to turn him down. I knew what kind of job he meant—he didn't want an actual professor but an adjunct instructor, the kind of gig that barely paid a living wage. I could make more money working retail, thank you very much, and I wouldn't have to grade any papers.

But before I could finish turning him down, he interrupted me. "Don't say no yet. I haven't told you the best part. One of the classes is called Literature of Horror and the Supernatural."

He paused to let that sink in. And irritatingly enough, I did like the sound of it.

I thought I'd let that old dream fade—making a place for myself in academia by exploring the disreputable stuff of nightmares. Wraiths and monsters, ghosts and clanking chains. I remembered the version of myself who met Fowler at SOFA. I'd given her up for dead.

"Go on," I said. "I'm listening."

He went on to explain how the professor scheduled to teach the course had become unavailable. Fowler revealed few details, mumbling something about him needing personal time to deal with some issues. As Fowler described the responsibilities that came with the job, I felt the more idealistic version of myself push away the dirt and reach up from the grave with a skeletal hand. That version of myself didn't care about the unpleasant reality of teaching college. Most people think college instructors make big bucks, enjoy jobs that come with limitless security. In truth, teaching part-time as an adjunct is strictly low wage, with work dependent on fluctuating enrollment. Everyone I knew who tried it ended up tending bars or working retail during their off-hours.

"You're right," I said when Fowler finished. "That's appealing. But the money's still not worth it." I paused. "Not unless it's full-time with benefits."

"Okay, no, it's not. Not exactly, *but . . .*" He let that word stretch out for an eternity, as if something really good would follow it. "There's an additional stipend to serve as an advisor to a student club. All told, not premium pay, but better than average. What do you say?"

"What's the club?" I edged closer to saying yes. The Shell Factory didn't pay so great either, and Erik and I needed money.

At the SOFA Conference where we met, Fowler demonstrated the smile he liked to bestow upon students caught cheating, one that combined malevolence with a certain kind of glee that comes from catching a troublesome rodent in a trap. Somehow, it made him look younger than his fifty-odd boozy, cigarette-huffing years. I imagined that smile as I listened to what he said next. I counted off the years since I saw him and wondered how it made him look now.

"They're called the Horror and Occult League," he said. "They fought hard to keep the 'occult' part in their name. A petition from the Bible Study Club nearly garnered enough signatures to get them to change the name. A lot of resentment still going on there. Anyway, *HOL*"—he pronounced this as *hole*, and once more, I imagined him with that grin—"they put together a haunted house every fall. Gets quite elaborate, you know? A little more than just scary sounds, makeup, fake blood, jumping out and screaming *boo!* at the suckers who pay five bucks to get in. The community likes it because they donate the proceeds to a good cause. Orphans, I think. Or maybe the mothers of orphans."

"Mothers of orphans? Do they send the money to a cemetery?"

"Maybe. By the looks of a couple of them, you'd think they live in a cemetery. Anyway, they need a faculty sponsor, and no one wants to touch it because of how involved it gets." He paused, perhaps to consider how unattractive he made it sound. "Students do the work, though. The faculty advisor just—well, advises. Makes sure they don't do something stupid, like pick an inappropriate theme. And it makes sense for the person teaching Literature of Horror and the Supernatural course to also advise *HOL*. Do you see now why I'm calling you?"

I did. I bit my lip. Already, I started imagining ways I could tie in the curriculum with the haunted house project, my brain already devising thematic links, extra credit assignments. The haunted house could function as an interactive text of sorts, one correlating with the written works we read in class. I felt my skin tingle the way it used to when I got a good idea for a journal article or a conference paper. I liked that feeling a lot.

Then a mental image brought it all crashing down. A familiar one that shut me down every time. A body, falling into the street, just in time for the wheels of a car to roll over it, crushing it horribly.

It. I called *her* an *it*. I didn't deserve to pursue dreams, not even their pale imitations.

But I didn't say no. Instead, I responded with practical matters in mind. "How much is the stipend?"

When he told me, I laughed. Snorted, mostly.

"Seriously? You call that *close* to premium pay?"

"You know what I make, Nat? I mean it when I say it's close."

"You make more than that," I said.

"Yeah, only because I chair a department."

"And you have health insurance," I said. "Do I get health insurance?"

In the pause that followed, I could hear the sound of his breath. I wondered if those sounds signified thinking or frustration. Probably both. No doubt he expected me to give him the answer he wanted. Maybe he came away from our last meeting with the impression he could talk me into anything if he just worked at it hard enough. I disappointed him then, and I would disappoint now. It didn't take a detective to see that Fowler held a high opinion of himself and expected other people to do the same.

When he failed to answer, I said, "Without the insurance, the answer is no."

"Let me get back to you on that. In the meantime, you have my number." He finished by saying "Call me" in a singsong way.

I hung up and walked around in a daze. Even if I wanted to agree to his terms, maintaining the house and taking care of my brother required money. And speaking of that brother, I remembered I'd left Erik alone to deal with the electrocuted bird. I normally pace when I talk on the phone, and I managed to travel halfway around the block without realizing it, leaving him out of my line of sight. I hustled back the way I came, worried that he tried to pick up the dead bird with his bare hands. For all I knew, he could suffer a residual shock or catch some awful, mutated flu.

But I saw Erik kneeling in the same place, a pair of oversized rubber gloves covering his arms up to the elbows. On the ground before him sat a shoebox, now entombing the dead bird. On my approach, he held it out to me. With him kneeling, it looked like an offering of some kind.

"There was tissue inside," he said. "I used it for padding."

I nodded. "You did good."

"What do we do now?"

I hadn't thought everything through, a lamentable trend lately. "Bury it, I suppose."

Together we surveyed our dingy neighborhood, with its weeded lots, its busted lawn furniture, cars with missing wheels, broken glass. The bird chose an inhospitable place to die.

"Where?" asked Erik.

I shrugged. "We'll figure it out later. Maybe we bury him without the box."

Erik looked at me as if he might start crying.

"Or *with* the box," I said. "We'll put him someplace safe in the meantime."

"Promise?" Losing both of his parents, Erik believed in treating the dead well. I, on the other hand, preferred ignoring them. At least as much as they let me.

"I promise."

I set the box on a crowded shelf in the garage. I returned the rubber gloves too, fully intending to keep my promise.

But I forgot, another item in a long list of failures. The bird sat forgotten in its makeshift coffin for a long while—long past the time it took me to come to a decision about Fowler's offer—not quite as dead as we originally thought but not really alive either.

Two

Fowler didn't wait for me to pick up the phone. Instead, he called back the next day to say he couldn't swing insurance. "But if you get sick with the crud or fall off a building, I'll personally pay your doctor bills if you take this job. That's a Fowler guarantee."

"Based on what you told me the other day, I wouldn't think you could afford that."

"I can't, but people pay good money for kidneys, I hear. Or is it livers? I hope it isn't livers because I only have one and I'm still using it. I think. How about it?"

It took me a moment to process he meant would I take the job, not whether I would consider buying his kidney. I considered the circumstances, as well as his apparent desperation. Would he, I wondered, put his willingness to pay medical expenses in writing? He wouldn't want to hear about Erik's circumstances, not just his need for medication to help with a stubborn mood disorder, one that exasperated the teachers who insisted upon calling him "Erika." Calls came weekly, along with pamphlets put together by "concerned parent" groups about how kids Erik's age couldn't make decisions for themselves yet, and anything outside the norm would only "confuse" other students. I couldn't ignore the calls, but I could throw away the pamphlets. Which I did.

After more haggling, I finally agreed to meet Fowler on the campus—a smaller "satellite" one since it served a modestly sized area, with only a few hundred students enrolled. Fowler said to find him near the lake that sat on the perimeter of the campus.

"Why there?" I asked.

"I wanted to show you where they set up their annual haunted house—or 'haunt,' as they like to call it."

"That's not until October, right? You make it sound more important than the class."

"Because it is *as* important as the class. Without one, there's not the other. And tuition pays the bills."

"And helps support the mothers of orphans," I said.

"See, you get it. Glad to have you on board. You'll fit right in."

"I haven't agreed to anything yet."

"You will." Then he rang off.

I pictured the lake as something dug out for drainage, but it looked much larger, more ecologically complex, with wild grass, birds, and alligators. The latter announced their presence with croaking, but no one could miss the *Don't Molest the Alligators* signs positioned around the lake by Florida Fish and Wildlife. Beyond it ran a woodland corridor, beginning just near the shore on the opposite side of the campus's few buildings. To reach the pavilion where Fowler wanted to meet, one had to walk a hiking trail that zigzagged around the lake. The pavilion, positioned ideally for biology students to study local plants and wildlife, now primarily served as the site of the haunted house. Modest in size, it functioned as the framework for the plywood that would go up and enclose the interior.

I found Fowler standing in the middle of the pavilion, staring at his feet. I assumed he hadn't noticed my approach, but then he decided to speak. "Good to see you, Nat." He didn't look up, his feet apparently too fascinating.

Only a few years had passed since I'd met Fowler, yet he looked much older than the white middle-aged guy I found mildly attractive and repulsive at the same time. Not simply because he looked a bit grayer with a more noticeable paunch, but because his face looked hollowed-out, with deep pits where I once saw lively hazel eyes. His cheeks looked sunken too. I wondered if some illness had befallen him, or if the stress of his job caused the changes.

I walked closer to see what occupied his attention.

A rust-colored stain covered a crack in the foundation near his feet. Using the toe of his loafer, he rubbed it, trying to clear it away.

"We ought to get this cleaned up," he said as if I already worked for him and needed to carry out his orders.

"That looks like blood," I said.

"You think? I thought it was nail polish. Of course it's blood. Like an alligator crawled up here to have its period." His voice trailed off as he switched to the heel of his shoe, but it still wouldn't go away.

"Alligators don't have periods," I said. At least I didn't think they did.

He didn't answer, and I almost asked if he'd like me to leave him alone while he worked on the stain. Then I noticed the flock of crows roosting in the exposed rafters overhead. They seemed to regard me in judgment, and I wondered if they somehow left that bloodstain for me to see, intending to convey a message. A warning, maybe, or perhaps a threat. A while back, while researching a paper on Edgar Allan Poe, I read articles about birds like these, birds that belonged to the corvid family—ravens, rooks, crows, and the like—and I learned that they possessed uncanny intelligence. They remembered human faces, and they even seemed to communicate with other birds when a particular human did them wrong. I wondered if news of the electrocuted crow had reached this congregation here and if they all intended to somehow hold me accountable. A familiar guilt came over me, one that I never could escape. A deep swell of anxiety filled me. I still hadn't done anything with the shoebox containing the dead crow. That needed addressing as soon as possible.

Fowler drew my attention away from the birds by pointing out the supports of pavilion, challenging me to imagine how the structure transformed with big sheets of plywood screwed in, creating what amounted to a modest-sized house.

"It doesn't seem like it would be that much," he said, "but you'd be surprised. It's remarkably effective, especially walls installed inside." Here, he pointed to the interior supports. Above us, the birds chattered, and I wondered if they became trapped inside.

"You sound like a fan of the final product."

"Not on your life. I stay away. I'm surprised you haven't come over and done a walk-through. It gets a lot of talk and publicity, all that shit. I figured you'd have heard about it, being a fan of the spooky stuff. You sure your credentials are in order?"

I began to wonder if I stepped unwittingly into a formal job interview and if he wanted to meet me here to see how I measured up. Although I decided I wanted the job, I didn't want to kiss up to him. No more doing that for men like him.

I shrugged. "What can I say? Never been here."

"I figured you had," he said. "At least, I got that impression when we met. You made quite an impact on everyone. A real whiz kid."

Apparently, since you saved my number. I didn't say it out loud, though.

He shrugged now, though I couldn't tell if he meant to mock me. "Doesn't matter. The students put it together. They're a committed bunch. Maybe even destined for commitment, if you get my drift. Some of them already belong in straitjackets. We keep the plywood locked in a facilities shed on the other side of the campus. It goes up in a weekend, assuming everyone pitches in."

"Everyone? Including you?"

"Ha, yeah, right. By everyone, I mean students and faculty advisor."

I didn't say anything.

"That's why the job comes with a stipend," he said. "Once the walls go up, you'll be surprised."

"Surprised at what?"

His voice changed, became serious. "At how big it suddenly feels. How the walls form a corridor that seems to wind further than it should, almost like it goes beyond the dimensions of all this." He held out his arms to signify the whole enclosure. But his eyes looked down, once more considering the rust-colored stain. I studied it as well, trying to discern a shape, a pattern, as if someone left it there to convey a message. But I saw only an inscrutable mass, the result of someone spilling a vat of liquid on this spot. Liquid like blood. A vat like a body. Again, Fowler rubbed at it with his loafer, causing some of it to flake away into the wind.

For some reason, that made him smile, stretching his face, making his gauntness seem all the way evident. I breathed the air, detecting some of the gin I remember on his breath, his face too close to mine. Or maybe time simply clouded my earlier memory of him. Until he spoke.

"What do you say," he said, "that we go somewhere else and get you hired?"

What do you say we go somewhere more quiet?

Not then, and not now.

"Did I say I'd take the job?"

His smile deepened, along with the crevices of his face. If he meant it to look friendly, he missed the mark. He knew he had me. I wanted the job.

"Of course you will. Let's get you some textbooks so you can get started on the syllabus for that course you've dreamed of teaching."

We set forth along the path, my mind retracing the steps of the conversation, realizing I let something slip by. Behind us, the birds grew noisy, forming a chorus of expletives to celebrate our parting. I made a mental note to see about the box containing the dead bird at home. I chanced a glance back, noticing that several of the birds flew down to where we stood just a few moments before.

"They've been peculiar today," he said, noticing the attention I paid them. "Almost pissed off."

I nodded and allowed myself one more glance back, in the process noticing something else. Although the crows now occupied the floor of the pavilion, they avoided the brown stain. Their sounds continued, as if laughing at me for nearly failing to notice his little slip.

If he'd never gone inside the haunt, I wondered, how did he know about how big it seemed on the inside?

Three

I came home with my arms full of textbooks and my fingertips stained with black ink. To process my employment, the college needed to check my fingerprints, something I failed to anticipate. The public safety officer on the staff handled the fingerprinting, a retired police officer from New York named Carter who didn't seem to enjoy my attempt to joke and make light of the process.

"Call me Sarge," he said in the sort of northeast accent I associated with the snowbirds who came into the Shell Factory.

"Nat," I said, introducing myself. "Say, Sarge? When you run those prints through your machine, how soon will you get the results?"

Sarge glanced up at me as he pressed my fingers onto card stock. I saw the slightest hint of irritation. Moments before, he'd explained how the state's efforts to slash budgets meant taking my fingerprints the "old-fashioned" way, using ink and paper rather than recording them digitally. True to police form, he pretended to not hear and thus forced me to repeat the question, maybe to see if I would divulge a guilty secret, implicate myself somehow. Never interrupt when the suspect starts talking.

"Because my guess is that the college won't hire a notorious jewel thief," I said.

Not even a smile as he returned his materials to a supply closet. He regarded me as he wiped his hands on the seat of his pants.

"Forty-eight hours," he said.

He watched my reaction, noting my respiration, counting my heart beats. His brown eyes watched me with such stillness that I wondered if he could use them to read my blood pressure.

"You get results in just forty-eight hours?" I asked.

"Give or take."

He continued to study me.

"Thanks for the information," I said. Fowler had already given me the textbooks, which I gathered into my arms before heading toward the door.

"Miss Miller?"

I stopped and looked back, expecting him to say he didn't need the results to detect a liar in his presence. But he said, "You the one who's going to start up the haunted house in October?"

As easily as I could, I let go of the breath trapped in my lungs. "Looks that way. Any advice?"

"Yeah. Watch yourself. I'm here to keep out the hooligans, but I need you to do your part. Don't let things get out of control."

"Things get out of control?"

He made a face, his hands waving invisible objects in the air, all to signify what a dumb question I just asked.

"People get rambunctious. Overenthusiastic. A little too creative in all the wrong ways."

"What are the wrong ways?" I put down the books, determined to defend students I'd not yet met.

"We had a little incident last year that I'd rather not see repeated. I'm thinking that if the students tone things down, maybe keep it wholesome this time, maybe we won't have history repeat itself. That's all I'm saying."

I moved closer, standing straight the way my mother taught me to do when people wanted to judge things about me, like how my hair kinked a little too much for a girl with green eyes. *Hold yourself tall, girl,* my mother would say when she tried to instill in me the kind of courage it took for her to make an improbable voyage across the water from Haiti to the beach where my father eventually found her exhausted and sodden. Already, I could sense that I might have problems with Sarge telling me how I should do my job, and I hadn't even passed my fingerprint check yet.

"What happened, if you don't mind me asking?"

"You could ask Tom Dash," he said. "Assuming you could find him. Good luck with that, what with his little sabbatical and all."

A beat passed as a tiny duel played out between us, neither wanting to surrender by looking away first. He spoke the name as if I should know it and to confess I didn't know it would award him some sort of victory. Tom Dash? Where had I heard that name? Then it dawned on me—the name in the textbooks Fowler piled into my arms. *Professor Dash*, the person originally assigned the courses I just agreed to teach. Not once had I thought to ask why Dash decided to step away from his position. Now, Sarge wanted to play some game where he expected me to hunt him down and ask him questions Sarge himself could easily answer.

"Why not just tell me your version of things?" I said.

"Not my job to fill you in. That's for your supervisor to do. I just want everything to stay on the up-and-up, and that means maintaining safety for our faculty and students. You been to the pavilion yet?"

I nodded.

"Well, did you notice camping gear anywhere around it? Trash and the like?"

I could recall nothing of the kind. Nothing besides the giant blood mark. And the birds. I considered mentioning the blood (assuming that it was blood) but decided against it. "No, I didn't see anything like that."

He huffed as if he didn't believe me. "Well, maybe they saw you coming and decided to keep out of sight. They prefer coming out at night—you know, when it cools down—so maybe they were sleeping."

"Who is *they*?"

"The homeless. Vagrants. Might as well call it a leper colony. We have a problem with them camping around here. Pavilion provides shelter when it rains. Best to tear it down, if you ask me. Come fall, when the haunted house goes up, they'll try to take up residence inside." A gruff laugh before he added, "They blend right in with the decorations. Some of them try to play a part by sitting up suddenly and saying *boo!* Not at all what we want at a wholesome family event."

"I'll keep that in mind," I said.

"You do that," said Sarge. He dismissed me by gazing down at the paperwork on his desk. As I turned, he said something under his breath.

I paced back to stand in front of him again, convinced he hadn't meant for me to hear him. "What?"

He cast his eyes up at me briefly before returning his attention to his desk. "Forty-eight hours. Usually less. For the fingerprint results."

I acknowledged him with as stoic a nod as I could manage, not letting my face relax into worry until I stepped outside and away from view. *Show no weakness,* I reminded myself as I walked back to the faculty offices, where I decided to have one more word with Fowler. With summer waning, the campus felt quiet and empty. My eyes shifted to the lake and the trees on the opposite bank, where the pavilion nestled, silent and brooding.

Unlike Sarge, I didn't fear or mistrust the homeless. I didn't call them *lepers.* In fact, it often felt like my situation only needed to worsen slightly for me to wind up in their ranks. So many of us just one step removed. Yet I did sense someone—or something—looking back at me, and I didn't like the feeling.

I found Fowler in his office surrounded by crowds of books and unfiled papers, his form slumped over an ancient-looking laptop. He closed it when he saw me standing in his doorway. Holding the books against my chest, I waved with my free hand.

He pointed at my fingertips. "That ink doesn't look dry yet."

"About that."

I paused, and he waited.

"There was a thing that happened a little while ago. A thing that happened to me. Or really, a thing I did. I still haven't completely decided which. The thing is, when I filled out that application you gave me, I didn't mention it."

Once more, he waited me out. I felt like I was talking to Sarge again, such men who let silence linger until the accused implicates herself. Fuck that. I would wait him out, see how he liked it.

Finally, he caved. "Did someone die?"

"Yes."

Another silence.

"Were you arrested?" he asked.

"Yes."

"And you didn't put it on your application." Not a question. Something in his expression changed. A hint of judgment, or maybe just the realization that the answer to his problems turned out to be a fuck-up.

I felt my palms sweat as I pressed the books tighter to my chest. Part of me wanted to drop them and run. The other part wanted to run and take them. Maybe I didn't realize how badly I wanted this chance to teach what I loved, no matter how shitty the pay.

"Look," I said, "you called me out of the blue. I didn't come to you. I can go back to my old job."

"The Shell Factory. I still don't know what they make. Do they really—"

I cut him off. "It was an oversight, okay? I just don't like thinking about it."

He blinked several times. "Were you charged with criminal action?"

"No," I said.

"Like you said, then: an oversight. Don't worry about it."

I started to protest. I didn't have the luxury of *not* worrying about it. I would *always* have to worry about it. Instead, I changed the subject. "I was told to ask you about Tom Dash."

"What about him?"

I considered my words carefully. We'd already established a pattern of evasiveness, so why stop now? I would speak as if I didn't really want this poorly compensated position very badly or that I didn't want to believe it could turn into something permanent and not just a short respite from the service industry.

"Any chance I could contact him?" I asked. "Get his advice on working with students here?"

"I'm the best, Nat. You can always get my advice. Here's just a sample: show no mercy for plagiarism. Cancel that. Don't even give them a chance. Avoid assigning any papers. While you're at it, never miss a chance to cancel class."

"Back to Dash," I said. "What if I want to borrow some lecture notes from him?"

I didn't need to borrow anyone's notes, but I thought it sounded good.

"Imagine that. She plans to lecture," he said, as if speaking to an invisible person in the room. "Listen, Nat, he's simply not available. But how about this: you can use his office. I mean, why not? It's just sitting there. We can call it another perk of the job."

He hoisted himself from his desk, and I followed him to a door in an adjacent hallway. Using a key attached to a wooden stick that reminded me of a grade school bathroom pass, he opened the door.

"Ta-dah. Nothing's been cleared out yet, but it's all yours." With the flourish of a circus ringmaster, he presented me with a desk, a file cabinet, and a bookshelf, everything overflowing in a cramped space. "Feel free to borrow whatever you find. Make sure you kill the silverfish. Supposedly, they don't bite, but all bets are off once they grow to a certain size."

Bookshelves always drew my attention. I never could walk past one without stopping, especially when entering the living space of a stranger. Even in its state of disarray, this one proved no different. I needed to know what people read, or pretended to read. On Professor Dash's shelves, *The Marrow of Tradition* by Charles Chesnutt caught my eye first, along with a paperback edition of *Frankenstein* (the 1818 text, I noted approvingly). Then I saw a copy of *Tell My Horse* by Zora Neale Hurston. Immediately, it caught me in its gravity, much in the same way it did when I read it for the first time after my mother's death. Perhaps subconsciously, I hoped it could fill the ache of her absence, even tell me about the things she never wanted to share about the folklore and myths of Haiti, the place of her birth. Born with an appetite for the supernatural, I craved stories my mother never found the time or patience to tell me about the *bokors* who raised people from the dead, the ceremonies that called forth the loas—or spirits—to inhabit human bodies. Hurston's book brought me one step closer to the things I couldn't experience for myself, and for that reason, I always felt a jealous sense of ownership whenever I saw that book on anyone else's shelf, as if such a book should only belong to me. Intellectually, I knew that feeling came from a need to fill an empty space in my own life, make up for a great absence.

I thumbed through the pages of Dash's copies, noting with amusement that he left annotations in the margins, using neat script in blue ink, very much unlike the chaos of his office. Then I realized that the ink on my fingers left black smudges on the pages. "Oh fuck," I said out loud.

I turned to see if my profanity earned a reaction from Fowler, but he'd already left. On the desk sat the key he used to open the door. Apparently, I didn't warrant a goodbye.

I made sure to take the key before I left. I also made sure to help myself to the copy of *Tell My Horse*, adding it to the stack of books already in my possession.

I arrived home with nervous energy, anxious to start prepping classes, my mind filling with plans for activities and (yes) lectures. I even felt more optimistic about advising students on their annual haunt.

The one thing I wanted to remember slipped my mind entirely. I forgot all about checking the shoebox containing the dead bird. And it stayed forgotten for a long time.

Four

Forty-eight hours passed. I even noted the hour, expecting a call to come in at any second, telling me that the employment offer went to someone else but thank you very much for the interest. I even planned to keep the books given to me for prep, including (just for spite) Dash's copy of *Tell My Horse*. I'd keep that one. For my trouble.

But no such call came, and I suppressed the impulse to call on the day that classes started just to avoid the embarrassment of showing up to the classroom and finding someone else teaching in my place.

Instead, classes began as planned with me at the helm, and the first day started off as boring as someone might expect, with me handing out syllabi and explaining the schedule of readings. I braced myself for questions about what happened to Professor Dash, convincing myself that no one would want to take the course with some woman who looked barely a few years older than the students. Most of all, I worried some of the students would remember that time they went with their family and friends to the Shell Factory for someone's birthday. I even had an answer prepared ahead of time in case some smug-faced student said:

Hey, aren't you the lady who let my grandma use her free admission coupon three different times so all us grandkids could go in for nothing that one Saturday?

Yeah, I'd say, *I must've done that too many times, or maybe your grandma's a snitch, because things didn't work out there. I figured I'd give teaching college a try now—at least until something better comes along.*

Or words to that effect. I even rehearsed a few different versions of that line, but I never got to use any of them. The students seemed either nervous or simply anxious to get the first day over with. Most of them had jobs or even families they needed to get back to at the end of their class schedule. They didn't attend a university—not yet at least. The college maintained an open-admission policy, the degrees it granted usually used to transfer somewhere bigger. A class like Literature of Horror and the Supernatural fulfilled a humanities requirement, and it seemed modestly popular, with more than half of the seats in the small classroom filled.

Confronted with their nervous faces, I improvised a little activity. On the whiteboard, I wrote the words *horror* and *terror*. Then I pointed to those words with the bravado of a middle-aged professor doped up on the big, beautiful gothic novels of Ann Radcliffe and challenged them to think of them as different concepts. Mirrors may fill us with terror, for instance, but when we look at our own reflections, we might feel horror.

Some of them snickered at that, which, okay, I deserved.

But I challenged them to consider their own mirrors—that is, metaphorically—and to tell me what made them feel terror.

Mostly generic answers followed. *Spiders*, for instance. Several students vocally agreed with that one. Pretty soon, almost everyone raised their hands to say *spiders*, so we established that no one liked spiders. "No more spider answers," I said. No one else except me laughed at that, and for a moment, no one wanted to raise their hands. Finally, after a brief silence, new answers started trickling in, all of them involving other animals, mostly reptilian, like snakes. I prompted them for something else.

"Drowning?" This answer came from a male student, who made it sound like a question.

That earned a snicker from a pale young woman with a nose ring and straight black hair in the last row.

"How could you possibly know what it's like to drown?" she asked when the other faces turned in her direction.

The other student gave her a look. "As a matter of fact, I do. In fact, I died. I praise Jesus's name that the good lord allowed me to come back so I can enjoy taking this class with you."

A pall of silence fell over the room. No one knew what to say. I watched the woman grimace. At one point in my life, I wanted nothing more than to look like she did, to have that kind of alabaster skin, corpse-white, with hair that lay long and flat so no one would look at me funny when I blasted Depeche Mode and Bauhaus from an open car window. I wanted to haunt graveyards on Halloween night, and I had the wrong notion that I needed to look a certain way to do it.

To get them back on track, I pointed to the other word on the board: *Horror.* Then I prompted them to share what horrified them, reminding them not to think of it as the same as *Terror.* Someone raised their hand and said, "Spiders." Everyone laughed at that, including me. Well, everyone except the goth girl in the back.

"Spiders laying their eggs inside of your body," someone else said when things quieted down.

Only a smattering of nervous laughter at that. *Good*, I thought, *that's good. They're getting it.* "How about one more?" I said.

A brief moment of contemplation. Then the goth woman spoke up without raising her hand.

"Dying," she said, "with no one there to bring you back."

Her words brought about a silence so complete that I could hear my own heart beating. The goth woman locked eyes with me as the clock ticked down the final moments of the class. *Maybe you're not cut out for this*, her expression seemed to say.

I brushed away the thought, knowing that I needed to meet with the club before the day finally came to an end. With class dismissed, I went into a restroom and splashed water on my face, wondering how I could let such a thing get to me.

You know why.

Maybe the voice that spoke those words came from my own head. I could never tell. Regardless, that voice was a familiar one, and it caused me to lift my chin and gaze into the mirror over the sink that I'd managed to avoid up until that point.

I already knew what I would see.

Not just my own face but something with a skull so traumatized it hardly looked human anymore. Before a car tire rolled over it, the face belonged to a woman with children who loved her. She just had the misfortune of stumbling into a street that ran through Ybor City, right in front of a distracted driver who failed to look up in time. A driver blaring Depeche Mode and Bauhaus through an open window at top volume.

"I'm so sorry," I said.

The face lingered, refusing to acknowledge the apology I'd spoken so many times. This phantom I'd conjured proved judicious about when it chose to speak. Not that it should possess that capability. Other than being dead—or *un*dead—with a crushed cranium that still oozed blood and brain, it possessed no functioning jaw, thanks to the weight of the car that rolled over it.

Once more, I rinsed my face, praying for the cleansing power of tap water. When I looked up again, I saw only myself. Someone who made a horrible mistake, who didn't belong here, who ought to pack up her books and return them to Fowler with sincerest apologies. How could I spend a semester talking about death with a group of students who signed up to learn something? All the reasons why I stopped pursuing my studies in literature came back to me.

I made a decision. I would finish the day, attend the meeting with the *HOL* students, and get them started on their plans for the haunted house they would stage later in the term. Then I would quietly depart. Go home and send in my resignation by e-mail.

Already a few minutes late, I entered the meeting room designated for clubs that sat next to the cafeteria in the college's poor excuse for a student union. I found only a handful of students waiting, each one of them meeting my lateness with a businesslike scowl, only accentuated by the oval table around which they sat. I recognized some faces, including the one seated at the head of the table, presumably the place for the club's president.

"Hey, Professor," the goth woman said with the air of comfortable authority.

I didn't feel ready to see her again, but turning and running didn't seem like a professional move. I forced myself to enter the room and take one of the unoccupied chairs.

"You can call me Nat," I said, though I could tell from their expressions that they would never do it. Obviously, a test from the new instructor to see if they would really do it. "Sorry for being late. What did I miss?"

"We were just talking themes," the president said. "But no worries, we'll get you caught up."

Next to me sat one of the other familiar faces—the student who thanked Jesus for saving him from drowning. He nodded at me and smiled. "That was a great class," he said.

"Save the ass-kissing. We need to get the professor acquainted with us and how we do things." To me, the president said, "You know Mark, of course."

"Of course," I said. The drowning victim smiled and nodded at me.

"That one over there is Ruth. Next to her is Mo." I waved to Ruth. She smiled in return. Mo pointed a finger cocked like a gun in my direction and winked. "And over there is Zach," said the president, gesturing toward a broody-looking male with dark hair who didn't acknowledge the introduction at all. "Me, you know of course as Isera, but I prefer Isis, if it's all the same to you, Professor."

I made a mental note of this name so I wouldn't make a mistake, my plan to resign momentarily forgotten. "Isis. Got it. Sorry if I made a mistake earlier." All the names from the previous class had not stuck.

"I didn't correct you. Not that you asked either."

"Yeah, I hate it when my professors don't ask me my preferences. They always fuck up my full name," Mo said.

"While we're on that topic, just call me Nat, not Professor."

Their expressions reminded me I'd already told them that. I started to explain the whole situation and how adjuncts didn't have full faculty status, but I decided not to go into it. I'd just bore them.

"Nah. You're our faculty advisor. I'm president here, so you're *Professor* as long as I'm in charge." Isis looked around the table, daring anyone to challenge her. "Everyone got that?"

I laughed. "Okay, Madame President. Whatever you say. So fill me in. Themes."

Isis leaned forward and laced her fingers together, each nail coated perfectly in black polish. "Ruth here wants to do what we did last year, only I'm not sensing a lot of enthusiasm."

Ruth's brow furrowed. "You didn't give anyone a chance to comment before you shot it down." She looked at the others, but Isis had a point—not a lot of enthusiasm.

"What was last year's theme?" I asked.

"Fairy tales," said Isis.

"That sounds kind of fun, actually," I said.

"Oh, it was fantastic," Ruth said. "Each segment involved an encounter with the Big Bad Wolf. Well, a werewolf, really. I was Little Red Riding Hood, and at the end, I crawled out of the wolf's belly, covered completely in blood. Mark was the woodsman, armed with the axe he used to cut open the wolf. It was *glorious*."

"It was repetitive. By the end, people were sick of the wolf. He stopped being scary," Isis said.

"As I recall, you were very scary," said Ruth to Isis.

Avoiding eye contact with everyone, Isis said, "You aren't trying to find a nice way to call me a bitch, are you, Ruth?" The faintest sign of a smile appeared on Isis's cheek. I couldn't tell if Ruth meant it as a compliment, but I could tell Isis liked it when someone called her scary. "Anyway, it doesn't matter because we aren't doing repeats. New ideas, people."

Ruth leaned close to me and pretended to whisper. "You should have seen the effect at the end. We built a false floor so I could crawl up through the wolf's guts."

"What did you use for guts?" I asked.

"You don't want to know, trust me, but I was cleaning it out of my hair for weeks."

"She smelled like a slaughterhouse for about that long too," said Mo. "Don't worry, we love you anyway. Even when you're covered in gore."

What Ruth said brought to mind the weird stain I'd seen at the pavilion. It suddenly made sense. "I think I saw the stain you left out there. Judging by the size of it, it must've been an impressive effect."

Isis shifted her gaze from me to Ruth and then back to me. "Wait, what stain? We didn't leave any *stains.* We cleaned our shit up."

"I was there not too long ago, and I saw a stain. Professor Fowler saw it too."

At the mention of Fowler's name, Mark formed a pretend flask with his fist and made a chugging motion. However, Isis didn't look ready to dismiss it. "Show us," she said as she began gathering up her things.

The others followed suit, though Zach, silent through all this, made a show of taking his time. Ruth smiled at me. "Field trip!" she said.

"Fact-finding trip," said Isis. "Besides, maybe the air will stimulate brain cells."

"Hopefully, the sun won't cause you to burst into flames," Mark said. He turned to me. "Are you going to come with us?"

I looked at the time and made a quick calculation. I needed to catch the bus so I could meet Erik at home. "Sure. Besides, I think my credibility might be on the line,"

"The only word Isis trusts," said Mo, "is her own."

We followed Isis toward the footpath that led around the lake. Both distance and the tree line made the pavilion difficult to see. Zach took up the rear of our dark little pilgrimage. His brooding made him seem a more likely candidate to turn to ash under the sun's rays. Isis led the way, Mark walking a few feet behind her. Mo and Ruth took up positions on either side of me like personal escorts.

Isis turned briefly, arms held out as if to cast a curse upon all Creation. "It's too fucking *bright,*" she called out to us.

Since Mark already made the joke about bursting into flames, no one responded. Instead, Ruth started talking about blood, almost as if to herself at first. "Lying in all that blood night after night gives you a certain perspective. Like what it means in a bigger sense to that story of Little Red and the Wolf. I didn't tell anyone, but I had a terrible period the last week. Like, truly awful cramps, worse than normal. Because of that, something about the story's narrative started to click. 'Little Red Riding Hood,' I mean. The *red* is period blood, the wolf some kind of metaphor of fertility, with me coming out of the wolf's carcass a kind of birth. Or rebirth, maybe, narratively speaking." She looked at me. "Assuming I'm not abusing that phrase."

"Blood is narrative," I said. Simultaneously, Mo and Ruth turned their heads to me quizzically. I shrugged. Even I didn't know where that came from. "Please continue. I want to hear more."

As did Mo, who said, "So you don't just want to recycle this fairy tale theme. You want to reinvent it. Give it what? A rebirth? Narratively speaking, of course." Mo shot me a glance, challenging me to repeat the *blood is narrative* comment again. Which I didn't. Not until I understood what I meant by it. My academic brain still needed to restart, but my academic mouth decided not to wait.

"Right," Ruth said. "It's what that old narrative needed. We fixated on the Wolf as the monster, but what if we ended it a little differently? What if Little Red sprouts fangs as the climax of the story and eats the woodsman?"

"As in a PMS-fueled rage?" asked Mo.

"I guess that's sort of the metaphor I had in mind. Anyway, I didn't get to say it before because . . . well, you know."

"Because I came in late and caused the discussion to come to an end?" I asked.

Mo shook her head. "You brought blood to our attention. We love blood. Bad periods notwithstanding. No offense, Ruth." Ruth saluted in a way that said *none* taken, so Mo continued. "Now look at us, going to see the gory details. Besides, Isis apparently wants a different narrative altogether."

I started to say something when I noticed Mark increase his pace to a short gallop so that he could walk next to Isis. Side by side now, his arm slid around her waist as if it belonged there. Speaking of narratives, that marked a twist I didn't see coming.

"They're dating?" I asked.

"Depends which narrative you hear," Ruth said.

"What if I ask Isis?" I noticed she didn't seem to return the display of affection. In fact, Mark's move seemed a bit aggressive. "She'd say they weren't dating, I take it."

"She'd say it was a sex thing," said Mo. "Which, between them, I imagine as pretty weird. Just look at them."

Ruth covered her ears. "I wish you didn't say that because now I'm imagining it, and it *is* weird. He was the woodsman, remember. Maybe she plans to *eat* him. Maybe that's the metaphor we should go with."

Mo told her to uncover her ears and keep her voice down. I fell back, letting the two of them get ahead of me, realizing that because of me, an interesting conversation about narrative turned into gossip about the romantic lives of college students. Wanting to stay out of that, I paused for Zach to catch up so I could walk beside him instead.

Zach took his time, making the wait feel awkward.

Even more so when he spoke.

"How'd you end up teaching here?" he asked.

It sounded almost like a challenge. It seemed that I'd exchanged one awkward situation for another.

Or maybe I just imagined it that way. I tried smiling. "Good fortune, I guess. I think I'm going to like it here. The students seem . . . nice."

"So you're here to stay. Not just a replacement."

A replacement. Again, a hint of aggression. Maybe he didn't mean it to sound that way?

"Well, I know I'm stepping into someone else's shoes," I said. "But who knows? Maybe you all will decide you like me."

As soon as I said it, I wished I hadn't. Now, I sounded like I was fishing for something positive. I decided to change the subject. Make it about him.

"You're not one of my current students, right?"

"No," he said a bit too flatly, like I'd made him uncomfortable. "Nothing personal. I'm just more into real life than literature."

"Literature *is* real life," I said. I believed it too. Or used to. I almost used Ruth's phrase. *Narratively speaking.*

A ghost of a smile crossed his lips. "*Supernatural* literature, you mean. Sorry, I'm just not into it. The true things are weird enough."

"Then why are you . . ." I didn't get to finish because Isis reached the pavilion and let loose a volley of expletives so profane that it disturbed a family of crows in the pine branches overhead, the voices forming a chorus to accompany hers. One flew down and perched on a trash can, where it eyed me suspiciously. Why had I returned? it wanted to know.

If crows can recognize human faces, as ornithologists claimed, then it should work the other way too. Shouldn't I recognize this bird as well? It seemed so unfair for the bird to have the upper hand.

Isis stood over the rust-colored blotch—blood, it looked most definitively like blood—her arms extended from her body like a sorcerer trying to summon a phoenix from a pile of ashes. Without meaning to, we formed an evenly spaced arc with Isis in the center, like the columns of some ancient temple where someone had just left us a secret code drawn with the blood of a recent sacrifice. It took me a moment to realize that Isis's outburst came from a sense of joy and amazement, not rage or consternation. The mark delighted her so much she seemed to forget the rest of us. From the crows came excited chatter, as if they shared her revelry.

"Don't you get it?" she asked, finally acknowledging our presence. "We could build our concept around this."

"This *what?*" asked Mo. "Someone please tell me it isn't what it looks like."

"It's blood. Unquestionably blood," Isis said. She turned to Ruth. "This isn't from where you crawled out of the wolf's intestinal track, is it?"

"Ew. No." But Ruth's eyes scanned the area doubtfully. "I mean, I don't think so. Once the walls go up, everything becomes so different."

Which seemed to confirm what Fowler told me about the illusory effect of the haunted house and how the inside somehow seemed larger than the outside.

Ruth walked a few feet away from the offensive blotch, her strides suggesting that she was measuring yards. "I think we set up the false floor here. Yeah, because people exited there." She used her hands like someone standing on a runway, directing an airplane where to taxi.

Heads turned, following her gestures—everyone's except Zach's. He approached the stain on the ground, careful not to let it come into contact with his shoes, his expression thoughtful.

"You owe the professor an apology," Mo said to Isis.

"I never called her into question. I just called it a fact-finding trip."

"And there it is," I said. "A fact indeed."

"Look, I didn't mean you were a liar or anything."

She didn't—not directly, at least. "It's fine. I would have wanted to see it too." I wondered if Professor Dash ever said anything that led to a "fact-finding trip." Perspiration caused my top to stick to my skin. I'd overdressed for work that day, wearing a top more suited for a job interview or a funeral, a mistake I wouldn't make again. I probably looked like I was trying too hard. No doubt they already saw my relative youth and inexperience as something that undermined my authority. They probably found me fake. Stuffy. Never mind my gender and brown complexion.

A replacement, Zach called me. If he meant it to sting, it worked.

Meanwhile, Zach squatted down and began scraping the blotch with a broken tree branch he found nearby. The others watched.

"He's getting a vision," said Isis, apparently anxious to change the subject. "Are you sensing a vibration, Zach?"

"What? He's psychic?" *I'm more into real life*, he said to me just moments ago. Did that include psychic powers?

"What? No, Jesus, I was joking. Zach, what's the deal, man?"

"I think it's real blood," he said quietly.

"That would be *fantastic*," Isis said. "We can only hope."

The woods around us stirred with a hot gust of wind. My friends the crows no longer hovered about, but I could feel their presence, observing these strange human proceedings while perched safely in the branches of the nearby trees.

"Why is that 'fantastic'?" Mo asked for all of us.

"Verisimilitude," Isis said. "Authenticity. We could build a narrative around this blood spill."

"There's already a narrative," said Zach. Still crouched near the blotch, his eyes met mine, and I realized I may have misjudged his age. He seemed to grow older as he held my gaze, more tired. *A veteran?* I wondered. I'd seen enough people my age coming home from foreign wars who looked like they'd aged decades. That would explain the stress lines around his eyes and mouth.

"Did you . . . murder someone here, Zach?" Mo asked. Her tone suggested she meant it in a half-joking way.

"*No.* But I'm surprised you all haven't heard this story. Aren't you all supposed to be interested in the scary stuff?"

"Ladies and gentlemen," said Isis, "our colleague Zach is about to revoke our license to run a haunted house. Or maybe he'll just get to the point and tell us what he knows."

"Is it a good story, at least?" I asked. "Narratively speaking?"

He stood, his knees creaking as he straightened them. Once more, his gaze bore down on me. "Depends on what you mean as *good.*"

Five

"This land used to attract some rough characters. I'm talking about long before there was a college or anything like that. Instead, you had people living off an untamed wilderness and instituting some questionable mob justice when the need arose," Zach said. He pointed toward the forested area beyond the pavilion. "If you go back there today, you'll find everything overgrown, the trees thick, mostly pine. Decades ago, there was a whole turpentine industry built on harvesting the resin from those trees, with crude paths cut through to allow for wagons. Supposedly, a tall oak still stands somewhere back aways, one especially suited for hangings."

"Don't you mean lynchings?" asked Mo, flinching at the very mention of the word. I understood. It triggered something inside me, too.

"There were *lynchings* here? For real?" Mark looked at me for confirmation, his expression reflecting a strange combination of excitement and shattered innocence. Such things didn't really happen, did they?

Zach nodded. "Oh yeah. People usually don't think of Florida as a scene for . . ." Here, he hesitated, looking for a way to sidestep the word. "For that sort of thing. But it happened here a lot."

"That's an understatement," I said, and I could have said more, like how it occurred at a higher rate per capita here than any other state in the former Confederacy. I could also have mentioned how angry mobs even murdered adolescents and children during those ugly decades, as well as pregnant women. *Save it for another time,* I told myself.

Besides, like them, I wanted to hear Zach's story.

"I mean," he said, "it's not like you'll find a rope still hanging from that tree—at least, not unless you're telling a ghost story—but some people around here still whisper about it when they tell the old stories, the ones passed down through the generations. You just have to talk to the right people."

"Or the wrong people," Mo said, nodding toward me. I nodded back, a silent communication passing between us. We both knew the sort of person they would have hanged from that tree. And who did the hanging. Mo had a point. Usually not the "right people."

"Right," Zach said, though without any real acknowledgment of what Mo meant. "Anyway, you all know how railroad tracks used to cross the road up yonder?"

No one answered.

"No," Zach went on, "of course you didn't. Anway, they stopped at a depot, where wagons and trucks would bring in newcomers looking for work, usually during the winter months. Some of them came looking for more than work. They hoped to find some good times too, something outside the view of the law. They usually found it, along with a little trouble too."

"How do you know all this?" Isis asked, the question on all our minds. "I'm not sure if I like the old brooding Zach or the new Zach who has so much to say."

If Isis meant the remark as an insult, it didn't land. Zach just rolled with it. "My family's lived around here for ages. My grandfather used to come out here as a little boy, looking for the hanging tree. He said that if the full moon cast its light just right, you can still see the shadows of hanging bodies, cast right there on the ground near your feet. Like I said, he did this long before plans to build a college here."

"And all that has *what* to do with this blood stain?" asked Ruth.

"I was just getting to that. Near that tree sat the site of a place called The Bloody Bucket. See, we're talking about a long time ago, way back in the 1930s when Prohibition took effect. The Bloody Bucket was what they called a juke joint in those days, a place where workers liked to blow off steam by listening to music and drinking. This particular place had a reputation because of its signature cocktail, a blend of moonshine the proprietor mixed up in a huge barrel and sweetened with strawberry syrup. People literally came out of the woods to drink it, even kids. You'd think the place got its name from the color of this elixir, but no. It became known as the Bloody Bucket on account of other things, like how the music they played could allegedly conjure the devil. But mostly, the name stuck because of a side business that took place here."

"Your grandfather told you all this?" Mark looked at the others, his skepticism showing.

Isis shushed him. "This is the most Zach has said in his entire life, and you want to interrupt him? Besides, I think he's getting to the good part."

"Yeah, my grandfather. He wasn't around that long ago, but the story was passed down to him from people who knew it firsthand. I'm not making this up." He looked at me as if I'd accused him of doing just that. Based on his expression, I believed him. I also sensed he didn't entirely enjoy becoming the center of attention. That sort of thing may have come natural to Isis, but not to Zach.

Not unless he knew how to fake that impression.

"This side business," I said, "I bet I can guess what it was."

His gaze hovered toward the lake, breaking contact in a way that suggested he felt embarrassed. "Yeah, that. Well, the proprietor worked on the side as a midwife, and sometimes that meant lending her services to the women who made their living in the Bloody Bucket, doing . . . you know . . ."

When his voice trailed off, Mo piped in. "Doing the clientele?"

"Well, yeah," said Zach.

"Sex workers," said Isis. "Prostitutes who got pregnant. I can't believe you couldn't say that out loud. How old are you, anyway?" Without waiting for an answer, she added, "This proprietor—what was her name?"

"I don't really know," Zach said. "I've heard different ones. Bonnie or Molly. But probably it was Ma something. Or maybe just *Ma.*"

Isis nodded slowly. "This *Ma* performed abortions for them. That's not exactly shocking, given the fact that pregnancy was probably a work hazard. Not like they had an abundance of family services or birth control options back then."

"Oh," I said, making the connection before the rest of them. "*Oh.* You're saying that she used a bucket for the—"

"Yes," Zach said, his gaze still drifting, avoiding eye contact. "And supposedly, she would stand on the shore of the lake and empty the contents of the bucket."

We all turned to regard the lake, where fish and insects caused tiny ripples on the water's surface while the sunlight created a silvery sheen. The longer I looked, the more I expected to see clouds of red billowing beneath the surface.

"Hence, the Bloody Bucket," said Ruth.

"That's not the whole story," Zach said.

He paused as we moved closer to him, compelled by the gravity of his story. Even Isis seemed to feel it, her attention fixed on him, no longer compelled to mock him. For a moment, I felt envy, wishing I could magnetize my students in this fashion. I didn't feel at all sure of myself, self-doubt still plaguing me with an inner voice that said I'd made a horrible mistake in taking this job. But for now, I felt the same hunger they did, a desire for narrative, to know what came next in a good story, even one rooted in such a hateful past.

Zach continued: "Word got around that Ma—let's just call her that to make it simple—Ma was dumping her bloody waste into the barrels she used for her strawberry-flavored moonshine. Whether or not she really did, I can't say. For all I know, it's true. Or maybe someone started the rumor as an excuse to steal her business away from her. Either way, a horde of men showed up at her door and waited for her to come back from one of her trips to the lake. They threw her into the back of a wagon so they could use the tree I told you about. They did more than hang her too. They mutilated her pretty good. Made an example of her."

"Mutilated her how, exactly?" asked Mo. "Do I want to know?"

"Probably not. They focused on this area here." Using his hands, he indicated the region below his belt, an attempt at tact that failed miserably. That just made it worse. Collectively, we cringed. All of us, that is, except

Mark, whose face bore a question that earned him a glare from Isis.

"They went to work on her lady parts," said Isis. "You need more explanation than that?"

"Jeez, no, I got it. You don't have to explain it," Mark said, though his reaction did leave me in doubt. Something about him told me he needed certain things spelled out. To deflect attention away from himself, Mark said, "How is it you know about this in such detail? It's not like you were there."

Impatient with how he kept hearing his authority challenged, Zach scowled. "I told you: my grandfather told me this story. But he wasn't even alive when it happened. Someone told him the story the same way he told it to me."

"Just a bedtime story," Isis said dreamily. "Once upon a time."

"You said he went looking for the tree," I said, "and that it's back in there?"

Everyone turned to look in the direction I pointed, back toward the woods looming behind the pavilion. Zach let the silence linger before he answered.

"Yeah. He said he would wait for the light of the full moon and go exploring back in there, hoping to catch sight of the shadows of those hanging bodies. And if you did see the shadow there on the ground, never look up. You do, and you might see her staring back at you. If that happened, she'd follow you back home, and her dangling innards, her . . . lady parts, would leave a trail behind her. He told me he woke up one morning and found a big bloodstain on the floor near his bed, and he knew that she caught him spying on her. She followed him inside his house and stood over him while he slept, leaving a stain a lot like this one." He pointed toward the mark on the concrete. "That's what reminded me of all this."

"Quite a curiosity your grandfather had," Isis said. She appeared to ponder something before adding, "Not to ask too indelicate a question—"

"God forbid," said Mo.

"—but the people who shared this lovely story with your grandfather, were they related to him?"

Zach blinked, apparently not expecting this question. "Yeah. I mean, I guess."

"Then how did *they* know what happened? I'm guessing they didn't read about it in the newspaper."

Again, Zach blinked. He looked at me for help, but I had none to offer. I sensed where the conversation would go next. An unpleasant place that Zach stepped into unwittingly.

"They heard about it, I suppose," said Zach. "It was an even smaller community then. People talk."

"Sure," Ruth said, picking up Isis's caustic tone. "Just talk. Of course your family didn't have anything to do with the crime itself. Of course they didn't wear white hoods themselves."

"I never said anything about white hoods," he said. "Who said anything about *white* hoods?" But his voice trailed off. No one spoke for a time, everyone watching Zach's face as a growing realization set in. He'd never considered the possibility that his own family had anything to do with an all-too-common hate crime.

I knew I should step in. Make it a teachable moment. What would Fowler say? Not to feel bad? Remind them that these events happened in the past, that they no longer mattered, that they had nothing to do with the present? But of course they still mattered and had everything to do with the present. The great contradiction. Like me, a woman with a complexion inherited from her mother, both wanting and not wanting the heaviness they now felt to sink in deeper.

I could tell them they needed these moments, reminders that ghost stories don't spawn on their own, that they require the spilling of real blood, the rending of actual flesh. I could tell them they needed to unpack the buried truths nestled inside repressed narratives and to feel the burdens they bring, not try to hide behind lies.

Me, a fine one to talk.

So I didn't.

A gust of warm air stirred the trees behind us, and a flock of crows took flight. Perhaps they roosted on an old oak where a phantasmal corpse continued to swing, abandoned and forgotten.

Finally, it was Mark who felt the need to say something. "Come on, it's not like *he* did any of these things." He faced me, looking for reinforcement.

"No, he didn't. You're right." My words sounded hollow, even to my own ears. What were we even doing out here? What was I doing, trying to play the role of professor to people not much younger than myself? They needed someone else. Afterwards, I decided, I would pay Fowler a visit, return the textbooks, tell him I made a terrible mistake accepting the job. I didn't feel ready. Not just professionally. Personally too.

"We're missing the bigger picture here," Isis said, breaking me out of my spell. "How can we use this?"

"Use this?" Mo spoke for all of us.

"This is our haunted house, isn't it? It's authentic. It's real. It ties in something relevant."

"I don't think it's appropriate," said Ruth.

"Too controversial," added Mark quietly.

"Oh, please," said Isis. "If that's the case, then maybe we need a little controversy." Carefully, she toed the stain on the concrete with the tip of her black boot. Until that moment, we'd all avoided touching it, but now Isis showed no hesitation or fear. I recalled how Fowler did something similar previously, only he tried to scrape it away. Isis wanted to preserve it. Not that it showed any sign of dissipating, the blood having seemingly fixed itself permanently into the concrete. "You're saying that this Bonnie or Holly or *Ma* was here. This was a sign that she's still out looking for revenge."

"No," Zach said. "I said no such thing. I don't believe in any of this stuff. I was just pointing out a parallel. This has nothing to do with the Bloody Bucket. It's too new." He looked at the faces in the group, his gaze holding mine the longest. "I mean, you all agree with that, don't you?"

"What happened to the original Bloody Bucket?" Isis asked. Fearless and undaunted, she now stood on the spot itself. "Where is it?"

Zach shrugged. "How would I know? Bulldozed? Burned down? For all I know, it's rotting away somewhere back in the pines."

"Or it could have stood right here. In this spot," said Isis. "It had to be close to the lake where she emptied her bucket. I can feel it. Her presence.

Can't you all?"

No one said anything. Zach shook his head. "I wish I never said anything."

"But you did, and it was amazing. Don't you all see? We have our theme. This year, we're calling the haunted house *The Bloody Bucket*."

"I don't know," said Mo.

"And you could play the part of the proprietor," Isis said, pointing to Mo.

"Me? Why?" Mo looked at me, the only other person in the group with brown skin, and once more, something passed between us, the understanding of what it meant to feel different from everyone else.

"Maybe we need another approach," I said. "After all, we're talking about actual people. Don't you want this to be something people can enjoy?" I let my voice trail off. Hadn't I already decided I wouldn't see this project come to fruition? Let it become someone else's problem. Still, Mo needed an ally. "Maybe you all can take a vote on it later. For now, we should call it a day. Reconvene on the subject when you have your next meeting."

"Yeah," Zach said, "I'd prefer my family's name not dragged through the mud. It's not exactly appropriate."

"That's what you're worried about? Your family name?" Isis showed him the palm of her hand. "I say we ought to consider it. We'll be scaring people *and* teaching them something at the same time. Don't they call that service learning or something like that?" She looked at me for an answer.

"Yeah, they do." I wanted to call it a day. The flock of crows had returned and surrounded the pavilion, cawing at us, demanding we leave. Stewards of the lake and forest and all the secrets they contained, they belonged here, not us. "It's time for us to go. I have a bus to catch."

I began walking away, not expecting them to follow. I heard someone mutter, *"She takes the bus?"* but I couldn't identify the voice. Maybe one of the crows spoke. When I glanced back, I saw that they'd formed a line behind me, all their energy depleted as they each retreated into their own thoughts. Only Zach remained behind. Still standing at the pavilion, he watched our exodus. I lifted my hand to wave, but he didn't wave back.

Six

A few years before, I killed someone.

It happened just after I finished my master's degree, setting another milestone for a family that never before counted a college graduate amongst its members. My father barely made it past high school, while my mother had even less formal education, though I remember her quick mind and ability to summon fountains of knowledge—just not the kind you would learn in school. Things like how to hold two baby chicks and tell which one would grow into a rooster and which one a hen, or how to determine from a dream she had the night before whether I should ride the bus to school or if I should go by foot. Once, I tested her wisdom, defying her when she said to ride the bus. That morning, as I walked, a neighbor's dog got loose and bit me so badly that I needed four stitches and a painful rabies shot.

"See?" she said as she pressed a bloody rag against my wounded arm as we sat in the hospital waiting room. "You don't question what I know. Never think you're smarter. You can't learn what I know from books or teachers."

Not that I could learn it from her either because she never taught me. Or maybe she tried and found me too stubborn and unwilling to learn. Besides, I loved books. And I loved scary things. "Tell me a scary story?" I would ask her sometimes, and she would answer by telling me how evil men in her country would raise dead bodies to labor for them in fields. That always ignited my ghoulish imagination. I would want to know more about these reanimated corpses. Did the flesh rot from their bones in the sun, eventually turning them into skeletons? Could they still work as just skeletons? Did they *eat* the living? But she would only sniff in derision and say, "No, they just keep on working until they died again." Then she would lecture me about how you must always treat working people fairly, as if I had any say in such things. Each time I wanted to hear one of her stories, she would turn it into something else, never giving me what I wanted to hear.

What she must have thought of me, this strange alien daughter she'd given birth to in a strange foreign land. I loved Halloween, with its witches, skeletons, and pumpkins. She scarcely understood the appeal of such things. In defiance, I went to college and pursued a degree in English so that I could cram my head with the kind of stories I craved and she'd denied, the more gothic and macabre, the better. When my mother suffered her untimely death, I pursued these things even more tenaciously, almost as a way to spite her and her resistance to indulging me.

That pursuit led me to kill someone.

After graduating with a master's degree, I spent an evening partying in Ybor City, something I'd never done before. For one thing, I usually kept to myself, always too bookish and withdrawn to maintain friendships. Books gave me the kind of relationships I felt comfortable with, and I spent most of my free time with them. Just once, I decided to leave my monastic shell and join my fellow grad students for a pub crawl to celebrate our achievements. Though my father never quite understood what I did or wanted to do with my degree, he saw how hard I worked and encouraged me to join the crowd and blow off some steam. We both knew I would go on to the PhD next, so he told me I needed a break. "Go out and have fun," he said.

And I did.

Then I killed a woman.

She has a name.

I killed Taryn Hall.

Struggling with addiction and living on the street, Taryn stumbled into the path of my car. Or someone pushed her. It depends on which witness you ask. Some of them said they saw me driving recklessly, speculating (correctly) that I was fiddling with the stereo—trying to find the right track from Depeche Mode's *Violator* to match the wild buzz I felt from hours of dancing at the goth club I'd left earlier. Others said that I seemed to swerve, possibly with the intent of running over Taryn Hall as she stumbled off the sidewalk and into the street. One person even swore that I chose that moment to speed up. Still others said they could see my face through the windshield, and they read an expression ranging anywhere between diabolically possessed to horrified, unable to avoid running over the person who fell backwards into the path of my vehicle.

My dad's vehicle, actually. Not only did the car belong to someone else but it also seemed that the experience did as well. I can't recall what happened. I don't remember what song played on the stereo or if I had really reached over to change the track. My hands might have gripped the steering wheel or fumbled with something that had fallen under the seat. What I looked like, I couldn't tell you, but alcohol played little or no part, as a blood test proved when the results showed me under the legal limit.

I only recall the sickening feeling as the front tire rolled over Taryn Hall's face, crushing her skull and killing her instantly.

The police arrested me, and I remained in a stupor through the finger-printing and mugshot. I remained in that state until the next morning when my father came to bail me out. Eventually, the police reduced the charges to reckless driving. Apparently, they decided that Taryn Hall's life didn't warrant a vehicular murder or even a manslaughter trial.

In the end, I decided to forgo the rest of my education. My own self-imposed sentence.

But somehow, I still found myself at the college, the latest in a life consisting of mistake after mistake.

The day after the club's meeting at the pavilion, I went to visit Fowler in his office, my plan to resign once and for all. With me, I carried the copy of *Tell My Horse* that I'd pilfered from Dash's office, along with the instructor copies of the books used for teaching.

I knew what I would say, the speech well rehearsed. I would have used a mirror to practice my delivery, but I knew I would find Taryn Hall's ruined face leering at me. The sight of burst skull and oozing brain matter always appeared alongside my reflection during vulnerable moments. Like the day of my father's funeral, when I tried to rinse away my tears at a bathroom sink while trying to avoid the sight of her grinning face, made even more hideous because of her broken jaw and shattered teeth. If anyone else shared that mirror with me, they never saw her. Never Erik, for instance, who would go on chattering to me with a mouth full of toothpaste, failing to notice the third person in the reflection or the fact that I seemed to tense up. Over time, I could predict when I would see her, and no amount of apologies for what I did could make her stop showing herself.

In any case, I knew what I would say to Fowler, my tongue armed with an apology as well as assurances that I would continue until the end of the week if he needed time to find someone else to fill in. If he protested, I would counter that I didn't have the kind of experience that made me feel competent. For one thing, the students needed someone relatable, if not someone they could actually look up to. If he pressed me, reminding me how he'd seen me present scholarship that impressed him enough to remember my name, I would tell him I'd lost my earlier passion and no longer wanted anything to do with teaching or academia.

If all that failed, I would tell him that I killed Taryn Hall.

She probably wanted me to say those words to as many people as I could.

Before trekking to Fowler, I stopped by Dash's office. I never properly moved in or had time to use it for office hours, but at least I could lighten my load by returning *Tell My Horse* to its place on the shelf. It didn't belong to me, no matter who was responsible for my birth.

But when I stepped across the threshold and turned on the light, I felt a blast of cold air that sucked my breath away, leaving me suspended in mid-step.

Then I saw something that made me gasp out loud. All the books in my arms fell to the floor.

A body, hanging by the neck above the desk. It rotated slowly, the back of its head turned so that I could see its leering face, grinning even in death.

Immediately, I recalled Zach's story of the Bloody Bucket, thinking I'd encountered the phantom of its proprietor, no longer hanging from an oak but somehow the office ceiling. The dead menacing me now somehow forming a legion. If I thought for an instant that the hanging body belonged to Taryn Hall, the wholeness of the skull and lack of brain matter quickly disabused me of the notion. Slowly, it rotated on what looked like a thick strand of twine, revealing a face I recognized. I also became aware that the figure didn't possess an adult-sized body.

A large doll, about three feet in height. More precisely, a replica of Slashing Sally, the title character in a recent series of horror films about a razor-wielding doll come to life. It continued to rotate, now seeming to peer down at me with a leering white face under a shock of wild red hair, its lust for murder made evident by a ludicrous smile. I'd seen these films—all four of them. Until now, I even liked their simple formula, as did Erik, who had joined me for a marathon of the series on a rainy Saturday night not long ago.

The commotion of me dropping the books brought Fowler out of his office, and he appeared quietly behind me in the doorway, startling me for a second time in a matter of seconds.

"Boo," he whispered close to my ear as we watched the doll continue to rotate. It finally stopped with its face in our direction. "It looks like you've been got," he said.

"*Got?*" I moved away from him, though I couldn't tear my eyes from the doll. "By who? Or what?"

"By the faculty, I'm guessing. They like to do this sort of thing when someone moves in to an office. Sort of a way of saying hello. Or 'welcome to the building.'"

"A plate of cookies is a hello. Shit, a *hello* is a hello." I reassembled the stack of books. He didn't offer to help, choosing to watch instead. "In other words, it's hazing."

He laughed, but it didn't sound genuine, as if he'd heard that one before. Or I struck a nerve. "It's all in good humor. Besides, everyone here knows what you teach. They thought you'd appreciate it."

"By 'everyone,' do you mean *you?*" I had not met or even seen any other faculty.

Again, that awkward laugh, but no denial.

"Well, I need to return . . . this." I gestured at Slashing Sally. "You at least need to let me know who the rightful owner is. You know, so I can . . . thank them. For the welcome." A vein throbbed in my neck, perhaps the beginning of a stroke. No more Slashing Sally movies for me.

"Oh, it's yours now. It stays in your office. At least until someone new comes along. Then you can pass it on to them. Assuming you're still here."

"About that."

I paused, and he waited for me to continue. But I couldn't, all the words of my prepared speech now gone, emptied from my brain thanks to the shock I'd just experienced. Meanwhile, Fowler struggled to read my expression.

Finally, he said, "Set down your books and come to my office."

Unencumbered, I found myself across from him, a desk cluttered with dust and ungraded papers between us. It did hold two picture frames, one holding a photo of woman I took for his wife, posing outdoors with snow-capped mountains in the background. In the other, I saw a little girl with braces, perhaps a little bit younger than Erik. She looked like Fowler around the eyes, likely a daughter, though I didn't know anything about his family life. When I met him at the conference, he came across as a single man, his flirtations stopping just short of inappropriate. I got the impression he wanted me to see his photos, though he said nothing about them. He would probably claim I flirted back, and I might have. A little.

"What are you trying to tell me?" he asked as he settled back in his chair.

"I'm having doubts," I said. Instantly, I became angry with myself for sounding anything but firm.

Fowler made it worse by offering assurances, or at least pretending to. "You've got this. I believe in you."

"Well, thanks, I believe in me too. Jesus Christ."

"Quoting Jesus now? What chapter and verse was that?"

I couldn't help it. I returned his smile.

"Ha," he said, pointing at my face, "got you."

I half expected him to open a hidden drawer in his desk and produce a bottle of cheap bourbon along with two shot glasses. A shame, as I would have taken him up on that. Maybe he didn't want to remind me of how he tried plying me with alcohol when I met him at the conference.

"Look," I said, "this doesn't feel right. Those students have ideas about their haunted house, but I'm no help. I feel out of touch."

"You're only out of touch when you start receiving the AARP mailings. If you don't believe me, just wait. It's quite a wake-up call. Then you realize you have no idea what your students are talking about. Come see me then. We'll go shuffle boarding together."

"Maybe you should talk to them. I'm pretty sure they'll tell you I'm a drag. They have ideas I'm not sure if I can get behind."

"A drag? You? You're the goddamn life of the party. And I know these students. What could possibly be complicated about their ideas?"

"I didn't say they were compli—"

He cut me off before I could finish. "It's a fucking haunted house. Ghosts, witches, scarecrows. Those are the ideas they should have."

Through the window behind him, I could see the lake in the distance. A thin haze hung over its surface, obscuring the woods on its opposite bank. A crow landed on the windowsill, a worm squirming in its beak. Its black eyes watched me as if it intended to report whatever I said next.

Noting the shift in my attention, Fowler turned, but the bird flew off before he could see it. We both gazed at the lake instead.

"Apparently," I said, "there's a hidden history here they want to use. From what I'm hearing, there's a tree in the woods that was used for lynching people."

Now wearing a poker face, Fowler regarded me in silence, content to let me talk without revealing the extent of his knowledge. I couldn't tell if he'd already heard this lore or not.

"A woman," I said. "A black woman. Hanged by the neck because she did things for other women when they needed help. And that bloodstain out there—"

"Bloodstain? What bloodstain?"

I gawked at him in disbelief. Did he really say *what bloodstain?*

"You saw it," I said, biting back the tone I normally used when someone tried to gaslight me. "The one we found when you showed me the pavilion?"

"Oh, that?" He waved his hand dismissively. "That's cleaned up."

"No," I said, "I was just out there yesterday." I told him about Isis's fact-finding mission and everything else Zach told us about the Bloody Bucket, though I left out the insinuation that his family had anything to do with its violent history.

Once more, as if to disperse some foul odor, he waved his hand. "You can't trust students to keep their facts straight. Consider what they have to say about Dash."

I leaned forward. "What about him?" I still knew little about the man whose classes I now taught and whose office I now had access to.

"You haven't heard what they say about Dash? Interesting that they haven't shared those rumors with you. You must frighten them, Nat."

"Just tell me."

Now, he leaned forward. I found myself recollecting the way a police officer once leaned across a desk to ask me if I'd taken any illegal drugs the night my car ran over Taryn Hall. In a hushed voice, Fowler said, "That he went into their haunted house and never came out."

"But that's not what happened, I assume."

Once more, he waved his hand, and it took all my will to resist the urge to grab his wrist and sink my fingernails into his skin. "Don't be ridiculous."

"What did happen to Professor Dash, if you don't mind me asking?"

"I don't mind at all. I'm an open book, completely forthcoming. The thing is, we've already talked at length about this."

I searched my memory and came up with nothing except his earlier evasiveness. "No, we didn't. You only told me he wasn't available in the event I wanted to discuss the course material with him."

"I'm sure I said more than that."

"I'm sure you didn't."

He sighed. "He took what you might call an unauthorized leave of absence."

Might call. Even when Fowler sounded forthcoming, he wasn't. Not really.

"Look, it's not worth discussing," he said. "He's somewhere. Probably convalescing. Getting himself back together. This job can take a lot out of you."

"I recall someone mentioning a sabbatical," I said. "I just thought he went off to write a book or something. You make it sound like he could be inside a padded cell."

Fowler didn't answer. He squinted as if fighting back heartburn or a kidney stone. Did he need me to find him an antacid?

"You're not telling me something," I said.

"No, I'm telling you everything. I'm an open book. A glass door so transparent you hardly know it's there. You can see right through me." The wrinkles around his eyes deepened as the straining intensified. Finally, he said, "It's just that we don't know where he is."

"So how do you know he didn't actually disappear in the haunted house?"

"Oh, come on, you sound like the students now. You've seen the dimensions of the slab out there."

I conceded I had, not adding that I also recalled his own remarks about how the area seemed larger once the walls went up. I also wondered about the contraption the students described, the fake floor used to create the illusion of Little Red Riding Hood crawling out of the wolf's exposed entrails. Could that have provided some means for Dash to perform a disappearing act?

"My point," said Fowler, "is don't listen to what the students say. In fact, I wouldn't listen to what that nutjob in public safety has to say either."

He meant Sarge. Then I remembered: it was from him that I heard the cryptic remarks about Dash taking a sabbatical.

"Sarge said that I needed to ask you what happened to Dash," I said.

"Do I look like my brother's keeper? Some public safety officer that guy is. Look, Nat, you need to keep the students' imaginations in check. Sway them away from bad ideas, like that theme they have in mind for the haunted house. What did you say the name of it was, the place that was supposedly out there?"

"The Bloody Bucket," I said, struggling to maintain a neutral tone.

"Yeah, that won't go over so well with the local clientele. Lots of churches out here. It's still the Bible belt, after all. Besides, I doubt it was real. It even sounds made up. Didn't it occur to you that you were being played?"

"No," I said.

"Well, they're devious cunts, these students." A pause to let the profanity sink in. I let the moment pass without response. I knew when someone was testing me. "Make them go with something safe. Fairy tales, for instance."

"Fairy tales aren't safe," I said. "Just ask the Little Mermaid about her surgical scars. Ask the stepsister with the mutilated foot." *Ask Bluebeard's wives*, I almost added, but I felt increasingly as if murderous Bluebeard himself sat across the desk from me. I didn't know Fowler at all, I realized. Who was this man, I wondered, who once again dismissed something I said with a wave of his hand?

"Safer than a Depression-era abortionist. Safer than the history of lynching. I hope this talk was as productive for you as it was for me. I remember why I liked you so much at that conference. Why you made such an impression."

I left him sitting there, realizing as I walked back to Dash's office to retrieve my things that I used none of the speech I prepared to tender my resignation. Not only that, but I had no such plan to leave my temporary position at the college, nor did I have any intention to dissuade my students from using the Bloody Bucket as the theme of their haunted house. As I turned on the light in Dash's office, once more revealing the suspended form of the Slashing Sally doll, I considered how I at least needed to figure out a way of dealing with the interpersonal issues in the group.

Gathering up my things, I once more felt cold, damp air on my skin. I almost blamed the doll, but turning, I found Isis standing in the doorway, her hand upraised in the act of knocking.

"Yo, Professor," she said, "we need to talk about Zach." Then, as if she felt the chill as well, she looked up at the doll's leering face, once more rotating on its own accord. "Hey, that's a *nice* Slashing Sally collectible you have there."

Seven

The doll continued to rotate restlessly as Isis carried on about her misgivings concerning Zach. More specifically, she found him a detriment to the group's morale, thus making her job as president more difficult than necessary. "Besides," she said, "I'm not even sure he's enrolled in classes. He's probably not even an actual student."

Sitting on the chair behind Dash's desk, I caught myself modeling Fowler's techniques. I hid my reaction behind a wall of deflection. Above us, Slashing Sally remained suspended like a possessed body in the act of levitating, its feet roughly at eye level. Through some silent communication, we both agreed to ignore it.

"Why do you think he's not a student?" I asked.

"Is he?"

"You act like you know the answer to that question already."

Isis sighed. "Well, he's not in any of my classes. He's not in your class, and doesn't that indicate a certain lack of investment in what we're trying to do?"

"Which is?"

"Scare the fuck out of people with the haunted house we're putting together."

I caught myself in the act of waving away her answer, a mannerism Fowler used on me just moments ago. How we replicate the apparatuses of power without intending to . . . Fortunately, I managed to stop myself. "I think you're jumping to conclusions. The class isn't some kind of prerequisite."

At least I didn't think it was.

"So he is a student? You've checked?"

"Yes," I said, even though I hadn't. Another apparatus of power: the bald-faced lie. I immediately wished I hadn't said that.

"Well, okay." She didn't sound convinced. "I think he lives back there."

"Back where?"

"In the trees. Camping or something. It's creepy."

This time, I exercised discipline and didn't fire off a quick response. I considered her words. Zach didn't appear homeless—but what can you ever tell about a person simply by looking at them? Never mind the fact that homelessness didn't make a person inherently dangerous or justify contempt. Perhaps she spoke the truth and Zach needed intervention. But where would I turn for the resources I needed? Certainly not to Sarge, who spoke of a homeless camp in the woods and referred to it as some kind of blight on the college. What if Isis went to him with this information? I needed to show care in what I said next.

"If that's the case," I said, "maybe we ought to check on him. Find out if there's anything we can do to help him. Make sure he's safe."

She sniffed. "He doesn't want our help."

"How do you know?"

Now she seemed to consider her own words. "Help isn't what he wants. Professor Dash tried to help him and then—well, never mind."

She must have noticed the expression on my face, the look that said I wanted to hear more. Clearly, she felt she'd said too much already. Or maybe she simply wanted to bait me.

She said, "Well, now no more Professor Dash. But I guess that worked out pretty well for you. You even get his office."

At some point in the last hour, I decided *not* to resign. When that happened, exactly, I couldn't say. But now my jaw tightened at the notion that I owed my position to a vanishing act performed by my predecessor. I could have laid before her feet the sad truth about what it meant to teach higher education as an adjunct, how it amounted to a form of low-wage slavery. How I just needed one bad accident or injury to fall into certain poverty. Stepping into the street in front of an oncoming car—

I stopped myself there. Not her burden.

"I don't know anything about Zach's situation," I said, "but it sounds like you miss Professor Dash."

"I'm in your class because of him. He was supposed to teach it, obviously. He mentored me on the way to becoming the club's president." For a moment, her voice sounded on the verge of cracking, but none of that emotion showed on her face. Her eyes remained dry, her expression stoic.

"Which you seem to take very seriously."

"Oh, I do." She leaned forward, fixed a pair of heavily mascaraed eyes on my own. "Let us do the Bloody Bucket. As a theme. We can tell the story, make the haunted house a kind of simulacrum." She waited to see if her use of the word *simulacrum* would impress me. "That means—"

"I know what a simulacrum is," I said. "I suppose that Professor Dash would agree to this proposal."

She nodded. "He sure would. He liked to promote the idea of service learning." Another beat. "You know what that is too, I take it."

I nodded, resisting the impulse to push back on the condescension. Her tone indicated she meant no disrespect. She wanted a coconspirator. I felt inclined to give her what she wanted, especially after my conversation with Fowler. He would hate it. *Good*, I thought.

Just one thing.

"You have a problem with Zach, but you still want to use his idea?"

She exhaled. "He's holding back parts of it. He can't be trusted. There's more to it. I can feel it. We need to get the whole story and tell it."

"In the name of service learning?" I asked. "Why teach them when you can just scare them?"

"Oh, we'll scare people. We will scare the living fuck out of them. But we'll do it by revealing the true history of this place."

I thought about it. Above us, Slashing Sally hung from her twine noose, her face slowly rotating. I looked up to see her uncanny expression, noticing that her painted eyes seemed to have shifted so that they now looked down toward me, trying to hypnotize me into agreeing and going along with it. Not that it needed to work very hard. More than anything, I wanted to say yes, let's do it. Once more, I felt a cold draft, and I shivered.

"Do you feel that?" I asked Isis.

She blinked. "Feel what? I don't feel anything. That's my superpower."

Evil is the absence of empathy, someone once said. I couldn't recall who, but I repeated those words to Isis.

"Then I guess I'm evil," she said.

"Somehow, I doubt that."

"Doubt all you want. Seriously, how about it? Can we do this thing?"

I tapped my chin, looking up once more at the rotating form of Slashing Sally as if she could bestow any wisdom about what to say next. Finding the doll as hollow and inscrutable as any other worthless deity, I let my gaze drift to the stacks of books I'd brought into the office, the ones I intended to return. *Tell My Horse* sat on top, its presence reminding of how its author became an initiate in vodou practices in Haiti. Something about that tugged at my subconscious, a connection trying to shape itself. Maybe I felt like an initiate, with Isis serving as a high priestess.

Or maybe goddess, considering her name.

"Professor?"

The word stopped my mental plummet. I came back to the conversation.

"I told you before: call me Nat."

"You seemed to vanish there for a moment."

"I'm still processing. What would Professor Dash say about this business?"

"The first rule of the Horror and Occult League is that we don't talk about Professor Dash. And you've made me break that rule already, Nat." She put a little too much emphasis on my name. I wondered if I ought to rescind that directive. "Besides, you're in charge now, not him."

"As club president," I said, "you're in charge."

"Then I say we go with the Bloody Bucket as our theme." She tapped her fist against her knee like a gavel. "But we need to do our research. For one thing, I don't trust Zach's rendition of things."

"For another?" I asked when she said no more.

"For another," she said, choosing her words deliberately, "I want to do this right."

"Which means, I'm guessing, another fact-finding trip in our future."

"Oh, yes, but a different kind. I know a librarian who specializes in this kind of history. The odd stuff, I mean. I know she'll help us. She's my tía."

"We have librarians here," I said. "It's a college, after all."

"Nah, the librarians here just want you to sit down at a computer. They even got rid of all the books and made everything digital. You ever hear of a library without books? That's not how I was raised, not with my tía in the picture. She taught me how to appreciate stories. And not just the ones people bothered to write down. No one knows local lore like her. She can tell where it goes to eat, fuck, and shit. In that order too." Her eyes gleamed as she spoke these words.

"I see. And which library does your aunt work in? Do we have to go far?"

"She's kind of a freelance librarian, always on the move. But don't worry, I know where to find her. I'll even drive."

"You'll have to," I said, "because I don't drive."

"Thought so after all that business about taking the bus. I guess you never learned. That's what happens when you keep your head in these." She picked *Tell My Horse* off the stack of books and waved it in the air. My heart winced as I curtailed the urge to snatch it from her hands. It felt as though she was waving my very soul around in the air, and if she dropped it, it might shatter into a million pieces. Once again, something tried to worm its way through my consciousness. A premonition, maybe? I let it go.

"Yeah," I said when I could think of nothing else to say, "I guess I was too busy to learn."

"Well, I'm the best driver you ever saw. In fact, my tía taught me herself. I even learned by driving the library."

"Driving the library, you say? How does one drive a library?"

But before she could answer, Fowler burst through the door, his lips stretched in a way that made his face look like a contorted mask. He brought with him a gust of cold air that made Slashing Sally spin even faster, her eyes roughly at the same level as his. The two of them looked like grotesque twins, their expressions nearly a match.

I wondered if he needed me to call emergency services to help him stave off a heart attack. He spoke before I could make that offer.

"Did you hear?" From the tone of his voice, I realized he was smiling, his face bloating into an exaggerated Halloween mask of evil glee. "Did you hear?" he asked again before we could answer, his delight impossible to contain. "There's a storm out there in the gulf, and it's turning. A hard right in our direction, heading right toward us. The campus is officially closed. Tomorrow, we get a storm day. We all get to *stay home.*"

Eight

No evidence of an impending storm appeared the next morning. Instead, sunshine filled the air, along with a brisk, steady breeze sweeping tufts of white cloud across a sky of perfect blue. It felt good to go outside, and I left Erik just as I anticipated: happy to spend the day by himself, in charge of the house.

"I'll make sure the batteries in the flashlights still work. Just in case," he said before I could say goodbye and close the door. I knew he would do it too, his mind always focused on safety. Every night, he checked the doors to make sure we remembered to lock them. He always looked both ways before crossing the street, even when he needed to evade the inevitable bully.

"Good idea," I said, though one look at the sky convinced me that we didn't need to worry about losing power. Overnight, the forecasts had become muddled with conflicting storm paths, most suggesting the college closed for nothing. The storm would likely veer further north. Besides, we didn't have much to worry about from a tropical storm.

I thought about how Fowler expressed the news with the elation of an undergraduate. Did that happen to everyone who worked in education for as long as he had? You hated coming to work that much? Maybe Fowler just had a rich personal life and appreciated the fact that a weather event gave him an opportunity to share time with his family. But I just couldn't see it.

As for myself, I surrendered to the idea of going on an adventure with Isis. She picked me up in a car that I heard before I saw, a cacophony of rusted gears leaking oil and puffing fumes.

The car backfired as Isis rolled to a stop and leaned across the passenger seat to look at me. "Fancy," she said.

I looked around, wondering what she meant.

"Your red raincoat," she said, recognizing my puzzlement.

My mother used to insist I dress appropriately for rainy days, and I suppose old habits die hard.

"We're probably still in for some rain," I said. "I'm just trying to be prepared."

Isis grunted dismissively. "These things always miss us. Remember Hurricane Irma? It went right up the state and did a complete loop around us and then kept on going. It's like the weather gods look out for us. In fact, I'd say they wanted us to take this trip by giving us a free day. You'll stay as dry as a bone. I guarantee it."

I thought about times when lightning and thunder shook our little house. My mother referenced a particular loa. *Agua is angry right now. You better stay inside.*

The quality of sky now supported Isis's predication. Still, I decided to keep wearing my raincoat.

"Climb in, Professor."

"Nat," I reminded her.

"Climb in, Nat."

I complied, and as I shut the door behind me, the engine coughed and stopped altogether. Isis swore and set about turning the ignition again. It took several tries, but she managed to get it running once more.

"How far did you say we needed to go?"

"Across the county line and into Vissaria County. However many miles that is."

I regarded her questioningly.

"Don't doubt Grendel, here. She'll get us where we need to go. She's never let me down before." Isis patted the dashboard, causing flakes of red paint to cloud the air around us. Without looking for oncoming traffic, she pulled into the street at about twice the legal speed limit, the car spewing black exhaust.

I could appreciate the fact that she named her ride after a literary monster, but neither the car nor her driving instilled confidence. "In *Beowulf*, Grendel was a 'he,' not a 'she,'" I said.

"Okay, then *he* never let me down," she said as she cut a little too closely in front of another car.

"Unless you're talking about Grendel's mother," I said. "Now, *she* was a monster."

"You sound alike."

"Excuse me? Who sounds alike?"

"You and Professor Dash. That's the sort of thing he'd say."

The sideview mirror hung from the passenger door at a disjointed angle, clearly useless to someone sitting in the driver's seat. It shook and bounced as the car rattled along like a bucket of loose bolts. If I twisted my neck far enough, I could see a portion of my own reflection. I could also see someone else over my shoulder, a figure sitting in the backseat with a pulverized head leaking blood and cranial fluid. I reached through the window and turned it further away, but not before I saw the broken jaw struggle to form a smile. Taryn Hall knew I didn't like cars, and she enjoyed my discomfort.

"Didn't you just break your club's first rule?" I asked, refocusing on what Isis just told me.

"We're off the clock. Away from campus. Some rules, we can loosen."

That felt like an invitation to ask a nagging question. "So what happened to Professor Dash?"

No answer at first. Instead, Isis pressed down on the accelerator and used the opposite lane to pass a slow septic truck. In the distance, I could see an oncoming vehicle closing in on us. Grendel groaned, its engine laboring to meet Isis's demand for speed. I knew that if I looked in the sideview mirror, I would see Taryn Hall still trying to laugh with a lolling, lacerated tongue. It seemed impossible we would make the pass before an imminent collision occurred, but a sudden burst of speed allowed us to pull in front of the septic truck just in time. The driver of the truck used his horn to express his irritation. Isis honked back and gave him the finger.

"Asshole," she said under her breath. Then, as if the world had finally given her enough peace to consider my question, she said, "Who knows what happened to Professor Dash. He just sort of went away."

"As in disappeared?"

"He left his mark, though," she said. A deliberate non-answer. I could sense she wanted to avoid my question.

What followed consisted of an oral history of her time at the college and the impact Professor Dash had on the institution's culture. Isis painted a picture of an affable, slightly bumbling mentor, someone who encouraged risk-taking. Hence why Isis saw opportunity in the Bloody Bucket story as a theme for the haunted house. She wanted to maintain the man's legacy.

"When it was clear he wasn't coming back," she said, "I almost quit everything—the club, college, the whole thing. I thought about becoming a freelance librarian like my tía."

I still didn't know what she meant by *freelance librarian*. "Since when do librarians work freelance?" I asked.

I thought she would hold off on answering until after she completed her next maneuver, overtaking a vintage convertible sports car with a *Don't blame me, I voted for John Kerry* bumper sticker, but even that didn't slow down her end of the conversation. I could see the appalled expression on the face of the convertible's driver as we went by. "It means she's not tied down to a single institution. You know, she works for the people. You play things right, she might give you a library card. She took mine away, but she forgot I had her on speed dial. So now she just doesn't answer when I call."

Droplets began to patter the windshield, the first obvious sign of a storm out in the Gulf of Mexico, hopefully just brushing the shore lightly, avoiding that direct hit predicted only a day ago. Things started to feel wrong, my getting into this car a mistake. The intensity of the rain grew, along with my anxiety, especially when Grendel's wheels went over a slippery section of asphalt, causing a subtle slide in the car's motion. If Isis noticed, she gave no indication. She acted as if nothing worried her.

Except for what she said next.

"You don't think that's his blood, do you?"

Even her voice sounded different, lacking its usual confidence. I saw worry in her face too.

"Whose blood? You mean the blood at the pavilion?"

She nodded, her eyes still fixed on the road. Our speed began to drop as she let her foot off the gas. *Good*, I thought, believing that she intended to turn around. Maybe she, too, recognized that this whole excursion now seemed like a bad idea.

But instead of changing direction, Isis let the car roll to a stop. When I saw what sat in the middle of our lane, I realized why. A gopher tortoise trying to cross to the other side. Sensing us in its vicinity, it retreated into its shell. Our conversation on pause and the car in park, Isis stepped outside and casually picked up the tortoise. I watched as she carried him to safety in the brush, well away from the road. Then she resumed her place behind the wheel, now looking like a goth demon, the rain having caused her mascara to run.

When she turned to look at me, I saw what big, brown eyes she had and that, quickly, the goth demon went away, replaced by something smaller, more vulnerable.

"Why would you ask me that?" I said. "I don't even know what happened to Professor Dash."

She didn't respond. She put the car into gear, and we took off again, hydroplaning as the wheels struggled to find purchase on the wet pavement.

"Do *you* know what happened to Dash?" I asked.

She glanced at me, and I saw that the goth demon had returned. Her eyes blazed red.

"Yeah," she said. "I killed him. Or the haunt did. It's the same thing, though. Right?"

Nine

Nothing further.

I killed him.

At most, the haunt served as an accomplice. No shifting of blame. No attempt to absolve herself of responsibility. In the mirror's reflection, the smile on Taryn Hall's broken mouth grew impossibly wider, distorting her features into something only a sadistic Cubist painter could have imagined. *Your turn to share*, that smile said. *Tell her about me.*

And I knew I would feel compelled to do just that, if in exchange for hearing her story. To have her explain what she meant would require a transaction. I would have to tell her everything about me. It would spill out of my mouth, and I would have no way of stopping it.

Because Taryn Hall would make me describe everything about how I killed her. So I didn't press Isis. Later, I told myself, when the time felt right, I would ask her to explain everything.

When I could make sure Taryn Hall had no mirrors to reach through to me.

Instead, Isis shifted the subject to our destination, sharing trivia about Vissaria County, a locale I knew very little about but which sounded like a locus point for everything weird and off-beat about the state where we both lived. Her aunt sounded like an unofficial historian, collecting local lore that came to her in the form of oral narrative.

"I used to think she collected it all in a notebook," Isis said. "I mean, she could be a writer if she wanted to. She loves books more than anyone I know. But now, I know she stores it all up here." She tapped her forehead as she recalled some of the more arcane stories, including ones that extended far back in time, well before any recorded history, making me wonder how much of them she made up herself.

For instance, as Isis explained to me, understanding what makes Vissaria County strange means coming to grips with what Florida is—or, more precisely, what it *isn't*. We fool ourselves into thinking of the peninsula as a land mass, but in reality, it's a corpse. A giant corpse, that of a great beast of unfathomable size that once wreaked havoc upon the world. Insatiably hungry, it devoured everything in its path—whole forests, mountain ranges, rivers, and early human communities. It continued to grow, becoming large enough to eat away portions of entire continents, and it seemed as if it would eventually consume the whole planet until those early humans set aside their differences and decided to band together to fight it. They eventually succeeded, using powerful weapons lost to time and memory, and the beast took its last breath on the southeastern edge of what would become the North American continent. There, its flesh decayed and rotted down to the bone, eventually becoming a giant fossil. Over time, forests grew upon its remains, swamps and rivers formed.

Fearing their descendants would forget what it once was and follow the animals that migrated to live upon it, those early humans carved out a great lake on its southern end, fashioning it into the shape of a skull. The ominous shape of this lake, they believed, would serve as a warning to their children and the children of their children: Do not go here. Meanwhile, the heart of the great beast didn't decay with the rest of its organs, but rather it lay buried somewhere in the region that became Vissaria County, still connected to the underground rivers that once served as the creature's veins and arteries.

Though buried deep and out of reach, the heart sometimes manages to produce a beat, like periodic aftershocks of its terrible life, and the people there can feel it beneath their feet. The sound fills their souls with a foreboding they can't explain, and many of them respond by performing evil acts that defy reason. For people did forget how to read the warnings their ancestors carved into the earth, and they did move onto the back of the great beast, building cities and canals. One day, that heart will manage more than just a beat, and blood will fill the beast once again. All of which will likely doom the whole planet because no one knows how to get along anymore, much less how to fight such a monster.

According to another story, Vissaria County owes its strangeness to its long-standing correctional facility, one that houses an inordinate number of serial killers and mass murderers, the perpetrators of crimes of so heinous a nature that their records remain hidden from public view. No trial nor any media preceded their incarceration. Instead, once apprehended, these criminals found themselves transported to that prison so that they could rot in a special ward, somewhere deep in the prison. For reasons that no one can explain, this special ward has no guards, yet the prisoners cannot escape. Either that, or they don't want to, having developed a world of their own making within the walls of that facility. According to one employee of the prison, the situation involves an ancient god that the indigenous people of the region once held captive on that parcel of land. When white settlers "acquired" the land through the usual means, like war and genocide, the surviving natives told them that if they insisted on becoming the new stewards of the land, then they needed to maintain that area as a prison and borrow some of the ancient magic to keep any evil presence there from escaping. Apparently, someone listened, and now we have the Vissaria County Prison. But either the ancient magic didn't work so well or the Europeans didn't apply it the right way, because some of the malignance leaks out from time to time. Sometimes, that makes people crazy, sometimes mean, and often both at the same time.

After nearly an hour of driving, as well as some near collisions that would have sent us both to an early grave, we reached our destination.

The Vissaria County Correctional Facility, as luck would have it.

It looked nothing like the fearsome, gothic edifice I imagined. Instead, we encountered a flat, gray, mostly featureless building that sat behind a high fence studded with chicken wire. Canals bordered it on all sides, forming something like a moat and further deterrence to anyone trying to make a jail break. According to Isis, a giant alligator named Gustav lived in one of those canals. Allegedly, Gustav had eaten at least three prisoners who tried to escape. While the Florida Fish and Wildlife office generally removed nuisance alligators of such temperament, the prison's warden had not only successfully lobbied to leave the animal unmolested, but he also treated it to a weekly ration of leftovers from the prison's canteen. Rumor had it that some of those rations had, in the past, included the bodies of prisoners who'd died while serving their sentences, their records mysteriously vanishing in the process.

Some of these details I later learned from Halia, Isis's tía, who occasionally parked the library in the parking lot of the prison. Once I saw the library—a huge parcel truck or moving vehicle in a former life, now painted black and stocked with shelves full of books in its cargo area—everything Isis had told me made sense. Essentially, Halia maintained her own mobile library within the borders of Vissaria County, though it never became clear if she kept a formal agreement with elected officials.

"I've even seen Gustav," Halia said regarding the monstrous, man-eating alligator, "and trust me, he's bad news. But he's not the worst thing in that prison. Not by a long shot."

We stood near the loading ramp of the library, though Halia maintained that it now served patrons in wheelchairs. "Got to keep ADA compliant," she said without specifying what federal or state agency she answered to. Books packed the truck's rear bay, numbering in the hundreds, maybe even thousands. Either way, more than I would have thought possible.

"You can tell her about Gustav later. We came for some specific intel."

Halia raised her manicured eyebrows at Isis. At this point, Halia had still not said one word to her niece, and she'd barely looked directly at her either. In fact, when we approached her initially, Halia kept her face hidden behind an old paperback, pretending that Peter Straub's *Floating Dragon* kept her too engrossed to acknowledge us. She seemed to warm immediately when I told her how much I loved that novel, even more so than *Ghost Story* or *The Throat*. "I like a girl who knows her Straub," she'd said, even as she maintained a cold silence while Isis criticized the sort of titles she kept on hand when she parked the library outside the prison during visiting hours every Thursday.

"People need lighter reading, Tía. I know you like peddling books, but you've got to consider what your patrons want. They've got enough horror in their daily lives. Sorry, Professor—I mean, Nat. I know you love that shit too."

Hearing that information prompted Halia to bestow me with a smile both warm and sardonic at the same time.

"I don't 'peddle' books," Halia said to me as if I'd made that comment. "I'm here because of library truancy. The inmates would probably be pretty good about returning books, but sometimes, it isn't so easy getting them back to me from behind those walls. If I actually collected fines, you know how much money would waiting for me behind that gate? A whole Fort Knox. But I'd rather have the books back, you know? People forget that a library's for lending, not giving away. I'm just trying to serve my goddamn community."

"That's why you keep sending more books in there," Isis said, apparently unbothered by her aunt's lack of attention or acknowledgment.

Instead of answering Isis directly, Halia fixed her eyes on me. "Everyone needs books, especially people who get locked up for life. I don't care what you've done, but being denied the written word is cruel and unusual punishment. You strike me as someone who'd agree."

"She's my fucking literature professor. Of course she'd agree."

"So, what is it you do?" Halia asked me, pretending to have not heard anything said by Isis.

For a moment, I thought about how I could see Taryn Hall in reflections, even as she remained invisible to everyone else. I resisted to temptation to poke Isis just to make sure she existed in physical form. Instead, I reminded myself that she drove me here, and as far as I knew, ghosts couldn't drive.

"I'm a literature professor," I said. Then I caught myself. "Actually, I'm an adjunct instructor." I thought again. "For now. I usually work retail. At least I make more money doing that."

"I hear that, sister. Librarians don't make shit either. If I could figure out a way to do it, I'd add a coffee shop back here for some much-needed funding." Then, as if noticing Isis for the first time, she said, "What the fuck are you doing here, anyway?"

"It's my volunteer day," Isis said, beaming proudly at her aunt, who finally hugged her. The sudden change in mood left me questioning how much of what I'd seen up until that point amounted to a performance. Either way, I felt instantly jealous of the connection I now saw.

It turned out that Isis really did some kind of volunteer work inside the prison. "I told you, I know all about service learning," she said. "Professor Dash helped me set it up."

"Jesus Christ, the sainted Professor Dash," Halia said. "He ever turn up again?"

"She doesn't know rule one," said Isis. "About how we don't talk about Professor Dash." She went on to explain how her service learning consisted of going into the prison and working in an area designated for babysitting.

"Babysitting?" I asked. "In a prison?"

"Spouses don't always have someone to watch their kids," she said, going on to describe how they kept an area designated for that purpose, complete with broken-down play equipment, ratty toys, torn books (though not, she added, to her aunt's relief, from Halia's library), and, finally, of all things, rabbits—though Isis conceded that she didn't know if they would still have the rabbits when she went inside. Apparently, the warden allowed the rabbits strictly as a courtesy to an eccentric prisoner named Leonardus Engel, allegedly the oldest and longest-serving inmate in the entire prison.

Isis couldn't pinpoint this man's precise age, and neither, he maintained, could he, though he insisted that Isis call him Len or Lenny. He looked, to her, like a lot of old people—his bald head covered in age spots, his mouth full of broken and rotting teeth—but she loved how he liked to make up stories, almost always about events in the distant past, some of them going back not just decades but centuries. When asked about what earned him a life sentence, Lenny Engel would say something different each time, though the word *piracy* came up often, as well as references to the nefarious influence the King of Spain held over his sentencing.

"If I ever get out," he once told Isis, "I'll exact my revenge and collect what's due to me."

"And what's that?"

He remained cagey in his response. "You can't possibly think he came by all that gold through pure luck, do you? Happened by it when he was walking down the street?"

"How would I know how much gold he has?" Isis said. "Does Spain even still have a king?"

Lenny Engel would sigh theatrically at that. "You should know the answer to that better than me. Time moves quite differently inside these walls."

He amused Isis with such quips, and she loved his funny accent. More to the point, she needed to work with Leonardus Engel because the warden gave him the responsibility of the rabbit hutches that took up a good portion of the children's area. In fact, the old man relished the company of children and enjoyed regaling them with stories about ancient kingdoms and civilizations so old that they'd become lost to time and imagination. He liked to seat the children in a circle, each child with a rabbit on his or her lap, as he hypnotized them with these tales. Listening in as she, too, held a rabbit, Isis would find herself transported to faraway places. Even the air would begin to smell differently as he spoke, and not always in a pleasant way.

"But I mainly go there to help out with the rabbits," said Isis. Each time she crossed the bridge over the canal and passed through the various security gates, she expected to learn that her beloved Lenny Engel had finally succumbed to age and been fed to Gustav. "Gustav might be as old as him," she said.

"Older," said Halia. "He's a goddamn dinosaur—literally. And hey, one thing before you go in there." She went to one of the bookshelves and reached for something on top. Isis seemed to know what to expect as Halia handed her a book.

"Really? Still?" Isis noticed me trying to read the title in her hand, so she held it up for me to get a good look. *The Werewolf of Ponkert* by H. Warner Munn. I knew of the author only vaguely, having seen the name in a concordance of pulp fiction from the early 20th Century. The garish cover depicted a demon with a green face looking down upon a werewolf holding an unconscious woman. "I'm telling you, no one in there wants to read this shit."

"I don't know," I said, "it looks like fun to me." It really did. I reached out for it, but Halia gently patted my hand away.

"Oh, no. That book is waiting for its real owner to come back. I'm hoping to find him. Using it as bait, I guess." To Isis, she said, "You make sure people see it, okay?"

"Yeah, yeah," Isis said, "just no more shit about the people I miss." She spoke at a volume that suggested she intended the remark only for Halia's ears, and nobody brought up rule number one. Clearly, they'd carried out this ritual before.

I busied myself by looking at the other books on the shelf and pretended to not listen as Halia reminded her about the person she hoped to find, apparently someone who would notice the cover of the book. A boyfriend, I supposed, or at least someone Halia cared about a great deal.

"You know I'm mainly around kids," Isis said. "And Mr. Engel."

"Just keep an eye out. Remember, he's tall. He stands out."

"Yeah, yeah," Isis said, but her demeanor indicated she would do what her aunt said.

"And you need an umbrella? I don't want that book getting wet."

"I brought a windbreaker," she said. We watched as she opened the rear door of her car and withdrew a yellow coat about two sizes too large.

I couldn't resist as I watched her slide her arms into the windbreaker's sleeves. "Fancy."

Isis smirked. "You wish you could be as fancy as me. Speaking of your amazing raincoat, you going to be okay out here braving the elements with the crazy librarian while I go inside and do my thing? If you want, I can probably get you in. I'm assuming you'd pass a background check."

The wind began to pick up, and as if on cue, the rain that chased us during our journey finally caught up to us. At that point, it fell lightly, not enough to make me concerned we had anything to worry about from the storm trying to make landfall. I tugged down on the hood of my raincoat while Halia opened an umbrella. Already damp, Isis just let the raindrops fall where they may as she waited for me to say something about how I'd do in a background check. I didn't want to hand over my ID and have someone find a record of what I did to Taryn Hall in front of Isis.

A prison. I let her take me to a fucking prison.

"We came to talk to Halia, didn't we?" I said, looking for the easiest way out of the predicament. "Plus, if we stay too long, we might end up driving through some rough weather."

"You've seen my skills. You've got nothing to worry about. You coming in with me or staying with the crazy librarian?"

"Let the crazy librarian and your professor talk," Halia said.

Isis shrugged and turned toward the small bridge that spanned the canal to the prison's gates.

"And keep that book dry," Halia called after her.

We watched as Isis stuffed the book under her windbreaker with one hand while flipping us the bird with the other.

"She's a goddamn truant," said Halia, notwithstanding the smile on her face. "But believe it or not, she's read practically every book in the library."

"I believe it," I said. "She's smart."

"You'd never know it from the way she barely squeaked through high school. In all fairness, I probably bear some responsibility for that. She spent a lot of time she should've been studying with me, helping me paint the library. You like the color?"

I said I did. I had my own affinity with black, despite my red raincoat, the color of every single one I'd ever owned. During one especially wet summer, my mother let me choose the color myself, stipulating I couldn't choose black. I chose red because of Nicholas Roeg's film version of *Don't Look Now*. My mother indulged me, having no idea I based my decision on the style worn by a knife-wielding maniac. Now, I always bought a red raincoat whenever I could afford one.

"We can sit inside," Halia said. "I'll keep the door open as long as the rain doesn't blow in and get the books wet. You can even browse if you want. Doesn't look like many people want to grab reading material today."

I nodded. "Got any Daphne Du Maurier?" I asked since I had *Don't Look*

Now stuck in my head.

"*Jamaica Inn*, bottom shelf. Still waiting for *Rebecca* to come back from a nice lady who keeps her mother's mummified hand in a china cabinet. She uses it on a Ouija board so she and her mom can still talk. I'll probably never see that book again, but you've got to cut your losses sometimes—especially when the person in question keeps human remains in their home. I can understand a box of ashes, but you know."

I didn't know, but I certainly had questions, just not the right way to ask them. Instead, I found *Jamaica Inn* and sat on a wooden box while I flipped through the yellowing pages, wondering what on earth to do with information like that. Halia sat on a similar one across from me. She bailed me out by returning the subject to Isis.

"I couldn't believe it when she said she planned to go to college," she said. "Do you think she's going to make it?"

From what I'd seen, I did. I told her about the club, talking up Isis's leadership, and it turned out Halia already knew a lot about that. That information opened the door for me to mention Zach's narrative about the Bloody Bucket and Isis's aspiration to incorporate the story into the haunt this year. Halia listened as the rain continued to fall just outside the library's open door. Occasionally, people passed by on their way to the prison, mostly defeated-looking women, likely wives and girlfriends of inmates. Some of them had children in tow. I couldn't imagine taking kids behind those bleak walls, but I supposed they could at least look forward to holding a rabbit. Halia nodded and waved to some of them, but except for a few curious glances, she received nothing in return. By the time I got to Isis's plan, Halia placed an unlit cigarette in her mouth.

"Jeez, that Isis sure likes to court controversy," she said. "But she comes by it honestly, being related to me." She paused and gazed thoughtfully at the prison in the distance. "It's not like they didn't murder women in those days. You know the name Stella Long?"

I did, but only vaguely, so Halia had to remind me about an infamous mass lynching that took place in the early 1900s in a town called Newberry. I remembered a photograph connected to the event—a group of well-dressed white men posing around six corpses strewn in the dirt near their feet. As in other photos of its kind, the men looked proud of what they'd done, though they'd gone to great lengths to hide the body of Stella, the lone woman amongst the victims. Her corpse lay buried under the bodies of the others. However, in close-ups, you could clearly see her face, though her heavily pregnant belly remained concealed.

"That happened before the time period of Zach's story," I said, "and besides, we're over a hundred miles away from Newberry. Plus, Zach didn't mention pregnancy, other than the woman being some kind of midwife."

"Not like they would keep reliable records on that," said Halia. "Public officials usually tried to sanitize or cover up records of these crimes. But that phrase, bloody bucket, complicates things further."

"How so?"

She went on to explain the oral history behind the "Bloody Bucket Bridge," a Florida legend involving an ex-slave woman who acted as the midwife for her community. "A lot of families in rural Florida faced extreme poverty, so she took upon herself to relieve them of unwanted burdens. The story goes that she went to extreme measures in doing so, usually killing newborns before they could draw first breath. But as time went on, the guilt weighed upon her more and more, and she started to hear ghostly crying sounds from the great beyond. Some mornings, she would wake up to find her cleaning bucket filled with blood, and she would take it to a bridge near her home so she could empty it into the river. Eventually, she either fell off that bridge or jumped—no one knows—but either way, she drowned. Supposedly, you can look down from that bridge today and see blood in the water."

I thought about it, sensing a thread of connection that just needed someone to tie it together. Before I could figure out how, Halia added more.

"Of course, in another version of the story, the midwife wasn't a serial killer of newborns at all. Instead, she knew how to help families end unwanted pregnancies well before anyone went into labor. I probably don't need to tell you that certain people have agendas that make her a useful scapegoat."

"And prejudices."

"Amen, sister. But regardless of that, the location is off. The so-called 'Bloody Bucket Bridge' is well north of here."

I thought about it, still unable to make everything harmonize. I thought of the Mark Twain quote about how if history didn't repeat itself, it did somehow manage to rhyme. Maybe we just needed rhymes instead of absolute accuracy. "Maybe Zach heard the story from somewhere else and is simply lying," I said.

"Or extrapolating. Stories migrate sometimes, especially when they exist as legends and folklore. It's not like you're going to open a history book and read about the Bloody Bucket. When people pull up their roots, their stories go along with them, and they grow new roots—the stories and people alike. Stories don't stay in one place without official documents pinning them down. They get up and wander on their own sometimes too."

"Like ghosts," I said, trying not to think of Taryn Hall waiting for me in the back of Isis's car.

"Sure, like ghosts. Jeez, it's really starting to come down."

Outside, rain battered the asphalt and turned the prison into a faint outline behind a veil of mist. "Do you need to close the door?"

"Only if the wind changes direction." She studied my face as if she saw Taryn Hall's reflection in my eyes. "You mind me asking how you ended up with such gorgeous green eyes?"

I laughed. "Why? Because they don't go with the rest of me?" I paused. Normally, I deflected compliments. I didn't like people getting too personal. But something about Halia made me want to answer, especially when I heard what she said next.

"They match the rest of you just fine."

I smiled, and she listened as I told her about my parents, the unlikeliest of couples, starting with how my father came from a family of mechanics and farmers down south in Homestead and how he allegedly found my mother wandering on a beach in South Florida, fully clothed but soaking wet. My mother told him she swam all the way from Haiti, and he didn't believe her, of course, but he saw no sign of a boat or raft anywhere. Even after they married over the objections of his family, she never altered that story, not even after she successfully applied for asylum in this country. Whenever anyone asked her, she stuck to the same account: she swam to get here, and my father happened to walk by at precisely the right moment to see her emerge from the surf at Key Biscayne. Afterwards, he took her to Denny's, where he fell in love with her as he watched her wolf down a hamburger and a plate of fries.

I watched Halia's reaction as I told her how I never once in my entire life saw my mother swim, so I had trouble believing the story. Halia maintained an expression of steadfast seriousness through this entire account.

"I believe her," said Halia. "I know this guy who walked all the way here from the Miccosukee Indian reservation, and that's who I'm trying to—hey!"

The veil of mist seemed to part, and we saw Isis coming forth, apparently finished with her volunteer work.

"It doesn't seem like she was gone that long," I said. In truth, I felt some relief. The rain made me anxious to return home, concerned that we'd underestimated the impact of some extreme weather.

"No, she wasn't," said Halia.

Something in Isis's gait looked different, her posture off somehow. I even noticed a slight limp.

"Is she okay?" I asked Halia.

"She better be okay." She called out: "Hey, chica, you got my book?"

Isis said nothing as she held up something and waved it at us.

"It's getting *wet*," Halia said. "Cover it up!"

"It's really starting to come down," I said out loud before I caught myself. Halia spoke those exact words only moments ago. Miss Obvious to the rescue.

Halia didn't reply, hopping down to the ground and gesturing for me to follow so she could close the back of the library. She opened her umbrella while I covered my head with the hood of my slicker. Quite suddenly, things felt wrong.

"Walk faster," Halia said, but Isis didn't change her pace. Halia stepped toward her but stopped. The rain seemed to twirl and dance around Isis like a small tornado, lessening just enough for us to stand together when she finally got close enough to talk. Her dark hair lay matted against her skull, all her makeup washed away.

"Here," Isis said, thrusting the book at Halia.

Halia looked momentarily frozen at the sight of the damp paperback, but she took it and began rubbing it against her shirt with the hand not holding the umbrella. "Didn't I teach you how to handle books? I expected better of you." She walked back to the library's rear door. "Come with me. You need to dry off while I rescue this book." She didn't look back as she opened the door just wide enough to slip in.

But Isis didn't follow, and neither did I. I stared at her, trying to understand what looked so wrong about her, and realized it had something to do with her other hand, the one that didn't hold the book. She kept it under her windbreaker, pressed close to her body.

"We need to go," she said. Her free hand reached into a pocket and extended a key chain to me. "You need to drive."

I stared at the keys. A stand-off ensued, neither of us budging, the keys dangling there, me not taking them.

"I don't drive," I said. "Not anymore."

After what happened to Taryn, I foreswore ever getting behind the wheel of a car again.

"I need you to drive." Her hand remained like that, stubborn and unyielding. "Please."

I saw then what looked like paint on her hand, red streaks that the rain caused to run in rivulets down her wrist. She hid something underneath her windbreaker—I knew that for certain. I could also feel the weather tighten its fist around us as the rain quickened. We'd made a horrible mistake coming here. Just how horrible, I wouldn't know until I saw what she kept hidden from sight.

From behind her came the sound of a siren. Alerting us to a tornado or an escape? I couldn't tell. Part of me wanted Halia to come back out and take charge. Part of me didn't.

"She's busy with her precious book," Isis said as if she could read my thoughts. "Look, I know you can drive. I know you ran someone over. I need you to take the wheel. We've got to go. Now."

Shaking, I took the keys.

Ten

The wind and rain grew much worse. I tightened my grip on the wheel as the weather caused me to recall other details about the day my father met my mother. It happened right after Hurricane Andrew devastated the southern end of the peninsula. My father still lived with his parents at the time, struggling to find a way to put his skill set to work. They lived near a nuclear power plant, something which I thought a great deal about in the days after he received a grim medical diagnosis. Before that, as a young man, he liked to tinker with gadgets and machines. He possessed an aptitude for not only fixing things but building them too. That made him invaluable at home after the storm blew through. All the damage meant long days made more difficult because of the sun and humidity. One evening, he felt the need to see the ocean. He didn't expect to find recreation, nor did he particularly want anything like that. He just wanted to break up his routine and feel the cool breeze blowing from the sea.

That's how he found my mother stepping out of the surf.

"At first, I thought I was looking at a mermaid or something," he told me. "She walked out of the ocean with such grace. She looked otherworldly. Especially since she came out fully dressed." I wondered if he just said that to preserve her modesty and his, so I pressed gently.

"Why did you think she was a mermaid? Don't they have fins instead of legs?"

He shrugged. "Maybe because she looked like a natural feature of the ocean. Maybe also because she said she swam all the way here. Sometimes, she would tell me she had some help from the surge created by the storm.

But that's crazy. Right?"

My turn to shrug. I didn't know. She never talked about what made her take the journey or what she left behind. She just wanted a completely new start, and the way my father fell in love with her so instantly gave her that chance. I like to think she fell in love with him that quickly too, but I don't know. I seldom saw her smile. Hardly more than I saw her swim, which was never. She remained a mystery to all of us, I guess. Maybe she really did swim all the way to my father and received help from a hurricane. Part of me, perhaps the better part, wanted to believe that.

If only I could rely on similar torrential forces for aid now. I gripped the wheel of Isis's car, struggling to see through the windshield. Only one of the wipers worked—the one on the passenger side, thus making things doubly difficult. Outside, the wind and rain conspired to create crazy patterns on the asphalt, sigils that defied understanding.

Next to me, Isis stared ahead blankly, her hand still hidden under the windbreaker. I risked quick glances toward her, noticing blood on her sleeves that the rain had failed to wash away. She kept quiet and stone-faced, even as I kept pressing her to tell me what happened to her and if I needed to take her to a hospital.

Finally, I threatened to stop the car so I could examine her myself. She answered brusquely, "I'm fine."

"But the blood."

"It isn't mine. Just drive."

"Then whose? What the hell happened to you in there?"

Irritated, she slowly unveiled her hand. I slowed the car, bracing myself to see some awful mutilation or injury. "Keep going," she said. "Seriously, I'm fine."

"But the rain," I said. *But everything.*

"There's no one here to run over. The road's empty."

The cruelty of her remark cut deep. I pressed the gas pedal. The car roared for both of us.

Finally, she showed me the source of the blood.

I couldn't tell what she held at first. It looked like something from a butcher shop. A heart or a kidney or—

"Oh, my god," I said. I now saw the newly formed ears, the closed eyes of the thing that would have become a rabbit eventually.

Satisfied that I'd seen it, Isis removed her windbreaker and wrapped it around the bloody remains. Carefully, she set it on the floor of the car. Once again, I let our speed decrease. Neither of us said anything. Behind Isis's tough exterior, I sensed unspoken trauma and pain.

Eventually, she turned to me. "I'm sorry for what I said a moment ago."

I couldn't return her gaze thanks to the worsening road conditions. I gripped the wheel so tightly my hands hurt.

"Forget it."

"No, that was a shitty thing to say."

"No, demanding that I drive while you held a dead thing was shitty. Isis, I'm going to ask again: what happened in there?"

A tense quiet ensued before she answered. "I think I sold my soul."

I didn't know what to say to that. I let the silence answer for me.

"But it was for a good reason," she said.

Then the words flowed forth.

Eleven

Isis's Narrative

Isis passed through the usual checkpoints without incident, undergoing the typical security measures she'd come to expect, the metal detectors, the pat-down. Thankfully, the latter came from a female guard and not the pervy middle-aged man from last time who paid too much attention to her inner thighs. Isis smiled to express her appreciation for keeping the pat-down professional, but the guard avoided eye contact as she picked up *The Werewolf of Ponkert* and began deliberately turning one page after another rather than flipping through it.

"Expect to find a file hidden in there?" Isis asked.

The guard regarded Isis coldly and started over again at the beginning, her concentration apparently ruined. This time, something did fall out, and Isis thought, *Oh shit, there really is a file in there,* but it turned out to be a gray business card with Halia's name and phone number on it—one of her "library cards," which the last reader of the book apparently used as a bookmark. The guard waited for Isis to pick it off the floor before handing over the book, her face set in a permanent scowl.

"Have a nice day," Isis said as she strolled past a group of miserable-looking visitors, very few children this time, she noted with some measure of relief.

Because she wanted some private time with Lenny Engel without any distractions. Later, I would find an old essay she wrote for Professor Dash in his office drawer that explained why. In this essay, Isis wrote:

I thought "this service learning" project would turn out to be dumb and boring.

Partly because I actually hate kids, and I'm not all that fond of rabbits either. Probably because they share something in common with kids that I don't care for; namely, all the pooping they do. But it turns out I really like Leonardus (or Lenny) Engel, who says he's the oldest living inmate in the Florida prison system. How old? I can't tell, but he looks about the age of my abuelo, which, in numerical terms, is old as fuck.

(I noticed that Dash circled the word "fuck" in red pen, the sole mark on the page. From what I can gather, he never returned the essay to Isis.)

The essay continued with some vague and, I assumed, imaginary anecdotes that Engel shared with her, including his strange recollection of becoming lost in the Florida wilderness and coming upon a warm spring that an indigenous woman promised would restore him to health, for he'd suffered an arrow wound during the course of his travels. The spring also apparently revived his libido, which he put to good use with the woman on the bank of the spring. Too many details about that for my taste. I wondered to what extent Isis embellished this part of the narrative and if she did so just to embarrass Dash. I skipped ahead, where I read the following:

While in prison, Mr. Engel has heard a lot and seen a lot. He's a wealth of information about the first people who settled in Florida, including how they occupied a great city that used to sit at the mouth of the Miami River. "You mean Miami?" I asked, feeling a little bratty, and he said with absolute seriousness, "Oh, much older than that." He says that traces of their civilization lie hidden under the waves and that someday a tsunami will wash away ours, the same way it happened with the older one. He says it occurs over and over like that. I think I like Mr. Engel, though I don't know why he's in prison. He says he'll get out eventually. Some day. As old as he looks, that day better hurry up and get here. In a way, I hope it never does. Who'll take care of all the rabbits? I suppose I do sorta like the rabbits.

As it turned out, Isis wanted to go to the prison that day not just so she could see her aunt but also so she could see Leonardus Engel. As expected, she found him amongst the rabbit hutches, wearing his usual orange jumpsuit.

"It's been a while," he said as he handed her the plump white rabbit he'd been stroking. "I was afraid you'd forgotten about your poor incarcerated friend."

"I'll never forget about you," she said. "You can be sure of that."

He raised his full eyebrows upon hearing these words. Isis described how high and arched they were. Only a few wisps of gray hair remained on his head, while the eyebrows remained a deep brown and grew so full that they nearly met in the center of his forehead.

"Never?" he said. "Do I have your word on that? It's very important to a person of great misfortune such as me to know he has friends in the outside world. People he can depend upon."

"I'll never forget you," Isis said, giving only the briefest thought to how leaving out a simple word like *about* changed the meaning of her sentence. She thought he said all these things as a prelude to telling her that he would die soon, that they would never see each other again after today.

But he just laughed. "I'll never forget *you*. Even when you're an old abuela yourself, sitting all alone in the ruins of your decrepit home, surrounded by rising water, about to take your last breath. Even as your skin withers and wrinkles, I'll hold your hand and whisper reminders of the beautiful woman you once were. As you are now, I mean."

"Aw, shucks, Mr. Engel." Used to his whimsy and macabre humor, she still felt uneasy about the specificity of the scene he described. Her, owning a home? Never. Ridiculous. She changed the subject and asked him if he'd ever heard of the Bloody Bucket.

It turned out that he had indeed, and he went on to provide details that went well beyond the anecdotal information related to me by Halia. He had not only heard of the rumored Bloody Bucket, but he could describe how its signature drink tasted, how its nuanced flavors surpassed more sophisticated cocktails, a thing of refinement too good for the ruffians catered to by Bon Manman."

"Bon Manman?" repeated Isis.

"A moniker she acquired from some of the Creole-speaking laborers, many of whom picked the strawberries she used. It means something like 'good mother,' though in her case, they may have used the phrase with more irony than endearment. Bon Manman knew how to use a knife better than most men, and pity he who failed to pay her girls for services rendered."

His rheumy eyes seemed to gaze at something faraway in the distance.

"You know, she used strawberries grown on the site of a Seminole Indian massacre. You can hardly imagine the devastation they endured as war forced them further south into that strange land. But from their blood came the most delicious strawberries, without which the Bloody Bucket would have been a pale shade of what it was. People came from miles and miles away just to take a sip of it. Don't you wish you could try it?"

According to Isis, she began to feel as she often did in Engel's presence—a bit light-headed, as if his words alone had a more intoxicating effect than any moonshine concoction. The idea of a massacre revolted her, but the more he talked, the more she did wish she could try it.

"Yes, I do," she said. To her own ears, her voice started to sound as far away as his own. During this conversation, they moved to a remote area beyond the rabbit hutches—the guards regarded Lenny Engel as too old to amount to a threat and thus he could wander about as he pleased without supervision. Isis still held the plump white rabbit, stroking it absentmindedly. There seemed even less guard presence today. Maybe the impending storm required their attention elsewhere.

Engel smiled and tapped her hand. "If you really do, there is a way. You can call her forth."

"Call who?"

"Why, Bon Manman, of course!"

As Isis listened carefully as he described what she must do, she looked down at the rabbit in her arms in horror. Her hand under its belly felt something stirring.

When Engel finished his instructions, she said, "I can't do it. I just can't."

"You can with this." From the inside of his orange jump suit, he produced a crudely made object, its tip sharpened into a lethal blade. She stared at the sight of something so forbidden, so clearly against the law. He held it forth without fear. What would happen if she called for help? She should. She he knew she should. But surely, he would cut her throat to keep her silent.

Or so she told herself to justify her lack of action. But complicity, not fear, motivated her silence. A part of her that she never knew existed wanted to take the weapon and follow his instructions.

"You'll not only do this for yourself," said Lenny Engel, "but for me. I feel as if my time in this prison has finally come to an end, and I must leave. Today. By doing what I ask, you'll assist me in that endeavor. For I can't do it myself."

The major part of the rabbit's remains, he said, must go to Gustav, the monstrous alligator inhabiting the canal outside those walls. "My true jailer. He'll never let me leave until he tastes my flesh. I cannot depart until he does—or until we fool him into believing he has. You do want me to leave, dear Isis, yes? When the waters rise around the ruins of your final home and your body has grown so weak and old that you can't rise from your own bed to escape, do you want to drown there all alone? Do you want me to appear by your side so that you can place your hand in mine and allow me to distract you from that awful fate? I'll remind you of the good times you and I have shared, repaying you for the kind distraction you have given me. Because it will happen. It has already happened. And it will keep on happening. You have no recourse except to make sure you're not alone. And only by setting me free today can I appear to you on that day."

Isis felt her eyes filling with tears. Somehow, she knew he spoke the truth. She said she dreamed about such a death starting a very young age. She knew what it would feel like when the waters rose around her and began filling her lungs.

"There's darkness all around," she said.

"I'll bring the light," he said.

He showed her where to cut, and he helped control the animal's thrashings as it died. Then he instructed on how to remove the tiny gestating form inside it, explaining how she must take it with her to use it in summoning Bon Manman. The rest of the remains they dropped into a cleaning bucket near their feet. Those, he said, she must toss into the greedy mouth of Gustav.

"But first," he said, and he took the knife from her hand and cut into his own wrist. She watched as black blood flowed from the opened vein. He allowed it to flow into the bucket, coating the white fur of the dead animal. "This will provide the right flavor. Fool him just enough for me to slip away."

Then he winked at her.

It must have happened during that wink, so fast she hardly noticed.

The knife in her hand nicked the tip of her finger. An accident, perhaps. Perhaps not.

"It looks like he'll get a taste of you as well," Engel said as her own blood dripped into the bucket. "But don't fear. If Gustav learns your scent and comes for you when the waters rise, I'll be there as well."

So much blood flowed from Engel's vein. So thick and black, it looked as old as time. How could he even be alive, she wondered, much less look so unaffected by its loss? Eventually, little of the rabbit's white fur remained visible, its hide now just a sticky blackness.

Finally, letting a few last drops of ichor fall from his wrist, Engel, like a cat, used his tongue to clean away the traces of what remained. Then he asked her to say back to him what she needed to do with the remains. He smiled in approval at her perfect recollection.

"But one little problem," she said as Engel dabbed the corner of his mouth. He waited patiently for her to continue. "Scratch that—one *big* problem. The guards. The check points. You expect me to walk out carrying this gory mess? They'll stop me. And you—what will they do with you?"

"They won't even see you, sweet Isis, Queen of the Nile. You remind me so much of your namesake, you know."

"Stop the bullshit, Mr. Engel. I'm not buying it."

Whether or not Isis actually expressed her feelings this way, I of course don't know. Whether or not any of these things happened the way she described, I don't know either. I have only her account. But according to her, Engel looked momentarily angry before his expression melted into one of hurt.

"I'm bestowing a great gift, Isis. I've waited for many years to find someone like you. I believed that I'd find the one I sought in one of the many children who came to visit the prison rabbits. I never expected you. And now you disavow me? Say that you don't believe me?" He sighed. "Believe your eyes, then."

With this finger, he reached out to her. Before he could touch her, she flinched. But he smiled reassuringly, so she let him do as he intended, pressing the tip of his index finger against her forehead as if drawing something.

"Drawing what?" I asked, my hands still gripping the wheel, afraid of taking my eyes off the road. Even as we passed woods and open field, I expected a figure to materialize out of the air, running into the road and in front of the path of the wheels. I expected to both hear and feel the crunch of bone as we rolled over them.

"I don't know. I couldn't see it. But I picked up the mess, including my tía's stupid book—I almost left it, but I knew she'd never forgive me. And I walked right out."

She described how no one gave her a second glance as she returned the same way she came in. In fact, they seemed to not see her at all, a notion she tested by pausing to say goodbye to the guard who'd sassed her earlier. "So I guess I'll be seeing you," she said, but the guard went on typing at her computer, her bored, dead eyes fixed to the screen. "I guess I'll just throw these dead rabbit remains into the canal," Isis said, "so Mr. Engel can finally leave the prison." The guard typed away and didn't even look up.

So Isis continued outside, pausing at the walkway over the canal. She tucked the book under her arm so she could give the dead rabbit a good throw. Hardly the athletic type, Isis didn't make it go very far, but just before it hit the water, a great snout appeared and a reptilian mouth opened wide, catching the animal in its jaws. Then it thrashed away beneath the surface.

With the other, smaller remains guarded under her windbreaker, she continued on, knowing that if she let the paperback get a little wet, that would divert her aunt's attention and allow them to slip away without her noticing anything wrong.

"The rain might have washed it off," she said.

"Washed what off?" I risked a quick glance and saw her pointing to her forehead.

"What he put here. Can you see anything?"

"I have to watch the road." But I thought of how Isis seemed to appear in the distance as she walked back toward Halia and me. Another quick glance in her direction, and I just saw a rattled, perhaps crazy young woman, soaking wet. But as she held back the hair plastered against her forehead, I saw the trace of something. An upside down cross? I couldn't tell.

"It doesn't matter," she said. "Just drive."

Twelve

A staticky voice on the car radio eventually told us two things: one, that the storm intensified in an unexpected fashion, and two, that a wobble in its course caused it to make landfall further south than expected. Its winds now battered the coast in a way that made driving inadvisable. Stay off the roads, warned the voice.

That almost made me laugh. I really wanted to cry, knowing I left Erik by himself with a bunch of flashlights.

The return trip took nearly twice as long, largely because I couldn't match Isis's fearlessness for death-defying speeds. The road remained mercifully deserted, though the wind shook the car mercilessly, often causing us to veer dangerously toward the edge of the road. I didn't want to stop, my mind on Erik. Reminding myself of his smarts and resourcefulness did little good. He inherited those qualities from our father, who would have expressed disappointment in me. Erik depended on me, my father would say, and I stupidly let him down.

A strong gust nearly blew us onto the shoulder of the road. Even Isis gasped and swore. I glanced briefly into the rearview mirror and saw the ruined face of Taryn Hall looking back at me, her broken jaw swinging open in joy. *Weeee!* she would say if she could.

Without meaning to, I said it for her.

That prompted Isis to exclaim, "What?"

"Nothing," I said, but Isis, noting the direction of my gaze, looked in the back seat.

"What did you see?" she asked, worry in her voice.

"Like I said: nothing." I resumed speed, feeling all the more like I'd left Erik in a state of danger. I abandoned him. I should have stayed at home, filled the bathtub like you did before a hurricane struck, helped him check the flashlights, maybe boarded the windows.

"Bullshit," Isis said. "You saw something back there." In a softer voice, she asked, "Was it him?"

"Who?"

"Lenny Engel."

I heard something in the name I missed before. *Lenny Engel. Len Engel.* Fallen angel.

No. Stupid. Absurd.

"Don't be ridiculous," I said. But the inference left me chilled.

"They'd say something on the radio, right?"

"About what?"

"About him escaping," she said. "But there's been nothing. We'd have heard by now, right?"

I thought about the sounds we'd heard outside the prison, the wails that might have come from sirens. I still didn't know what I'd heard. Or if I really heard anything at all.

"You can call your aunt," I said.

Isis shook her head. "She'll still be pissed I let any water get on that book. I doubt she'll talk to me for weeks."

Another gust of wind blew us to the shoulder, and this time, I didn't fight it. I stopped and put the car into park. I didn't look toward the mirror again. I already knew what I'd see. I knew that if I kept driving, I would kill more people, so I told Isis she needed to take over the rest of the way. I expected her to argue, at least huff with exasperation, but she simply nodded. Before she exited the car, I once more saw the faint outline of a cross on her forehead, like the reminder of some perverse Lent. Outside, we crossed paths without saying anything, and by then, the rain washed away all signs of her weird baptism.

Back in the passenger seat where I belonged, I kept my feet tucked in close, far away from the remains Isis left on the floorboard. I suppose I expected her to move them out of consideration for me, but at least she agreed to take the wheel.

"You could call her," she said as we began moving again.

"I don't have her number."

"She didn't give you a library card? She probably forgot. There's probably one in the glovebox. Go on and look."

By opening the glovebox, I unleashed a flood of tissues, condoms, and overdue traffic tickets, along with a photocopied drawing of a man with long hair. *Have you seen this man?* read the caption beneath. Under that, I found a business card with Halia's name on it.

As I dialed, Isis said, "If she starts yelling, hang up."

"I'm not hanging up," I said.

"She probably won't yell. I can tell she liked you. You'll probably get special library privileges."

I didn't know what that meant. Either way, I couldn't get through, the ringing eventually bleeding into static. With my hands free now, I tried calling Erik, with the same result. "A cell tower must be down," I said.

I started to return the card to the glove box, but Isis said to keep it. "She'd want you to have one. Besides, me and her will be on the outs for a while. Once she finds out I sold my soul, she'll be doubly pissed."

Thirteen

The storm only seemed to grow worse as we drew closer to home. Instead of letting me off at the bus stop where she picked me up earlier, Isis took me all the way home. I expected to find our street flooded and breathed a sigh of relief when it wasn't. I couldn't imagine Grendel making it very far through rising water.

Nor did I expect Isis's luck to hold much further. "You should come inside," I said, pulling down the hood of my raincoat before braving the elements to get to the door. "It's not safe."

Downright dangerous, in fact. I didn't know what she'd do if she got stuck in standing water. Earlier, Isis muttered curses and invectives about global warming and rising water as a new voice on the radio warned of the likelihood of flooding and tornados as the storm stalled and all but stopped over our area.

"You'll just have to leave that," I added, indicating the dead rabbit fetus near my feet.

"Negative," she said. "I need to do what I was told. I think the storm is part of the plan."

"Plan? What plan? For God's sake, Isis."

But she kept the car running and waited for me to open the car door. "Don't worry. Grendel will get me home. She never quits, especially not for a little water."

I thought of saying something about the fate suffered by the literary Grendel at the hands of Beowulf but decided to let it go. An adult, Isis could make her own decisions. Still, I cared not to speculate what she planned to do with the unborn rabbit. I didn't want to know.

Erik met me at the door. He wore a baseball cap with a flashlight fastened to it with duct-tape. Rounding out this look, he held a flyswatter. "I'm all right," he said before I could ask. "But you should really answer your phone."

I helped him push the door shut behind me, dreading to see how many missed calls I would later see on my phone. The wind kept beating at the door, even as Erik threw the deadbolt closed. For good measure, we pushed a heavy chair in front of it. No sooner than we had it in place, Erik handed me a towel he'd kept ready near the entrance. As I wiped my face and hair, I reflected on how much I loved my brother and vowed I would never again leave him to deal with a weather event by himself. What was I thinking?

Outfitted with the light strapped to his head, he looked like a short and very determined miner, especially with the flyswatter.

"We need to keep the chair there," he said. "The wind's been crazy. I was so scared something would happen to you."

I nodded and hugged him. "Never again. That was stupid of me."

"I thought the worst of it would miss us. Everyone did, I think. No one expected it to be this bad. Don't even look in the backyard." Not that I could because he kept our hug going by holding on to me. "There's a tree down, but it missed the house. I taped the windows even though I know that won't do much good if the glass actually breaks. At least it'll keep pieces flying everywhere—if we're lucky."

We finally let go, and I had to shield my eyes from the beam of his flashlight.

"Maybe we can look for some wood later and build ourselves some panels. For the next one," said Erik.

"I'm sorry," I said.

"Sorry for what?" No irony or sarcasm at all in his voice. So much of our father in him. Dad would have stood in the rain and covered the windows with panels by himself.

I didn't know how to answer. It felt like I had so many things to answer for. I needed to get it together, starting now. Take charge. I pointed at the flyswatter in his hand. "What's with that?"

He looked at the flyswatter as if he'd forgotten he held it.

"Nothing," he said, but he was not a good liar, another trait he inherited from our father.

"Tell me," I said, trying to make good on my conviction to take charge and not leave it to him to perform the role of the adult.

He paused to consider his words as the wind howled outside.

"There's something in the house," he said, his voice hushed as if he didn't want someone else to hear. "Something flapping around."

The lack of sun and electricity allowed shadows to gather at will. Unable to see much beyond the beam of the flashlight, I listened to the sounds around us, all but dominated by wind and rain.

"Like a bat?" I asked, straining to keep my voice low.

"Maybe," he whispered back. "But I doubt it. It's big."

We both knew how animals liked to crawl into the attic sometimes, usually just squirrels nesting in the rafters. Though our father would never have tolerated their presence, we left them alone. Other intrusions proved less welcome, like the time I opened the toilet and found a rat staring back at me. I drew the line there. But with something flapping around the house, we'd entered unfamiliar territory.

"There! I hear it again." His head and the flashlight beam whipped toward the kitchen. "I saw it that time for sure. It *is* big."

I saw nothing, nor did I hear anything that sounded like flapping. "Is this a practical joke you're playing?"

"What? No, *no*."

"Because I wouldn't blame you for feeling frosty. I shouldn't have gone off like that."

"I'm not mad. And trust me, if I wanted to play a practical joke on you, it would be so much better than this. Wait—" He ducked, and so did I, though I didn't know what we meant to avoid. "It's definitely in the kitchen."

"Is there another flashlight?"

Erik nodded before procuring me one from his arsenal.

Gripping it, I thanked him. "I'm just going to hold mine," I said, switching it on. "No hat for me." The additional light made his face visible, and I saw how frightened he looked.

"I'm really glad you're home," he said. "I was fine until a moment ago. I don't want to deal with this alone."

Another wave of guilt. "Nor should you have to. I'm so glad you took care of the flashlights. Imagine what we'd be doing without them."

"Candles," he said. "I made sure we have those too. You want me to light some?"

"Go ahead. I'll see if I can find the source of the flapping."

He got to it as I treaded softly into the kitchen, armed only with a flashlight. I felt genuinely unnerved. When the rat appeared in the toilet, I'd quickly closed the lid, wetting myself slightly as I rushed outside the bathroom and shut the door on the vile thing, intending to leave it trapped until I could find someone who would deal with it. The only exterminator I could reach that late in the evening said he would come out in the morning.

"In the bathroom, you say?" the exterminator had asked. Judging by his slurring, he'd started celebrating the weekend early. "You better put a towel or something under the door. Those little fuckers can flatten themselves and crawl through tight spaces."

I did as he said, and all that night, Erik and I could hear the infuriated animal crashing and thrashing behind the door, wholeheartedly wrecking the bathroom in every way it could. When the exterminator—an obese white man wearing a shirt at least two sizes too small—finally arrived, I had to restrain myself from hugging him, even when he burped his hello and held up a metal pole. "Show me the rat," he said.

Erik and I watched as he clutched the metal rod like a weapon—it's actual purpose, it turned out—and slowly opened the door. Much more gracefully than I would have expected from a man of his size, much less one with a hangover, he slipped inside and quickly shut the door behind him.

"Is he going to catch him and take him somewhere?" Erik asked.

"Yeah. Probably?" I had no idea. In fact, I doubted it.

A flurry of loud noises followed before the exterminator emerged. He held up a clear plastic bag for us to see. It contained the carcass of the gigantic rat. "Caught him sleeping in a waste basket," he said. "The way he was curled up was actually kind of cute." He handed me an exorbitant bill, and after accepting payment (which I doled out from the last of our emergency fund), he gestured toward the bathroom. "You and the kid'll have fun cleaning that up." Then he took the dead rat and left.

"You think the rat bit him?" Erik asked as we worked on restoring order to the ravaged bathroom.

"I hope so," I said. Despite the damage, which seemed extensive for a medium-sized rodent, even one so clearly enraged, we still felt pity for it.

I reminded myself of that pity as I followed the flashlight beam into the kitchen. Unable to see clearly, I stepped on the shards of a broken coffee cup and felt them break under my foot. The flashlight revealed other signs of destruction on the counter—a toppled bowl of cereal, a glass on its side but still intact. I wondered if the deceased rat's friends had descended upon us to exact revenge. I reminded myself that bats counted as rodents, wondering if they'd allied themselves with their earthbound cousins. I despaired at the thought. I didn't want to call the drunk exterminator again.

As it turned out, it was neither a bat nor a rat.

I saw the source of the chaos perched on top of the refrigerator.

"Erik," I said, my voice a register or two above a whisper, "come in here. Please."

It took a moment for him to respond. Out of the darkness, he appeared like the figure in a strange Rembrandt painting, still wearing the flashlight on his head but holding a lighted candle too.

"Wait. Do you have shoes?" I asked, remembering the shards on the floor. I used the flashlight to show him where to watch his step.

He paused but nodded.

Then I turned the beam of the flashlight toward the refrigerator.

Erik gasped.

Perched like something from an Edgar Allan Poe poem, a crow looked down upon us.

It tolerated the light but only for a moment before it opened its wings and took flight. We both ducked as it flew out of the kitchen.

Erik took a late, errant swing at it with the flyswatter before we followed it into the dining area. We couldn't find it at first, not until it let out a mocking caw.

"There," said Erik, his turn to flash a light upon it.

Once again, the bird expressed its irritation and flew, this time to another part of the house.

The chase went on like that for several minutes. I anticipated the crow flying into a wall or window, but it expertly navigated the doors and passages of our house as if it had lived there with us for several years.

Or days.

I thought of the electrocuted crow.

"How did he get in?" I asked.

In the glow of the candle, I saw Erik's mouth move wordlessly, his shoulder shrug.

"Is there a broken window, maybe?"

"No," he said.

"Let's check and make sure."

"I'm telling you, there aren't," he said, but we still checked each room—first Erik's, then mine, before moving on to the room once shared by our parents. All the windows looked intact, though the rain and wind battered them relentlessly.

Then, facing our parents' bed, still made with the linens I used to make it after the last time my father slept there, the crow flew in after us, landing expertly on a bureau against the far wall as if to mock our confusion.

"Erik, what did we do with the—"

I didn't want to complete the sentence. To do so would test the fates even more than we had already. What sort of bad luck came from disrespecting the remains of a crow? My mother would know.

Erik knew what I meant.

"We buried it," he said.

"I didn't. Did you?"

He shook his head. Quietly, we turned and left the room. Pausing, I pulled the door closed behind me, casting one last glance at the thing sitting on the bureau. I flashed back to performing a similar action with the rat imprisoned in the bathroom.

Erik led the way through the kitchen and toward the rickety door that led to the garage. Finding the shelf full of forgotten hardware, he set down the candle and found the box where we'd laid to rest the electrocuted crow. Its lid was askew. He opened it and held it out for me to see.

Empty.

I swore at myself, though I didn't know why. Had we buried it, we obviously would have consigned it to a horrible death, leaving it to suffocate under the ground.

Or did something else occur?

Thunder rumbled, the air around us full of electricity.

On Erik's face, the traces of a smile began to appear.

"It's a good thing, right? That it's not dead? That we forgot to bury it?"

Mentally, I counted the days. Too many for it to just lie there unconscious, not eating, not drinking. With what happened at the prison and now this occurrence, it seemed as if the storm blew in something else besides wind and rain.

"We need to get it out," I said. The need felt urgent.

The expression on his face suddenly changed. "But it's dangerous out there. It could die."

Could it? I wondered. *Twice?* "It doesn't belong inside," I said. "We need to open the door, try to make it fly out on its own. What did you do with the flyswatter?"

Muttering more protests, he went to look for it while I returned to the bedroom where the crow lay in wait for us. From its perch, it glowered down at me. No need to call the rat-killing specialist. Instead, look up an exorcist. Or maybe we'd already received a visit from a *bokor*, the kind of magician from my mother's home that could revive the dead by capturing their souls in a container. Did we unwittingly do that when we placed the bird in a shoebox? I remembered something about salt serving as a possible antidote. Feed the zombified individual salt, my mother may have said, and you would reverse the process, restoring the person's soul to its rightful place in death.

Before I could go look for a saltshaker, Erik returned with the flyswatter.

It didn't make me feel confident, but I took it. "Be ready by the door."

"But the storm . . ."

"It'll be fine. Besides, I think it's already dead."

Sensing our intention, the bird flew into another room, once more challenging us to find it. We did, and it flew again. The game went on like that until we cornered it in our tiny bathroom, where it sat upon the shower curtain and regarded us coldly. I closed the door behind us, and the light from Erik's flashlight surrounded us. Behind it, the window overlooking the bathtub gave me an idea.

I ducked underneath it so I could reach the window. Unopened for years, the lever resisted my efforts to turn it, but I finally managed to slide it open. A flurry of wind and rain rushed in.

"Close it!" Erik shouted, but I already realized my mistake. The wind blew open the door, and the crow escaped, flying into yet another corner of the house.

I swore as I struggled to close the window again. It proved as difficult to close as it was to open. Finally managing, I swore again, turning as I did to Erik, who looked crestfallen and injured.

"Don't call me that," he said. "It wasn't my fault."

"I didn't say it was. I just—" I didn't know what else to say as I stood there in the bathtub, soaked to the skin and starting to shiver. I felt so tired, so spent. I just wanted the bird to go away. For reasons I couldn't explain, it spelled danger. Maybe it would wait for us to sleep and then pluck out our eyes. That and other irrational fears that came from the deep, dark gulf of my soul.

"I heard you," Erik said, and he started repeating those words over and over, finally screaming them as he ran from me. Somewhere, the crow hid from sight and watched me chase my brother until I finally caught him. I wrapped my arms around him and rocked him until he stopped crying and shouting. Even with his warmth, I continued to shiver, but experience taught me that nothing else would quiet an attack like the one that just came over him. They happened infrequently, but when they did, they could prove intense. As he finally quieted, I told him the story of La Sirene, a tale once told to me by mother—how La Sirene existed as both a mermaid and a spirit that protected secret knowledge. Woe until those who didn't treat her with the proper respect, for La Sirene could use her fish tail to drag you down into her underwater lair, where no one would ever see you again. Treat her right, however, and she would allow you a glimpse into the mirror that divides the world of matter from the world of spirit, thereby granting you great knowledge. I wondered, as Erik's breathing grew even with sleep, if I owed my issue with mirrors to my mother telling me that story. Would I see Taryn Hall's face if not for that tale?

Take a tour of our house and you won't find very many mirrors, certainly not in the few spaces I called my own. When I showered, I used a towel to cover the bathroom mirror. I didn't want anything on the other side to see me.

Finally, I slept too, but not before catching a glimpse of the crow in the shadows over my dresser. How long it sat there and whether or not it heard me tell the story, I couldn't say.

II

Part Two

"Mountains overawe and oceans terrify, while the mystery of great forests exercises a spell peculiarly its own. But all these, at one point or another, somewhere link on intimately with human life and human experience. They stir comprehensible, even if alarming, emotions. They tend on the whole to exalt."
—*Algernon Blackwood*

One

When it reopened a day later, much too soon considering the impact of the storm, the college looked like a very different place. Not the buildings, which suffered little damage beyond minor leaks in ceilings. Not the walkways, where broken tree limbs and branches lay strewn about, having somehow missed breaking windows. Instead, the effect of the storm became evident in the surrounding landscape, which managed to look all at once both sparser and wilder. The scene left the impression that the storm peeled away the glossy coating of reality itself, revealing the chaotic core underneath.

Near the pavilion where we would eventually stage the haunt, it revealed something else as well.

A wooden sign, unseen for decades, rotted and faded.

The improbable existence of the sign inspired theories. Rumors began to proliferate. A road must have cut through the woods at some point, one that wound its way well beyond the pavilion's foundation. The prevailing thought held that time and the demand of modern vehicles called for a straighter, less complicated route, and with the construction of new roads, it didn't take long for people to forget this older one, hence leaving it for the trees and foliage to eventually swallow everything whole.

The unearthed sign advertised a roadside motel, the lettering worn faint by time but still readable:

WHITE NITE LODGE

A crudely painted graphic decorated the lower right portion of the sign, just underneath the final E, as faded as the lettering: a caricature of a snoozing rooster sporting a white sleeping cap.

Or a white hood. It appeared ambiguous at best. Just enough to remind you about the seeds of hate planted long ago on this land.

At least, it left that impression on me when I finally saw it for myself, which didn't happen until after I paid my office a visit.

This time, Slashing Sally didn't startle me. I anticipated seeing the doll where I'd left it, still hanging by the neck over the desk. It lost its power over me, or so I wanted to think. I just didn't expect to find the office occupied by another visitor as I opened the door.

Isis. Planted at my desk, her face buried in her arms, snoozing.

My surprised gasp roused her.

Snorting, she lifted her head and rubbed her eyes, her mouth twisting into a silent yawn. She still wore the same clothes she wore on the day we went to the prison. She smelled like it too.

"I did it," she said when she recovered the ability to talk without yawning. "And Mr. Engel wasn't lying. It got results."

She explained what she meant as I worked to regain my breath. When, I wondered, would I open my own office door and not have the life scared out of me?

Those results mentioned by Isis included more than just the appearance of the sign. She took credit for that, attributing it to how carefully she followed Engel's instructions, which she divulged in only the vaguest terms. "He said not to tell anyone the words," she said.

"What words?"

"The words to the speech before and after I threw it into the lake. You know. The thing."

I knew what "thing" she meant. How could I forget the sight of what she carried out of the prison? Whatever the case, I pictured the improbable scene she went on to describe: driving to the campus after she dropped me off at home, bracing herself as she pressed forward against the wind and rain, the elements themselves conspiring to push her back into the car. But she forged on, carrying her dread burden to the edge of the shore, where she spoke those memorized words and then tossed those pathetic remains as far as she could. Maybe she only imagined the wind picking up with even greater intensity as it floated briefly before disappearing beneath the surface, compelling her to carry on. She took off her clothes and stood there naked, holding her arms out to sky as she spoke the remaining verse.

"Verse?" I asked. "So it was like a poem?"

"It even rhymed. Sort of."

"Recite it for me."

She regarded me coolly. "I just told you: I can't."

After that, her memory became fuzzy, but she recalled hearing the sharp snapping sounds of breaking tree limbs rising against the howl of the wind. The noise made her suspect an approaching tornado. "But then I saw her, standing on the opposite bank, completely unaffected by the storm. It seemed at times like the wind could lift me up. I really started to think my time had come. But as for her—she just stood there like it was nothing. But she could see me. I know it. Then I did a thing Mr. Engel told me not to do."

I waited to hear the rest. Cold air filled the room, its source a vent right over the desk. Isis began to shiver, and I could hear her teeth chatter. The stirring air caused the hanging form of Slashing Sally to rotate, and I noticed something new, something that gave me great pause. Isis must have seen something in my expression. Only she must have misinterpreted it as a response to her story because she stammered through the rest. "I spoke directly to her. I called to her. Not just that. I sort of invited her into me. You know, to *inhabit* me. Don't think bad of me, please. I know it was stupid. But I'm pretty sure she heard me and accepted. At least, I think she did. Not in words, but by floating toward me, right across the water. Just watching her made me feel dizzy. I must've blacked out before she could reach me."

"You're saying that all this happened during the storm," I said. "You stood on one side of the lake, while she stood at the other?"

Isis blinked, taken back by the question. "Yeah, duh, that's what I said."

"How far is that distance? At least a quarter of a mile?"

It didn't take long for the insinuation to dawn on her. She bristled. I knew enough about Isis to know she didn't like it when people challenged her. "It really happened."

"Answer me this, then," I said. "How could you see clearly enough to recognize anyone in all that rain? From so far away?"

Again, the blinking, slower this time, as her anger mounted. "I didn't say I saw anything 'clearly.' I just know who it was."

"I'm not even sure you really went inside the prison. Maybe you planted that disgusting rabbit fetus outside and only pretended to come out with it. And now this story. For what purpose?" The words came spilling out of me. "Do you hope to scare me? Impress me? Evoke awe and terror? Is that what you're hoping to create? I *teach* this material, Isis. I know how to tell the difference between fiction and reality."

She stared at me. She expected me to believe all of it. I picked up a book within reach—Bram Stoker's *Dracula*—and waved it at her face. Even as her mouth remained in a set, rigid expression, I could see a tremor begin near her jaw. The tears wanted to start, and I didn't care. Let them. She needed to feel pain.

I said, "We're supposed to be creating a haunted house to entertain people and raise funds for a good cause, not to mythologize people and events from the past. Not to bamboozle people. And speaking of bamboozling people, which one of you did that?"

I pointed up at Slashing Sally. From the doll's neck jutted the handle of a knife, a blade of significant size now stuffed deep inside it.

"Was it you?" I asked. "Or was it Zach? Because I can tell, Isis. I can tell the two of you are in on this. I'll hand it to you, though—everything has been well orchestrated. I do congratulate you for the performance. Both of you."

She lifted her eyes to the hanging doll, a subtle change forming in her expression. Surprise, perhaps? Maybe Zach improvised that touch and forgot to tell her.

When her eyes found me again, they burned with defiance. "I didn't do that."

"Of course you didn't," I said, now mocking her with irony. "I want the key back. I may be new around here, but I suspect the college doesn't go around giving students the keys to faculty offices."

Without letting her gaze waver from mine, she reached into her backpack and rummaged around. Then she extended her hand to me, a key dangling from her fingers.

"Professor Dash gave it to me," she said, providing the explanation I didn't care to hear. "He said I could come here when I needed a place to get away."

That just made it worse. I let the silence say it for me. I clasped the key in the palm of my hand, felt its coldness.

"A safe space to cool off," she said. "Sometimes, I get angry and need to get away from people." A pause to grant me the opportunity to reply. Then: "We weren't doing anything inappropriate, you know."

"I didn't say you were."

"Not out loud, you didn't." She got up to leave, and I looked away, deliberately avoiding the fact that she wore the same clothes she wore the day we went to the prison. I also pretended to not notice the funk of her unwashed skin, nor the ruined makeup, nor the faint outline of the inverted cross on her forehead. She could have done that to herself, I reminded myself. Before disappearing through the doorway, she said, "You know, you got all of that wrong. Most of it, at least."

"I have to start prepping for class," I said. "I hope you did your reading."

Before we could exchange another word, she left. I exhaled when the door closed behind her. *Good*, I told myself. Time to get serious. She needed to get ready because I planned to dazzle her class today, convince them—and myself—of what a superstar I could become right before their eyes. Who needed Professor Dash when they could have a hotshot instructor like me? Watch what I can do with today's assigned reading, "Schalken the Painter" by Sheridan Le Fanu. No dread or fear here.

Because what makes Nat feel terror? The faces of all those students, especially Isis, who hate her but nevertheless must sit behind a desk and hear what she has to say.

What causes Nat to feel horror? Having nothing to say.

I planned to recycle some of my grad school research, including a paper I wrote on the "Death and the Maiden" motif in Victorian fiction. Show confidence. Ignore the murderous stare that would surely come from Isis.

Demonstrate that it had no power.

But thanks to the crow and a house without electricity the night before, I couldn't review my notes or material as I planned. Instead, Erik fell asleep against my shoulder, the two of us huddled close as I read aloud from Dash's copy of *Tell My Horse*, the last candle providing waning light as it melted into wax. I don't know where the bird finally settled. Exhausted, we gave up trying to evict it. Occasionally, I would hear the rustle of feathers, so I knew it never went far, perhaps close enough to listen as I read Hurston's description of La Gonave, an island which, when seen from the shore of Port Au Prince, apparently looks like a sleeping woman.

"Everyone knows that La Gonave is a whale that lingered so long in Haitian waters that he became an island."

I lingered on that sentence, reveling in the playfulness of that voice, its distinctiveness, before moving on to the account of how Damballa commanded the whale to carry one of his wives, Cilla, across the sea to Port Au Prince so she could reveal the secret of peace to the people living there. The whale took its task seriously, so as Cilla stretched out across its back in anticipation of a long journey, the whale made extra effort to avoid storms or tempestuous waves. Evidently, he did such a good job of making the trip serene and relaxing that Cilla fell into a deep sleep. Even with the journey completed, Cilla would not wake out of her slumber, and the whale did not want to wake her. Thus, the whale would swim out to sea every day to do all the things that a whale does before returning in the evening to its place off the coast of Port Au Prince, just on the off chance that Cilla would finally decide to wake up from her long nap and deliver the gift of peace to the people of Haiti. But she just refused to awaken, so now the whale had become an island, one that looked from a distance like a woman sleeping.

Reading those words brought to mind the years of unending political violence and upheaval the people of Port Au Prince endured. When they looked out to sea toward the island of La Gonave sitting on the horizon, they must have wondered why that woman wouldn't wake up. Maybe they called out to her. More than anything, I wondered if the island still remained visible, if it had sunk beneath the waves, or if the whale got tired of playing host to a sleeping woman. Maybe he finally decided to swim away, no longer have people mistake him for an island. Or perhaps Cilla finally did wake up from her nap, but she'd stayed asleep for so long that she'd forgotten whatever message her husband had sent her to deliver. Maybe she instructed the whale to carry her elsewhere. Maybe she got tired of riding on top of a whale—or the whale became tired of hosting such a tired woman, so he brushed her off his back, and she wound up swimming on her own until she finally washed up on a beach very far away, where she found a new husband.

I lay there, feeling a bit like the whale in the story as I felt Erik's weight on me and his breath against my skin. He mumbled in his sleep, and I wondered for the millionth time what other life my mother left behind when she came here. Did she have another family who wondered where she went? Maybe even another husband?

I found myself growing tired as well, and with the candle almost burned away, I started to put the book aside when a folded piece of paper fell out from its pages. Had it always been there? I failed to notice it before.

Unfolding it revealed a document headed by the college's seal. It looked official, but as I read it against the dying light of the candle, I grew doubtful of its authenticity. It came from the Office of Academic Accommodations. Addressed to Professor Dash, it began with the kind of standard language that usually preceded instructions for giving a student extended time on tests and assignments, usually due to some kind of learning challenge or disability. I'd already seen such documents at the college, and they usually avoided mentioning the specific issue out of respect for student privacy. Usually, they involved something more common, like dyslexia or attention deficit disorder—conditions that generally required the diagnosis of someone with clinical knowledge.

But this particular document not only mentioned the student's name— Isis—but it specified her affliction in a strange, blunt paragraph.

The student in question, it read, *suffers from the debilitating effects of a rarely seen and even rarely documented condition. While state and federal laws normally forbid us from specifying medical conditions, this student's needs stem from a condition that falls somewhat outside these categories, granting us some latitude for transparency. Indeed, the nature of her condition, we feel, requires not only this transparency but some context. Please note that we have not sacrificed the normal diligence we take in confirming a diagnosis. Specifically, the student suffers from demonic possession, which causes dramatic mood swings, lapses in attention, and verbal outbursts which we might liken to Tourette Syndrome (though for the sake of clarity, she does not suffer from the latter). Hence, the student requires additional time in completing essay assignments and exams, as well as the understanding of her instructors that she may need to stand up periodically for leg-stretching exercises. Any questions may be addressed to—"* Here, someone used a heavy black marker to obliterate the name. I held it to the light, trying without success to read it. I eventually gave up, instead taking note of the handwritten note scrawled at the end of the document:

IT IS REAL!

Underneath that, an illegible signature. Whoever had signed it apparently used the same pen to redact the name listed as the official contact.

I refolded the document and returned it to its place inside the book. Then, as the candlelight finally died, I lay there in the darkness, listening to my own heartbeat.

What did it mean? Despite the handwritten note, I believed none of it. I knew that either Isis convinced someone in the Office of Accommodations to put together that farce of a document or she got hold of some blank letterhead and forged it herself. Or maybe she and Professor Dash intended it as a practical joke, targeting some impressionable, perhaps gullible instructor.

Like me.

After all, someone left the Slashing Sally doll as an effigy for me to find.

Maybe someone expected me to pick up this particular book and planted this forgery inside of it for me to find. Perhaps Isis herself. She could have slipped it inside during one of her visits to my office. Just a quick sleight of hand. Or maybe Professor Dash himself tucked it in there, intending it as a ruse to haze his successor.

A seemingly endless series of possibilities cycled through my brain as I listened to the dying fury of the storm. I barely slept that night, and in the morning, I staggered toward the shower. Still no power, and the sun had barely risen, so the only illumination came from the gray light coming in through the window. The water felt lukewarm at best, neither hot nor cold enough to help me wake up. I almost dozed while standing on my feet. Then came a surge of electricity—or more like a gasp, the lights flickering with hesitation before they managed to come on. As I rinsed soap from my eyes, I saw something that made me freeze.

The silhouette of a figure visible on the other side of the shower curtain. Just standing there.

"Erik?" I said.

No reply. I saw a figure both too tall and too wide to be my brother. Creeping fear and my sense of vulnerability kept me still. I waited for the figure to move until, once more, the light flickered and went out. I dared not move. Then came another surge of electricity and, finally, bright light.

I knew when I looked again, I would find the silhouette gone, and I could discount it as a trick of the senses.

But no. It remained.

It seemed even larger this time, tall enough to peer over the shower rod and look down at me. It just needed to move closer.

If someone invaded our home, I couldn't just stand there. Erik needed me to protect him. I needed to do what I should have done the day before. Be there for him.

I gripped the shower curtain, wondering if I should slowly peer around it or yank it open.

It didn't take me long to decide. Two deep breaths, and I flung it aside.

At first, I saw nothing there at all. Then, as the water began cascading over the tub, I saw it.

The crow, sitting on a towel rod. It regarded me with eyes that had begun to fog before casting off, flying away through the open door of the bathroom.

The door I thought I could remember closing before I disrobed to start the shower.

But of course I simply misremembered. I felt spent, exhausted, and thus prone to believing the impossible. The story of my life, thanks to my mother

Whales didn't turn into islands. People didn't sleep for centuries. Women didn't swim hundreds of miles across the sea and make men fall in love with them over breakfast. Electrocuted birds didn't magically come to life. And most certainly, mirrors didn't contain the aggrieved souls of dead women.

No such thing as demonic possession either.

I came to work that day determined to repair the ruptured boundaries around me, starting with Isis. I'd allowed her to infect me with her imagination. I almost started to believe the things she wanted me to believe. Maybe Professor Dash encouraged her to play out these fantasies for his entertainment.

But I would not.

Later, I stood before my class lectern and pressed my way through my lecture. I willed myself to recall the words and concepts I once used to impress my audience at the SOFA conference. Barely more than half the students showed up for class. The ones there regarded me with sleepy faces as I read aloud from the assigned reading, pinpointing crucial moments in the narrative to make my point about why they should care that the Death and the Maiden motif remained persistent in art and literature for centuries and not just in the assigned reading by Sheridan Le Fanu. I reminded them of the tragic fate that doomed poor Rose, the "maiden" in "Schalken the Painter," forced by her uncle to marry a living corpse. How even after that wraith, that *thing*, carried her off to some unimaginable hell, she somehow managed to escape, eventually finding her way back to her uncle and his protege, Schalken.

I paused at this moment in my lecture to look out at their faces, trying to impress on them the gravity of this moment. Yet I could read on their faces how so few of them even seemed to care. Didn't they want to be here? I wondered. Hadn't they paid good tuition money to listen to me share the expertise that Fowler seemed to believe so much in?

At first, I didn't see Isis at all, then I saw her in the back, her head tilted down as if asleep, just like how I'd found her earlier in my office.

I moved through the rows of desks, continuing to make points, asking questions that no one could answer, then providing the answers myself. I moved closer and closer to Isis, noticing the way her hair hung slack over her face, providing a membrane between herself and everything else. Another boundary I meant to rupture, this one intended to shut out the world. To shut me out.

None of the other students mattered to me at that moment. My voice began to crescendo, timed in a way she would find it impossible to ignore. She needed to hear me read a crucial passage out loud, and I would do it as I stood over her. She needed to understand the point I wanted to make. I would force her to look up and see me and understand the importance of what I wanted her to hear.

At least the other students had their books open. At least they went through the motions of following along as I directed their attention first to this passage and then that passage.

But Isis remained fixed and unmoving, her eyes cast downward. No book on her desk to follow along and annotate, no notebook to jot down key ideas. From where I stood, I couldn't tell what held her attention as I continued to roll my way through what I believed had become a pretty terrific lecture, maybe the best lecture of all time, and what a damn shame it was that Fowler hadn't chosen this day to come in to observe me putting my skills to work. No longer at the lectern, I maneuvered my way through the rows of student desks, moving closer in a way intended to grab Isis's attention, my book open in my hands. I began to enunciate those crucial words spoken by Rose when she begged those men for help, pleading with them to protect her from her undead husband, who would surely appear if they turned off the lights or left her alone in the room. He would appear out of the darkness, I reminded them as I edged closer to Isis, the words flowing from my mouth as I prepared to tap her on the wrist so she could hear the most important passage of all, the one she needed to hear.

"The dead and the living cannot be one."

With those words, the character Rose sums up the horror of her doomed existence, this unholy marriage.

The dead and the living cannot be one.

Isis needed to hear this appeal to establish a clear boundary between the living and the dead. Earlier in the lecture, I used the overhead projector to display images so that my students would understand what lay at stake in Rose's declaration that the Dead and the Living could not be one. I heard the muffled responses of the students as one image after another passed before their eyes, some of them several centuries old but all of them conveying some version of the Death and the Maiden scene: a decaying corpse, somehow animated with a desire, trying to grope a young woman in some state of undress. With the help of this reading assignment, we would address what such images mean as metaphors for oppressed women, for fleeting youth, for toxic relationships, yet all the meanings coming down to that elegant phrase spoken by Rose in Le Fanu's story.

The dead and the living cannot be one.

I timed the passage perfectly, coming to those words just as I reached out to Isis, her eyes still gazing down toward her lap, her hair an impenetrable black veil concealing her face from view.

I realized then, just before my fingers could make contact with the bony white wrist, what an awful, terrible mistake I'd made.

The head lifted and the veil of hair parted, revealing half of the ruined face that now smiled at me with a broken jaw and shattered teeth, one good eye bloodshot and steaming with delight at the shock that prevented any other words from forming in my mouth,

Not Isis at all but Taryn Hall. Sitting in my classroom.

Her mouth moved, and a bloody glob of drool rolled off her ruined tongue. Even with a voice capable of garbled sand instead of coherent speech, I knew what words she tried to form, quoting that sentence for me.

The dead and the living cannot be one.

Silence followed her attempt to form words. No one in the room said a word. She leaned away from the desk so that I could see what held her attention.

A rabbit fetus.

Immediately, I looked away and saw the faces of my students staring back at me. Did they see her too, now that mirrors no longer confined her? Now that she'd escaped? To my left, I saw Ruth, her concerned eyes gazing back at me. Next to her sat Mo, who looked away when I made eye contact, rifling through the pages of her book instead. Behind them sat Mark, his mouth hanging open as if he meant to say something.

None of them seemed to notice Death in our presence.

They looked as if they felt concern for me, as if I were the problem.

I looked back toward the desk where Taryn Hall sat, hoping I would find Isis gazing on me in triumph. Maybe she'd just pulled off a spectacular stunt, tricked the adjunct professor into thinking the victim of her vehicular manslaughter sat in her classroom. After all, Isis led a student club that worked with special effects and makeup. And she evidently knew what I'd done to Taryn Hall.

But I found the desk empty. As it probably had been since the beginning of the class period.

I said something eventually, I think. Something about not feeling well. "Class dismissed," probably. Someone, I think Ruth, approached me and asked if I needed anything, like a bottle of water. Mo paused at the door and asked me if I wanted her to call Sarge at public safety. I said no, perhaps too emphatically. I waited until everyone left the room and cried. I cried until I felt myself gulping tears.

* * *

Eventually, I went looking for fresh air to clear my head. With my bus not due for over an hour, I had time to wander the path that ran around the lake. Debris floated in the water, mostly tree branches, along with a few stray tiles blown from the roofs of nearby buildings. In the wake of the storm came an unseasonably cool day. The wind made me shiver, something unheard of during that time of year in Florida. I welcomed the discomfort as something I deserved and pressed on until I came into the presence of the pavilion.

While the forest line suffered during the storm, the pavilion remained stubbornly intact and impervious to the destructive winds. I stepped across its threshold and looked down at the concrete slab, where the brown smear stubbornly remained. Not even rain could wash it away.

It only appeared larger, having spread further around a widening crack in the foundation.

From above me came the squawking of crows roosting in the rafters, still angry at me, perhaps blaming me for the weather that displaced them. Behind me, the lake seemed closer than before, its levels elevated from the rain. Ripples of brackish water now came within a few feet of the path and the pavilion itself. Standing now within its borders, I looked down at the brown stain. Did the mark represent an attempt to communicate? I noticed swirls in the pattern I'd not recognized before, likening it to a letter in some ancient alphabet, or a sigil in a magic spell.

Much like the one allegedly cast by Isis when she tossed that pathetic thing into the waters. She wanted me to believe that something emerged here, responded to her bidding by crawling out of the depths of the underworld.

Beyond the pavilion, the once impenetrable wall of trees and brambles now gaped open, an angry maw split wide by nature's fury.

I stared at it, fascinated, its depths seemingly endless.

Not far back, I saw the sign and its garish script, stubbornly legible after decades of weather and termites.

White Nite Lodge.

Who knew it stood back there this whole time, concealed by vines and ferns? A silent witness to changing decades, a reminder that we might forget the past, but it never goes away. The caricature of the rooster and its ambiguous cap looked back at me, mocking me with its droopy eyes and hang-dog expression. *Step into the trees and take a look*, it seemed to say. *Come on in and have yourself a little rest.*

I might even have taken a step or two forward, until a real voice made me fall back.

Sarge, calling to me from the path. He rode toward me in golf cart emblazoned with the college's logo.

"I said, you can't be here," he said before the golf cart finished coming to a complete stop on the foot path.

My mind immediately went back to my fingerprint check and the possibility that some awful report finally came to the college's attention. Do not hire this woman. This murderer.

His wheels finally came to rest between the pavilion and the lake. "Don't you see?" he asked as he hoisted himself up from behind the wheel. Adjusting his pants so they rode higher on his hips, he hobbled over to where I stood as he pointed toward the golf cart.

I remained frozen, staring at the cart, an unpleasant association beginning to form, one that I'd never shared with anyone,

When I didn't answer, he once more thrust his finger in that direction. "Do you?"

I didn't know what he expected me to see. He couldn't possibly know the feelings that the cart triggered in me.

But then I realized that he meant for me to see something near the waterline. Just above the waterline, an enormous snout and the glare of reptilian eyes, followed by the ridge of a gigantic tail.

The alligator looked impossibly long, a monster even by Florida standards.

"I've been chasing people away from that thing all day long," Sarge said. "It probably found its way here during the storm, maybe came up through a storm drain. They live in the sewers. That's a fact. You know why it's trying to get close to you, don't you? It's lost its natural fear of humans. Some fool's been feeding it meatloaf or something."

I thought of Isis. *Rabbit, not meatloaf,* I almost said out loud. A cunning intelligence lay behind the alligator's eyes as it glided closer. It approached me in a way that suggested we had unfinished business. Like we shared a mutual acquaintance.

"Fifteen feet at least."

"What?" I asked, Sarge's words snapping me out of my reverie.

"I said it's at least fifteen feet long. Might be some kind of record for a beast like that. Belongs in the Everglades. Or a Toho film. Jesus, I never should've left the northeast. Imagine someone feeding a monster like that. Can't they read the signs?"

He meant the signs near the water that warned people not to "molest" any alligators inhabiting the lake. But reflexively, my attention turned toward the sign advertising the White Nite Lodge and that infernal rooster. Beyond that, somewhere deeper in the woods, I detected faint movement.

"Oh, that," said Sarge, noticing where my attention strayed. "We'll have that cleaned up soon enough. Who knows what else is back there. Or who else. I told you about the camps. For all I know, the remains of that lodge are back there and they're putting it to use."

"Who?" I said, trying not to sound alarmed. "Who's 'they'?"

"The lepers," he said.

More movement beyond the sign, causing my attention to revert there. This time, a new form came into view. On four legs, it stood just within my line of sight as if it intended to reveal itself only to me. Sarge prattled on, evidently unaware of the presence.

"That's what they are, you know. All the vagabonds camping out there. They're lepers. That's right, it's a virtual leper colony. And I mean actual leprosy. You can see signs of it all over their skin. It's a real problem down here, believe it or not. It comes from people eating roadkill. Wild armadillos especially."

But I saw no armadillo. I saw something else entirely. Something impossible.

"Best be getting on," Sarge said. "I'm cordoning off this area. You and those upstart students of yours'll need to cancel that haunted house of yours. Not unless you all want leprosy. It spreads, you know. A regular fucking health crisis."

I didn't answer as I got into the golf cart beside him. We wheeled away just as the alligator finished hauling itself onto the bank of the lake. It watched us disappear, its attitude one of privileged expectation, as if a prior life of guarding the boundaries of a prison had taught it a supernatural capacity for patience along with a taste for human flesh. But it was here now, many miles away from its previous home, having followed the one who tricked him, and it intended to make it known that no one would ever again deceive it with rabbit meat. No one, absolutely no one would make it a fool like that again.

Of course, I could easily convince myself I saw an entirely different reptile receding into the distance. Just a quirky fantasy on my part. However, I couldn't explain away the other animal I saw, the one that emerged briefly in the clearing just beyond the sign. The presence of *that* one defied any reasonable explanation.

"Storms, reptiles, and leprosy," Sarge said as he drove. "Enough to make you think we live in a place unfit for human habitation."

I didn't answer. I kept my gaze fixed back the way we came, wondering if what I saw would reappear. Hoping it. Dreading it.

Because I watched it die ages ago.

A goat with a misshapen horn.

Two

The goat happened because of my mother.

She never gave me sweets or candy, she never baked me a birthday cake, and she tolerated my passion for trick or treating during Halloween with quiet indifference.

But she loved to indulge me with mangoes.

She had a talent for finding them too, always driving with the windows down, ready and alert for some sign of ripe mangoes for sale in the morning air. Her ability to detect even the faintest scent of them was unparalleled, and more than once, she took me on wild detours, often miles out of the way. Sometimes, it appeared as if she took these detours simply as an excuse not to take me to a different destination. A place I wanted to go, like a movie theater or library. She had no use for movies, and she didn't care for libraries. She treated both activities like monumental wastes of time, and because of that, I assumed that her aimless treks would lead nowhere and that she'd lied about following the scent of anything.

Inevitably, she would prove me wrong every time. We always found whatever it was she pursued. Sometimes, the journey led to a lone individual standing on the side of the road next to a homemade sign advertising the mangoes they picked themselves. No matter what price the person asked or what quality of product they offered, my mother always found their selection lacking, and she always managed to talk them down in price. Later, as she showed me how to peel the skin to get to their meat, our hands would become sticky as we giggled together at how she got the best of the salesperson. I always loved these moments, and I forgave her for not getting me to the library or wherever else I wanted her to take me.

On one of these trips, we came upon Rebel Farms.

Until that moment, I thought my mother had finally lost her touch. It seemed like we'd spent the day driving aimlessly for miles. The time inside the car moved especially slow because of my mother's foul mood. That week, she and my father had argued more than usual. Money had become tight, a situation exacerbated by the fact that my mother's car trips with me cost them more than what they budgeted for fuel. That day, she seemed intent on making the drive last as long as possible, perhaps to prove a point, and things became so miserable that I couldn't concentrate on the book I'd brought to keep me company, a collection of stories by Edgar Allan Poe. I kept the bulky volume open on my lap as my mother spoke softly to herself, muttering curses at my father for being so unreasonable and at herself for failing to properly track the scent of the mangoes. We even had to stop and fill up the station wagon soon after crossing a bridge that looked unfamiliar, one that led across an inlet and onto a small key north of where we lived.

Even though we lived close to the water, I rarely saw the ocean. Despite what the family lore said about my father finding my mother on a beach, she seemed to avoid going anywhere near water. Especially the sea.

Not this time. Whether out of anger or sheer determination to find the mangoes, we continued our trek on a rustic key with quaint shops selling beach souvenirs and old wooden fish shacks. We didn't stop. We drove the full length of the key, eventually bypassing the tourist district, and further in to where mangroves still grew wild and untouched, finally coming upon a side road that lead to Rebel Farms. A large Confederate flag waving in the breeze announced its presence. Though young, I knew and read enough history for the sight of that flag to create a bad feeling in my gut. But my mother paid it no mind as she rolled right past it and into a dirt lot, where she put the car into park and ordered me out. She didn't bother waiting for me. She exited so quickly herself that I had to hurry to catch up with her. I certainly didn't want to sit in the car by myself.

Under a canopy attached to an outbuilding not much larger than a shed, a fruit stand awaited us. Beyond that, rows and rows of mango trees extended well into the distance, interrupted only by a small pen that held a single animal: a goat.

I wanted to leave. Something didn't feel right, especially with that flag waving high above us, its presence stark and unashamed for anyone to see. Intuition told me that the people here would not welcome us, but my mother seemed to not give it any thought at all. They had mangoes for sale, and she wanted to buy them—the only thing that mattered to her as she marched toward the stand.

A man roughly the age of my father waited there for us, his white face smiling as if he expected us. Even when he spoke in a friendly tone, I held firm in my suspicions.

"What'cha reading there?" he asked as we drew close.

He meant the library book I held pressed to my chest like a shield protecting me from harm. I'd carried it along without even thinking about it. I showed him the cover, assuming he would recognize Poe's name, but he only took note of the image on the cover. It depicted the demonic creature from one of Poe's earliest gothic stories, a horse with fiery red eyes.

"A pony book, I see," he said. "I'll bet you love animals. We happen to have us a goat you can go visit." He eyed my mother, giving her a quick evaluation before adding, "For free."

I started to correct him. Of course I loved animals, but the appeal of the book in my hand had nothing to do with animals or horses. I started to object, hesitating so as not to seem foolish. Even though I'd read the story twice, I still didn't know the precise pronunciation of the title: "Metzengerstein."

My mother sensed the attitude simmering in me beneath the surface, and she didn't want me sitting in the way of a good deal for this man's delicious mangoes. Even I could smell the rich aroma that found its way to us in the warm sea breeze. To forestall whatever I might say, she made a condescending remark about my reading habits. Something about how she often had to pull my nose out of all those books I took home from the library every week.

That succeeded in breaking the ice. Apparently, the man didn't care much for books either. Before long, the two of them began discussing the varieties of mangoes he harvested. In a Dixie accent that he made sure to emphasize, he explained how he and his family owned several acres of trees on the key and how we picked the right time to show because everything had just started coming into season. Despite his drawl, he seemed intent on demonstrating that our complexions didn't make us unwelcome, though he did look me over a few times as if trying to make sense of how a woman as dark as this prospective customer could produce a child who looked like me. Perhaps, as he welcomed us under the canopy of the fruit stand to sample his product, he assumed that my mother worked as a nanny of some kind.

Either way, he put on a good show, providing sample after sample, each one presented to us in a tiny paper cup he placed carefully on the wooden bar under the canopy. My mother met his performance with one of her own, sniffing each sample before knocking it back like a cowboy with a shot of whiskey. I found them all delicious, but my mother looked unimpressed.

Her businesslike demeanor only added to the man's growing amusement. When we reached the end of the samples, he said, "None of these good enough for you?"

"No," said my mother, "they're not." She made a show of looking around. "Where's the freezer you've been keeping these stored in?"

The man fixed her with a serious expression and leaned toward her across the bar. My mother met his gaze and raised an eyebrow.

I braced myself for something awful to happen. Everything up to and including our murder.

Instead, he burst out laughing. After a moment, my mother joined in. I watched, wondering what had just happened, my confusion growing as he playfully wagged a finger in my mother's face.

"You're good, you're good," he said. Then he came out from behind the bar, congratulating her on her expert palate. "What you say I take you out into the grove and show you around. I'll let you pick what you want right from the trees."

She hesitated and turned in my direction like she needed my permission. The man followed her gaze. They both stared at me.

The man seemed to understand the unspoken question behind her silence.

He looked at me and asked, "How would you like to visit my goat while I take—" A pregnant pause lingered in the air as he once more tried to work out our relationship. My mother watched him, waiting to see what he would say next, enjoying his uncertainty. When he finally continued, they shared another bout of laughter—at my expense, I couldn't help but feel.

"Your mama. While I take your *mama* for a little ride in my golf cart. She'll bring you back lots of juicy mangoes." They shared another laugh as he turned to her. "You like them juicy, don't you? I'll give you a good price too."

He followed that by winking at me, a gesture meant to reassure everyone. One that said only a fool wouldn't feel at ease around him, and never mind that flag blowing overhead in the breeze. It only meant that good down-home people lived here. The type we call salt-of- the-earth. The real Florida.

It also meant unlearning everything experience taught me, including an unpleasant trip my father took us on to meet his family in Homestead. During a tense two days, I saw lots of those flags emblazoned on tractors, rear bumpers, and even on the cash register used in the feed store where one of his cousins worked. That experience at an early age gave me my first lesson about the meaning of its symbolism, before history taught me the rest.

But it seemed to not bother my mother at all. She agreed to ride off on this man's golf cart while I waited behind with the goat to entertain me. The man unlatched the gate to the pen and held it open for me, as if inviting me in to join my animal brethren.

"Go on," said my mother when I held back, my book pressed against my chest. "What are you afraid of? Go play with the nice goat, Nattie."

The goat stood at the farthest corner of the pen, sizing me up, daring at me to step into its domain. One of its horns appeared bent at an odd angle, either from an injury or birth defect.

"You can read the goat a story out of your animal book," said the man. "He won't even mind if you have to sound out the big words."

"Go on," my mother said before I could reply to the implied criticism of my vocabulary.

Something in her eyes warned me not to talk back. Reduced to playing a part in a game I barely understood, I resigned myself to the hope that she would at least come back with something that made it all worth it. Feeling scorned and rejected, I watched them sally forth to the man's golf cart before riding off toward the trees, leaving me with only a judgmental goat for company.

The animal and I remained frozen like that for several minutes. Immediately, I began counting down the seconds my mother spent away. My mind went back to the people in my father's family, like the cousin who stood at the cash register in the feed store, looking right through me as if I didn't exist. I wondered if I should have made a better show of resistance. Clearly, they both wanted me to stay behind. For what reason or purpose, I didn't know.

Finally, I decided to at least try to make friends with the goat. I did like animals. I just didn't fawn over them the way most girls my age generally did. I inched forward with an outstretched hand, all the while trying to avoid the excessive amount of goat droppings everywhere. "That's a good goat. Here, goat, come here." I didn't know how else to address such a hostile-looking animal.

As I came closer, the goat lowered his head in what looked like an invitation to pet him on the head.

But a voice halted me in my tracks.

"Stop!"

I turned to see a boy a few years older than me come from the direction of the stand. He wore a dirty white t-shirt and could have passed as the younger brother of the man who just took my mother away somewhere.

"Who the fuck let you in there?" he said as he stomped his way toward the pen. "This is private property. You know that animal could gore you to death, don't you? Or are you just stupid?"

My head swiveled back to the goat, its head still lowered.

Only then did I take full stock of how the misshapen horn appeared aimed at my mid-section.

The boy continued speaking as he entered the pen. He seemed unconcerned about planting his feet in goat shit. He wore mud-caked jeans that fit snug at his waist, and when he turned to look at me, I saw that something didn't look right about him. It took me a moment to realize the source of that impression: his eyes didn't line up correctly.

One of them didn't work. Which one, precisely, I couldn't tell.

I remained fixated on that mystery as he stomped his way toward me, eventually stopping between me and the goat.

"Didn't you hear what I said? This animal is evil. Look at what it done to me."

He tapped his left eye—glass, it turned out, the one that no longer worked. Jagged scar tissue surrounded it. "It done that when I was nothing more than baby, and he won't hesitate to do it to you too. That horn there," he pointed toward the one that looked deformed, "it's bent just right to rip your eye out of its socket."

Then I watched in horror as the boy kicked the goat. It bleated in surprise and ran toward the other side of the pen, where it regarded us both with an expression of pure loathing.

Then the boy turned to me. I waited for him to try to kick me next. *Just try*, I thought. I swore to myself that I would kick him right back, maybe give him one extra for the goat. Instead, he pointed a finger toward the gate.

"Get," he said, commanding me like livestock.

I held my ground, prompting him to repeat the order. The goat sniffed the air, daring me to trespass on its space.

"Go on and stay, then. See if he don't pluck out your eye and eat it for breakfast before you so much as scream," the boy said. Then he grinned. "He likes girl eyes the best. They're his favorite."

That broke my resolve. I left the pen, taking pains to not hurry, my library book still positioned against my chest, a protective barrier between me and the world. The boy huffed at my show of defiance. I barely made it out before he slammed the gate closed and shuffled back the way he came, a slight limp in his step, like an old man in a young person's body. He never turned back, eventually disappearing behind the outbuilding and leaving me to wonder what manner of psychopaths my mother's nose for mangoes had led us to. Now outside the fence's perimeter, I gazed back at the goat and its odd horn. It regarded me with antagonism. Still, I felt sorry for the animal and its isolation. If not for a genuine fear of losing an eye, I might have defied the boy and gone back into the pen to have another go at making friends with the animal.

Only I didn't. Eventually, the golf cart came rambling back, alleviating my suspicion that the man took my mother off somewhere to murder her. On the contrary, I heard laughter as the cart rolled to a stop within a few feet of me, and she disembarked with an elated expression on her face. She'd never looked so happy.

Strangely enough, she also appeared soaking wet, as if she'd been submerged in water. Her sundress clung to her body, accentuating hips and hardened nipples.

Embarrassed, I looked away, surprised she would let a stranger see her this way.

The man hopped to the rear of the golf cart, where two full crates of mangoes sat perched. "Your mama sure has an eye for the good ones," he said to me. "You make friends with old Milton?"

At first, I thought he meant the mean boy who appeared out of nowhere.

But then he pointed toward the goat, who maintained its defensive position at the back of the pen, watching and judging the humans in its vicinity.

"No," I said, wondering if I should mention the boy who kicked the goat. Would I just make more trouble for myself?

"Well, you can try again when you come back. I hope to see you and your momma again real soon." He winked as he stacked the crates on top of one another. He hoisted them as if they weighed nothing, his attention returning to my mother. The sight of her caused him to beam. "Load these up for you?"

Without hesitating, she accepted his offer, more unusual behavior on her part. She never accepted help from anyone, not even when employees at the supermarket tried to carry out groceries for her. But something about this man made her respond differently, and she laughed freely with him as they said their goodbyes.

I realized later that I never saw my mother pay for the mangoes. Nor would she tell me how she'd become so wet. "Don't be foolish, Nattie," she said when I asked her if she went swimming. Besides, her clothes dried completely by the time we arrived home, where she added the mangoes to the curry she prepared for dinner.

"All these mangoes," my father said, marveling at the sheer quantity of them.

"Where'd they come from?"

She gave a vague answer, but he seemed not to care. The curry left him too full and satisfied to pursue it any further.

The following week, we made the first of several return trips to Rebel Farms. Every time, we returned home with more crates of mangoes, each one personally loaded into our car by my mother's new friend—Mr. Dennings, I eventually learned to be his name. Each time, my mother rode away with him alone on his golf cart, only to return soaking wet but in good humor. Often, as we drove away, my mother hummed along to some tune playing in her head, perhaps a song from a previous life. It all seemed strange to me. My mother never hummed or sang to me. And she never explained why she always returned soaking wet, even her clothes.

I gave up asking. Instead, I concentrated on a task of my own. If she would force me to take these long car trips with her every week, I would make friends with the goat.

Each time we arrived, Mr. Dennings would say, "Well, now, there's the girl who loves animals," and he would prod me toward the pen so that he could have my mother all to himself.

For a while, the boy with the glass eye didn't show up again. That left me free to try enticing the goat to approach me close enough for me to pet him. I always carried a book with me and kept it pressed firmly against my chest, just in case the goat decided to charge me. Whether it would provide a reliable defense against that deformed horn of his or not, I didn't know. What the boy said about the goat eating human eyes made me wary.

"Here, Milton, come here, boy," I would say with my hand extended, calling him like a dog. "I won't hurt you."

But Milton always maintained his distance, leaving me unfulfilled as I returned home with my soaking wet mother and a car filled with ripened mangoes.

Soon, their scent filled our home. Everywhere you looked, you saw mangoes. Every meal involved them, to such an extent that my father joked that his skin began to develop an orange tint.

"Seriously," he asked at one point, "what's with all the mangoes?"

I waited for my mother to tell him about her new friend. But she withheld that detail. I wanted her to tell him more. Then I could add something about the cranky goat, maybe even mention the boy with the glass eye. But something about the way she dodged the subject insinuated that I needed to keep this information to myself.

Which frustrated me.

Because over time, I'd finally begun to make some progress with the irascible goat, and I couldn't share it. Normally, I felt closer to my father even though I spent far less time with him than I did with my mother, a circumstance hardly his fault since he worked all the time. But unlike my mother, he encouraged my passion for strange and macabre stories, telling me that I probably inherited that inclination from his grandfather, who used to regale the family with tales of skunk ape sightings in the Everglades, as well as strange, unidentified lights flying over the Florida Keys. This man died well before the time of my birth, and my father stopped short of saying that he would have taken a shine to me. Everyone knew his family disapproved of his marriage to my mother, and some of them considered my very existence an abomination. After they made their feelings clear, my father cut ties with them. Maybe that explained my mother's apparent secrecy about where the mangoes came from. Either way, I unwittingly became her co-conspirator.

At first, the mangoes had softened my father's mood. The more my mother responded to his questions about the mangoes with secrecy and obfuscation, the less he responded with jokes. Their arguments turned into all-out fights. I remember yelling, slammed doors.

To hide from the growing tension, I fell even deeper into my reading, as well as my efforts to tame Milton and make him my friend. I started bringing food with me to tempt him closer—pieces of dried fruit, like raisins, small enough to tuck away without my mother seeing.

One time, I grew bolder and stowed away an apple, planning to finally tempt Milton close enough for me to pet.

The reappearance of the one-eyed boy ruined this plan. Before Milton could take a bite, the boy yelled out as he stepped purposefully toward us, closing the distance quickly.

"Don't you try to feed that animal," he said.

At first, I ignored him, focusing instead on the wild eyes of the animal, trying to hypnotize him into getting close enough to pet. Maybe he would have done so if not for all the yelling and swearing coming from the one-eyed boy. Long before, I already suspected that the boy regularly mistreated the animal, and I hated him for it. He probably liked to deny the goat food just for the joy of watching him suffer. My kindness would balance the boy's cruelty, so I defiantly kept offering the apple to the goat.

But the boy wouldn't stand for it. He opened the gate and rushed toward me. Before I could react, he grabbed the apple from my hand and examined it. "I see what you're doing. Trying to give my goat rotten fruit." Then he threw it outside the pen and shoved me to the ground before stomping away.

Burning with anger, I gathered myself upright, finding myself covered in goatshit. Some of it even got on my library book. That infuriated me the most. I looked around for the one-eyed boy, intending to give him a taste of his own medicine. But like a ghost, he'd already vanished.

I worried about what my mother would say about the goat shit on my clothes, but upon her return with Mr. Dennings, she seemed distracted, withdrawn, displaying none of the good humor and joy his company always generated. Mr. Dennings helped with the boxes of mangoes as usual, but he also appeared dour and quiet. We drove off without the usual banter between them. Nor did I see his figure receding in the distance, waving goodbye as usual. The trip home proceeded in silence. Even the mangoes smelled faintly rotten.

We didn't return for a long time after that. In the meantime, we found out my mother had become pregnant. I never thought I'd have a brother or sister. My mother used to tell me that one baby was enough for her, so I gave up hope a long time ago.

Still, that news alleviated some of the tension around the house, but not all of it. A kind of shadow now followed my father wherever he went. He touched my mother noticeably less since they'd started fighting. He acted as if news of the pregnancy had interfered with his plans to avoid her. For her part, my mother seemed amused by my excitement, but if she shared it, I could hardly tell.

Sometimes, I'd ask her when we could go back to Rebel Farms. I kept thinking about poor Milton the goat, stuck there with that evil boy. If Milton really caused him to lose an eye, then maybe he deserved it. I never saw him treat the goat with anything but disdain and cruelty. In my mind, I'd somehow already tamed Milton, and he missed me as much as I missed him.

But my mother shushed these requests. She acted like that place never existed. We never discussed why, leaving me to wonder if I deserved the blame. I'd done something wrong. We even stopped taking those long drives together with the windows rolled down in anticipation of my mother's preternatural nose catching some delicious scent that we could track down. The distance between us grew. If I asked her, she would use her pregnancy as an excuse, explaining that the doctor wanted her to limit her driving until the baby was born.

When that day finally arrived, she presented my father with their newest offspring. My father looked at the scrunched face and seemed to not know what to do or say.

"Another girl," he finally said when he held the baby for the first time. "I'm really outnumbered now."

My mother tilted her head as if listening to a whispered secret. "Maybe," she said.

"Maybe what?" asked my father.

"You'll learn in due time. Let the child decide when to tell you."

She would never live to see the day that the child they christened Erika would want that changed to Erik. I still wonder if my mother somehow knew this would happen before anyone else.

But I can't ask her. I can't ask her anything.

Because months later, she told me to get into the car. "A little trip like we used to. Just the two of us," she said with my father out of earshot. We stole away together, leaving him home with the baby, something different in her mood. Something more expectant. Conspiratorial. She said nothing about our destination, but somehow, I knew anyway, even before the appearance of the old landmarks and the first hint of something sweet carried by the ocean breeze. When I saw the drawbridge, I knew it for sure: we were on the way back to Rebel Farms.

Everything looked the same, including the abominable flag blowing in the wind and, behind that, rows and rows of trees.

Whether or not Mr. Dennings expected us, he gave no clear sign. He looked several years older, even haggard, as he stepped out from beneath the canopy with a slight limp. Time, it seemed, passed differently here.

"I see y'all are back," he said, a toothpick rolling around in his mouth. He looked at my mother like she forgot to bring something with her before turning to me with a smile. "Well, hello, Miss Nat. I suppose you want to visit your old friend Milton while I take your mama to do some picking." Then he looked at her again. "You came for picking, didn't you?"

"I came for picking," she said tonelessly.

"Well then." Back to me: "You bring a tasty treat for Milton? I almost forgot what pretty eyes you have."

That threw me off guard. He'd never said anything about my eyes before. If he meant I should offer them as "treats" for Milton, I couldn't tell. He also never let on that he knew I'd made attempts to win over Milton with food. No one answered him, so he just went on talking.

"You know what Milton really likes?" He reached into his pocket and pulled out a stick of jerky. "They say you shouldn't feed meat to a goat, but I swear to you, that animal has quite an appetite for it. He ate a whole chicken once, all by himself. Now, they say that ain't a natural diet for a goat, but

I'm telling you the lord's truth. Why, he might even eat a human baby if you give him half a chance."

I could feel my mother shift her weight behind me.

Did he know my mother had a new baby? That filled me with dread, and I didn't know. Someone needed to change the subject, so I tried.

"He ate a boy's eye," I said,

"What? What boy?"

I didn't know how to answer. He made it sound like I said something wrong. My mother made a scolding sound through clenched teeth and pinched my arm. Hard. It occurred to me that the one-eyed boy appeared when I was alone. Did he belong to the grove? He always acted as if he owned the place.

Before I could recant, the man pointed over his shoulder. "You mean Dorian? Dorian told you that? Goddamned liar."

Then he stomped off toward the shed connected to the canopied fruit stand, leaving us standing alone. My mother gave me a rough tap on the back of my head. "Why are you lying like that?" she said

"I wasn't. That's what he told me."

"Is that what you do? Believe what any fool tells you? Listen to me: you stay away from that animal."

"Then what am I supposed to do?" I hadn't even brought a book with me.

"Just behave," she said. "Sit somewhere. We won't be long."

Hardly had she finished her sentence before we heard a flood of epithets coming from the building. Then sounds of violence: slapping and a horrible crash, followed by the voice of a boy calling out for mercy.

Seconds later, Mr. Dennings re-emerged and walked purposefully toward us. I braced myself for an altercation. Even if she'd just mistreated me, I planned to put myself between him and my mother, determined to do everything in my power to protect her.

But he stopped within a few inches of us and smiled just like he used to.

"You ready to do some picking?"

She nodded, and within moments, they rolled away together in that golf cart just like they used to. I looked down at my hand, holding the jerky. In all the commotion, my mother hadn't bothered to take it from me. If she really wanted me to stay away from Milton, I reasoned, she would not have forgotten. Thus, I wasted no time.

Once the golf cart rolled out of sight, I walked toward the pen, where the goat waited.

True to form, Milton positioned himself to face me directly, his eyes tracking my movement with suspicious intelligence. He maintained an adversarial distance as I closed the gate behind me, showing no inclination to get any closer. All that progress I'd made before apparently lost. But that changed when I held out the jerky. His demeanor became visibly different as he marched toward me. Miraculously, he ate the jerky from my hand, the two of us suddenly like old friends. With that deformed horn just inches from my face, I risked touching him. He accepted the contact, even seemed to welcome it.

"Good goat, good," I whispered, elated that after all this time, I finally succeeded in making friends with Milton.

A voice behind me broke the spell. "*Goddamn you.*"

I swiveled to see the one-eyed boy, Dorian, coming through the gate, a bucket in his hand.

"Goddamn you *to hell,*" he said, stomping his way into the pen.

Closer, I saw blood dripping from the corner of his mouth, and his one good eye now looked swollen and discolored, marks of the violence I heard earlier.

Violence he now intended to bring to me.

Buoyed by my victory with Milton, I would respond with ferocity. I would stand my ground, defend myself if necessary. Milton had finally accepted my advances, and in some strange way, that meant he now belonged to me. I had every right to keep petting him.

But it quickly became apparent that Dorian didn't want me. He wanted Milton.

"Goddamn you," he kept repeating, the only words he knew, and he used his shoulder to shove me out of the way. At the same time, he used his free hand to grab the goat by its misshapen horn. The animal bucked and bleated, but even when limited to just one arm, the boy's strength proved too much. With cold deliberation, he dropped the bucket, and from within it, he drew forth a long, curved knife.

At first, I misjudged what he intended to do. I thought he planned to pluck out the animal's eye, a delayed revenge for what the goat did to him long ago. Just as I started to voice my protest, he did something else. Something worse. Without regard for my outcry or the goat's resistance, he ran the curved knife across the goat's neck and forcefully held it over the bucket. Milton cried and shuddered as its blood filled the bucket.

The boy watched me the whole time, grinning.

He did this to hurt me. And it worked.

****

I don't remember what I did next, not until Mr. Dennings found me wandering through the grove. I must have walked there, looking for my mother and becoming lost in an aimless daze. Mr. Dennings rolled up beside me, the seat next to him empty.

I spoke first. "I didn't do it." I kept on walking. To where, I don't know.

He slowed his speed enough to keep rolling along beside me. "What? Done what? We been looking all over for you."

"I didn't do it," I said again.

"No, you didn't," he said. "It was an accident. Nobody's fault."

I tried protesting, tried telling him I saw what one-eyed Dorian did out of pure cruelty and meanness. I wanted Mr. Dennings to inflict more violence on Dorian, to punish him for what he did. Only I couldn't form the words.

Mr. Dennings interpreted my muteness another way. "You want to sit here next to me?" He tapped the empty seat beside him, the one that normally held my mother. Only then did her absence make an impression. Him wanting something from me left me with misgivings. He must have read it on my face because he said, "Don't look at me like that. I ain't going to lay a hand on you. Go on, get in. I'll drive you back. Ambulance is waiting."

Ambulance? For a dead goat? That made no sense, not in the least. But I obeyed the command, and together, we rode in silence back toward the big ugly flag waving over the road.

Where, indeed, an ambulance awaited.

We came upon it just as they loaded the gurney holding my mother's dead body.

Mr. Dennings consoled me by saying he let her have her pick of the finest, freshest mangoes. "No woman had an eye for ripeness like hers," he said. But according to him, no sooner had she stepped away from the golf cart than she started complaining about pains in her chest. Her breathing became heavy. She sat down on the ground to gather herself, and within a few minutes, she simply closed her eyes and died. Didn't even topple over. She just leaned up against a tree and seemed to go to sleep.

The cause of her death became mired in confusion. Corroborating Mr. Dennings' account, the coroner cited cardiac arrest as the cause of death.

"Makes sense," said the coroner when he finally granted my grief-stricken father a meeting. "For a woman her age, I mean. I saw signs of many other contributing factors. Lots of stress."

"A woman her age?" my father asked. He bounced the baby on his knee as I sat next to him in a cold, antiseptic office.

The coroner nodded like he'd heard a yes or no question. "I was surprised to see evidence she went through childbirth recently. For a woman her age, that would have been a contributing factor."

"A woman her age?" my father asked again. He held up my sibling for the doctor to see. "This is the baby."

The doctor stared at the wiggling form in my father's arms. He wore a pair of glasses that made his eyes look large and curious.

"Very interesting," he finally said, as if gazing upon a strange lab specimen.

In the weeks and months afterwards, my father pored obsessively over the documents pertaining to my mother's death. His face started to look perpetually gaunt and tired. The man who once resembled a youthful Bruce Springsteen transformed overnight into an old man as he read and reread sentences that proved to him that my mother died because of some malfeasance on the part of Mr. Dennings.

"Look here," he would say to me with glasses perched on his nose. Until then, I never knew my father even wore glasses. I followed his fingers to the words on the page. "Doesn't this sound like they think she drowned? Nat, she died on dry land, and they seem to be saying that she had water in her lungs."

I nodded, though at such a young age, I didn't understand the possible nuances of what I read. Maybe they meant she had fluid in her lungs. Still, I thought it among my mounting responsibilities to affirm my father's suspicions that the coroner's report held some conspiratorial secret about what really happened to my mother. He read it countless times, and eventually, he started making unwelcome visits to Rebel Farms so he could confront Mr. Dennings. More than once, my father's accusations became physical, and I would later have to help him treat a blackened eye or a bloody lip. The first time I saw my father take a swing at Dennings, I noticed how alike they looked, though Mr. Dennings proved more agile and always got the best of him.

"Go on, get out of here," he would say as my father pulled himself off the ground. "And take that mongrel child with you."

He pointed toward where I stood holding Erik, who we still called Erika at the time. I remember wondering which child he meant. He couldn't mean me, could he? Behind him, I could see the empty pen that once held Milton the Goat, and I felt doubly sad for all of us.

So began my father's long descent into despair. Eventually, Dennings petitioned for a restraining order against my father. Legally barred from going to the grove, he still went to the key and wandered along the beach, scanning the water as if he hoped to see my mother emerging from the surf the way he did years ago on a different beach. At night, he sulked in front of the television, watching movies about middle-aged men on violent revenge quests for dead loved ones. Each movie contained the same plot and often the same actors playing essentially the same widowed men with different names, but that didn't seem to matter to him. He became a ghost that we learned to live around.

Until an early death took him away for good.

I suppose he wasted all that time living as ghost so that he wouldn't have to haunt us in death.

Sometimes, I wish he would. If I had to endure any ghost, I would want it to be his.

140

Three

"Y ou look like you seen a ghost," said Sarge as he wheeled me across campus, the cart winding between groups of students, sometimes coming within inches of rolling over feet and toes. For a public safety officer, he showed little regard for actual safety, drawing more than one angry glare from pedestrians forced to step out of the way. Some of the faces belonged to my own students, their stares following me as we passed them within a hair's breadth. I knew if I looked back, I would see them pointing and whispering under their breath to their friends. First, that scene in the classroom, and now it appeared that I needed a personal escort off campus.

Hoping to change those optics, I said, "You can stop here. I'll walk the rest of the way."

He shook his head. "You'll miss your bus."

I couldn't conceal my surprise. Nor could he hide his pleasure.

"It's my job to notice that kind of thing," he said, responding to the unspoken question lingering in the air. "I keep track of the cars in the parking lot. When people arrive, when they leave, what they drive. It's my business. All of it. Security. And I had you figured you out the day you came in."

"Had me figured out?"

Ahead, near the faculty offices, I saw someone who looked like Isis duck around the corner. She moved quickly, vanishing before I could confirm her identity. Would she come looking for me after what happened that day? Not likely.

"I sure did," Sarge said. "I know what troubles you."

"If anything troubled me, you'd be the last to know."

He laughed unkindly. "You probably thought I meant 'women's troubles.' You ladies, your whole lives coming down to tubes and passageways, cycles and flows, like that's all there is to life. I know all about it. I have daughters. But let me set your mind at ease, because that's the furthest thing from my mind. I took sexual harassment training, so I know not to bring up anything like that. No. What I'm talking about is—"

Up ahead I saw my bus turn in and head for the stop. But instead of going faster, Sarge decreased our speed.

"—that day we did your fingerprints. You didn't ask for a parking permit. I thought, 'Well, that's something.' You don't see that every day, a hotshot college instructor who isn't asking where to find the faculty lot. I'm ready for that question because hardly anyone ever believes me when I say there ain't one. Everyone parks in the same place, see?"

We coasted along at a leisurely pace. A group of students waiting for the bus stood and gathered their backpacks as it came to a stop. Its door opened, and they began to board. I could make it, I realized, if I stepped quickly. I would need to hurry, but I could do it. But even at our crawling speed, I still risked falling or turning an ankle. I would need Sarge to slow just a bit more.

Still, part of me wanted to hear what he said next, where he intended to go with this uncomfortable conversation.

"All that uppity attitude you had. And you people call folks like me privileged. I thought for sure you'd ask where you could park some pretty car. I took you for someone who drove a nice tight compact. Probably purple. With a dented fender."

The boarding of the bus paused as one of the passengers paused in mid-step to ask the driver a question. Sarge's speed remained consistently slow but still too fast for me to jump off. He seemed to know what I considered doing, just like he somehow knew the kind of car I used to drive. I dreaded hearing what he would say next.

And for good reason.

"On top of that, you acted squirrelly about the fingerprint results. Sure enough, they came back clean, all right. But the way you acted kept nagging at me. My special cop senses, you know. They're still sharp. I couldn't have survived forty years as part of New York's finest without staying keen. I'll bet you can appreciate that."

The boarding proceeded, with two more entering the bus. The one behind them stopped to tie his shoe.

"So I did some poking around, called a few people I knew. And guess what? A little birdy told me where you earned your degree, and before long, I talked to someone in Tampa who did late night duty in Ybor City one warm evening."

The student checked his other shoe before straightening up and climbing the rest of the steps. Just one more behind him.

"That's how I learned about your purple compact and a certain woman named . . ."

I didn't want him to say the name. Already freed from mirrors, she would follow me everywhere if people started speaking her name out loud. That would summon her, and I would never, ever free myself of her memory.

So I made the plunge, not so much jumping as falling out of the golf cart. I grunted in pain as my feet struck the pavement, timing it just right so that Sarge's attempt to say *Taryn Hall* morphed into an exclamation of surprise, even as he continued to roll past where I stumbled, miraculously managing to keep to my feet. His head turned, his jaw slung open in the middle of a syllable I couldn't hear, not over the roaring in my ears as I willed my feet to move, move, move. I began running diagonally across a stretch of manicured grass, crossing the shortest distance between me and the bus, which against all probability, somehow still waited there with its door open, a refuge that would close if I didn't hurry, hurry.

As I ran, a memory resurfaced, something that until that moment remained buried, lost to time . . .

After watching the knife slice through the goat's neck, I ran through the rows of mango trees, calling for my mother. Only after I became lost and exhausted did Mr. Dennings find me. I now wondered if my panicked grief somehow caused her heart failure, if she heard my distress, and unable to find me, she simply quit and died. How I wanted to call her now, and why couldn't she appear to me the way Taryn Hall did?

Seconds before the bus door could close, I managed to stumble aboard. The driver's face told me I made quite a sight. Maybe I startled him a little. For whatever reason, the door remained open behind me as I fumbled for my pass, all the while trying to assure myself that I was safe. As soon as I scanned my pass, he would close the door, giving Sarge no time to follow me on board. But the bus remained motionless as I walked as steadily and calmly as I could toward an empty seat, my legs shaking. I avoided the curious and concerned looks I received from the other passengers, most of them students. And still the bus remained in place.

"I'm all right," I said over my shoulder to the driver, thinking maybe he didn't want me to stumble. Behind me, I could see the door still hanging open. "I'm fine," I said, even though the driver didn't inquire as to my well-being.

Drive away, I wanted to say. *Why won't you just drive away?*

I got the answer I feared when Sarge's imposing form filled the doorway to the bus. He leaned against the handrail as he took stock of all the faces that now turned toward him. How many would provide testimony on my behalf if he put his hands on me? Would they all say I instigated the conflict somehow? I wondered if Sarge assessed the same questions as his eyes searched for and eventually found me. The other heads turned in my direction, some with expressions of relief. I was the prey, not them. Did he, a retired police officer, still carry handcuffs, and would he try to use them before escorting me off the bus? Would they take out their phones and begin filming if I resisted and he responded by wrestling me to the pavement, pressing his knee down on my neck until I started to gasp and cry out for air? Would I call for my mother?

No one stood to block his passage as he strolled along the aisle of the bus, taking his time, enjoying the tension, until he came close enough to me so that I could smell the lunch on his breath when he leaned over.

"You left this," he said.

He dropped Dash's copy of *Tell My Horse* onto my lap.

Hoisting his pants so that they rode higher on his midsection, he turned back toward the front of the bus. His hips swayed with a kind of rhythm that looked strange until I recognized it for what it was: a strut.

I'd given him my fear—my terror—and he accepted it, devoured it like meat.

I couldn't let him have it. If he made it outside the bus before I said something, I would lose part of myself forever.

"It's not mine," I said, even though people who look like me often suffer when they talk back to people with badges.

Sarge stopped and turned. He tried to look amused, but I could see a glimmer of uncertainty. "What's that you say?"

"The book." I held it up for everyone to see. My witness. My shield. I fanned the pages at him. "It belongs to Professor Dash. But I'll see that he gets it back."

Cocking an eyebrow, he inched his way back to me as if trying to read the words that skirted past his eyes. "Who authorized you to take possession of—"

I cut him off. "I have all the authorization I need. Thank you for your service, Officer. Have a nice day."

His lips parted, but the words died in his mouth. He grunted something unintelligible and left with a little less victory in his step.

With him gone and the bus finally in motion, I finally exhaled. I put the book on my lap and sorted through the pages, hoping my carelessness didn't cause the documentation about Isis's accommodation to fall out. I hadn't meant to leave it behind when I made my break for the bus. I wouldn't do anything that careless again.

Especially not with that book, its effect in my hand like a talisman. I even thought some of that power came from that document tucked in its folds. Professor Dash obviously had no business storing such sensitive information about Isis inside a book—but I sensed that by doing so, he meant to give the document more power or authority.

But it was gone. I looked all around me, under my feet, across the aisle.

I felt sick. Though inconceivably strange, it still contained sensitive information about Isis. Maybe Professor Dash had no business storing it inside a book, but I made everything so much worse by misplacing it altogether.

The possibility of Sarge having it nagged me. If so, I would never forgive myself.

But maybe—hopefully—I would find it when I returned home, safely set aside on the table near my bed.

I thought about my earlier conversation with Isis, the things I said to her, my lack of empathy, understanding, or compassion.

I wished I could take back those words. Listen to what she tried to tell me. Maybe she really believed the things she said. Or perhaps she didn't. Either way, instead of giving her a chance, I shut her down.

To take my mind elsewhere, I opened *Tell My Horse* as the bus came to one jerking stop after another. Passengers came and went, but I managed to keep the seat to myself. Maybe everyone wanted to avoid me. I scanned the book's pages, noting the passages underlined in Dash's pen. One section talked about Guedé, a powerful loa, or spirit. The underlined passage read: *He has charge of everyone within the regions of the dead, and he presides over all that is done there. He is a grave-digger and opens the tombs, and when he wishes to do so, he takes out the souls and uses them in his serve.* It went on to describe how this being revealed himself by *"mounting"* a living being—*as a rider mounts a horse,* wrote Hurston, *then he speaks and acts through his mount. The person mounted does nothing of his own accord. He is the horse of the loa until the spirit departs.*

I wished I'd noted where I found the document about Isis, recalling that it fell out of the book's rear section—if not between these pages, then somewhere close. I wondered if Dash deliberately chose to tuck away that document near this description. Did he see a connection between the preposterous situation of Isis and the words written here? Did he think of Isis as a horse? I shivered as the next possibility came to mind. Did he *want* her to see herself this way?

So many mysteries I could not penetrate on a bus trip, not after what happened. My heart still hammered away in my chest. Now and then, the driver's eyes met mine in the rear-facing mirror, and I knew what his gaze meant—a warning not to cause any more trouble.

My father would listen to my complaints about such looks and preach patience. "Give them a chance to get to know you," he would say, never understanding that people thought it only took one look to know me pretty well. My mother better understood, but she thought such experiences would toughen me. "Look right back, and never let them see you cry," she would say. She wanted me to grow into woman like her, impenetrable as steel, infused with the kind of strength that would allow her to swim across the sea. So as not to disappoint her, I let no one ever see my tears. Not even her.

Another glance at the mirror, and I saw the driver still watching me. This time, he gave me a nearly imperceptible nod. What he meant by it, I couldn't tell. Did he intend some kind of reassurance? Not that I needed or wanted that from him. Then I realized we'd arrived at my stop, so maybe he didn't want me to miss it. He didn't want me on the bus any longer than necessary.

I exited the bus, the book clutched in my hand like a religious artifact.

As I passed the driver, he reached out and touched my arm. "I didn't want to say anything, but—" He paused to reach for something folded next to the wheel. "This fell out when that campus cop climbed up to put on his little show." Then he added quietly, "You need anyone to have your back, just tell me."

I gave no hesitation in unfolding the sheet of paper to confirm what I thought. Yes, it was the accommodation form, the document about Isis. Not lost at all.

My relief grew back into apprehension as the driver's gaze lingered. Like he wanted something in return.

"Thank you," I said, trying to sound casual and not relieved. I wondered what my mother would have said. Something in her native Creole, the key to the incantation that, for all I knew, made her mighty enough to swim across the sea.

I needed that now because the driver kept the door closed. From behind me, the other passengers stirred. I could sense their apprehension.

Something else would soon happen, making them later to wherever they needed to be, work or appointments or home-cooked meals.

The driver pointed to the document. "This girl, I know who she is. I've seen her. She waits at my stop sometimes—not for a ride but to curse me with the evil eye. Don't let her try it on you. If she does, you do what I do." He displayed his left hand, holding his thumb wedged between his middle and index finger. "That little gesture wards away evil. My grandmother, she taught me that, and now I'm teaching you. She came from the old country, where they knew what to do about evil like that. You know what I'm talking about, right?"

I expected him to say burning at the stake. People always thought of fire as a way of dealing with witches.

But he held his fist over his head and pantomimed a broken neck. Hanging.

"Just remember this," he said, repeating the thumb gesture. Finally, he opened the bus door.

"Go on," he said. "Be good."

Which sounded less like a blessing and more like a warning.

The world around me seemed to swirl as I made the short walk home, the book still clutched in my hand like a religious artifact. It alone would not keep me sane. I needed the safety of a familiar environment, cleansed of all the malignancies that relentlessly followed me. I expected to find Erik already home per our normal schedule. Hopefully, he had luck in relieving us of our unwanted guest, the crow that defied death. If not, I felt renewed determination in seeing it gone.

Instead, I walked in to find the crow perched on the back of a chair, enjoying pieces of cereal fed to it from an unfamiliar hand.

The hand's owner turned to me, a smile forming on an ancient face.

"Natacha Miller," said Leonardus Engel. "I've looked forward to meeting you."

Four

"At times, it reminds me of a Ribera painting. Do you know the one of which I speak? *Saint Jerome and the Angel.*"

Lenny, as he invited me to call him, meant the film playing on the television while he and the crow shared a bowl of dry cereal. I recognized the film, the third in the Slashing Sally franchise. I didn't know the painting he referenced, but later, I looked it up. He had a point. At that moment in the film, Slashing Sally, the killer doll animated by an ancient evil, hid in the rafters of an attic as she stalked the old man who unwittingly purchased her at a yard sale. The old man's expression of horror as Slashing Sally fell upon him did resemble Saint Jerome in that 1626 painting, his wizened face in open-mouth shock at seeing an angel look down upon him from the heavens.

Lenny Engel matched the mental image conjured from Isis's description. His face a map of crevasses carved out by age. Sparse white hair barely covering a scalp mottled by age spots, thick eyebrows that nearly met. But for a man incarcerated for so many decades, his skin still maintained a deep bronze color.

"Time passes," said Lenny as he used his fingers to feed the bird a bite of cereal, "but nothing really changes. The world turns and turns and somehow still manages to stand still."

He still wore prison clothes.

"Where's my brother?" I said, forcing my voice to remain calm despite the fact that an escaped inmate had taken refuge in my home. "If you've hurt him—"

"Your remarkable sibling has undertaken an errand. Don't act so alarmed. Please, sit down and enjoy this delectable feast with me." On the opposite side of the table sat an empty bowl. Lenny Engel tilted the cereal box over it, filling it so carelessly that it overflowed onto the table. "Please make allowances if my manners appear unrefined. I've been denied civilization for so long." He fed himself the same way he fed the bird, prompting an angry squawk. Lenny Engel responded by feeding it a piece that had overflowed onto the table.

He gestured again at the television, where Slashing Sally continued to hack at the bleeding old man. "My jailers failed to dull my taste for violence. But art has a way of making us see beauty in all things. The blood, for instance. Not even the Flemish masters could achieve such a lush shade of red. If I can claim no other revenge against the king, my ability to still take pleasure in art will have to do."

"King?" I asked.

"The king of Spain, of course. My business with him remains unresolved." He used the corner of a napkin to dab at his lips. "But other tasks await me first."

"Why are you here?" I also could have asked *how*. He looked physically incapable of making such a long journey.

"Where else could I go? I fear that Isis made things difficult for me." With the napkin, he gestured toward the chair opposite him. The crow flew to the table and began pecking at the cereal that didn't make it into the bowl. More feathers had fallen from its body since I last saw it. In some of those places, I could see the whiteness of bone. "Please sit. We have much to discuss. Principally, Gustav."

The alligator. My face betrayed me.

"You've seen him," Lenny Engel said.

"It's just an animal," I said, resisting the premise that a reptile inhabiting a canal bordering a prison could have migrated all those miles to the college. But after everything I'd witnessed that day, nothing seemed impossible.

"It has plagued me for what feels like an eternity. Allow me to explain." And so Leonardus Engel told me his tale.

* * *

"Before my incarceration, that creature, that *monster,* pursued me through a sea of grass that extended from one end of the horizon to the next, its jaws snapping at my heels as I, lost and alone, struggled for survival in an environment more inhospitable than any living soul could imagine. Giant cats stalked the night, searching for prey, and each time I lifted my foot, I expected to set it down upon some awful venomous serpent. Many times, I waded across water that extended to my neck, and at night, I shivered under great cypress trees, listening to the strange knocks and howls that came to me on the night air. Once, I parted a curtain of sawgrass and spied a family of strange creatures, human in form but larger, their bodies entirely covered with hair. But nothing stalked me with the persistence of Gustav, his presence never far behind as I sought any sanctuary I could find—but I could find nothing, nothing at all. For sustenance, I ate the raw flesh of tiny lizards and spit out their skeletons. The dysentery was unimaginable, but often, I spied signs of human civilization in the distance, leading me to continue my march, only to find that I'd hallucinated when the vision evaporated.

"Except one time. From a distance, the fortress at first resembled a cathedral I knew in my youth. When I saw the spires emerge from across the marsh, I thought my madness finally complete, my sanity irretrievable. I laughed like a lunatic as my boots sank deeply into the muck, yet I didn't want to stop and let the monster finally have me. Still, as the hours passed and I drew closer, the image remained and became more distinct. I hastened, even as I lost one of my boots when it became stuck in wet silt. The sound of snapping jaws behind spurred me onward, leaving it behind. Closer now, I could see that the spires belonged not to a cathedral but to a great fortress, its walls seemingly having grown from the muck itself.

"Once I reached it, I found my energy nearly depleted. I could not count the number of days that passed since I'd arrived in this terrible land, my displacement caused by a tidal wave that lifted my vessel and left me here without any of my earthly possessions. They now tell tales about that doomed ship and how it still floats in undiscovered channels, a fortune still hiding beneath its wooden planks. As for me, I abandoned the ship with only the clothes on my back. Now with those clothes torn to shreds by the elements and only one remaining boot, I stood before the wall of that improbable fortress, worn down in body and spirit, and with no time to spare before the jaws of that pursuing monster found me. 'Hello!' I called forth to the top of the wall, where I could discern a guard tower. 'Have mercy on a poor lost wretch!'

"No answer at first. The sun blazed down from overhead, nearly blinding me, but I thought I could see a head topped by a familiar type of helmet, the kind favored by the conquistadors. A strange sight indeed, but not as strange as the fortress itself. How did it not sink into muck? But I had no time to puzzle over its stability or the inhabitants. A monster pursued me, so I called out again.

"This time, I saw signs of others gathering above, as well as the sound of mocking laughter. That someone should enjoy my misery brought me to a fury. I looked up and declared my wrath to heaven. I swore that if they didn't allow me ingress to their abode, I would curse them and their descendants to an eternity of sorrow and misery. Would you believe that thunder spoke in reply? Not a cloud in the sky moments ago, just unrelenting sun, and suddenly, great barrels of dark clouds called back to me across the watery plains as if our malignant creator offered a personal reply. Lightning struck the tower, prompting me to laugh like the lunatic I'd become. From above, merriment turned to terror as they came to the absurd conclusion that my words carried the weight of the heavens. 'He curses us,' they said. 'Let the devil in before his words cause more mischief.' My mad laughter grew louder as an aperture in the fortress's wall opened and a group of guards poured forth. Did I care that they shackled manacles to my wrists and encircled my neck with iron? Not at all. Not if it meant my salvation.

"As they led me toward the entrance of the fortress, I heard the guard behind me call out in alarm and terror.

"The reptilian beast fell upon us, but instead of me, its jaws found one of my captors. The poor man fell and screamed as its teeth broke through his armor and penetrated the flesh of his abdomen. The other guards cried out as the beast began tearing their comrade to pieces. Instead of coming to his aid, they pulled harder on my chains in the direction of the fortress. During the whole ordeal, I continued to laugh like a madman, even as the thunder shook the land. Trembling, they dragged me across the threshold of the fortress and bolted the heavy gate behind us.

"Only then could I see the state of their poverty and filth. 'You've brought curses upon us,' they said, 'and monsters.'

"Still unable to control my paroxysm of laugher, I said, 'Oh, that's just Gustav. My old crewmate.' Why that name came to mind at that moment, I don't know. But without meaning to, I'd christened it with a name it would retain, and so the legend grew for the duration of my capture.

"At once, they led me through their fortress toward a trap door made of old wood so water-logged that it barely covered the opening. It took two of them to lift it. Without a second's hesitation, the strongest in their number pushed me into it, and I fell from such a great height that, if not for the water down below, I might have broken every bone in my body. When my senses returned, I found myself confined to a half-flooded dungeon, the water high enough to reach my knees and filled with eels which I would have to fight for the meager portions of bread they fed me.

'Cannot the king of Spain afford better provisions?' I asked in the rare moments that my jailers opened the trap door and showed their faces. 'Surely, he can if he can fund such a magnificent fortress in the middle of a swamp.' My insolence received contempt in reply.

'You fool,' they said, 'we didn't build this place. We found it after we suffered a terrible shipwreck. Our vessels lie at the bottom of the sea, and everything here—the natives, the animals, those hairy creatures who walk on two legs—conspires to kill us.'

"But to look at them, you'd think them already dead, their faces so covered with open sores and blisters that they appeared to lack the ordinary features of mankind. The simplest movement seemed to cause them unbearable pain, though they tried unsuccessfully to hide it in my presence. They clearly feared showing any signs of weakness to me, but I saw enough evidence to know that I'd come upon a colony of lepers. I only wondered at what point their affliction would strike me.

'What do you intend to do with me?' I demanded. 'Put you to death,' they said, 'once the king signs your death warrant.' Naturally, I recognized that as an excuse. Either they felt too weak or sick to execute me, or they hoped to derive sadistic pleasure from my prolonged suffering.

"Soon, I stopped eating the scraps they threw me and instead began living on the raw flesh of the eels that swam around my feet. I became quite adept at catching them and tearing them open with my hands and teeth. The sight of me gorging on slimy flesh must have disgusted my jailers because they visited me with less and less frequency. Sometimes, I would go several days at a time without seeing their horrible faces. I even wondered if they began to die out.

"For distraction, I studied the curious walls of my prison cell. These walls felt spongy to the touch. Lichen and other fungal forms grew so freely upon their surface that the whole dwelling seemed organic in nature, as if the fortress itself grew directly from the soot beneath my feet. What had those Spaniards said? They'd not built this place but rather found it after they suffered their own misfortune. In the end, they made it their harbor, as well as my prison, all in the name of the king.

"The passage of time became difficult to measure and noticeable only as the faces that appeared above me began to change. The languages I heard changed too, with Spanish giving way to English, as well as periods of time when I heard the heathen tongues of the natives. At one point, I even heard French. The provisions thrown to me changed, even improved, but I never lost my taste for the raw flesh of eels. I even protested when my jailers insisted upon moving me to a new cell.

"That happened when, one day, the hatch above me opened and someone exclaimed in surprise at seeing me down below. They threw me a rope and insisted on me climbing up. I clasped an eel in my hand and shook it in their direction. 'Will the king of Spain allow me to keep my eels?' They swore at me, calling me a lunatic, and insisted that I climb out unassisted. I admit that I felt glad when they replaced my rags with an orange suit and moved me to a place where my feet could stay dry.

"Yet no one questioned my crime or my sentence. If they asked, I would have called upon them to inquire with the king. I still craved eel, especially when they insisted on feeding me dry, tasteless meals. I asked for the return of my eels, but they laughed and offered me rabbits instead. 'Not to eat,' they said when I asked how I would prepare them for supper. 'They're for the entertainment of children.' Children! I couldn't imagine children in such a terrible place. But that's how I met precious Isis."

Five

The sound of her name was like a fever breaking suddenly and causing the invalid to sit up and say, "Where am I?" What had Isis herself said about his way of making the impossible come to life with his stories? Describing events he could not have witnessed or experienced in a way that created something like a spell. Had he hypnotized me and used Isis's name as a trigger to snap me back to the real world of the present?

I took stock of him and saw just an old man, a fugitive from the Florida Correctional System taking refuge in my house, sharing a bowl of stale cereal with a wild bird. I even failed to notice the television still running, now with a scene of an unsuspecting child climbing the attic stairs, where she would find her grandfather's corpse slashed to ribbons by a murderous doll.

Her peril reminded me of Erik's lingering absence. "Where's my brother? You need to tell me now." I feared for his safety, but I also dreaded the thought of him coming home and finding me shredded to bloody pieces. He had only me. And I only him.

"In due time," said Leonardus Engel as he resumed alternately feeding himself and the crow. His lips opened to reveal canines unworn by time or age. I pictured him biting into the flesh of a wiggling eel and looked away, focusing on the cereal box instead, its packaging a depiction of a cartoon rabbit.

"Isis and I," he continued, "took to one another instantly. I don't believe I've ever met anyone with such insatiable curiosity. But your predecessor seemed less interested in quenching her thirst for knowledge than in pursuing his own aims."

"Professor Dash? What do you mean, exactly?"

"Was that really his name?" Lenny Engel asked. He paused to toss the bird a piece of cereal, smiling with approval when it caught it in its beak. "Or does 'dash' signify a lacuna of sorts? I never learned if his name was simply being omitted from the conversation in the manner of old manuscripts. You know what I mean, I'm sure."

I did. Writers used to omit names and offensive words by substituting a dash for missing letters. Did Professor Dash mean Professor – ? I shook my head in frustration. "You're trying to distract me. Everything you say is just a giant distraction." And I hated to admit how well it worked.

With a wave of his hand, just as one would do with a pesky fly, he dismissed my irritation. "Perhaps his name doesn't matter. Or maybe it matters a great deal. Either way, Professor Dash saw Isis as a kind of vessel waiting to be filled. With his own ambitions, that is, which went well beyond the scope of academia."

"That's rich, coming from you," I said. "You *used* her. To get out of prison. You don't get to pretend to be her champion."

"I pretend nothing." His condescension took the form of a smile that accentuated the contours of his face and transformed him into a grinning skull. "From what I could gather, your predecessor fostered a preoccupation with the occult, and he hoped to use Isis to further that pursuit. I suppose he sent her to me with that aim in mind. If I may sound shameless, he likely wanted to find out if I really existed and gather anecdotes. He had a willing pupil to send out for testimonials. But perhaps I flatter myself. In my defense, I am prone to loneliness. Additionally, I cannot resist an audience. The children who came to pet the rabbits rarely sat still long enough to hear my stories. But I could often sense that Isis wasn't acting in her own agency. I sensed that she had someone—or something—acting through her."

"You act like you care about her or her agency." My voice rose. I found myself practically shouting at him. "What was that business with the rabbit fetus and that spell you taught her? If what you say about Dash is true, you're as bad as him. He made her think she was *possessed.*"

"That idea didn't come from him, I assure you. As for what she did with the offspring of the rabbit, I'm afraid that was her own improvisation. It was simply time for me to leave, and I undertook the necessary measures to carry out my departure. An act of self-interest, true, but one that wouldn't have endangered Isis, even if she did play a minor part in offering a diversion. In the name of Judas, have you been starving this creature?"

He meant the crow. The bird pecked at the fingers of his right hand. Leonardus Engel grunted and poured the last remnants of the cereal directly onto the table so that the crow could continue its meal. Periodically, it lifted its head so it could stay abreast of the conversation. I realized only then that only one of its fogged eyes remained. Perhaps the other one finally rotted away.

"You said Dash treated her like a vessel waiting to be filled," I said, my thoughts in turmoil. "But that's no different from you. You used her and tossed her away."

Something in his face changed, his expression so piercing I needed to look away. I looked down at the table. Instead of the colorful contents from a stale box of cereal, I saw wriggling maggots, the table covered with them, the crow feasting on them.

I squeezed my eyes shut. "Stop it," I said, feeling certain he caused the illusion.

"Stop what?"

"Whatever it is you're doing. Just. Stop."

I rubbed my throbbing temples as he continued to speak. "I've only done what was necessary. The veil was already punctured. Split at the seam. I simply opened it wider—with some help, of course."

"You did it with butchery," I said, thinking of the rabbit.

"The blood started spilling long before. It seeps up from the ground beneath your feet. It's the rising tide around you. You've been bathed in it." His voice softened. I opened my eyes and saw his severe expression replaced with something that on anyone else would have looked like sympathy. He reached over and squeezed my wrist. His flesh felt cold, but the pounding in my head stopped. I looked down at his left hand and saw six digits, an additional finger next to the middle one.

"It's time to close the veil. For my sake and for Isis. I'll never be free of that reptilian beast otherwise. Eventually, its jaws will find me, but I intend to delay that inevitability for as long as I can. For many, many years, if I'm successful, when the last seals are finally broken. By then, he will have grown into a dragon large enough to devour the world, and no one will be safe. What Professor Dash wants to do will only peel back the veil further and harm poor Isis in the process."

"But he's gone. I'm here in his place." I could hear the absurdity in my own words. I may as well have waved my HR paperwork in his face.

What he said next, I somehow already suspected. "Oh, he's not gone at all. He's closer than you think. He wields the puppet strings and makes others dance around him."

I thought of the Slashing Sally figure dangling by the neck in the office I occupied, the knife stuck in its throat. On the television, the film continued with a scene in a decaying house, where a group of teenagers gathered in a circle around the subdued form of Slashing Sally. They closed their eyes and held hands as one of them recited the words from a book of arcane magic. Those words conjured a field of blue electricity around Slashing Sally as they harnessed the same sorcery that brought her to life to now cause her to melt into a pool of hot plastic. The chanting grew louder and louder until Slashing Sally finally exploded into a thousand gory pieces, though some hapless fool would resurrect her in the next sequel.

"Professor Dash," continued Lenny Engel, "may have not known about the Bloody Bucket by name, but he knew something restless stirred there. Anyone with occult sensitivity can sense where it lingers beneath the surface. It's felt in the way the land blooms and grows wild and unhindered. If he could just find a way to peer beneath the surface, he would find the source of it. He could talk to it. Connect with it."

"Says the person who made Isis kill a rabbit," I said. "You scheme, lie, and manipulate."

"I?" Lenny Engel pointed to his chest with an expression of innocence.

"I did no such thing. She needed none of my guidance. Someone else showed her the way to expose the rabbit's innards. She wielded the knife like someone trained to hunt wild game, not those pets we kept in the prison. 'This is the right decision for everyone, Mr. Engel,' she said. She well knew my intention to abbreviate my long sentence and merely offered her own assistance. She knew my feelings about the king and how he'd already taken enough of my life. But my foremost concern lay with Isis. She has a long life ahead of her, one that I plan to see to the very end. Imagine my surprise when she next turned the knife on me."

He displayed the inside of his left wrist, where darkened blood marked the place of Isis's cut.

I shook my head. "She said you did that to yourself."

"I? I?" Again, that look of confounded innocence. "I hardly knew what had happened. 'To show my thanks, Mr. Engel,' she said. Apparently, she intended to trick the waiting monster with the blood from my veins. Had she given him a more complete meal—my liver, for instance—it might have worked for good. Otherwise, she merely provided a diversion sufficient for me to make a hasty, if unplanned departure. She tossed the rest of the burden into an altogether different body of water, and now the beast awaits me there."

"The college," I said. "You didn't tell her to do that?"

"For what purpose? To agitate the spirits that roam there? Why should I help anyone bend the invisible world to their will? Why would I do that, Natacha? Especially when it puts Isis in such grave risk?"

Not just Isis. The crow stopped foraging on the table to look up at me as if waiting for me ask the question I dreaded asking. The place where Erik dropped his backpack every day remained empty, and the hour grew later and later.

"Where is my brother?"

"Waiting for you. But first, you need to understand what is required of you. What *I* require. What Isis requires. She has become the host to a manifestation that will overtake her completely if no intervention takes place. You must, shall we say, remove the rider from the horse."

Did I detect a twinkle in his eye? Had he deliberately repeated the metaphor at the heart of *Tell My Horse*?

"I don't know how to do that," I said, thinking if I had that ability, I would have long ago divested myself of my own angry spirit, Taryn Hall.

"You will. It simply requires resourcefulness," he said, a definite twinkle in his eye as he continued: "Did I mention my poor brother? You'll never guess what his name was."

Six

Lenny Engel's Narrative

"Gustav," said Lenny Engel, "suffered a cruel fate, thanks to the snapping fangs of a mad dog. Granted, we lived under such cruel conditions that we suffered many afflictions. A canal ran not far from our home, and as precocious siblings, we often played near its shore, unmindful of its heavy volume of sewage. Still, we thought dysentery a small price to pay for finding the occasional treasure thrown from passing vessels. We found many lost trinkets and speculated about their origins and the fantastic places they'd come from. I dreamed of becoming a sailor someday and escaping the misery of our surroundings, as did Gustav. We recounted our dreams and fantasies to one another. Though younger and a full head smaller than me, his imagination dwarfed mine by comparison. Such scenes he imagined in lands populated by strange and unusual beasts!

"But a more common beast undid him. As I said, a mad dog bit him, causing him to experience such an extreme change in temperament and personality that all who saw him believed he'd been possessed by the devil. Naturally, word of his affliction reached a priest from the nearby cathedral, prompting him to our home to perform the holy rite of exorcism. My mother met him at the door and explained how I, a foolish, careless sibling, allowed the dog to bite Gustav. She never forgave me. It happened after she sent us to the marketplace to beg for a bag of flour. Gustav saw a flock of ducks emerging from the water and expressed his intention to catch one, contending that, if he succeeded, our dear mother would lavish him with kisses. Like many city dwellers, we had so little to eat in those days, but Gustav only cared about pleasing her. She treated him with favoritism, and she even accused me of jealousy, of letting it happen deliberately. Nothing I said could dissuade her of that notion. I even feared what the priest would say when he heard this accusation.

"But the priest took pity on us and requested to see Gustav himself. By now, the affliction made it impossible for Gustav to swallow water, and he hallucinated such hellish visions that my mother couldn't allow him inside our modest home. She kept him outside in a wooden box given to us by a neighbor, its size barely larger than a coffin. The priest listened to the mad ravings coming from inside the box for a few moments before requesting that we go back inside the house. There, he requested paper, ink, and a clean place to sit. This request embarrassed my mother. She lacked the first two things, and the furniture inside our hovel did not suit the finery worn by the priest.

"The priest sniffed at the surrounding mess and sent one of his servant boys on an errand to find the materials he needed. When the boy returned, the priest pointed to me and demanded that I get down on all fours. At first, I thought he intended to bugger me in front of my own mother, and I lacked the will to object, thanks to the guilt that still lingered within me over what happened to my brother. I couldn't even sleep on account of the way my brother raved and pounded upon the box's lid all night. I thought I had no choice but to let the priest have what he demanded, so I began pulling off my breaches. That earned me a hard tap on the forehead. 'Foolish boy,' said the priest, 'I need something to sit on.'

"Once more, he directed me to assume a position on all fours, and after I complied, I felt his full weight on my back as he began to write. The whole process seemed to take forever, and my arms began to ache and grow weak, for the church offering plate kept the priest well fed. At one point, I looked up to see the face of the servant, a boy no older than me. His lips trembled in mocking laughter. I surmised that on more than one occasion, his body served the same function for the fat priest.

"Finally, the priest finished writing and told me to stand. 'Can you read

Latin?' he asked me. I could not. 'No,' I answered. He leaned forward for a closer scrutiny of my stupidity. 'Can you read anything at all?' he asked.

"I wanted to say I could read what Gustav and I believed to be a treasure map we found on the shore of the canal one day, but I thought best to answer honestly, so I shook my head, once more regarding the servant boy, who no longer pretended to stifle his laughter. I felt myself blushing with anger and almost missed hearing the priest's instructions.

"He explained that I must go in search of the mad dog that wounded my brother. Once I found it, I must make him eat the piece of paper he handed me.

"I stared at the paper in my hand and the shape of the sloping script. 'It will cure the dog, and the madness will lift from your brother,' the priest said. Could words alone do that? I squeezed the paper in my hands, hoping to feel the magic for myself. That earned me another cuff from the priest. 'Don't crumple it,' he said. 'Go now. You know what you must do. Find the dog and stuff the paper into its jaws. That alone will save your brother.'

"I saw the expectant look on my mother's face and knew that only this action would redeem me in her eyes. Craving her love, I departed as instructed. I walked along the canal toward the market, retracing the steps I took the day the dog thrust out its head from a pile of garbage. I had no idea how I would fulfill the responsibility entrusted to me. I'd seen how the madness affected my brother—the jerking movements, the incessant drooling, the eruptions of violence, the fear of water. How could I force the paper into the dog's mouth without suffering the same fate? I knew that I must not only trust the priest but the mysterious writing he produced. It felt as if I carried with me words spoken directly from God into the ear of the priest, for what else could cure the blight of a mad dog? Imagine it: such power in a simple incantation written on a humble piece of paper!

"Still, a different thought weighed upon me. If I managed to force the dog to ingest the script in my hand, I would no doubt suffer a bite and become mad myself. My brother would be cured, but his affliction would befall me. I did not know if I had the courage to trade my well-being for my brother's. I also felt the shame of the servant boy's mockery. Why should I sacrifice myself when even the servants of the Lord treated me with such derision?

"Lost in thought, I walked blindly, passing the market stalls without noticing any sign of the mad dog. Before long, I found myself outside the home of a man my mother warned me to stay away from. The people in our town didn't consort with him because of rumors that he was a witch. He saw me before I could take notice of him. Had I seen him, I might have turned and run away. Then again, I might not have done that at all. I always had such curiosity about him, not simply because of the awful rumors and accusations but also because I harbored a suspicion that this man was some sort of relation to me—perhaps he was even my father, about whom I knew nothing.

"Seeing me, he called out to me, demanding to know how I'd found my way to his home. Regardless of what I suspected of his identity, the sight of him filled me with great terror and rendered me practically speechless. I held up the paper given to me by the priest, thinking it held the power to ward off evil. But the man simply snatched it out of my hand. His brow furrowed as he read it. Then he laughed as he thrust it back to me. 'That's weak magic,' he said. 'Come in, and let's see if you're too stupid to learn the real thing.'

"From the outside, his home looked like a tiny place of squalor, no better than where we lived with our mother. But somehow, the inside seemed much larger, with every space filled with burning incense and curious treasures from all over the world. So many items looked too frightful to touch—things like human skulls decorated with patterns of brightly colored studs. But some I could not resist reaching for, like a length of wood carved into the form of a creature with a long snout. Its form suggested some manner of animal I'd neither seen nor heard of, and though frightful in appearance, the artist included carvings of men riding atop its back.

My new benefactor slapped away my outstretched hand. 'You are a fool indeed. Show some reverence for what lies beyond your comprehension. That,' he said, lifting the object, 'comes from a faraway land. It's the great crocodile god Atchakpa. It honors children drowned or eaten in rivers, not fools like you. I acquired it through great risk of life and limb, and not so an idiot like you can paw it.' Carefully, he returned it to its place. The place where his hand struck me stung as if bitten by a hornet, but as I rubbed it, something else drew my attention.

"The head of the mad dog that had bitten my brother. Its mouth hung open, displaying its yellow fangs, and blood dripped from the stump of its neck into a bucket situated beneath it.

"I stared at the strange display, feeling a mixture of fascination and sadness. I could no longer achieve what the priest sent me to do. I looked at the man who did this, and he misread my expression. 'It can't harm you, stupid boy. Look, the rest of it is here.' He gripped the remains of the dog's body by the scruff of its severed neck and lifted it. 'We'll skin it now, you and me, and I'll show you how. We'll create a girdle to sell to some idiot who wants to transform into a beast. In fact,' he added, shaking the dog's body, 'we'll create several. I might even let you wear one of them to try it out. But first, I have many things to teach you.' He held up the piece of paper, snatched from my hand, curling his lip as he re-read it. 'Just scripture, badly penned at that,' he said. 'The story of the demons banished into the bodies of pigs. Well, I banish thee, scripture—to the pit of this idiot's stomach!' He handed it back to me and demanded that I eat it myself. Obeying, I put it in my mouth, and as he watched, I pretended to chew and swallow. Surprisingly, my deception worked 'Did it taste good?' he asked. 'Do you feel any different?' I shook my head, keeping the paper tucked in the corner of my mouth so that I could remove it later. 'Good! So begins your true education by unlearning what others have taught you.'

"And for many years, he taught, and I learned, often so slowly that he rapped my knuckles incessantly. Before I even knew how to spell my own name, he taught me ancient, forbidden alphabets and the many names of the beings that inhabit the invisible world. He taught me to understand the connection between energy and form and to understand that matter was an illusion. He taught me many things until the fateful day came when people in our town went mad and burst through the door.

"Some children had gone missing, leading to rumors that my disreputable teacher had kidnapped them and boiled them in a big pot in order to feast on their flesh. They even alleged he used the leftover fat to coat his body, thereby giving himself the ability to fly about the land. But I never saw evidence of that. I managed to hide when they broke in. Though I'd not seen my mother in years, I recognized her as part of the mob, her face marked not only by age but also by fury. I wondered if she suspected he'd eaten me too. I wanted to ask her why she waited so long to do something about it.

"Still, I remained out of sight as they dragged him out of his home and toward a stake driven into the ground, where they tied him before placing kindling around him. When they set it ablaze, he called out my name, demanding that I use the magic he taught me to set him free. But I found myself frozen where I hid and watched in secret. I couldn't move. I watched my mother in the throng, dancing around the flames with all the others. I thought of Gustav, imprisoned in his box. Of course, I never saw him again. He died soon after I left. I'd assumed my mother died as well, but there she was, dancing and celebrating. As the flames rose and engulfed him, my benefactor and teacher, the man who clothed me and fed me and taught me countless lessons, continued to call out for me. Eventually, his pleas turned into curses—not against those who burned him alive but curses for me. With his last breath, he cursed me to a long life of suffering. He needn't have bothered because I considered myself already cursed. If only I'd found the mad dog in time to feed him what the priest had written. I hid until the next day, when I managed to sneak aboard a doomed ship docked nearby."

* * *

Leonardus Engel's eyes filled with sadness.

"Do you know then what you must do?"

The question snapped me back to my surroundings. At some point, his story had caused the world around me to dissipate. If earlier I felt hypnotized, I now felt a deeper immersion into something else, his story encroaching on my consciousness, my reality. Somehow, I did know what I must do, but I did not want to let his burden become mine. This monster, wearing an orange suit bearing the insignia for the Florida Correctional System, had kidnapped my only sibling, my last remaining relative whom I loved. A deepening shadow filled the space that should have contained Erik's backpack, betokening all manner of disaster, including death. Why should I care about his sibling when he might have done something unspeakable to mine?

I moved out of his view, toward the sink, where we typically left knives before cleaning them. I kept my movements as casual and unhurried as I could. His question lingered in the air without answer, but he didn't bother turning to track my movement.

"You must think me a foolish old man," he said with his back to me. "Full of stories that don't matter. Why would you listen to me? How could I possibly understand your own pain?"

In the sink, I saw what I hoped to find: a knife with a serrated blade. Reaching for it, I thought of how when he last spoke to Isis, she also held a knife. I wondered if he used his voice the same way on her. It occurred to me that I now knew how he manipulated her into dissecting the rabbit.

He kept his back turned to me, unconcerned about what I planned to do. But the crow.

With its single eye, the crow watched for him.

My hand barely gripped the knife before the crow left the table, its squawking shrill from decaying lungs as it flew into my face in a fury of feather, beak, and talon. Startled, I dropped the knife and heard it clatter to the floor, where it bounced twice before landing near the feet of Lenny Engel. Only then did the bird relent and fly back to the table. The knife now in his hand, Lenny Engel touched the blade with his finger and made a face at the drop of black blood it produced.

"Please don't make the mistake of assuming that I survived my incarceration through charm and affability." He put the knife on the table, within my reach, but we both knew I wouldn't reach for it. The scratches on my face burned, but at least the crow's beak had not cost me an eye.

"Now, I asked if you knew what you must do," he said. "Answer and I'll tell you where you need to go, though I suspect you already know."

It turned out I did. Once he told me the rest, I knew I would need help.

Seven

"What kind of trouble has my sobrina caused now?"

Halia kept the motor of the library running as she asked me this question, and she didn't ask to come inside. A good thing too, since I didn't know how to explain the fact that a fugitive and a zombie crow had taken up residence inside my house.

I didn't know who else to call—not Fowler, and certainly not Sarge. If I never saw Sarge again, I would rejoice. How to reach Halia vexed me, especially since I couldn't find my library card. Lenny Engel solved this problem for me by reaching inside his orange jump suit and producing a piece of paper.

Unfolding it, I half expected to see Latin scrawled in the hand of a priest, but instead, I once again set my eyes on a man with indigenous features pictured under the words: *Have you seen this man?* At the bottom of the page, the phone number that reached Halia when I dialed it.

"What? Yeah?" The voice that answered sounded breathless and anxious, like she knew trouble had found Isis. Then it occurred to me that she answered hoping for a reply to her flier, not a crisis that required her to drive miles across the county line to meet me.

Because of its paint job, the library at night blended well with the darkness, especially with only one of its headlights working. "Get in," she said, looking at me over a pair of dark glasses perched on the tip of her nose. She read my expression. "Don't worry, they're prescription lenses. They help me see at night. Come on, if just half of what you told me is true, then we need to get going."

And I only told her half of what I truly believed. Mainly that Isis had gotten caught up with a group of troublemakers at the college and that my own brother somehow became entangled as well. The kind of problem that required the intervention of two fierce women.

I looked for a seat next to her but saw none. Just an open space filled by a wooden crate tipped on its side with a few paperbacks spilling out of it. She urged me in. "It'll hold you. Unless you want to sit in the back. Passengers, when I have them, usually sit there."

I searched for a seatbelt that wasn't there. "Are there seatbelts back there?"

"No. Just settle in and don't worry. I'm a great driver, the best ever."

Remembering what Isis said about learning her driving skills from Halia, I tried to relax. She watched me shift around on the crate before pointing to the copy of *Tell My Horse* I carried with me. "You the kind of person who brings her own books to a library?"

I smiled. "Actually, I am. I hate going anywhere without reading material." Under normal circumstances, I would have told her more, but I already felt pressed enough to explain things.

"My kind of gal," she said with little indication of humor. I understood. She felt pressed too. She came to help Isis, not to fraternize with someone she only met once and hardly knew.

"I didn't like how she acted outside the prison," Halia said. "She might not have the warmest personality, but I'm the closest thing she has to a mom. Her dad's still around, but he's a piece of shit, pardon my language. I try to look out for her without getting into her business."

I nodded, wondering what it would have felt like to have had someone like Halia to turn to, especially when she came with all those books.

When I didn't answer, Halia asked, "What was she hiding from me that day?"

She looked away from the road to steal a glance at me. The way she peered over her glasses warned me not to hide the truth. It didn't look like she really needed those lenses to see at night. She didn't even seem to look through them. It also appeared that she maintained a generous opinion of her own driving. More than once, her abrupt turns left me grasping for something to hold on to.

"Dead rabbit remains," I said.

"Jesus. No, not Isis. She might be willful and stubborn, but she's a gentle soul. She'd murder me for saying this out loud, but she has an affinity for cute, furry things."

I told her the conflicting versions of what happened—how Isis said she mutilated the rabbit under Lenny Engel's direction, whereas Engel claimed she came to him with the intent and knowledge about how to apply the cuts. I reported this information as neutrally as possible, but Halia made it clear who she believed.

"He's a lying bastard. No way. He likes to mythologize himself. Thinks we'll all believe he's some harmless old man who got locked up by mistake. But it's no mistake. The records are muddy, to say the least, but you can't hide information from a librarian."

For a moment, we listened to the hum of the engine. If she meant that last part as a warning to me, I couldn't tell. And I wouldn't bite. "What did he do?" I asked.

"You really want to know?"

I thought of his narrative of shipwrecks and rabid dogs. His story lingered, a virus infecting my imagination. "Sure," I said.

"Ritualistic murder." Halia spoke those two words with a casualness most people would use to mention jaywalking or speeding. Which she continued to do as I bit my tongue, her words sinking in.

"Yeah," she said, correctly interpreting my uneasy silence. "His own brother. Can you believe it? It happened long enough ago that the records never made it into a database. But I knew where to look. Until now, I've kept it to myself, thinking if Isis found out, she'd never lose interest in him like I hoped she would. I kept imagining what she would do if she knew the truth. Get this: he believed a human sacrifice would earn him an audience with a demon."

I swallowed hard. I wondered if Isis found out anyway. "Go on," I said.

"He cut out his brother's heart and ate it. It happened in a cabin somewhere in Okeechobee, a cabin in the middle of nowhere. I found an account that didn't mention him by name, but it's him, I know it. They found him hunched over the corpse with his face covered all over in blood, growling like an animal. Based on that, they judged him too witless and pathetic for the death penalty but still dangerous enough to lock away for life. Decades pass, and he ages into an eccentric old man with a penchant for bullshit stories. I guess they assumed they'd rehabilitated him enough to put him in charge of a prison petting zoo, but the joke's on them. He probably had everything planned out before Isis got there. How he managed it is beyond me."

She looked away from the road in time to catch me gazing at her. That earned me another look over the dark glasses.

"Don't tell me you bought his bullshit," she said.

"No," I said. Only maybe I did. At least some of it. I had a plan, much of it predicated on what he told me.

He'd sent me with instructions I needed to follow if I wanted find Erik and keep something terrible from happening to Isis. *The walls of my prison have merely shifted*, he said, explaining that his ultimate freedom hinged on what I must do and why I needed to carry with me the copy of *Tell My Horse*.

"Because if you need convincing," Halia said, "I can pull over and let you read the whole sordid account. It's back there." She indicated the rear compartment of the library, accessible through a narrow passageway behind me.

I sensed something there along with the books, a darkness that uncoiled like a tentacle. What had Lenny Engel said of me? That I'd bathed in blood. "You're like an open wound," he'd said before Halia arrived, "unable to stop bleeding, just hemorrhaging secrets."

I didn't want to hear any more.

"What was that?" asked Halia.

I thought I might have unwittingly said something out loud. But she didn't mean that at all. Because then I heard it—a sound coming from the darkness at the back of the library.

"Did you bring someone with you?" Halia looked at me with suspicion. I wasn't prepared for how much her suspicion hurt.

"No," I said, but did I know for certain? He already demonstrated a talent for crossing thresholds, like a vampire who didn't bother waiting for an invitation to enter.

"You wouldn't lie to me, right?"

Again, a look that made me tremble. I might not be the most forthcoming, but the accusation stung. Of course I wouldn't deceive her—at least not on purpose. I didn't feel sure of anything anymore.

"I wouldn't lie to you," I said.

Her expression softened. "Okay. Maybe something fell over. You know, I have a pretty good shelving system, but that doesn't mean books won't fall down now and then."

She took a sharp turn up a service road that led to the college, throwing me off balance and producing another sound from the back. "Yeah, that sounded like the big-ass edition of *Uncle Silas* I keep on one of the top shelves. It likes to fall sometimes."

"Le Fanu," I said quietly. I didn't know if she guessed the source of sound correctly, but it made me uneasy. I peered into the accessway.

"What?" she asked.

"Oh." I looked back at her. "Sheridan Le Fanu. He wrote *Uncle Silas.*" In reality, the thick veil of darkness behind us invoked his name. Not long before, I'd talked about that other Le Fanu text and poor Rose, abandoned to a room devoid of life, allowing her wicked husband to whisk her back to the land of the dead. "The dead and living cannot be one."

I hadn't meant to recite that line out loud, but it got her attention. This time, she regarded me more with approval than suspicion.

"'Schalken the Painter,'" Halia said. "You know your Le Fanu."

"Is it true?"

"Is what true?"

"That the dead and living cannot be one?"

"Sheesh. How should I know? You're the professor, so you tell me." A pause as she slowed our speed. We'd arrived at the college, and it looked eerily quiet. The humid air created a haze that muted the few lights that remained burning. A thin haze hovered close to the ground. It looked like it would rain soon.

I said, "I always thought the phrase meant something carnal. Like . . . like . . ."

"Carnal as in fucking? As in necrophilia?"

I almost laughed. Halia noticed. She smiled in a way that encouraged me to let it happen. But I couldn't.

"Yeah," I said. "But now I think it means something else. The veil between worlds collapsing. Losing yourself." I pressed my book against my chest the same way I did all those years ago when my mother took me to Rebel Farms. If I could press that book all the way into my chest, I would, just to add some extra armor around my heart.

"Here's my position on the whole matter," Halia said as she parked the library under a flickering yellow lamp. "I respect the dead. They deserve our reverence. My grandmother taught me that. She talked to her dead ancestors while she did her gardening—trivial stuff, like the weather, who disrespected her when she went to the post office, that sort of shit. I'd help out and listened to these one-way conversations. Finally, I asked if these ancestors ever talked back, and she'd say sure, all the time. Then I'd ask her if she saw them. She would get real serious and say, 'Chica, you would know if I did, because I would run like hell, and you'd never be able to catch up with me.'" Halia turned the ignition key, and the engine of the library came to coughing halt. She turned to me, and in the lamplight, I could see her delicate features, the beginnings of faint lines around her eyes. "I like to think I take after my grandmother, but I won't run if you don't."

In her expression, I saw a definite family relationship to Isis. With that recognition, I felt that familiar pang of guilt in my chest. If I could relieve myself of just one burden . . .

"When I saw Isis last," I said, "I wasn't nice to her. I came down hard on her."

"You did, huh? And you're worried that she can't take it? Or that she won't like you anymore?"

"No." The sound of that word stretched out longer than I intended. As we stepped out of the vehicle, I wondered what I really needed—just forgiveness, or did I crave more love and approval than I wanted to admit?

"Because," Halia said when our paths crossed at the library's bay doors, "she can take it. I taught her how to be tough. And to always be on the right side of a fight. Because that's what we're walking into. Right?"

Precious minutes continued to pass, but seeing what she now wielded caused me to stop in my tracks. A metal baseball bat. Where the metal baseball bat came from, I didn't know, but judging by its scuffs and dents, someone had put it to use. She hefted it onto her shoulder like she knew how to swing it. Her eyes gleamed.

"I played softball at Vissaria High School. I won't tell you what year because I like to let certain things remain a mystery. I'm also too modest to report my batting average, except to say it was halfway decent." Her eyes found the book I kept clutched in my hand, the copy of *Tell My Horse*. "Of course, we could also defend ourselves with a quality paperback. I believe in the written word, Professor, I really do, or I wouldn't be the badass librarian I am, but you really need to consider your choice of weapon."

I didn't answer because we heard the knocking sound again, once more coming from within the back of the library. The vehicle shook from the movement of something inside.

It stopped as abruptly as it started. Halia turned back to me, her expression full of suspicion, her voice a whisper. "You sure you don't have something to tell me?"

I whispered back, "I swear."

She studied me for an uncomfortable moment before finally nodding. Gesturing for me to get ready to open the doors, she assumed a batter's stance. "On the count of three," she said quietly.

I marveled at the way she stood, her hands gripping the bat with her feet wide apart, her lips pressed in concentration.

She counted out loud, and on three, the door swung wide open. I ducked as Halia swung.

Eight

At nothing.

Just shadows and dusty volumes. The pages of an overturned book turned in the warm night breeze. Seeing the title of the book—*Uncle Silas*—I resisted the impulse to congratulate Halia for her prescience. She knew her shit.

I didn't see what I feared most. Not Lenny Engel. I knew he wouldn't come here. He didn't want to face the creature in the water, not after Isis had made her offering, her bloody pact, though I still didn't know whether to call it fear or something else.

What I feared the most would have lurched forward on broken legs. I would have seen a spine bent by the wheels of my car, a broken, disfigured face.

But nothing like that at all. The space in the back of the library appeared empty.

Until something flew forth on black wings, feathers brushing the tops of our heads. I ducked as Halia called out. She swung the bat, missing everything but air.

From my crouched position, I looked up at her astonished face. Our chests rose and fell in unison.

I expected her to blame me for the stowaway, and I probably deserved it. It was the crow I tried to entomb in my garage. How it got into the library, I had no idea. Yet I felt certain that it had come along with me, determined to never leave me in peace.

I waited for Halia's accusation.

Except her face broke out in a smile I could see in the yellow light.

"That," she said, "was fucking amazing. And I wish I could say that's the first time that sort of thing ever happened. Last time, it was a bat." She gestured with her weapon. "I mean a bat with wings. Not this kind of bat."

"A bat," I said, "in your library."

She nodded. "Don't look so surprised. I have plenty of gothic selections on those shelves. It's completely understandable for a bat or two to get in. They make a mess, though. Not excited about cleaning up after something like that."

"That wasn't a bat," I said.

"Oh, I saw. It was a crow. How it got in there, I have no idea. But you know what I think we should do?" She didn't wait for an answer. "Follow it. It's here for a reason. It's going to tell us where to go."

"You sure it's not an omen?" I left it at that. She didn't know the bird's history and probably didn't need to know. I couldn't imagine it leading us anywhere good, but I led the way toward the lights that marked the beginning of the path around the lake. It felt right to get moving, despite air so thick with humidity you could drown in it. We used our phones for what little light they provided, moving in silence until we finally made it to the trailhead, where rows of sawgrass grew from the water itself. Nearby stood an old bulletin board used for announcements and notices. Halia stopped in front of it and used her phone to illuminate something that drew her attention.

"What is this shit?" she asked.

I padded over to see what she saw.

She pointed to a white flier held in place by pushpins. We stared at the words in silence.

DON'T GET REPLACED!

DON'T BE ERASED!

Education, not Indoctrination.

Claim Your Narrative.

Join Our Movement in the

GREAT REAWAKENING

*as we embark on an endeavor to recover
the HISTORIC White Nite Lodge!*

Under those words appeared the same sleepy, hooded rooster featured on the unearthed sign at the border of the woods, along with information about when this exploration would occur. I didn't know who posted the flier or what they had in mind by searching out the site. Nevertheless, it sent a shiver through me.

Halia turned her light on me, forcing me to shield my eyes. "'Don't get replaced.' Isn't that charming. I knew we were living in troubled times, and I come across this shit daily. But replacement theory on a college campus? You know what that is, don't you?"

I did. Like almost everyone else, I'd seen the images of angry white men carrying tiki torches flashed, heard their threatening chants directed about people they believed would replace them as rightful sovereigns of this land. They saw anyone who looked or sounded different from them as an enemy.

"This is the kind of shit that scares me," Halia said. "It's why I taught Isis to believe in fairness and justice. To stand up for herself and anyone else who gets kicked to the curb. But this . . . this . . ."

"Halia, the light."

"Sorry." She turned the phone away from my eyes. "This is disheartening."

I tapped the flier. "That's where we're going. I think."

"I'm not joining a movement, if that's what you have in mind."

"No, that's not what I have in mind at all."

Something fluttered over our heads, causing us both to duck. We swore and cursed at it, whatever it was. When we looked up, we saw it once more. The crow, now perched atop the bulletin board.

Halia shined her light on it and uttered another curse under her breath. "Fucking bird likes to do that. I'm starting to think it's personal."

I thought so too but kept the reasons to myself.

"It doesn't look . . . healthy," Halia said.

Of course it didn't. After all, I kept the creature entombed in my garage for days. But now, hand-fed by Lenny Engel, it clearly enjoyed stretching its wings, despite the wiggling parasites on its body visible in the light of

Halia's phone.

After displaying itself, it took flight again, following the footpath that led around the lake and beyond the relative safety of the lights.

"You were right before," I said. "We need to follow it."

"I hate being right all the time."

"Keep your light on it. I need to try to call again."

For the hundredth time in the past few hours, I dialed the number to Erik's flip phone, wishing, as it rang and rang, that we set up location services so that I could find him that way. As before, it continued to ring instead of going to voicemail the way it should. Even technology couldn't escape the effects of what had taken seed out here.

Halia had already watched me try this a few times while riding next to her in the library. "Still no luck?" she asked.

"None," I said and went back to using the phone as a flashlight. We walked so closely next to each other that our shoulders touched several times. From the stalks of grass growing out of the lake came the croak of something unnaturally large. Halia turned toward the sound and bumped into me. "The fuck is that?"

"It's Gustav," I said.

"How could that be Gustav? Gustav's just a story. A legend to scare inmates at a prison."

I shook my head. "It's Gustav."

"And I took you for a rational person."

"And now you have doubts. I get it. You're not alone." I expected her to stop, to return the way we came, abandoning me to navigate the rest of the path on my own. But we both maintained our pace. Heat lightning flashed in the distance, and for the briefest second, everything around us looked beautiful. "Not having second thoughts?" I asked.

"I'm still walking, aren't I?"

"And I took you for a rational person."

"Me? I'm walking around with a baseball bat. You clearly had me all wrong."

We both laughed, and it made us feel good. The laughter felt powerful enough to repel whatever timeless thing lurked only a few feet away in the brackish water.

"How'd you end up with it?" I asked.

"The bat? Because of my old man. You really want to know the story?"

"Why not?" I said, preferring a story to walking in silence.

"Okay. He came to this country with three things: the clothes on his back, a burning hatred for Fidel, and a passion for baseball. Those three things left no room for anything else. Somehow, he wound up with a kid like me who had her head in books all the time. In his mind, that amounted to a sickness of some kind, and he got the idea that he could cure me by making me try out for the softball team at school. Only problem was I couldn't hit for shit. He figured he would fix me by making me go outside with him on his day off from delivering packages. But with every ball he tossed my way, no matter how gentle, I ended up hitting nothing but air."

As we walked, she took a slow practice swing, precise and lethal.

"That looked pretty good to me," I said.

"Yeah, well, I got better. I'm coming to that. He would keep tossing me these slow, easy pitches, and as I missed each one, he would mutter something about how God had cursed him with a girl instead of a boy, eventually building up to what a useless piece of cono I was. That finally did it. He tossed the next ball, and I belted it good, sending it sailing over his head to where he kept his parcel delivery truck parked in the driveway. Bam! I cracked the windshield good. Felt proud of myself too. You'd think that would have made the sour pendejo happy, but he really let the curses fly then. Who knew he'd been holding back. And he didn't stop there."

A pause as Halia let that sink in. The area around us became strangely quiet, as if all life held its breath, waiting to hear the rest of the story.

When the silence became too much to take, she continued. "His mood healed before my bruises did, and he made it clear I could prove my worth only by trying out for the softball team. I lied and said I would. Instead, I hung out in the library after school, only to come home and have him ask me if I made the team yet. I made up something about them not announcing the roster yet. 'Listen, chica,' he finally said, 'you better hope you make it, or I'll make you pay for that window you broke.' I started to tell him I had no money, but when I saw the look in his eye, I knew he meant I'd pay him in some other way—with blood or something worse. So finally, I went to tryouts, and once more, I couldn't hit for shit. I missed everything, one pitch after another, until I imagined his parcel truck sitting somewhere way out there in the distance, waiting for me to put another crack in the windshield. That did the trick. I sent the next ball sailing way out to left field. That worked every time." She sighed. "But he never could cure me of books. When I finally broke free of him, I decided to steal his truck and take it along with me. I filled it up with all the books he hated and rode the fuck out of Dodge. Later, I painted the truck the way I liked, and I kept the bat as a souvenir."

Halia gave me a meaningful glance.

"Not many people know that story," she said. "You owe me one in return. Something you don't normally tell people."

I smiled uneasily. So many things I could tell her.

"Later maybe?" I said.

"Okay, but make it a good one."

But we fell silent as we reached the pavilion. In the darkness, I could make out a crumpled shape leaning against one of its stanchions. The sight of it caused my heart to sink.

"Oh god, is that a person?" Halia asked, giving voice to what I saw and feared.

We hastened our steps, and as we drew closer, the form revealed itself more clearly. Not a person at all.

We found something else that caused my stomach to sink.

We found Erik's backpack.

Nine

"**I** don't understand," said Halia. She held the flashlight as I crouched down to go through the pockets of the bag. "Why would it be here? You sure it even belongs to your brother?"

"I'm sure," I said, perhaps too gruffly. I recognized the anime characters that decorated the outside of the bag and the small unicorn hanging from a metal clip. In the side pocket, I found what I dreaded: Erik's flip phone. It still maintained some power, so when I opened it, I expected to see my missed calls and unanswered texts. Instead, I found a message from someone identifying themselves as a college official. It informed Erik that a classroom mishap left me indisposed, thus delaying my arrival home, and that he needed to come to the campus and meet me here himself. Who sent the message, I couldn't tell, but instead of replying, Erik tried calling me. The phone log showed these as missed calls.

I never received them.

From my crouched position, I read the messages out loud.

"Who would send that to a kid?" Halia asked. She tried using her phone to illuminate the surrounding area, but the light didn't make it very far.

"I don't know. But Lenny Engel knew he would be here."

"I'm telling you, he's dangerous. Still, how would he even get his number?"

"Maybe it wasn't him at all." I thought about who might have access to it. My mind went back to all the paperwork I filled out the day of my fingerprinting. One of those forms asked for an emergency contact number, but I thought I left it blank. Only now I couldn't say for sure. Maybe I did list Erik. If so, that left a likely suspect.

"Sarge," I growled under my breath.

"Who's Sarge?" Halia turned, and the light in her hand formed a halo around her silhouette in the darkness, revealing the baseball bat still hefted on one shoulder. How I wanted to grab that bat from her and hunt down that man. Assuming my suspicion proved true. "Nat . . ." Halia's voice grew soft as her light found another place within the pavilion. "I don't want to say this, but—"

"What now?"

She pointed down. The light had found the jagged crack in the pavilion's slab. It had expanded since I'd last seen it, and it now looked wide enough for me to slide my hand into it. Something dark flowed from the fissure.

"That looks like blood," Halia finally managed to say. "It can't be."

But I knew it could, having already lingered over that spot, first with Fowler and then later with the students of *HOL*. Now, having gathered up Erik's backpack, I gazed down at the same spot with Halia. What earlier looked like a dry rust-colored stain now resembled an open wound in the earth itself.

Leaning over for a closer look, Halia dipped her finger into it. Using her phone light, she showed me a finger now glistening with red. "If I were made of tougher stuff," she said, "I'd taste it." She held out the finger to me.

"I'll pass," I said, waving her away.

"Aren't you a professor? Where's your academic curiosity? Your relentless pursuit of truth?" She looked around for something to use to wipe her finger.

"Wherever it is," I said, "it doesn't come with being a vampire."

She shook her head. "Maybe it's because of all the rain. Red clay or something."

I shook my head. "That's in Georgia, not here."

"Well, the earth doesn't bleed," she said.

"It does here, apparently," I said.

Once more, we heard the flutter of wings. Neither of us ducked this time. Halia forgot all about her finger and gripped the bat. We raised our eyes to the rafters of the pavilion, where my light captured the crow. It flew away, this time toward the gaping maw in the thick line of trees.

In silent agreement, we followed. Halia muttered something about her shoes as our feet sank into the wet earth. Our bodies collided as we struggled to find our footing, nearly causing us both to tumble into a patch of nettles.

"Careful," I said. "Those'll sting."

"Don't I know it," she said. "I grew up close to here."

"Same." We trudged on, both of us groaning when our feet found water that went up to our ankles.

"We'll need to establish a pact of sisterhood when all this is over," said Halia.

I felt like arguing on that point. I thought we'd established that pact already, starting when she agreed to come get me so we could proceed on this trek. But movement in the woods ahead brought me up short. I froze and looped my arm around Halia's. We both stared into the darkness.

"The fuck is that?" she asked softly.

I thought she saw what I did, but her light found something else: the ancient sign for the White Nite Lodge.

I forced myself to look away from what I'd seen. Not far ahead, something with four legs disappeared into the shadows. It vanished so quickly that I couldn't rule out a hallucination, but that vision of Milton the goat seemed so real. Maybe I wanted to see him again so badly that I imagined him. I forced myself to focus on the sign that drew Halia's attention.

"I'm sensing a sign isn't all that's left of this place," she said, aiming her light at the infernal rooster, that perennial symbol of white supremacy. "It's still standing back there." She gestured ahead.

I shrugged. "Maybe. Something's back there. We need to see."

She turned to face me, her features lost to shadow. "If anyone hurts Isis," she said, the silhouette of the bat on her shoulder, "I'll crush their skull. And it won't look pretty."

"I won't stop you."

Another voice answered, one I didn't recognize at first. It came from someone hidden in the wild growth before us, as if the trees themselves spoke. "You finally made it back here."

The voice spoke flatly. No malevolence. Simply stating facts. I struggled to detect their source. I struggled to see where it came from, certain that it didn't come from Erik. Too deep for that. Isis, perhaps?

Movement revealed the outline of a tall figure. Enough of it became visible for me to realize that I knew the voice.

"Zach?"

The figure froze. No one moved.

Zach spoke again, an automaton programmed for one pattern of speech. "You finally made it."

Halia stepped forward. "If you know where my niece is," she said, "you better start talking."

Zach's silhouette tilted its head as if trying to place Halia in the scheme of things. Somehow, he expected me but certainly not her.

Once more, the familiar flutter of wings as the crow crossed our view, just enough to disrupt the murky scene before me. When the shadows reassembled themselves, Zach was gone.

"Where'd he go?" Halia asked.

"Through there, I think." I touched her elbow and pointed to what looked like a clearing. The same winds that toppled trees and revealed the forgotten motel sign had flattened the brush and revealed an area that might have once served as a narrow road. "That's where we're headed."

"If you're leading, you might want my bat. Unless that book has lethal powers I don't know about."

I'd almost forgotten I held it crushed up against my chest. Just like I did as a child so long ago.

"Seriously," Halia said, "maybe you should keep your hands as free as possible."

I shook my head. "I need it. I think."

"You *think*. Right."

"Just stay close to me," I said. "But if you need to swing that, try not to hit me, okay?"

"Sure. And I guess you should try not to hit me if you decide to throw the book at anyone."

"Deal," I said. "But I recommend ducking. My aim isn't anything to brag about." We began moving like the character in that old, reliable narrative, but not with a basket seeking Grandma's house and with no woodsman waiting in the forest to rescue us. In our version, Little Red Riding Hood must find a way to save herself. The deeper we went, the more the night sounds of the forest surrounded us. Halia whispered something I couldn't hear.

"What did you say?"

I could feel Halia's breath on my cheek as she leaned closer. "Did I ever tell you what my batting average was?" she asked, louder this time but not by much.

"You said it was pretty good."

"Yeah, well, to be honest, it wasn't that hot."

"Just imagine swinging for your dad's windshield, and remember—"

"—to miss you. Yeah, got it. But don't forget what I said about ducking."

She punctuated her remark with more swearing as she slipped on uneven ground. We moved slowly, guiding each other around obstacles and supporting one another each time one of our feet sunk into the sodden earth, still soaked by the massive rainfall brought by the storm. Whenever we stopped, the sound of wings summoned us in the right direction. I recalled following the crow from room to room with Erik not that long ago. The thought of him propelled me onwards. I would not let him down again.

Eventually, a faint illumination met our eyes. A flickering light piercing the gloom. It led us to a clearing bordered by wild palm fronds. From clouds hanging low on the horizon came lightning, followed by low gurgles of thunder, a half-hearted promise of rain. By that light, we saw the crow perched on what looked like a wild heap of fungi, a wall of chaos growing from the thicket that dominated the clearing. A new sound came from our right flank: what sounded like the bleat of a goat. I didn't want to look, fearing I would see an animal with a malformed horn and a neck still bleeding from the cut of a cruel owner.

If Halia heard it, she gave no sign. Instead, she advanced past me, approaching the structure before us. It now resembled a small fortress, something spawned by nature in imitation of a human habitat.

She recognized it before I did.

"Oh, my god, it's—"

She didn't need to finish her sentence.

We'd found the White Nite Lodge.

Ten

Here is the version of the story I learned, the one I trust the most: Once upon a time, before the advent of highways and interstates, back country trails and roads wound their way up and down this peninsula, traversing fields of pines and crossing over waterways on narrow, rickety bridges, beckoning visitors further and further south in search of fortune and sunshine. Old industries built on the backs of working men and women gave way to roadside attractions, fleecing tourist money in exchange for glimpses of wildlife slithering through their natural habitat, as well as indigenous populations pushed to the brink of extinction. Motels began to dot the landscape, uninspired rectangles built upon land already spoiled by blood and violence.

Once upon a time, greedy men stole such land under the pretense of justice. For years, they bided their time as workers with brown, aching backs sought respite and pleasure inside a place called the Bloody Bucket. From a distance, these greedy men listened to the music coming from within its wooden walls, watching as drunken men staggered outside with a woman under each arm, their bladders nearly bursting with the sweetened concoction that gave the place its name. They witnessed such scenes in silence, harboring disgust at the shameless way men and women laughed as they relieved themselves together, watering the land that grew unhindered outside that ramshackle building, unrestrained by law or what polite society saw as good Christian manners. And they saw what offended them above all else, the fact that people different from them found a home within their borders, flaunting the authority of the ruling class.

From church pulpits, they railed against the way the proprietress flaunted custom and morality, allowing men and women to express their love and joy in naked abandonment and without the blessing of marriage. In sermons, they painted a scene that instilled both horror and terror. A house of fornication where evil rituals took place. A heathen priestess who sacrificed the unborn in terrible ceremonies, tossing the waste into large vats containing that special elixir she served her customers. A special unholy ingredient, you might say, one that provided additional potency. To let such crimes go on would mean an affront to the god they worshipped and adored, not for His love and kindness but for granting them dominion over the land. Their lord and savior expected them to act in His name.

One day, they finally decided to make their move. They hid and waited until morning hours, when the music finally ceased and anyone remaining inside could not so much as raise an eyelid. If anyone overcame the surprise and managed fight back, they would receive a bullet as their reward.

Most of all, they wanted the proprietress, the woman who bought the land for a song and the spit on her palm. For her, they reserved a special punishment befitting her crime. When they took her to the tree, she didn't scream or resist. It seemed as if she expected them to come for her eventually. In her time of waiting, she devised a curse to level upon their heads and those of their descendants. Let the land swallow up anything they tried to build their in her absence. Instead of fresh water from the nearby lake, let their buckets fill up with real blood. *Her* blood. Let that blood rise from the soil itself so no one ever forgets what they did to her and those she cared about. She didn't stop uttering these curses, even when the rope squeezed her windpipe, nor even when they used a blade to open her up and let her insides dangle there in the morning air. Let them bury her in an unmarked place because the land would continue to reverberate with the beat of her heart. Her ruined flesh would spoil that land and bring pestilence unto them who defiled her.

Those words undoubtedly chilled them. But when she finally grew still, they buried her quickly in a place they intended to forget, never understanding the implications of her curse. The land itself would remember. It would also not let their dominion go unchallenged. The land would remain wild, resisting their attempts to pave through it. Saplings arose in defiance. Vines choked progress.

If someone actually managed to find their way to the White Nite Lodge, they would also find a dead end.

Seeing it now hearkened back to Lenny Engel's account of how he blindly wandered through the swamp until he came upon a walled compound that appeared to grow out of the muck itself, eventually becoming his prison. The structure before us only marginally suggested the work of a human architect. Somehow, that design underwent a radical reconfiguration of root and vine. Tree branches jutted from apertures that vaguely resembled windows, while kudzu draped over walls, forming gaps where traces of the original construction remained, withering and rotting.

Nature took those ruins and created its own haunted house.

And now, a ghost appeared. It stood close to what looked like a barely functioning entryway, illuminated by flicking light that came from within like the flame of a jack-o'-lantern.

From a different direction, I again heard what sounded like a goat, another ghost I dreaded seeing.

The ghost before us seemed to fidget, and its outline became clearer. Standing next to me, Halia gasped, and I felt the kind of uncanny recognition that occurs when you find an old, forgotten picture of yourself. It both looks and doesn't look like you, and you feel like you've just seen your own ghost.

I believed I saw mine now, frozen at the age when I watched Milton the goat slaughtered before my disbelieving eyes.

"Is that . . . ? That's not . . .?" Halia asked, her voice barely a whisper.

"Me?" I asked

"No. I mean Isis."

The figure in the doorway lowered its shoulders, appearing to arrange the shape of its head before straightening again. Somehow, it had reformed its skull into something larger, almost malformed. Then a beam of light shone upon us, and I realized who I saw.

"Erik," I said.

Eleven

"He said you were back here," Erik said when he finally managed to peel himself away from my embrace.

Closer now, Halia and I could see the source of the light, the same hat with the flashlight duct-taped to it that he wore during the storm. With a little space between us, its light faced us directly.

"The light, Erik," I said, shielding my eyes.

"Sorry." He reached up to flip the switch, causing the darkness to rush back. "Hey, you found my bag."

I removed it from my shoulder so he could take it. "Why'd you leave it?"

"I didn't think I needed to go that far. Plus, I figured I didn't need a bunch of schoolbooks to weigh me down. Especially if I needed to run. It's creepy back here. Plus"—his voice dropped to a whisper as if it might hear him—"there's a big-ass alligator in that lake. The biggest one I've ever seen."

"Gustav," I said, sensing Halia's skeptical response before she had a chance to speak.

"If Gustav ever decided to cross that much land," she said, "he'd show up on satellite images. There'd be reports of dinosaurs roaming the earth. True reports. Gustav hatched from an egg over a billion years ago, if you ask me." That sounded like a joke, but she moved the bat to a ready position in case that creature burst from the brush and tried to eat us. A lot of good it would do—unless she planned to wedge it in its mouth to keep it from closing its jaws.

I turned back to Erik. "Who told you I'd be back here?"

"The boy with the goat," he said.

I trembled. The fact that he saw what I saw meant I couldn't deny the reality of its existence. The material world had truly ruptured. If Milton and that evil boy walked these grounds, then anything could. Anything was possible.

Halia made it worse by saying, "I thought I heard a goat back there. I figured it was my imagination."

"Where were you really?" Erik asked.

The accusation in his question stung.

He didn't wait for an answer. "I got a message saying I needed to come here for you. It said something happened." Erik felt around in his pocket.

"You left your phone in your bag," I said. "I got scared when I couldn't reach you."

"*You* were scared? How do you think I felt?" Erik began going through the backpack, stopping only when he saw that I held out his phone. He took it with a sigh. "I hate it when I do that."

"You remembered your crazy hat light, but you forget your phone?" I tapped the flashlight, hoping that gentle teasing would help make peace between us, but he grumbled and pushed my hand away.

"My hat is cool. Plus, if you think about it, power can go out anywhere, and I hate sitting in the dark. And what good is a phone if I can't reach you? I couldn't think straight. I was afraid something happened to you. What would I do without you? Where would I go?"

Halia cleared her throat. "We can discuss this later. Where's this person you saw? Did you say he was with—"

"He probably means me. I'm right here."

Zach's voice came from farther away, closer to the flickering lights. His familiar form filled what remained of the entryway to the White Nite Lodge.

"It's time for you all to come inside," he said.

"I don't know where the goat went," Erik said softly enough for just us to hear. "Don't say anything about it. They might want to eat it or use it for some kind of sacrifice. The girl inside, she's another story. Someone needs to help her."

"There's a girl in there?" Halia stepped forward, the bat gripped tightly.

"Is the girl's name Isis?"

"I don't know anyone's name," Erik said, "but there's something wrong with her."

I called to Zach. "Do you have Isis in there?" Part of me wanted to grab Erik by the arm and run back the way we came. But we couldn't do that, not without everyone.

Halia needed me.

Isis needed me.

"Answer, pendejo," Halia said when Zach didn't respond.

"She's fine. Come in and see. We're going to perform a ceremony." His voice sounded distant, just words without belief or conviction. He seemed vastly different from the last time I'd spoken to him.

Halia took a step forward. "What do you mean by ceremony?"

"There's someone else in there with her," Erik said. "Claims he's some kind of professor."

A lump formed in my throat. Without him telling me, I knew who he meant. Not Fowler. It could mean only one person.

"I think he wants to hold a séance," Erik said.

Twelve

To create a haunted house, know the necessities.

Not just the raw materials purchased in a hardware store. Not just the plywood needed to construct corridors that confuse the senses and make the thrill-seekers feel trapped. Not just a clever façade to suggest a decaying mansion or a crumbling insane asylum.

Or a forgotten motel hidden in the trees.

More than actors sporting makeup to hollow out their eyes and render them into grinning skulls. More than fake blood spattered across walls and bodies alike. More than cobwebs hanging from chandeliers or strobe lights to accentuate the unnatural movement of crawling ghouls.

For a truly haunted house, you need unresolved trauma.

Abandoned people. Forbidden places. Untold secrets.

My whole life should have prepared me step inside the ruins of the White Nite Lodge. All that gothic literature I read and studied should have hardened me. It should have made it easy to face what lay before me. But it didn't. I had embraced the darkness of my imagination so I would never have to step across the real threshold and confront what dwelled in the true night-lands. I hoped that every haunted book I read would form a spell to keep my real demons at bay.

But such things would not remain hidden any longer. They would not stay contained.

Closer now, I could see the tree branches extending from what remained of the roof transformed into luminous fingers by the lightning shattering the darkness every few minutes. Crouched over all of it, the limbs of a great oak with clinging drapes of Spanish moss. With the storm moving closer, the air filled with electricity, etching the impression of a body hanging from one of its branches.

Maybe I only imagined it. No one remarked on it as we approached Zach at the entryway. I could see his face now, drawn and pale.

"No light," he said to Erik, his hand reaching out to take away his hat.

"Don't touch him," I said. I didn't need more light to see Zach's sunken eyes and the swollen bumps and rashes that had formed on his skin since the last time I'd seen him.

He seemed to weigh my challenge before finally removing his hand from the top of Erik's head. What I saw looked less like hate than a resignation to exhaustion and pain. Sarge spoke of something like a leper colony back here. Maybe I shouldn't have dismissed the idea so quickly.

The idea of a colony implied several.

Who else would we find back here besides Isis?

Meanwhile, I tried to recall what little knowledge I possessed about leprosy. Was it contagious? I thought it resulted from eating tainted meat, but did I need to worry about us contracting something back here in this hovel? My skin began to itch as we crossed the entryway into this very haunted house.

The dead crow entered as well. Strangely, I experienced no more reticence about thinking of him as dead. I knew from literature that houses could go insane. Thus, the irrational may inhabit this rotten space. The flutter of the crow's wings could no longer surprise us, not even when it decayed down to hollow bone. Surely even then, it would retain the power of flight.

The light flickering within summoned us like moths to a burning wick, and space itself seemed to expand around us within the structure.

"Be careful where you step," Zach said, meaning the crumbling debris piled in mounds all about us. It formed a path through a corridor that seemed to run the length of the structure. What remained of the walls looked like ramparts of fungi, thriving there in the dark humidity.

The building itself felt alive.

And sick.

Full of leprosy, like the people inhabiting it.

To our right, we could see white faces illuminated by a circle of candles, the source of the light we saw outside. They flickered, agitated by the thunder, which sounded closer this time. The ground itself seemed to rumble in reply.

"Goddammit," Halia said, tripping over a portion of collapsed ceiling. I managed to catch her, and she thanked me. "Assuming we leave here alive, don't tell anyone what a klutz I am. We librarians have it hard enough as it is. I have a reputation to uphold."

"I promise." I looped my arm around her waist and squeezed gently. "And we'll get out of here. Everyone will."

From the candlelight came the sound of laughter. I ignored it and turned to Erik. Cradling the book I still carried, I reached for his hand now. "We will. I promise," I said.

"Keep moving," Zach said from somewhere I couldn't see.

Closer to the light, I felt a breeze that made it through the gaps in the wall. Until that point, the smell of mold and damp earth overwhelmed everything, but now a different odor reached me, one that made me want to retch and heave.

Mangoes. The scent of ripe mangoes.

"Is that her, Zachary? Is that my protégé?"

I didn't recognize the voice, and it didn't dawn on me right away that the voice referred to me. I was no one's protégé.

"It's her." Then to us, Zach said, "Keep moving."

Closer, I could see that the candles formed a ring atop a round table. They cast a light on two faces situated at opposite ends, facing one another.

One of those faces belonged to Isis.

In form, at least.

When her eyes shifted to regard us, I felt the presence of someone—or maybe some*thing*—else.

I didn't recognize the one who spoke.

Thin skeins of wispy hair covered half of his face, doing little to disguise the signs of the same affliction that marked Zach. He tilted his head in our direction, revealing a long, narrow nose, its shape marred by warty growths that made him look like a witch straight out of a fairy tale.

"That's him," Erik said.

"Him?" asked Halia. Seeing Isis caused her to radiate with energy. She gripped the bat with two hands now.

"The professor," said Erik.

"And a hello to you all," said the witch, speaking as if we'd all gathered casually for coffee. "It's wonderful to finally meet you in person. I'm Thomas Dash."

Thirteen

"She's channeling," Professor Dash said. He maintained the casual manner, even when Halia threatened to bring the bat down on his skull if he didn't release Isis from whatever influence he held over her. "I'm not doing anything, I assure you. She's quite a marvel. She truly is."

"Isis? Can you hear me?" Halia forgot about the professor for a moment. With the bat resting against her shoulder, she waved a hand in front of her niece's face.

Isis didn't respond. She fixed her gaze on me and pulled back her lips in a smile that chilled me. When she spoke, my knees trembled.

"What language is that?" Halia asked.

I already knew the answer before Professor Dash spoke. "Creole. At least I think it is. Beautiful, isn't it? Maddening, but beautiful."

"Isera doesn't speak Creole," said Halia. She put emphasis on her niece's given name.

"Like I said, she's channeling. And she's quite good at it. Aren't you proud of her?"

He intended the question for me, but Halia answered for both of us. "Fuck no, I'm not proud. I'm terrified."

My terror stemmed from something different. Isis spoke with a voice I recognized.

Dash read my expression. "Can you translate? I take it that you understand her, given your . . ." He trailed off as he searched for the appropriate word, finally landing on "background." He smiled in self-approval, a horrible sight as his lips pulled back to reveal receding gums.

I moved around the table, closing the distance between me and Isis. Her eyes followed me as her smile widened, revealing teeth that looked as if they wanted to nibble on me.

My mother rarely spoke Creole to me. She spoke English with the refinement of someone who learned it formally, though she never revealed to anyone what sort of education she received. She reserved Creole for rare, unguarded moments of affection, using pet phrases that I often wondered if someone—a mother or grandmother—used for her.

I heard such words come from Isis's mouth but in a voice that sounded like my mother.

"Hey, doudou, kòman ou ye?"

A simple term of endearment, followed by a question. How was I? I wanted to laugh at the absurdity.

I probably didn't make it easy for my mother to express herself to me this way. It embarrassed me. I never answered the way she expected me to. If I said anything at all, I probably said I was fine, followed by a request to not call me *doudou*, even if it meant something affectionate. As I continued to grow up, I pretended not to understand her. In darker moments, I told her I didn't believe that she'd swam onto that beach where my father found her, that maybe she never lived across the sea at all but probably worked somewhere cleaning hotel rooms or some other job I saw as undignified and beneath me.

This time, I wanted to answer her question the way she taught me. The words started to form. "I'm—"

From the mouth of Isis came new words, still in that familiar voice and a language only I understood. "I know. You're strong. I always knew. You were always so ashamed of me, but I knew your strength, and I wanted you to know too."

"What's she saying?" asked Erik, who never had those words spoken to him, too young to remember our mother's voice.

"Yes, I want to know too," said Professor Dash. "I need to know." He needed only a pointed hat and boiling cauldron to complete the image of a crone watching a spell manifest itself. Around us, shadows stirred as the wind outside began to rise. At what point would these walls finally succumb to nature, collapsing on everyone inside? The sound of coughing reached us. Who or what else watched us from those shadows?

"Isera, what's going on?" With her free hand, Halia reached out to touch her niece.

"Not while she's channeling." Thunder punctuated Professor Dash's words, causing us all to draw back, including Halia, despite gripping a weapon she could have used to bash his brains. That chance passed when Zach's hand reached out of the darkness to wrench it away.

Halia yelped in surprise. Zach's size didn't deter her from trying to grapple with him, a fight she wouldn't win, but not before showing him her fingernails and vowing to scratch out his eyes if he fucked with her again.

"You'll do nothing of the kind," Professor Dash said, never leaving his seat. "Not if you ever want to get out of here."

The shadows seemed to press closer. We could all feel it—the presence of something else stirring. Everyone grew still, including Halia.

Professor Dash regarded me meaningfully. "Think of this as a classroom. We're all here to learn, and to learn, we need to settle down and let order prevail. This is an academic endeavor. As my successor, you can understand that, I'm sure."

"I only understand that you've done something to this woman," I said, still uneasy with the way Isis gazed at me, her face having become a mask for something else.

Zach breathed harshly as he hovered around us. His confrontation with Halia sapped some of his energy but not enough of it. He seemed so different from that first impression he made on me when he seemed so skeptical and aloof. So out of place. So like . . . so like . . .

It hit me then.

So like a zombie. Not an undead creature who craved the flesh of the living, but a body divorced from its soul and forced to labor for someone else. A bokor would know how to capture the part of a person that gave them agency, personality, and consciousness—their petit bon ange. From there, the bokor could control their physical function—or their gros bon ange, as my mother called it.

If that explained what happened to Zach, then what did that make Professor Dash? Not just a witch. A kind of bokor.

Noticing the attention I paid to Zach, Professor Dash answered these questions for me. "I need Zach to be my eyes and ears—and yes, protector if necessary." He shifted in position, allowing his features to become more distinct in the candle flame, and I could see then how severely the leprosy marked him, even with most of his features hidden behind the lankness of his hair and beard. A rotten smell emanated from him, the odor of decay and open sores.

"Why can't you do those things for yourself?" asked Halia. She rubbed her shoulder, apparently sore from grappling with Zach.

"*Because I can't leave here,*" he said. "That's why we need to channel *her.*"

"Channel who?" Halia asked, not realizing what I knew. What none of them knew.

My dead mother, manifesting herself through Isis.

By "her," Dash could not possibly mean my mother.

It seemed as if he might not answer. His eyes reflected the flames of the candles.

"The one they call Bon Manman," he said finally.

Fourteen

"You've heard that name," he said to me. "I can tell by your reaction. I want to hear you say it."

"It doesn't sound like a name," I said. "More like a description."

He attempted to laugh but ended up coughing instead. He extended his hand. From where he hovered in the shadows, Zach supplied him with a soiled rag to wipe his mouth, a wordless act so automatic and mechanical that I thought again of zombie lore.

"True, true," Professor Dash said when he could speak again. "I know enough to understand it means the 'good mother.' Who knows how it became a name or where it came from. Racial prejudice had to play some role. I'm sure I don't need to explain the degrading perception of women of color during those times. Society deemed them either whores or idealized maternal figures. That's how they were kept powerless. Marginalized. Well, I'll tell you something. I don't know whose mother she was, but she isn't *good*."

He paused as if he'd said something so profound that he needed to let it sink in.

"She's trapped me here," he said. "Trapped. I can't leave. *And I do not know what she wants.*"

Halia and I traded glances. Like me, she wanted to know what had driven this man so barking mad. What would she think, then, I if I told her I'd heard the speech of my own dead mother come from the lips of her niece? She didn't yet know the extent of the insanity that surrounded her. How alone she was.

"You're not trapped," I said, though I felt very much trapped at the moment.

"I can't leave here," he said, the despondency heavy in his tone. "Zachary? Tell these smart women what happens when you try to help me find my way out of here?"

Flatly, Zach said, "It's true. He becomes confused. Disoriented. It doesn't matter how closely he follows me. I eventually . . . I lose him."

"I wind up back here, somehow," said Professor Dash. "Each time. It's the damnedest thing. Zachary leads the way through that infernal wilderness, and we walk, walk, walk for an eternity. 'Are we almost there, Zachary?' I'll say, and I hear an answer that clearly sounds like Zachary—"

"I never hear the question," Zach said, interrupting.

"—but we inevitably arrive right back here. Then the person I've been following turns around, and I see it's not Zachary."

"Who is it, then?" Erik asked.

"One of them," Professor Dash said quietly.

Halia responded for all of us. "One of *who*?"

Professor Dash hissed to her to lower her voice. "They're here now," he said, whispering. "They can't leave either. They're listening to everything we say. They're hoping we'll show them the way."

My eyes probed the darkness, the shifting shadows forming the impression of faces watching us. The boundary between illusion and reality shifted and moved. How many people shared this room with us? I couldn't tell.

"I can't get out now either," said Zach. "The last time I tried, I walked for days." He indicated Isis. "Then I found her. I brought her here."

"It's good that you did, Zachary," Professor Dash said, "very good. She has natural talents. We'll use them to discover what she wants. Find a way out."

"You won't use her for anything," said Halia. "You both need help." To Isis: "Snap out of it, girl. We're leaving this place. A storm's brewing."

Zach filled the space between them. "You'll need to wait it out. It isn't safe."

Halia laughed. "You think it's safe here? This whole place looks ready to come down."

Professor Dash made no effort to hide his condescension. "It's not coming down. It never will. Its roots extend deep into the land. Not even hurricane winds could topple it. The trees wrap their branches around these walls, protecting them, preserving them, becoming one with them."

Isis continued to regard me with that unsettling smile. Once more, she spoke to me in my mother's voice, her accented words intended only for me.

I knew just enough to translate: "Is this man the kind of person you aspire to be? Your head, always in books. Look, you even have one with you now."

Impulsively, I looked down at the book in my hand. *Tell My Horse*, its cover creased and damp from the sweat of my palms. Without meaning to, I'd clutched it hard, as if our lives depended upon it. According to Lenny Engel, they very well could.

Professor Dash noticed the book for the first time.

"Good. You found it on your own. When Zach told me about you, I knew getting it into your hands would be key to everything. I even told him where to look on my shelf, but he couldn't follow those simple directions."

Zach stiffened at the insult. "It wasn't there," he mumbled. "The whole area is cluttered. No sense of order." For a moment, he appeared less blank and more present. Good, I thought. Maybe he was not entirely lost.

"I told you the exact spot," Professor Dash said. "Start at the top shelf, count down three rows *exactly*. Then look for the ninth book to the right, and there, *voila*." He held up his hands like a magician accepting applause.

"He's like you," Isis said in my mother's Creole. "Move one book and you'd be infuriated. Who could understand your system? But I tried, believe me, I did."

I stared at her as the others regarded me mutely. How should I respond to that? Was I that difficult?

"You *need* to tell me what she's saying," Professor Dash said. 'I need to know what she wants."

"She says you were wrong." I waved the book in his direction. "It was the fourth shelf down and the eleventh book over."

The entity I knew as my mother used Isis to laugh. I'd forgotten about my mother's laugh, such a distinct sound. "Very good. That was a fine taunt."

Professor Dash's eyes flashed between us, unsure of where to focus. So did Halia's. "The fuck?" she said. "Was that a laugh?"

"You're lying," Professor Dash said to me. "I can tell."

"So you say. But I have the book." Once more, I held it high for him to see, all the while maintaining the distance between us. I didn't know if he'd try to grab it, forcefully remove it from my gasp. He would have to fight me for it.

"Well, someone must have moved it, then. So what? It doesn't matter," Dash said, though from the way he said it, it sounded as if it did very much matter, "because you recognized the clues and found me."

Clues? I gripped the book so tightly my fingers throbbed. I recalled how its presence on the shelf stood out to me, practically announcing itself. I couldn't say it called to me—not exactly. The idea that he left me clues to follow made me think of the terrible effigy hanging above the desk. Did he mean that too?

"What other clues?" I asked.

"It doesn't matter. You're here now." He regarded Halia and Erik. For the briefest moment, Zach too. "You're all here. Each of you will help bring this unfortunate episode to a close, and then we can resume our lives. Return everything to the way it was before."

"Before what?" asked Halia.

He turned his crone face to her. "Before I went into that infernal haunted house."

Fifteen

Professor Dash's Narrative

Student evaluations. A necessary evil, I suppose. I would read mine at the conclusion of each semester to find out what students liked and didn't like about me. "An easy grader." That one came up a lot, and Fowler always mentioned it during annual reviews of my job performance. He alleged that only one natural relationship existed between students and professor: conflict.

I pushed back on that one. No, no, I would say, we need a more peaceful form of co-existence, to which he laughed and called me a bleeding heart. Still, I pressed him to understand that the pursuit of knowledge and wisdom became possible only when trust and benevolence came into play. More laughter, along with his promise that my students would lie and cheat their way through my courses if I gave them half the chance.

Determined to prove him wrong, I set about to make myself as much a part of my students' lives as possible. I interjected myself in their conversations. I interacted with them on a personal level, even outside the borders of the classroom, and that led to the founding of HOL, the Horror and Occult League. The germ for that idea occurred when I made a show of bemoaning the uninviting walls of the classroom. How could anyone expect them to learn under such confining conditions? "Let's take a walk, everyone," I said, and I headed out the classroom door, not even sure if they would follow me. If I shared Fowler's cynicism, I would have expected them to assume I'd gone mad or just found an indirect tactic for dismissing that day's class. But to my relief, they gathered their books and followed me. Maybe they expected an interesting method of discussing "The Willows" by Algernon Blackwood, the assigned reading for that afternoon. So as not to disappoint them, I led them to the path circumventing the lake. I could sense Fowler watching from his office window as I led that cadre of students to the pavilion situated on the opposite bank. Knowing that he probably mocked us from afar, I held up a middle finger. The students needed no encouragement to follow my lead in the gesture. Everyone's middle finger extended into the air, though I imagine they didn't realize we were flipping off a specific individual. Perhaps in their minds, we intended the gesture for the college as an institution, or perhaps society itself. Maybe they thought of their parents as they joined me in the salute.

Either way, Fowler saw it. This I know because he refused to speak to me for several days afterward.

Once we reached the pavilion, an underused structure apparently once intended as a place for students to bring their lunches, I instructed them all to sit in a circle around me. I chose an especially humid day for this activity, so perspiration covered their expectant faces. Still, no one complained. I encouraged them to observe how the pavilion was bordered by the water on one side and a thick wall of forest on the other. Realizing I didn't feel like talking about Blackwood and his nascent form of cosmic horror, I instead started using the surroundings as a tenuous metaphor for learning and academia. Quickly, they began to look bored, so I chose another tactic.

"What secrets do you think hide back in there?" I asked them, pointing toward the wall of trees. I paused to give them time to consider. Their eyes shifted to one another. Someone laughed, but that laughter contained nervousness, a touch of fear. None of them had ever ventured past the tree line, not even to satisfy a craving for sex or drugs. I forged ahead, inviting them to imagine what past sins and indiscretions lay trapped and repressed back there. Realizing that I could still loop in "The Willows," I challenged them to consider what Blackwood wrote. Hadn't that author demonstrated to them how nature itself might be haunted?

It turned out that many of them failed to complete the reading assignment, so they didn't understand what I meant. Rather than follow Fowler's approved tactics and shame them, I asked them to imagine what sort of haunted house they would build for themselves out here. One of them, a young man who often struggled to grasp abstract ideas, took my question literally. He considered the structure of the pavilion itself, observing out loud that some plywood bolted into the base and rafters of the structure would enable us to section off rooms and closets, even a hidden passageway.

Two other students, both with experience from working construction jobs in the summer, stood and began assessing the size and sturdiness of the building before adding their agreement. Before long, everyone completely forgot about Algernon Blackwood in favor of designing the interior walls that would bring visitors to various scenes of horror and wonder. The energy became infectious as some students began sketching designs and brainstorming themes and concepts in their notebooks. To my delight, they even began incorporating elements and themes from the stories I assigned to them. I imagined myself saying, *See now, Fowler? They do take their coursework seriously.*

And that was the moment that gave birth to the Horror and Occult League, principally to give students the organization they needed to implement their haunted house by the end of October. To give it academic legitimacy, I explained to Fowler and other skeptical colleagues that the organization could charge money for admission and donate the funds to some worthy cause, thereby making the whole endeavor an exercise in service learning. "Pray tell, what would they actually be learning?" asked Fowler. I answered that question by tasking the students to research materials we could use in the implementation of the haunted house. Folktales, myths, rituals, and the like.

In no time at all, my classroom became a hotbed of discussion and investigation—all student-led, with my role evolving into more of an advisory direction. Lectures got in the way, so I suspended those, along with the required readings, and instead tasked them with forming sub-committees and pursuing any area of inquiry that could serve our ultimate project. I could sit back and watch, reveling in how I'd fulfilled the dream of every instructor. Oh, I still taught lessons, but only to supplement what they discovered on their own—for instance, when I brought in Angela Carter's writing to provide a foundation to their understanding of fairy tales, one of the more popular themes as this project took root.

Each year, the haunt became a final exam of sorts, a living embodiment of all our studies and research. When we finally transformed that lowly pavilion into an incarnation of their fears and fantasies, I couldn't have anticipated how successful it would become, a truly otherworld spectacle, thanks to the committed group of students inside, dutifully playing their parts. Everyone contributed, whether donning makeup or hanging decorations or building interior walls, which surprised even me with their singular effect of something positively labyrinthian when you stepped inside.

One year, I even convinced the irascible Fowler to go inside it. "Why?" he asked. "You think it could count as a classroom observation?"

"Of course!" I replied. I even slapped him on the back as if we'd become old chums. He grumbled, but he surprised me by showing up one evening. After forcing the cheap bastard to pay his entrance fee, a donation to our cause that year, I offered to lead him through the haunt personally.

And what an experience that turned out to be. I never imagined that Dick Fowler would turn out to be a jumpy coward, but he became so overcome at times that he practically clung to me. By the time we made it to the end, I found myself supporting much of his weight. He even needed a moment to collect himself. As he stood there, bent over with his hands on his knees, I asked him what he thought.

"What the fuck, Tom? What was that?" he said. "How long did that actually take?"

I could hardly suppress my delight. I may even have giggled out loud.

My delight ended when the next words came out of his mouth.

"That woman," he said, "with the bucket. That was a student? Christ, was that real blood?"

I didn't know how to answer. Our theme that year involved ghost pirates, all based on historical lore, and we had no one dressed as what he made sound like a washer woman of some kind. No one with a bucket.

To mask my confusion, I asked him, "You liked it, then?"

"No," he said, "I very much fucking did not," thereby concluding the first and only time he ever visited our haunt.

Before the evening concluded, I went through the haunt several more times, trying to figure out what Fowler saw.

At no time did I encounter anything like what he described. It all followed the script we meticulously constructed.

Just to make sure, I mentioned the woman with the bucket to the students. Perhaps one of them improvised something special without seeking the approval of the group or, for that matter, me. A deckhand pretending to mop the floors of the ship, perhaps? But no one came forward, and all of them seemed genuinely perplexed by what Fowler saw.

Someone joked good naturedly that perhaps our haunt had summoned an actual spirit. Hardly an original occurrence, of course. The most famous haunted attraction of all sits in a massive theme park east of us on I-4, and that one allegedly contains real ghosts thanks to the number of grieving parents who have smuggled in the cremated remains of their dearly departed children, leading to supernatural manifestations interfering with animatronics.

But our little enterprise?

At first, the suggestion merely amused us, but in the days ahead, it became clear that Fowler's vision planted a seed. It inspired several students to make further inquiries into the occult. One student brought in a Ouija board, and after closing the window shades and lighting a candle, she invited her colleagues to gather around and use it to find out if we had a new visitor. That experiment yielded no results, though. The planchette remained stubbornly in place, despite the eager fingers that touched it.

Did that setback discourage others from taking a sharp turn toward the occult? Hardly at all. Another person endeavored to learn how to read Tarot cards, becoming practiced enough that she designed her own "Spread of *Mis*fortune." We all got a kick out of it, including me. The student wore traditional Romany clothes, allegedly handed down from a great-grandmother who escaped Hitler's concentration camps. I remember distinctly what the student said when she used the cards to foretell my own "misfortune."

"Professor Dash," she said, "I pulled the Chariot. You know what that means, don't you?" I had an idea, but as any good educator would do, I let the student tell me. "Don't take any long trips. That'll be your ultimate misfortune."

"Yikes," I said, not taking it seriously.

Well, look at me now.

At the time, we all shared a good laugh over the reading, especially when I told them what a community college professor makes in a state that cares so little about education. I couldn't afford to take *any* long trips, I assured them.

Our activities progressed from there into further areas of exploration, including dowsing rods and seances, but like the exercise with the Ouija board, they failed to yield any results.

Even so, year after year, each incoming group of students brought with them a fearless determination to make the haunt better and better, to always top the group that came before them. Any interest in exploring actual paranormal events began to wane, the students having grown more pragmatic in their philosophy. They judged such pursuits a distraction from the real goal: to put on a good show and raise money for charity.

Still, what Fowler said about the woman with the bucket continued to nag me. It haunted me, you might say. Maybe it came down to jealousy, the fact that such a cynical, cold-hearted bastard like Fowler could be granted a glimpse into the numinous realm of the supernatural while the same forces denied me such an experience. Occasionally, I'd hear of something strange occurring. For instance, the appearance of a group of disheveled, disfigured men, all sharing a common skin condition, that no one recalled checking in at the ticket table. We explained them away as residents from the homeless encampment rumored to exist close by. Many of its inhabitants no doubt suffered the effects of opioid addiction, and perhaps they'd wandered into our haunt. Fortunately, they harmed no one and disappeared as stealthily as they appeared.

Privately, I plunged into my own research of the woman with the bucket filled with blood. The searches led to dead ends—mostly. Reviews of a Roger Corman movie about a deranged artist, for example. But also an interesting, if apocryphal story of a bridge a short way to the north, where a midwife used to dispose of the remains of murdered children, causing the river to turn red with blood. The woman allegedly met her demise by haplessly falling into the river where she emptied the contents of her buckets. One account suggested that she'd become so overcome by guilt that she found it necessary to end her own life by jumping from the bridge. All very intriguing, but not very well documented, and thus little more than a folktale to spice up the atmosphere of a Halloween evening.

The lack of anything concrete frustrated me, to say the least. I considered many possibilities. One, that the woman's death in the river never happened and that she simply moved her operations to our area. Two, that she didn't travel, but her story somehow did. Or three, she never did exist in the first place and Fowler made up the whole thing as a practical joke for the sake of revenge. After all, he owed me for giving him the bird.

Eventually, I dismissed that last possibility. Hadn't I witnessed his reaction myself? Did I not have to bear his considerable weight after he became overcome by his vision? Besides, I could sense something hiding in the thick trees on the edge of the campus, something unseen and forgotten. If not a spirit, then something like a spirit.

For all their dabbling into the occult, none of my students showed any real aptitude in summoning the spirit world.

And then Isera came along.

Before joining HOL, she visited my office so we could discuss the special needs accommodations she arranged through Student Services. Such notices arrived at the start of a semester and usually involved the requirements of extra test time because of a disability. I hardly knew Isera, much less about her preference in name—Isis. That, I found amusing, attributing it to an inflated sense of self. How little I knew before that meeting, when I planned to explain that her accommodations didn't matter because I didn't give tests. Then I read the paperwork.

"Am I to understand," I asked her, "that you've received accommodations based on the premise that you experience psychic manifestations?"

I avoided using the language on the document, intending to seize an advantage over her by employing more academic phrasing. *Possession*, the paperwork said.

Bear in mind, I considered myself a staunch defender of a student's right to receive necessary accommodations, especially when people like Fowler derided them. But this case clearly went a bridge too far.

Isera—or Isis, as I now call her—maintained eye contact and smiled. "Absolutely," she said without a trace of hesitation. "I think you'll find everything in order."

A stand-off ensued, the two of us engaging in a staring contest like two middle school children. I knew a practical joke when I heard one. Someone put her up to this, I thought, maybe Fowler, who wanted to mock what he saw as a lack of academic integrity in my courses. He didn't approve of the fact that I found ways to tie all my coursework into HOL.

Yet, part of me wanted to believe.

Finally, I broke the silence.

"Show it to me. This demon, I mean."

She answered by raising an eyebrow.

"Go on," I said. "Prove it. Reveal to me this entity that cohabits your body."

She sighed as if it pained her to deal with someone so dense. "I can't just call it up. It's not on speed dial. Do you say the same thing to someone suffering from epilepsy? Have a seizure? Show it to me?"

"You're likening yourself to someone with epilepsy?" I couldn't believe the audacity, but she went on as if it didn't matter.

"Or do you say that to the person who struggles to deal with social anxiety? 'Have a panic attack for me. Show me what it's like.'"

"Those are real disorders," I said.

"I have a 'real disorder,'" she said with air quotes.

I would lie if I said a small part of me didn't enjoy this repartee.

I said, "If I'm understanding you correctly, you have a disorder I can talk to. That's certainly unique. Go on, then. Let's summon him. Or is it a her?"

Without answering, she began to gather her things.

"What name does it go by?" I asked.

She stood, but I didn't want her to leave. I waved back to her chair. "Oh, come on. Don't be like that."

She didn't sit, but she paused near the door, regarding me. "I was told you would understand," she said. "That I should go to you. Speak discretely to you about my special circumstances."

Wondering briefly if I'd made a mistake, I considered the document on my desk.

No. If not Fowler trying to teach me a lesson, then perhaps someone in the office that handles accommodations. I would eventually find the real prankster. I knew my reputation. What others said about me. How I let things go a little too far in my classroom. Rumors of how easily a student could earn a high passing grade.

Still, a small doubt lingered. What if Isis spoke the truth and really did experience some form of psychic manifestation?

"Join HOL," I finally said. "I want you to play a role in the haunt this semester."

"What about my accommodations?" she asked.

"They won't be a problem at all." I also told her about a service-learning opportunity that had arisen lately, one that had surprising occult connections. If she had no problems with going into a prison, then it sounded perfect for her. Especially given her penchant for self-invention.

She agreed, naturally. Nodding, she started to leave, then hesitated. She turned to face me again. I waited expectantly, wondering if I would receive a confession.

But she said, "I won't play a supporting role. No victims. In the haunted house, I mean."

I smiled. "Something predatory?"

I don't know what I expected. For her to return my smile, maybe? Her face to light up with gratitude? I saw nothing of the sort. Just, for the briefest moment, something else. A hint of a presence behind her eyes. Something that lit up at the word I used. *Predatory.*

That fast, it vanished.

But she started attending meetings, this young woman who I found could appear at turns both shy and aloof. She kept her distance from others, speaking up only when planning moved on to role assignment.

She looked at me expectantly when the more senior members of HOL began claiming the more coveted roles and responsibilities. Isis expected me to speak up for her, to intervene.

But no. If you want to play a predator, you have to act like one. Not witless prey.

Sure enough, when her silent challenge to me went unanswered, she spoke up for herself.

"The wolf," she said. "I want to play the wolf."

Her gall received the expected reaction. Those in leadership roles looked at her with amused disdain. After all the time and energy they invested in the project, were they supposed to let this upstart come in and claim the role of the wolf for herself?

By that point, I'd grown tired of the fairy tale theme, even though it maintained popularity with both the performers and the community. Principally because of the wolf costume.

It was, to put it mildly, *really fucking cool.* Unquestionably the most realistic piece of work we had, thanks to a student who had a godparent or uncle—I can't remember which—working at a theme park in Central Florida. Not only did the costume resemble an actual wolf standing upright on its haunches, but its jaws functioned with a long, extending tongue, just like a real werewolf, if such a thing existed.

Besides having no seniority in the ranks of HOL, Isis also lacked the physical stature needed to wear the apparatus. (I hesitate to call it a "costume," a word that would diminish the full effect of its function. You don't wear it. It wears you.) Based on his height and build, everyone assumed that Mason Crane, a former pitcher on the local high school baseball team, would fill the role.

Everyone liked Mason too. His affable personality made up for a lack of intelligence. That affability made him amenable to playing a different role. He simply didn't care so long as he earned his passing grade. But others voiced their objections, leading to one of the only heated arguments I can recall occurring during a HOL meeting. I chose to let it play out, even when it became intense enough that I wondered if physical violence might erupt. Admittedly, I took a small fraction of pleasure from seeing how much they cared about our little venture. If nothing else, I could justly call it a teaching moment, providing them with the space to resolve their own conflicts, no matter how one-sided. Anyone could see that Mason not only had the required physical dimensions needed to play a monstrous wolf, but he even possessed lupine features, such as a narrow face and a snout-like nose, making his eyes appear closer together than on most people. Logic heavily favored those who wanted him to play the wolf.

Isis exchanged glances with me. I wondered at first if she wanted me to interject and tilt the argument to her favor. Maybe she wanted her accommodations to come into play. When I did nothing, a shadow fell over her features. Rightly or wrongly, she assumed that I'd subjected her to a sadistic test of sorts, one that would determine how far she would go to get what she wanted.

I soon found out.

When Mason failed to show up for the next meeting, no one suspected that something awful happened. Not until his next failure to make an appearance did anyone think to check on him and discover that he'd been hospitalized thanks to an attack by some sort of wild animal.

"He was practically mauled," the concerned student reported. "They had to stuff his guts back inside him.

I studied Isis as we processed this news, reactions ranging from horror to disbelief.

Only Isis's face remained impassive. Not even a flinch.

"I'll bet she has something to do with this," someone whispered loud enough for everyone to hear. Evidently the goal.

We all watched her now.

Not even a tic to indicate that the accusation bothered her.

"No," said Mason's friend. "He said it was a wild animal. He described what almost sounds like a coyote, but a massive one. He says it stood as tall as the roof of his car."

The ensuing conversation went in several directions at once. Some pointed out that coyotes never reached that size and certainly didn't go around attacking people. A bear, perhaps? Someone else used their phone to show the others what a bear looked like when it was starved and wet. I looked at the image myself and can attest that it looked surprisingly canine. If Mason saw something like that in the dark, especially when it decided to attack and maul him, he might have mistaken it for a coyote. And though uncommon, bears do sometimes make their way into our area.

Attention drifted away from Isis, but not mine. I moved closer to her.

"I suppose you're the wolf now," I said, keeping my voice low enough for only her to hear. "Assuming you can make it fit."

"I took the liberty of making some adjustments," she said, matching my volume. Noticing my reaction, she added, "I took it home, but don't worry, I'm no thief. I brought it back."

At the end of our meeting, I asked her to remain.

"That was not only presumptuous but dangerous," I said. I went on to warn her that tampering with the property of HOL would likely cast more suspicion on her. "Besides, I only advise in my capacity here. The leadership rests in the hands of your peers, and they won't take kindly to what you did."

"Just wait until they see what a great wolf I'm going to make. They'll have a change of heart then."

"If they don't ban you first."

"I see," said Isis. "Maybe it's time for a change in leadership."

"Not likely. You're too new."

"Well, if I can't change hearts, I'll just have to start eating them instead."

An evil twinkle in her eye dared me to wager on how serious she was.

And when the time came for her to wear the wolf costume, everyone agreed: she looked fully capable of rending human flesh. As the time reached the eve of showtime, with all the props and pieces in place, hardly anyone could play their parts thanks to how Isis's appearance left them thunderstruck. On multiple occasions, thrill seekers who paid a small donation to walk through the haunt became so overcome that they required the help of paramedics.

Transformed, Isis left us in complete awe. Adding to the effect, she went through the process of putting on and taking off the costume in private, leaving it a mystery as to how to she managed to fill all its space. Some speculated that she simply used a considerable amount of padding.

Only I had a different theory, one I shared with no one. After all, I couldn't divulge the nature of the documentation that came from the Office of Accommodations. That *thing* inside Isis filled the space for her. It did the real work, the costume allowing a display of its full monstrosity for all to see. It moved the mighty haunches it used to approach you in the darkness. As it towered over you, it opened the jaws that held those magnificent fangs. Some visitors complained that it even slavered on them and showed us evidence that it had done so, despite the fact it contained no mechanism that could achieve such an effect.

Had Isis managed to drool on anyone? Unlikely.

Still, I began to question everything.

What moved her arms? What voice spoke from her mouth? I no longer felt certain that Isis—or Isera, for that matter—even existed.

Just a body.

A horse for something else to ride. Something that wanted to roam free but needed her lungs to breathe.

I watched the way she stood, solitary, gazing out to where the forest began when the evening concluded, donations counted, everything stored away for the night. Whatever looked out of her eyes wanted to run wild through those trees and pursue real game. It no longer wanted to pretend.

I dared to say as much to her, prompting her to turn to me with feigned perplexion.

"Whatever's riding you now," I said, "does it feel good to let it out?"

"Riding me?" she said. "I don't follow. But that sounds nasty."

I reminded her about the letter of accommodation, the psychic manifestation. She had to the gall to laugh. "Professor Dash, that was a joke. I thought you knew that." Then, after studying my expression, she said, "I was kidding around. I thought you'd get a kick out of it."

I let it go, telling her that she certainly had me convinced for a while. In truth, I knew that Isis harbored something, even if she herself remained innocent and unaware of it. After all, something compelled her to play her little joke on me. All our fictions contain some element of truth, sometimes without our awareness.

"Jesus, Professor, you seem like you're getting ready to perform an exorcism or something. Don't throw any holy water on me, okay?"

Oh, no, Isis, far from an exorcism. I wanted to draw it out. Let it ride. Play witness to it in all its glory.

Even more so, I wanted to coax it into myself. Make me its horse.

Just a different level of what we did with that lonely little pavilion—inhabit it with our bodies. Haunt it for the pleasure of others.

I wanted to feel that on the inside. Haunted.

With that end in mind, I made myself a constant fixture in the haunt, at first following groups inside and wandering close behind their footsteps. Eventually, I began lingering, much to the consternation of the students trying to play their assigned roles. Rarely did they voice their aggravations. By rights, I didn't need an invitation. I could come inside whenever I wanted. If I stood in their way, they would work around me. In the event that anyone asked, I had an answer ready. "I'm the Invisible Man," I planned to say. No one ever did ask, yet I began to feel truly invisible.

Perhaps I had stumbled upon the key. Not invisibility per se, but to feel emptied out. Ready to receive.

I fell into reveries, even trances like that, sometimes finding myself becoming lost within the haunted house.

"Professor? You okay? You need help?" That question came in various forms by the end of the night, along with a hand to guide me back outside.

Sometimes, that hand belonged to Isis, and I resisted the urge to say, *No, no, leave me inside. I belong in there.*

"Come along, Professor," said a faint voice, the darkness settling in so thickly that I couldn't see the hand's owner, though I believed it to belonged to Isis. She led me on a path that seemed to stretch for an eternity. The ground became uneven and thick with brambles. I kept stumbling and even fell at one point. I couldn't find my feet without my guide's assistance. "Come along, Professor," she said again, ignoring my complaints about how the tumble left me with scratches or the clouds of insects forming around us. The intermittent breeze offered no relief from the growing humidity.

"Are we still in the pavilion?" I asked, even though I knew the answer to such a stupid question, so stupid it didn't even warrant a response. A break in the clouds allowed in enough moonlight that I could see that we'd reached a clearing.

At first, I took what lay before me as a natural formation. Maybe the remains of an old levee, designed to hold back floods. But then I saw shapes that suggested windows, then open doorways, some still with numbers inscribed overhead. Though it sagged dangerously, the roof somehow avoided a completed collapse. Trees now grew from the soil that settled upon what I now correctly perceived as the ruins of a building.

"Are you ready for a late check-in, Professor?" said the figure leading me. The moonlight failed to penetrate the shadows cloaking my guide. It spoke with Isis's voice, a good trick. If only the shadows would lift. She allowed Fowler to see her true form—this, I firmly believed—so why not me? This act of ventriloquism only added further insult.

"Speak to me in your true voice," I said.

An audacious command, but I had the right, didn't I? Hadn't I created a means for this entity to materialize? To ride borrowed flesh? I believed what people often said of spirits—that they watched the living with jealousy, wanting, above all else, to live through us, to enjoy the sensual pleasures denied to them by death.

Yet what now led me into these ruins wouldn't fulfill even such a simple request. To take physical form would require energy, I had no doubt. But at least it could let me hear its true voice. Instead, it mocked me by answering in a language I couldn't understand, a form of French Creole by the sound of it.

It led me through one of those doors, its touch growing colder and colder until, inexplicably, my flesh seemed to burn. The inside of the building smelled of mold and rotten vegetation, the putrescent odor of offerings left to spoil in a forgotten temple. It forced me to sit as it hovered over me, waiting for me to do something, the outline of a shadow inscribed on more shadows.

"But I'll starve if you force me to stay here," I said, because I somehow sensed she intended to do just that—enclose me in that awful space and never allow me to leave. "What will I eat?" I added when no answer came, giving no mind to how much like a child I must have sounded, only concerned with maintaining my own biological functions. What would a decent psychoanalyst make of that? It pains me to admit I even started crying. I didn't expect an answer to my question.

But I got one.

"The same thing we eat."

The sound of that voice, coming from some unseen source, sent a chill through me. It seemed to originate from the hidden spaces around me, where rats chittered and something far worse than snakes slithered.

I realized then that I didn't have this prison cell to myself.

"There's meat if you know where to look," added a different voice, "and if you can't stomach it and try to spit it out, she'll force it down your throat."

"And she'll wash it down with her elixir," said the first, "that sweet, sweet elixir."

The voices came from the opposite side of the enclosure, where a shadow detached itself from the wall. It lumbered toward me, eventually materializing as a person with form and mass. "I'm no ghost," it said, anticipating the thought that ran through my mind, "but I'm still dead."

"We all are," said the owner of the second voice. "Hurts like hell too. Even her elixir don't do nothing to fix the pain." He moved no closer. As my vision adjusted more to the darkness, I could see why. Vines and branches had grown around him, pinning him to the wall.

"Elixir?" I asked.

"What she uses to wash down the food she forces us to eat," the first one said. Unlike his companion, he seemed to have freedom of movement. He moved in close enough for me to smell the fetid odor of his breath. He laughed when I recoiled. "She carries it in a bucket. It's full of blood. Her blood."

"I refuse to take another sip," the other said.

"We all refuse," said the first. "That's why she brought you."

"Me?"

"You," said the second. He shook the vines that held him bondage as if to test their strength. As if he intended to come after me and do me harm. "She's chosen you to be her night watchman. She's getting weaker. She can't hold us here much longer. She intends to use you."

The other one laughed without humor. "I know my sins. A minister tried to absolve me once. Said the blood of the lamb would wash away the sins. But it didn't work. The lamb was no good. Now I bathe in the blood of the goat."

"What did you do?"

The unabsolved sinner either misunderstood my question or simply wanted to avoid it. He pointed at the ground near my feet.

"That's him there. The minister."

I looked down and saw them. Human remains scattered at my feet. Bones with clinging bits of dried flesh and a grinning skull topped with a wig of moss. The eyes of the skull reflected my own face, and it took me a moment to realize why. Perversely, the skull still wore a pair of round silver-rimmed glasses.

"He might be able to absolve you, though," the second one said. "Especially if you do what needs to be done."

"Do it without fear or shame," said the first. He pushed aside what looked like an old bed frame. I wondered how many travelers actually found their way here before it became this.

And how many were still here.

The bed frame's upheaval revealed something of interest to the tortured soul. He lifted it from the ground and presented it to me. At first, I mistook it for a snake and lurched away from him, prompting laughter when I fell on my ass. "It's only a rope, you coward."

He loomed over me with the rope in his hands. In the uncertain light, it seemed to writhe in his hands.

"Was the preacher's own rope," he said. "Sturdy, strong, and blessed in the glory of the lamb." He extended his arm so that I could take the rope. It ended in a noose. "In his name."

"In his name," repeated his bound companion with surprising conviction.

"I'll trade redemption for freedom, though," said the first. "As her night watchman, you can help us put this where it belongs: around her neck."

Already, I felt my sanity teetering, and the thought that they wanted me to slip that noose around someone's neck left me reeling. I heard laughter and wondered where it came from before finally recognizing it as my own.

"You want me to hang a ghost," I said. "A phantom."

"A spirit," said the first. "One that uses heathen magic. That's how she gets inside you."

"Gets inside me?"

But he delayed answering, his attention having shifted to something else on the ground. He bent at the waist, and when he straightened, I saw that he held an object crafted out of tiny branches and packed mud. It formed a head, torso, and limbs. Over time, I would find many of these objects myself, their precise function a mystery, though I speculated they were types of fetish objects. Eventually, I came to theorize that the whole building constituted a larger version of the same sort of thing. Seen from the air, I speculated that the amalgam of natural growth forming around the building would suggest some sort of design, an arrangement of trees and vines that served some sort of magic.

He tore the head off the fetish object and tossed it into a corner. "How else do you think you'll serve as her night watch?" he said, finally answering my question. "She'll move you like a puppet." He held forth the now-headless object. "Doing this makes her weaker."

"So he says," interjected the second one.

"*It makes her weaker,*" the first repeated, enunciating each word forcefully. "And we want her weak, but not *too* weak. She needs to be strong enough to get inside you without overpowering your will. That's when you exert control and do your part."

"My part?" I said, moments away from the first of my many failed attempts to run away from this place. "What is *my part?*"

They responded with laughter, cruel and without a hint of mercy.

"To put your head inside that noose," said the second one when the laughter finally ended.

"Do what we all tried to do before," said the other one. "All of us, including the preacher. But do it right this time. End her for good so we can finally leave this hell."

Sixteen

Professor Dash ended his story there, his body slumping as if the effort left him winded. Haggard, sick, and likely insane, he looked like a thousand-year-old leper. Except in his eyes. There, a glimmer of light remained, a hope that we would see what his story meant and why he needed all of us there, me, Zach, Erik, and Halia.

And, most of all, Isis.

I studied Halia's expression to see if we shared the same sickening understanding.

She focused on Isis instead. I could hear the librarian muttering under her breath. A chant of some kind? A prayer? I couldn't tell until I leaned closer to take her hand. Only then did I hear the words.

"Baby girl, whatever's got you in its clutches, you need to make it let go. Fight it."

Thunder answered, shaking the ancient boards under our feet. They labored in their rot, our weight causing them to bow, dying to surrender and let the earth below swallow us up. Isis peered at us with feral cunning. She cocked her head, twin candle flames reflected in eyes dilated into total blackness. Or maybe they'd filled with blood. Halia's voice continued to beckon her into ridding herself of what held her in thrall, ignoring the truth of the evidence before us.

That Isis welcomed her rider, just as she loved slipping into the skin of the wolf.

I tried to imagine the sensation and what it offered her. Freedom? Escape? I spent so much time locked within my own self that I couldn't imagine how that could feel.

She must have sensed the question in my gaze because she answered—again in my mother's voice and in the language I alone understood.

"This is not the time for jealousy, my sweet pea. I know you craved closeness and connection. That's not what this is. This doesn't replace anything between us."

"What is it then?" I asked. I tasted tears before I even knew I was crying.

"What? What's she saying?" Professor Dash found the energy to stand. He leaned against the table.

"That man," my mother said, "is a fool. He wants me to put a noose around my own neck. He thinks that will end the curse that hangs over this place. He thinks it will set everything right so that he can just walk away from here. But let me tell you, he does not know what he's messing with. He does not understand it. There is an angry spirit here. A hungry one. He thinks violating it will make it go away and release him."

"I need to know what she's saying," Professor Dash said, still without a clue that an altogether different spirit rode Isis.

Still wielding Halia's bat, Zach shifted his weight nervously, the signs of leprosy palpable on his face. How much time before it infected the rest of us? Erik stepped closer to me, and I felt the weight of my responsibility for him.

Then he said something that caused my heart to sink.

"Mom?"

That single syllable hung in the air. For what felt like an eternity, no one moved or said a word. Even Isis seemed to hold her breath.

Professor Dash finally broke the silence.

"Why did you call her that?"

My arm circled Erik's shoulders. I pulled him closer to me. "He didn't call her anything."

"No, I heard him." Then he moved with a quickness none of us expected, hoisting himself upright and reaching for the back of Erik's neck with a clawlike hand.

"Let go of him," I said. I tried to make myself an obstacle, but he pushed back at me with strength I thought he lacked. I heard Halia call out, followed by the sound of her struggling with Zach again.

"Say it!" said Professor Dash.

"Mom," Erik said through gritted teeth. Not a question this time.

"No. *No.* That's not who she is. What you need is a history lesson."

Erik tried to twist away from his grip. He sucked air through his teeth and regarded Professor Dash with an expression of pure loathing. My sweet, sweet baby brother transformed into someone who would happily murder Professor Dash for that assault, and I would happily offer my assistance.

"Be smart," said my mother through the mouth of Isis.

I drew in a breath and nodded. "Bon Manman," I said, "that's what she was called."

From outside came the sound of thunder, and above us, what remained of the rafters groaned and leaked. The building itself seemed to tilt like a wounded ship about to sink into the sea.

Seventeen

Bon Manman's Narrative

Eventually, she knew, they would come for her.

When exactly, she couldn't predict. She just hoped they wouldn't choose a good day to ruin. For such a feckless thing, time certainly demanded a great deal of attention in this world. In return, it only caused problems, inconveniences.

It certainly didn't start off like a good day. One of the women who lived with her woke up with fever—Beatrix, who never let a good party pass her by and already feared she would miss the next one.

"You always say we have to live for the good times," said Beatrix, "so I need to get better."

Bon Manman wiped the sweat from her brow. "You just like Robert and want him all to yourself. You're possessive."

"I like his *singing*," Beatrix said. Then she shivered despite the warm air coming through the window.

"We all do. You think he's singing just for you? I'll bet that's news to him."

Robert showed up on foot with a cigarette dangling from his mouth and a guitar hanging from his shoulder. He'd heard of the Bloody Bucket and thought it would make a good stop before he needed to start moving on again to his destination—a town somewhere east of them called Eatonville, where he intended to share his story with a budding writer there. Bon Manman had not heard of the writer—Zora something—and at first glance, she didn't think much of Robert either. But once he started strumming his guitar and singing, his voice did the impossible and made the strawberries she mixed with the liquor all the sweeter. She just wished the smell of sulphur didn't cling to him quite so much. Still, she let him use one of the beds in the upstairs of the Bloody Bucket and noticed that the smell didn't keep women from trying to join him, including poor, sick Beatrix. In younger times, Bon Manman herself might have left her own shoes under that bed. Even now, she had a certain notion.

But that smell.

He noticed her wrinkling her nose at one point and apologized. "You try washing it out?" she asked.

He nodded. "Doesn't do any good. Ever since that man I told you about taught me to play, it's stuck to me."

During his stay at the Bloody Bucket, matches became scarce. They went through them quickly since the smell of burning proved the one sure thing that could mask the smell. But every time someone ignited one of the matches, Robert looked uncomfortable. Thinking that he felt self-conscious about his odor, Bon Manman assured him that nobody meant anything by it.

"It's not that," he said. "It's just that it reminds me of where I'm going."

Bon Manman thought she knew what he meant, but she pretended that she didn't. "Where do you mean? A match factory?"

"No," he said, his voice maintaining a somber politeness. Then he pointed down to his feet.

Bon Manman still acted as if she didn't know what he meant.

Robert shook his head. "Don't make me say it out loud. Someday, those hounds chasing me will finally catch up and drag me off."

Bon Manman planned to make an offering in his name that day, but first, she needed to do something about Beatrix's fever. She didn't want it spreading through the Bloody Bucket.

"You drink what I prepared for you," she said to Beatrix, knowing that her friend would turn up her nose.

"It tastes like swamp," Beatrix said.

Perhaps true. After all, the fever came from the swamp, and to the swamp

Bon Manman went for its cure.

She liked her treks there. She knew where to find footpaths that kept her away from the alligators, not to mention the panthers that liked to feed on deer but wouldn't turn down a meal on two legs when it suited them. Sometimes, she sensed the presence of more elusive creatures, like the wild man covered in hair that left behind large footprints and strange droppings. She knew that so long as she didn't disturb its den, it would leave her in peace, content to study her from a distance.

Not so when it came to other eyes. She didn't trust those eyes, the ones that belonged to the preacher and his flock. They liked to spy on her, and then on Sunday morning, they told colorful tales about the special rites she practiced. It amused Bon Manman to hear these accounts from Beatrix, who still attended the preacher's services. "I only go so I can find out what they say about you."

She waved away the girl's excuse, tired of explaining that her beliefs and practices did not conflict with the preacher's—at least not entirely. "It's all part of the same mystery," Bon Manman said, "but it's your time, and you can use it or waste it as you see fit." *There I go again*, she thought, *musing again on time.*

Undaunted, Beatrix said, "They say you take off your clothes."

Bon Manman nodded. "Well, I might do that now and then."

"Then they say you get down on all fours and wait for the one they call 'the Adversary' to float down out of the sky and mount you from behind."

Bon Manman found that amusing and wondered out loud if her sagging backside could still appeal to the Prince of the Air. Maybe a few decades ago. She'd never met him personally, at least as best she could recall. She'd met some of his deputies and lieutenants, and they all went by different names. She'd even witnessed them inhabiting bodies on various occasions, depending upon the type of offering used, and she'd seized upon the opportunity to speak to them personally. But she'd never had any desire to fornicate with any of them.

Overhearing this conversation, Robert offered his own observation. "The one I met was all business, but he certainly had his predilections and appetites."

Beatrix cocked an eyebrow. "You fornicate with him?"

He winked at her. "I just got music lessons."

"Well, he's a fine teacher, then."

Bon Manman laughed too, but her thoughts returned to the preacher. He encouraged the stories about her because he wanted his flock to regard her as evil and heretical. That way, he could easily manipulate them into doing what he wanted done.

Such as taking the Bloody Bucket away from her.

She oversaw its construction herself, though she'd had help, sometimes in the form of human hands, but sometimes she received other forms of assistance. Like the spirits that originally led her to this spot. They guided her to the right ground, close to the tallest oak she'd ever seen. They helped her find materials, including the boards and planks that formed the walls and the roof, sturdy enough to contain the music and joy that called out to others for miles and miles. And Bon Manman welcomed everyone—at least the ones with money and who could behave themselves. She even cared for them when they grew sick.

Or she tried to, at least.

She recalled how Beatrix resisted her tea, the girl claiming that she made it too strong.

"Drink it," Bon Manman commanded. "Don't make my work count for nothing."

Remembering how Beatrix flinched, Bon Manman now regretted her tone. Perhaps she could blame the weather for making her feel uneasy, the air humming with the electricity left behind by the thunderstorms that tried to drown the world every day. She noted how rising waters altered the borders of her world with each passing week, the nearby lake's boundaries stretching and spreading, doing its damnedest to engulf everything around it. Even the high ground could become treacherous, and she took care not to join the bodies of the unfortunate things she'd seen floating near her path. A rabbit, a squirrel, even a tiny fox, its teeth bared to the sky in anger. It hurt to see such small things suffer, but she would not trade places with any of them for all the world.

Her trek led to the shore of the lake, where she made offerings to La Sirene, a water spirit who migrated there from the sea after hearing the music and joy coming from the walls of the Bloody Bucket. She transported these offerings in a simple pail, and in return, she only asked that La Sirene give her fair warning of when the preacher would finally make his move.

Her pail contained a portion of what she served in the Bloody Bucket, its deep red color the sources of that name. Everyone who tasted it knew the sweetness it left on the tongue and lips as well as how just a few sips could make you feel higher than the tallest tree. It never made anyone mean or violent. It might cause you to crave a little too much affection sometimes, but only someone like the preacher would see that as a bad thing.

She knew that he sent people to spy on her on her as she poured the contents of her pail into the water and how their accounts became the source of wild rumors, such as how tiny legs and feet floated in her pail, wrested from the wombs of ailing mothers. Make no mistake, she knew how to care for the women who sometimes came to her in times of crisis, but she did so with discretion and didn't make a show of such things.

No, she just wanted to offer a prayer to La Sirene and maybe receive something in return.

If not protection, then a warning, perhaps? Guidance?

Spirits didn't always make the best guides. Sometimes, she needed to let her own two feet judge the way for themselves. To make matters worse, some spirits liked to deceive.

* * *

Once, when she first came to the place where the Bloody Bucket would eventually stand, she heard something calling to her from well beyond the swamp, further south, where rivers of grass stretched for an eternity. Along the way, she'd heard stories about an old, lost ship that still floated ghostlike in the most hidden recesses of the sawgrass pools, occasionally revealing its rotting masts and decaying hull to surprised onlookers. No one could agree upon that ship's origins—Spanish, according to some, while others insisted that it belonged to a Dutch trader, allegedly lifted by a giant wave at the behest of a dark magician. This wave carried it over the land, well beyond the sea where it belonged, and now it was damned to float crewless and lost. Some said that to see it meant good fortune would come your way. Others said that curses followed anyone who beheld it.

Bon Manman decided she would brave that curse so she could set eyes on it for herself.

It contained a lot more than a curse, as it turned out.

As she finished pouring the contents of her pail, she pondered whether or not La Sirene rode a similar wave. That would explain how she ended up here, well away from her true home, the sea.

Her pail emptied, she turned it over and used it to rest her rump. She listened to the birds as she rolled a cigarette. All around her, life carried on with its usual business. An alligator swam past her, and she thought she recognized it as the same one she saw last week, a monstrous thing with scars crisscrossing its back and a tortoise trapped in its jaws, argument suspended in mid-sentence. She wondered if that beast ever had its meal or if the tortoise managed to escape. Either way, it appeared moody. She looked around to make sure it didn't have its young nearby.

"Don't look at me with those hungry eyes," she warned it when she saw no sign of a nest. "And take your ill temper someplace else." She blew smoke through her nostrils and decided to leave half the cigarette for La Sirene. If she stayed on her good side, maybe La Sirene would provide her with some valuable protection.

But as Bon Manman started to place the cigarette onto a fallen pine she used as an improvised alter, she froze.

She saw someone on the opposite shore of the lake, where the land grew lush and wild.

A young woman. Just standing there, gazing back with the same air of wonder and puzzlement she herself felt. Briefly, she wondered if she beheld La Sirene herself, but the young woman didn't possess the kind of scaly skin that befitted a water spirit. And Bon Manman saw plenty of skin. This trespasser wore not a stitch of clothing.

She suspected that something more than physical distance separated the two of them. What had she said before about time? Here it came again, time rearing its ugly head. Yes, much more than a lake spanned the distance between them, though Bon Manman would probably concede that time had a lot in common with water. Time, like water, tended to slip through one's fingers. Hell, the strange woman even looked like a reflection in the water, a figure consisting of rippling waves. No clouds in the sky here—not yet at least—but over there, the day looked gray and windy. The girl staring back at her from another time even looked soaked to the bone.

Bon Manman held up her free hand and almost waved a greeting before she stopped herself. She sensed no malice in this visitor, but something still felt wrong. Finally, it dawned on her. She realized what the girl intended to do.

Close the distance between them. Bend time to her will.

You do that, and you run the risk of drowning the whole world.

"Oh, no. I won't be a party to that," said Bon Manman, though she doubted the girl could hear her. They existed as little more than spirits to one another. Ghosts. "I'm not passing through any gateway. Not today. No, no, no, no."

Sure enough, the girl held something, and Bon Manman surmised what she intended to do with it before it happened. Whatever that girl held looked small and pathetic. A dead rabbit, maybe? She could almost smell its blood.

Someone had taught the girl how to use that blood in a ritual.

Before Bon Manman could cry out a warning, the girl threw the bloody thing into the water.

A tiny splash from a tiny thing. But a rising wind carried the girl's voice across the lake and time itself, echoing with words in a forgotten language that would cause that splash to become a huge wave that would come crashing down on everything.

A day destined to go bad suddenly became worse. The rising wind turned and lifted Bon Manman off her feet, trying to carry her over the water to where that woman waited.

"No, no, no, no," she said again. It took some fighting, and at one point, she saw water beneath her feet, but she finally won and got the wind to turn back. On dry land again, she cast a final admonishing glance toward the woman and hurried back the way she came. She ignored the complaints of her joints, as well as the ankle that never completely healed from the sprain she suffered from jumping off a moving train. She didn't even stop for the snake that crossed her path, and she paid no mind to the bobcat that tracked her with wily eyes. She wondered what the girl hoped to achieve by doing something so foolish. Did she intend to awaken an unruly spirit?

* * *

Bon Manman knew firsthand that such spirits could not resist an opportunity for mischief. Take that derelict in the swamp, with its broken masts and rotting planks. When she discovered its location, she found herself in awe of how it could remain afloat under the weight of the misery it contained, still traversing hidden waterways with a heap of lost souls trapped within its hull. Most of them victims of kidnapping, longing to escape and return home, where they could finally rest. She'd set herself at a distance, wondering what she could do.

As she sat, a voice entered her consciousness. *Come aboard,* it said. She knew that the voice came from the ship.

"No, thank you," she said aloud. If it just felt lonely and wanted someone to listen to its stories, she'd oblige. But it wanted more than that. What spoke to her would not respect the sovereignty of her existence, a quality that seemed in short supply everywhere she traveled.

The ship barely fit in the narrow channel formed by cypress trees. Spanish moss clung to its splintered wood like a burial shroud. Its bow butted against the shore near her resting spot, as if to nudge her. She detected a whiff of sulphur, a trait not uncommon in the water that bubbled up from the aquifer. But in this case, she knew it came from the trapped occupant aboard the vessel that spoke to her.

What's in your pail? the voice asked.

She lifted the mango she'd found growing in an abandoned row of trees. A feeling of petty meanness came over her, and she used her knife to peel its skin so she could bite into it. She planned on saving it but couldn't resist taunting the trapped thing by indulging in an earthly pleasure.

Is it good?

"Very," she said with her mouth full.

Describe it for me.

She paused to think about it before finally answering. "Sweet." In truth, it tasted a little rotten.

What else is in your pail?

The question hung in the air. She could have answered the truth and cited the strawberries she'd found, the prime ingredient in her special elixir. You could find them growing in the wild if you knew where to look. But she thought of the despair of the ship's other occupants, their long-endured suffering and what she shared with them. "Blood," she said. "I'm carrying blood."

Blood in a bucket, the voice said. *That's what you are. A bloody bucket.*

She'd already risen to her feet and turned when she felt the ground beneath her feet shake. She turned to see that the ship once more butted against the land, this time more insistently. As if on its own, a rope ladder fell from the bow and plodded near where she'd stood a moment ago.

Won't you come aboard? asked the voice.

"I will not," she said, and she resumed walking, the thing still talking behind her.

You could carry me away in that bucket of yours.

But she didn't stop, even though it continued to call after her. *I'll be back,* she quietly vowed to the ship's other occupants. *I'll set you free.*

When she returned to the ship later, she brought along five of the strongest men she could find, all newly arrived on a boxcar traveling on Mr. Flagler's railroad. After agreeing to her terms, they traveled by wagon along the border of what had become known as "the Devil's Garden," an area of dense cypress trees that retreating Seminoles used to shelter from the soldiers hunting for them. At one point, they stopped so that Bon Manman could gather sage, and they heard ghostly war cries coming from farthest reaches of the trees. "Just echoes from the past," she reassured the restless men, though she recognized it as a warning to them to make haste and not to linger. Their trek resumed, and they eventually found that the derelict ship had drifted into another channel, now abutting against a dense group of mangroves.

In the short time since she'd seen it, the ship had incurred even more damage, but it still stubbornly floated on, like something lodged in the guts of a great beast that had swallowed it. A cloud of vapor even hung about the vessel, an ailing digestive system unable to break down an unwanted object. Once again, she marveled at the ship's ability to navigate the narrowest of waterways. Its new position made their job more difficult, but not impossible.

First, she made sure they all had protection against the thing still aboard the vessel. She combined the sage she gathered with tiny bones and placed them into small bags. She gave one bag to each of the men and instructed them to keep those bags on their person at all times. That would insure that unclean spirit on the ship would not use any of them as a means of escape by possessing them.

Thus protected, they all boarded the ship, though Bon Manman needed help from one of the men to get aboard. The planks groaned and wailed under her feet as she instructed the men to begin removing the wood that made up the main deck. Watching the men remove section after section, she determined that she'd judged their strength well. At one point, the rain cooled them, and they even sang songs together as they wrenched away the wood.

Then the unthinkable happened.

The man standing next to Bon Manman, the one who spoke the unfamiliar language, suddenly vanished.

It happened so quickly that it took her a moment to realize that the deck under him collapsed and he'd fallen into the darkness of a lower deck.

At first, they feared him dead, but in short time, they heard him crying out for help, and with the help of a rope, they managed to pull him to safety. To their amazement, he suffered no discernible injuries. But Bon Manman took the accident as a sign that the unclean spirit intended to thwart them. The time had come to leave.

Before returning to dry ground with their takings, she touched the shoulder of the man who'd fallen.

"You still have that bag I gave you?"

Smiling and nodding, he tapped the pocket of his pants.

"Good," she said, not realizing until minutes later that the man seemed to understand her perfectly. Only when they unloaded the wood at the site of what would become the Bloody Bucket did she notice that he no longer cast a shadow. The truth struck her like an arrow. When he fell, he must have lost the protection, and the unclean spirit might have seized on the opportunity to use his body to escape.

Using the planks salvaged from that vessel, she started the construction of the Bloody Bucket, thinking it could serve as a sanctuary for wanderers, both the corporeal and noncorporeal alike. She would even welcome the souls that managed to free themselves from that awful derelict. After all, that was the point of dismantling it. She regretted letting that unclean spirit get away, though. Where it rode off to, she didn't know. It went wherever the foreign-tongued man went, and she never saw him again. Yet she recognized the experience as lesson in humility. She couldn't protect everyone.

Especially herself.

* * *

Hence it came as no surprise when the preacher and his flock finally made their move. She knew she couldn't stop men so practiced in taking what didn't belong to them, so accustomed to seeing the world as rightfully theirs. Maybe that girl standing on the opposite shore set everything into motion by stripping down and performing her ritual.

Either way, it came as no surprise when the walls of the Bloody Bucket came within view and she saw the men waiting.

The preacher's round glasses glinted in the sun. You never could see that man's eyes properly on account of the way those lenses reflected the light. With a Bible gripped in one hand, he held his arms upraised as he intoned a blessing of some sort.

Not that his followers looked like the praying types. Most held firearms. One of them, Bon Manman noted, held a thick coil of rope. That one saw her first. "There she is," he said.

But the preacher didn't stop his praying. His voice only rose as he declared her den of sin a blight in the eyes of the lord, one that they would wash away with the blood of the lamb.

Bon Manman stood apart and assessed her options as the others joined him in intoning amen.

"There she is," the one with the rope repeated.

The preacher hardly glanced her way. Instead, he tucked his bible under one arm and began cleaning his glasses with the hem of his shirt. Bon Manman tried to get a glimpse of the color of his eyes, but they remained downcast. It wouldn't have surprised her to discover that he had empty holes in his face. Maybe that was how all the light managed to flee from him so long ago—they flew out of those holes and left behind nothing but dark pits. He managed to return the glasses without satisfying her curiosity.

Once a sure-footed young woman, Bon Manman would have turned and run in times past. Back when she went by another name, she ran away from who purported to be her father as he horsewhipped her mother to death. At other times, she'd run away from thieves and murderers, devils and demons, even a pack of hounds loosened from the bowels of the earth with glowing embers for eyes. She heard Robert sing a song in the Bloody Bucket that rekindled that last memory, a short blues number about a hellhound on his trail. When Bon Manman heard it the first time, she asked him, "You too?" and he'd nodded sadly before explaining that this particular hellhound never stopped chasing him and wouldn't give up until it latched its jaws on his throat and shook him to death.

It occurred to Bon Manman as she regarded the throng of the preacher's men standing near the Bloody bucket that she'd been running from that preacher her whole life. Now, she'd grown tired of running.

Still, she wondered if the Bloody Bucket had emptied out like she told them to when this day came. Run clear of the place, she told everyone. Don't look back. She thought about borrowing a page from the preacher's book and warning them that they might turn into a pillar of salt, but that seemed all too dramatic, not to mention unlikely. They could do their worst to her, but she didn't want anyone else getting hurt. One gun in the whole place, and only she knew its hiding place.

Too bad she didn't have it on her now.

But then she saw Beatrix in the crowd, her arms held behind her by one of the preacher's own sons. One of her eyes appeared swollen and shut, and blood ran from her nose and over her mouth. Tears streamed from her good eye. She still wore her underthings. They didn't even allow her the dignity of getting dressed.

Bon Manman struggled to hide the swell of distress she felt. She didn't want to give these men the satisfaction of her despair. She took three steps closer. "Make you a drink, preacher? We can talk inside."

"I'll have none of your heathen potions, you vile creature." The preacher's tone sounded casual. He maintained the demeanor of a man commenting on the weather. His glasses fogged, but he didn't clean them this time. She wondered how he even saw anything. Holes for eyes, she reminded herself. "You're not the rightful owner of this land. All you've done is pollute it. It's time we washed it clean of you."

Bon Manman sniffed in contempt, hoping that it conveyed a lack of fear. She continued her march forward, all the while alert for something she could use to cause a commotion, something to buy enough time for Beatrix to break free and run.

But the girl already looked defeated. Her body trembled as if the ground shook beneath her feet.

"Just let her go," said Bon Manman. "You scared her enough."

She recalled how she liberated Beatrix from a bootlegger in Ybor City. The bootlegger, a Mr. Charlie Wall, came to Bon Manman because he needed a curse lifted, one of his own making. The ghost of a man he killed haunted an underground tunnel where he stored his merchandise, causing all that good liquor to turn into spoiled milk. To make matters worse, none of his men would venture down into that tunnel because the sight of the ghost was such an awful thing to behold, its face nothing but a hole thanks to the close-range rife blast that killed him. Bon Manman harbored no fear of such things, so she agreed to go into the tunnel and convince the ghost to move on. A difficult thing to do because once a ghost becomes set on revenge, hardly anything will convince it to just up and leave. It takes some powerful persuasion. But Bon Manman knew what to say. She could hardly bear to look upon the ghost, thanks to its lolling tongue, the only intact feature that remained of its mouth, but the ghost listened and found a new place to haunt. Hence, thanks to her effort, movement of contraband resumed in the tunnel, which made the bootlegger happy. As payment, he insisted that she take several cases of his best Canadian whiskey. Later, she found that this whiskey mixed well with some molasses and strawberries, but at the time, she didn't feel so agreeable. She insisted that Mr. Wall also let her have Beatrix, at the time a hospitality worker in one of the man's speakeasies and a frequent victim of mistreatment. When Mr. Wall balked at the demand, Bon Manman started walking away, but not before mentioning that leaving her dissatisfied meant risking the ghost would return to haunt the tunnel once more.

"Very well," said Mr. Wall, "I suppose I got plenty of whores. This one's useless anyway."

Tired of beatings and broken noses at the hands of men in Ybor City, Beatrix wasted no time in packing her things. "Never worked for a woman before," she said, "but I'm sure it beats this."

Mr. Wall overheard this remark and stiffened. Bon Manman wondered if either of them would make it out alive. Instead, he smiled and shook his finger at them.

"You know what the Cubans call me, don't you?" he asked.

If Beatrix knew, she didn't answer. Bon Manman said she had no idea. She cared to know nothing more about this man. She wished she'd never met him.

"El Sombre Blanco," said the bootlegger. "The White Shadow. You best remember that. Because my shadow extends *everywhere*. Anywhere you go, you still fall under me."

Now, as the preacher's men gripped her tightly by the arms and with Beatrix sobbing next to her, she wondered if she took Mr. Wall too lightly. Maybe she really did fall under that white shadow, the preacher himself just an extension of it. She felt no regret for herself but only for Beatrix. The freedom she secured for her turned out only temporary.

"Let this woman go," said Bon Manman to the crowd gathered near the Bloody Bucket. "What crime has she committed?"

"Associating with you is crime enough. We know what sort of business takes place in your establishment. People can hear the cries of the unborn coming from the lake at the midnight hour. That correct, Eustis?"

The one called Eustis came to her door quite often, drawn by the music from within. He stood outside, then begged for admittance, but Bon Manman had seen the injuries he inflicted upon the women he'd lain with and barred his way. "Yessir, that's correct," said Eustis. He breathed through his mouth, and even with some distance, Bon Manman could smell his rankness.

Bon Manman scanned the faces of the crowd and noticed a few women, noting in their expressions a lust for violence that, in some cases, exceeded that of the men. One of those faces belonged to the preacher's unwed daughter. The daughter met her gaze briefly before turning away. Bon Manman knew worry when she saw it. Not worry for Bon Manman and Beatrix but worry for herself.

Bon Manman understood the source of that worry. She could tell everyone now about the time the preacher's daughter came to her in secret, desperate for help. Bon Manman couldn't turn away a woman in need, especially when she divined the truth—that the father was the preacher himself. When she brought the remains of what the preacher planted in the womb of his own daughter to the water's edge, she asked La Sirene to adopt whatever soul might have followed it. She knew an abandoned spirit could become angry and pollute whole tracts of land.

She sought eye contact with the preacher's daughter, wanting to assure her she wouldn't reveal her secret. But the other woman now avoided her direction.

As for Eustis, she doubted he really heard anything. He just told the preacher what he wanted to hear.

"Who has the rope?" asked the preacher.

The man with the coiled rope held it up for the preacher to see.

"Throw it over yonder oak," the preacher said. "That branch there. You see the one I mean?"

The man didn't move at first. He studied the rope in his arms as if he couldn't discern how it worked. Bon Manman knew this one too. He'd taken a shine to Beatrix at one point, a fact likely unknown to the preacher.

"You don't have to do anything that man says, Donald." She hoped by using the man's name, she could appeal to his better self. "He worships a bitter god."

"That god will wash your sins away, Donald. Do what I say."

Donald shifted his attention from Bon Manman to the preacher. Back and forth like that, two or three times, as if he couldn't decide what to do.

"Do it," said the preacher, "and the blood of the lamb shall be your reward."

Donald nodded and resumed movement, the preacher's words like a magic spell. One of his legs stopped growing at the age of twelve, so Donald walked with a distinctive limp. His neck bore lesions that Bon Manman offered to treat before the preacher warned Donald away from having any contact with her. Only a matter of time, she knew, before those lesions spread to his entire body.

Donald cleared a space in the crowd and made a feeble attempt to throw one end of the rope toward one of the tree's sturdier branches. After three unsuccessful tries, the preacher said, "He needs something to stand on. John Lee, may we use your wagon?"

John Lee saluted like a military officer, and with the help of two men, he moved his wagon so that its back end sat under the branch. Everyone watched as Donald climbed aboard. His shorter leg meant that the act required more time and labor. Once standing atop the wagon, it still took him more than one try with the rope. When the third attempt proved successful, even he looked surprised. Bon Manman expected applause.

"The noose now," said the preacher.

"He don't know how to tie knots," said the man still holding Beatrix. "Let me do it."

He must have loosened his grip because Beatrix suddenly moved. How she'd managed to hide the gun wearing those scant underthings, Bon Manman had no idea, but that pistol Bon Manman had hidden away instantly appeared out of nowhere and in Beatrix's hand.

She pulled the trigger, and the air exploded.

Yelping in pain, the preacher hunched over, his arms too late in shielding his head.

Good, thought Bon Manman, *you got him. Now run away and don't look back.*

But instead of running, Beatrix pointed the gun at the man who, a moment ago, held her by the arm. Again, she pulled the trigger, but no explosion this time. Just a click. She'd already fired the only bullet in the chamber.

Having regained his senses, the preacher's son snatched the gun from her grip and threw it onto the ground.

"Just for that, she's first," said the preacher. He stood upright again, now with his hand pressed against his ear. Blood trickled between his fingers. "The lord preserved me and my ear," he said to his astounded followers. "His miracles show no bounds. Thanks to His intervening hand, the bullet only grazed me. 'Tis nothing but a scratch."

Standing on the wagon, Donald gazed upon the preacher in wonder, the un-noosed rope still in his hand.

"Donald," said the preacher, "you come down here and switch places with my son. He knows how to tie a noose."

Donald continued to stare at the preacher, and for a moment, Bon Manman wondered if he'd resist. "You'll wash my sins away?" Donald finally asked.

The preacher nodded. He held out a bloody hand. "With this blood I shed for you."

Donald grunted in agreement and climbed down to relieve the other man of his burden. "Damn simpleton don't know how to tie," the preacher's son said under his breath as he let go of Beatrix and began forming the dangling rope into a noose.

It took him a while. The empty gun lay in the dirt like a headless snake. Despite the blood running down the length of his neck, the preacher appeared unfazed. He leaned over and lifted the gun so he could examine it.

"Wasn't even hers," said Bon Manman. "It's mine. It was my fault she had it. Show some mercy and let her go."

"Was the lord's mercy I survived." He opened the chamber, and out fell another bullet. "Praise Jesus the hammer didn't fall on that one."

"She was just scared," she said. "Please."

"Caught up in the web of your sin. She has to pay." To his son, he asked, "All done?"

"All done."

"Okay then. Donald? Quite your sniveling and get her up there."

"I want to do it," said Eustis. "Let me do it."

"Okay, then," said the preacher.

"You leave her alone." Bon Manman heard a foreign note in her own voice. It sounded like pleading. For the first time in her life, she felt truly helpless as Eustis dragged Beatrix to a standing position on the flat of the wagon. The woman sobbed as Eustis tightened the noose around her neck.

His face twisted in disgust. "She pissed herself."

"Just make sure it's tight. Donald, help him out."

"The blood of the lamb?" asked Donald.

"The blood of the lamb."

Donald used his sleeve to wipe away snot and obliged. Then he and Eustis climbed down from the wagon, leaving Beatrix standing alone. They didn't need instructions on what to do next. Together, they rolled back the wagon so that Beatrix's feet dangled above the earth. Her body jerked and shook before finally going still. For a time, they all watched her sway there in the rising wind. A gap in the branches allowed in enough light to cast her dangling form into a shadow on the ground.

That shadow continued to writhe and struggle for air long after its owner expired. It wouldn't have surprised Bon Manman if that shadow remained there for generations to come. It would never stop struggling, for the pain of unjust death was eternal.

To her executioners, it appeared that Bon Manman kept her eyes downcast out of shame.

No, she simply couldn't tear her eyes away from that shadow on the ground.

She didn't even look up when she overheard talk of setting up a camera. *So we can preserve this moment for posterity,* someone said.

Bon Manman wondered then if no one else could see the shadow. They didn't need to take a photograph, not when that shadow bore testimony to the pain they caused. Touch it, and it would stain your fingers. But let them take their photograph. Someday, it would serve as a curse to their descendants. They would hide from it in shame, and that curse, too, would seep into the land like poison, just like that shadow she now beheld.

When it came her turn to wear the noose, she considered using her last breath to bestow that curse upon them, to give it shape and form so that they would know it and recognize it. Didn't accused witches always do that before the hangman completed his work? Claim responsibility for all misfortune that would follow?

Nah, not her. These people were their own misfortune. They would have to face the fruits of their own evil. It wouldn't come from her. It would come from themselves.

As if in agreement, the wind intensified while they carried out their work, blowing in hot and angry from the west, and the clear sky quickly filled with clouds.

"Look at that," someone said, "we best hurry. It's about to turn ugly."

No sooner did he speak those words than the rain began to fall, though it brought no relief, raindrops sizzling on the earth like water from a boiling kettle. Maybe these men didn't realize it, but as she stood upon the wagon, Bon Manman knew. Without her offerings, La Sirene would become angry and eventually fill this land with stinging water, wash away whatever these men hoped to build, drowning them and all who came after.

Without warning, the wagon abruptly moved, and her feet suddenly became free of the earth, as if floating. Though her air constricted, she was surprised to feel no pain.

Another unexpected thing occurred as her last thoughts drifted, settling on the memory of that strange naked figure she saw on the opposite shore of the lake and that sad, bloody thing tossed into the water. She'd encountered many phantoms in her lifetime, but she'd never seen one like that. It struck her that she'd not only witnessed a scene from the future but that it constituted a message, an attempt to communicate with her personally. In Bon Manman's experience, the dead sometimes still had useful things to say. Perhaps that included her. Perhaps even in death, hers would remain a necessary presence in this beautiful, cursed place, and maybe she should work out a way to stay around in case someone like that misguided woman—not much older than a child, really—happened to need her.

Funny, then, that even with the rain coming down heavy and blistering and bringing no relief, another shadow formed on the ground below next to Beatrix's. Her own.

And though it didn't continue to writhe like the one cast by her friend, hers did another curious thing.

It formed wings and flew away.

Eighteen

There.

I said it.

Bon Manman.

The name hung in the air like a guilty verdict, and Professor Dash, our Grand Inquisitor, made me say it like an obedient puppet.

"It's time for the rope, Zachary," he said. "It's time to end this once and for all. I have classes to teach, duties to perform."

He placed his hands on the table to support himself as he rose again. Until then, I'd not realized how tall he stood, even with a back curled into a noticeable hump, as if he'd spent far too long gazing into a crystal ball. He looked like an animatronic Halloween decoration struggling to work after years of disuse. I gasped out loud, prompting him to face me with a ghastly smile of satisfaction.

"Fowler thought he could find someone to replace me. A delusion, obviously, especially if he chose someone like you."

"Someone *like me?*" My cheeks burned from a rush of blood. His words seemed to trigger something in Isis too. Her pupils vanished, leaving just the whites. Did my mother still inhabit her body? I couldn't tell, and that wrecked me. I would never talk to her again, and I wanted to hear her voice one last time. That woman who broke my heart and left me all too early. A different sound came from her lips then, a low growl from the back of her throat. Not a language, at least not one that I recognized, but something elemental, loosened from deep within the earth, ancient roots breaking free of the soil. The rumble of forgotten rivers hidden underground rising and pushing to the surface. A vocabulary that preceded memory rising forth like a tidal wave. It stirred something in me, gave me the words I needed.

"You don't know me," I said to Professor Dash. "Our lives, our stories—you don't know them. They don't belong to you. Our *bodies* don't belong to you."

Would my mother have felt pride hearing me say those words, that woman who kept her own story to herself, never willing to share it with the person who craved to hear it the most? To fill the void she left, I sought the stories of others, narratives that might contain traces of her.

Including the one still in my hand. The one Lenny Engel said I would eventually need.

You'll know when the right moment arrives, he'd said to me.

That moment arrived with the appearance of the dead crow, its frame crawling with maggots but still managing to defy gravity with skeletal wings. It coasted majestically before landing on the table Professor Dash used to support his bowed frame. With a single fogged eye that still conveyed uncanny intelligence, the crow regarded me before turning its attention to Professor Dash.

He hesitated as he struggled to place this creature in the crumbling order of things. Meanwhile, the low growl coming from Isis intensified, her lips spreading further. The old wooden boards under our feet began to shake, making standing difficult. The bird opened its beak as if to imitate her, and the cacophony rose even higher. Outside, the rising torrent of wind and rain pounded the roof, testing the integrity of this aged structure.

"I'm standing in water," Erik said.

I looked down and saw that I was too. We all stood in water. It ran down from the rafters while also seeping up from the floor below, as if the building had come unmoored and now drifted on the high seas, nowhere near seaworthy.

"Zachary," said Professor Dash, using the table to brace himself as the building began to tilt, "use your bat to kill this thing."

"*My bat*, you bastard," said Halia. She lunged, but the building's tilt sent her sideways instead.

The candle holder slid across the table, but the crow wouldn't budge. It stood steadfast, challenging Zach to do his worst. Zach hesitated, his brain already taxed by having to follow two commands. Hang Isis, kill the crow. The building tilted again, this time in the other direction as if waves lolled beneath the floor.

The candle reversed direction, now sliding off the table. It landed in standing water, its flame going out with a hiss. The lightning from outside illuminated the strange stand-off between Professor Dash and the crow.

"Smash it, Zachary. Hurry, so we can hang the girl and end this."

That achieved the reaction he wanted. Zach lifted the weapon and prepared to bring it down.

"No!"

That plea came from Erik, no longer the kid who once chased the bird around a darkened house with a fly swatter but now its defender. His cry proved enough to distract Zach, giving Halia an opportunity to get back to her feet and make her move.

"That's *mine*," she said, grappling for control of the bat and causing Zach's swing to go wide. He struck the table with enough force to split its wood but brought no harm to the crow.

Forced into flight, the crow aimed its beak at Professor Dash's face.

As Halia and Zach grappled, it went for the man's eyes.

Professor Dash shrieked and tried to defend himself, but death only seemed to make the bird more relentless. Fresh blood streamed down his face.

Meanwhile, the low drone coming from Isis's throat grew deeper, more intense. Her jaw unhinged like a cobra preparing to feast.

I remembered Lenny Engel's instructions. At the time, I had no idea how I could accomplish it.

"You'll recognize the moment when it arrives. What sounds impossible will become quite doable," he'd said to me as he sat at my kitchen table. *"But you'll need the page of a sacred text. One that means something to you. Magic you can trust and believe in."*

I'd asked him what he meant. As an answer, he showed me an aged scrap of paper with a scribbled passage in Latin. *"The scripture I was given to feed Gustav. You'll need to do the same with Isis, though I hope you'll choose a more reliable text. Something less orthodox. Perhaps this?"* He'd tapped Professor Dash's copy of *Tell My Horse*, perhaps noticing how close I'd kept it to myself. *"A special page, maybe?"*

I opened the book. No, the book opened itself. It opened for me. It knew before I did the page I needed. The twelfth chapter. Page 133. The story of La Gonave, the whale that became the island home to Cilla as it transported her sleeping body across the sea. The story's beauty remained fresh in my mind, having read it aloud to Erik not long ago.

"Look at it closely," Lenny had said. *"What else does it say?"*

Something else on the page spoke to me, a kind of magic hovering around the edges. I could sense it. Stubbornly, it wouldn't reveal itself.

"Relax your eyes. Let it materialize on its own."

I did what he said. My eyes lost focus, and the words seemed to move through a will of their own, rearranging themselves on the page.

Until I finally saw it.

I needed a marker—quickly, before I lost it. I almost knocked over my chair as I resituated myself, using the marker to blacken out some words while leaving others, my intuition determining each decision. Eventually, a series of black streaks ran across the page, allowing the important words and phrases to stand out. They formed a jagged message, one that revealed itself first to my unconscious mind. The scattered arrangement of letters read:

————————————————————————————————————*a*—————
woman————————————————————————————————————
————————————————————————————————————*prayed*
——*for*——————————————————————————————————
————————*invocations*——————————————————————
to——————————————————————————————————————
————————————————*transport her*———————————
——*to*————————————————————————*safety*———
so quickly——————————————*that*———————————————

she——————————————dared———wake——————-

A poem, an incantation buried in the page, waiting for me to find it. One that, with any luck, would perform the magic I needed when the right moment arrived.

And that moment, with Halia struggling with Zach and Isis's mouth widening unnaturally like she wanted to swallow the sea, finally arrived.

I tore the marked page from the book, so hastily I feared that I left out some of the words I needed. No time to make sure, not with everything happening at once. The building itself began to come apart, and the water around our feet was rising faster, as if the floor itself had begun to sink.

Halia swore and called out for me to help her, but I had no time to spare. I crumbled the page in my fist and fed it into Isis's waiting mouth. As I did so, I recited the incantation.

"A woman prayed for invocations to transport her to safety, so quickly that she dared wake." After that, I recited it again, shouting each word into Isis's face, calling upon her to return, to claim herself. Every word I spoke was a plea for her to awake and for whatever possessed her to relinquish control of her body. But Isis snarled and snapped at my fingers, an angry, feral thing of the wilderness. Big and white, her teeth rended the page to shreds, and the portions that fell, I fed back into her mouth, even if I didn't know if it would work. Not when I just had Lenny Engel's word to depend upon.

Something tugged at my hair, and I turned to see Professor Dash's bony arms extended across the table. Though sightless now, his hand found me, and I felt his fingernails press into my scalp. Blood streamed from empty eye sockets. "Leave her. She's mine," he said.

Erik grabbed me, kept me from losing my balance and falling into the water that continued to rise around us. From somewhere close came a crashing sound, unleashing a torrent of wind and rain into our faces. I clawed at the professor's fingers, trying to pry myself loose.

He only let go when the floor beneath us finally gave way.

Everything collapsed, and we fell.

All of us.

Later, Erik would liken it to a huge drain. "It sucked us all down. I saw you force-feeding Isis what looked like wadded up paper with that guy trying to grab you. Then you were suddenly gone. Almost immediately, I felt my nose filling with water. It felt like a . . . like a . . ."

"Whirlpool?" I said.

"Yeah, that's it, a whirlpool."

A Poe story I read as a kid came to mind, "A Descent into the Maelstrom." Poe's narrator described himself clinging to a barrel as his ship broke apart in such a monstrous vortex. The experience turned his hair white, but at least he survived to tell his story.

Likewise, I survived, as did Erik. But not all of us did, not with that building coming apart around us, its aging boards and beams snapping like twigs as the vortex formed around us.

"And then," Erik later said, "I got of a glimpse of that . . . thing."

I caught more than a glimpse. Its massive tail propelled its body against the direction of this vortex that remained determined to suck down the entire world. Not that reptilian beast, though. As it surged by, its great eye managed to find me, sizing up the sort of meal I would make. In that brief instant, I sensed a brooding intelligence that felt all too human.

Gustav.

I would have spoken his name, acknowledged his lordship over this domain, but I couldn't afford the air it would cost me. No time for a big breath with the building collapsing. Eventually, my lungs would give up with the water continuing to pull me down further and further into the underworld that lay hidden beneath our feet. With death seeming inevitable, I marveled at the sight of Gustav surging past me, a force of nature deserving of my reverence and worship, his form made visible by refracted bursts of lightning. *This is the way a god demands to be seen*, I thought. If I could have prayed, I would have prayed for him to take us all upon his back and carry us to safety, anywhere, even across the sea.

But he showed no inclination for mercy. He wanted to feed. Just not on a puny morsel like me.

The whirlpool provided something better.

Professor Dash, blind, flailing, and, most of all, defenseless to the jaws of the beast. He could have swallowed him whole, bitten him in half, but Gustav wanted to soften the man's flesh, carry him down deep and let his body moisten and putrefy into a more satisfying meal. His jaws clasping the man's torso, Gustav turned and swam with the current now, the professor's face frozen in sightless horror.

I pitied the man. Truly. And not just because of the unspeakable horror of his fate, but because he would never see the awful magnificence that brought him to his end. Monstrosity shaped into purest, more perfect form.

Me, I would just drown. Or so I thought as I watched it recede into the darkness, me in its wake.

Then a violent tug around my ankle.

I didn't see the rope, also trapped in the jaws of the leviathan. Its noose snagged me, pulling me along with it, carrying me faster now, to a point where darkness spread like the wings of a crow.

Erik witnessed none of that. "I could barely keep my eyes open with all the silt in the water. It's still in my nose. God, I'm going to smell sulphur for the rest of my life." Then he blew into a rag and stared in horror at what came out. I waited for the question I knew would come next. "How you managed to find me is anyone's guess. I still don't know how you pulled yourself out. How did you find that opening?"

"Just luck, kiddo. That's all it was," I said. I hugged him tightly, intending to hold him like that for as long as I could, hoping the silence would help me conceal the lie I'd just spoken.

But Erik pushed himself away and regarded me.

"Seriously," he said, "how? I couldn't have pulled myself up through that crack without your help. How did you do it on your own?"

I smiled and made a show of flexing my muscles. "I'm *strong*. Didn't you know that?"

Erik continued to study me. "No, there's something you're not telling me."

What could I say? Officially, a sinkhole chose that moment to form, thanks to erosion caused by the storm. We'd fallen through a natural cavity in the limestone, and when it filled with water, it drained everything into a subterranean tributary.

"We should have died," Erik said when the silence became too much. "All of us."

I nodded, thinking of how I pulled him up through the crack in the pavilion foundation. All the rain and shifting of land caused it to widen enough for a person to crawl through. Just barely. Miraculously, the underground tributary passed just beneath it, and only by luck did my outstretched hand find Erik's shirt. With sheer will, I managed to pull him up and out through that crevasse.

After that, I needed his help with Halia. At first, we didn't think she would make it through. Only when her head came up sputtering and spitting water did we realize why.

She'd managed to grab hold of Isis.

"I helped out when she was born, you know," Halia told me later. "This experience was like a second go-around, all that pulling and pushing a real group effort. The first time was easier, you know."

What we did took strength and willpower, Halia pushing from below, Erik and I pulling from the top. But up came Isis's limp form, followed by Halia, who barely kept herself from drowning during all the effort.

With Isis, it looked too late. Stretched out on the remains of the foundation, her eyes stared out at nothing, her chest refusing to rise and fall. She appeared dead.

"She came out of my sister like that," Halia later said. "All blue. Even the doctors looked ready to give up. Give her a chance to live, I told them, don't give up. I think I scared them into not quitting. This time, I was the one who was scared, but no way was I going to give Death a second chance. Not on my watch."

Halia went to work performing CPR on Isis, filling her lungs with what little breath she retained and pumping her chest with clasped hands, occasionally calling out to any god in the vicinity with pleas and promises, as well as one or two threats about what would happen if they didn't respond.

Eventually, they did listen. Isis suddenly vomited a stream of foul water, as well as soggy bits of paper. I wondered if they did the work they should have or if I only hastened her near-death experience. I wouldn't know until she could speak. Whose words would we hear? Whose voice? Her own, hopefully.

Other problems demanded my attention. With one of us unaccounted for, my job wasn't finished. I already knew Professor Dash's fate, but what about Zach? I leaned into the darkness of the crevasse, hoping I would see some sign of him. I called out for him and heard only the sound of rushing water in reply.

Behind me, Isis coughed and sputtered. Halia cried with joy. But I felt sick. I wanted to crawl back down after him. I might have done so if not for Erik's hand on my shoulder.

"Don't," he said as if able to read my thoughts. "You're all I have. Don't leave."

Being soaked to the bone couldn't hide the tears. Not for either of us. I held him tight there on the edge of the crevasse, and he held me too. I promised I wouldn't let go of him, and he swore he'd hold on to me, and our sobbing turned into laughter when we heard Isis mutter the first words of her rebirth.

"Worst waterpark ever."

It started slow but grew. The laughter became infectious, all four of us collapsing there into rapturous, relieved laughter until we found ourselves once more gasping for air.

We would have laid there in exhaustion if not for the rising water eventually forcing us to move. It came up through the crevasse and flowed across the remains of the foundation.

"Look." Erik pointed as we dragged ourselves out of the way.

Overhead, the clouds began to part, and by the light of a tired moon, we saw what drew his attention.

The color of the liquid spouting from the scarred earth appeared red.

The land bled.

Buckets and buckets of blood.

Nineteen

I hid away the truth about how I managed to crawl through the crevasse before anyone else. I hated lying to Erik, but I could tell no one what found me in the darkness.

Some of what I said is true. Thanks to sheer desperation to live, I did some of it alone, like freeing myself of the noose. But even that wouldn't have happened if the beast hadn't slowed, allowing the rope to loosen. The rope might have broken free eventually—nothing could survive those jaws, not even that—but by then, I would have drowned. I managed to wiggle myself loose before that could happen, thinking that if I must die, I refused to die while connected to such a vile object. Faint light made it possible, its source unknown, until I saw that Gustav had turned and fixed upon me a single glowing eye.

Once again, I sensed a very human intelligence. The remains of Professor Dash still hung from its jaws, one of his arms floating within a few inches of my face.

Now freed, I had one last task to perform, assuming the beast would let me live. I knew it would cost more precious seconds of air, but that glowing eye made me believe in the possibility that this monster really did house the angry spirit of Lenny Engel's little brother.

And perhaps it wanted me to do something.

I'd lost the book when the floor collapsed, but I still had the fragment of scripture from Engel's storied past. Whether the water ruined its legibility, I didn't know. But if his account contained any truth, it had survived much worse.

"An opportunity will arise," he'd told me. *"When it does, feed it to that monster. Do what I should have done. Then I'll be free of it."*

"What about us? Will we be free of you?"

He'd smiled in a way I didn't find comforting. *"Do it, and you won't ever see me here again."*

I thought about his choice of words. *Here.* Everything he said concealed a potential trapdoor. Maybe not *here,* but another place, another time.

But drowning left little time for such nuances. I pressed the scrap of writing into Professor Dash's hand and closed his dead fingers around it. Not the most reliable delivery system, I know. Kind of like hiding a cat's medicine inside a treat. Besides, I doubted I would live long enough to see if it worked.

With only the vaguest sense of direction, I pushed myself away and let the water have me, watching as Gustav's glowing eye faded into darkness.

That meant I couldn't see the hands that found me, that pulled me gasping and spitting through the crevasse that opened like a gaping wound in the land itself. I couldn't see who reached under my arms to pull me completely free before crawling back into the shadows as I lay upon the concrete, my chest searing from the effort of holding air that long.

When my eyes cleared enough to see, I didn't anticipate what I would see. The shattered, ruined features of Taryn Hall.

No longer confined to mirrors or my imagination, her broken mouth formed the approximation of a sad smile before she scuttled away like a crab into the darkness.

The desperate moments that followed left me with little time to reflect on what that smile meant. Only later could I ponder it.

For so long, I sensed nothing but malice in my visions of Taryn Hall, just resentment at me for ending her life in such an awful way. I'd assumed she appeared in my mirror to torture me, to remind what I'd done in a moment of carelessness. It didn't matter if she appeared as an actual phantom or as a manifestation of my guilt. She felt real enough. Besides, her appearance that night seemed to settle that question.

But why would she save me like that if she meant me nothing but ill will?

I wondered if my death would mean she could no longer torture me. Maybe my death would mean the end of her afterlife. Her revenge would remain unexacted.

Maybe she didn't think I would find the strength to save Erik, Halia, and Isis. Maybe she wanted me to live so I could experience their loss, further evidence of my own ineptitude. Proof I couldn't save anyone.

If so, I foiled her plan.

Or maybe I had it all wrong and her actions signified forgiveness, the very thing I could never grant myself. And if she only existed as a projection of my psyche, did that mean I'd finally given myself that forgiveness?

Maybe. The most potent ghosts haunt our minds, not our houses.

Either way, I stopped seeing Taryn Hall in mirrors after that. Something pierced the veil, allowing her slip away.

That doesn't mean I never saw her again. Not at all. The show, as they say, would go on.

Twenty

Thanks to a generous endowment, the college replaced the pavilion with a new one. It took a rigorous petition campaign led by the students to make it happen. As the petition gathered more steam and signatures, the college finally relented, but it insisted on a compromise: the new pavilion needed to occupy a different space, one closer to the campus buildings. They cited safety as the reason. The real reason, they insisted, had nothing to do with calling attention away from an embarrassing tragedy involving one of the college's most esteemed faculty members.

"I knew he was unstable, but Jesus," Fowler said when we talked about the revelations concerning Professor Dash. "To think he was always right there, not very far away. Who knew?"

"You must have known," I said, "or at least suspected." I pointed out all the talk about the homeless encampment. "It had to be an open secret. Besides, everyone was cagey whenever his name came up. Including you."

Fowler shook his head adamantly enough to leave no doubt that the accusation offended him. "If I knew those woods were thick enough to hide secrets that big, you know how many bodies I'd have disposed of back there?"

My turn to look offended. "Not funny. Seriously, don't go there."

"I meant *student* bodies, but okay."

The destruction that occurred revealed more than the ruins of an old, forgotten building, evidently someone's long-ago pipedream to build a stronghold for white supremacy. The construction materials drew the curiosity of local historians. The fragments they unearthed contained specimens of wood that predated most pioneer settlements in the area. One historian posted about it in her blog, noting curious aspects of the wood, including the fact that it appeared Flemish in origin. She identified it as *Quercus robur*, a type of oak typically used in 15th Century shipbuilding. Another curious aspect went beyond the origin of the wood. "One remaining wall," she wrote, "contains an inscription of sorts. It appears illegible, but if I had to guess, I would say it resembled the name of a sailing vessel."

That revelation didn't surprise me as much as the discovery of human remains.

"Two women," said one forensics expert, "both with broken necks. Lab work will help us determine more about them, like age. But if you ask me, I'd say it looks like a lynching."

When Halia heard about the plans to replace the pavilion, she just shook her head. "They need to devote that space to some kind of memorial. They should put me in charge, goddammit. Who *is* in charge? Names, please, so I can remind them about how the past doesn't vanish simply because you want it to. This is what librarians are for. To keep the assholes from throwing dirt on top of history."

"I expressed the same sentiment to Fowler," I said.

"And what did he say?"

"He shrugged and said something about his hands being tied because it was up to the state."

"Just another pendejo. Then no one remembers—or pretends not to. That's how you get hauntings. You should remind him of that. Ghosts are there to make sure no one forgets. That's what every ghost wants. To insure memory."

"Not everyone believes in ghosts, Halia. For a lot of people, they're just stories."

"Yeah, well, people need stories. Narrative is the lifeblood of everything we know and see. Once upon a time, right?"

Fowler certainly didn't buy the idea that anything supernatural occurred in those woods.

"Nat, I think your chosen area of expertise has left you a bit touched," he said. "I mean, what is it with you SOFA people? You all get a little too immersed, if you ask me, and you forget where to draw the line between the real and imaginary. You start believing that things really do go bump in the night."

"Maybe they do. And you might have a different attitude if you'd experienced what we went through."

He grunted dismissively. "It was all a natural occurrence. When a big storm pushes away water, it comes rushing back eventually, sometimes even a few days later. That's what happened. There were no whirlpools. Just a massive sinkhole. It was just dumb luck you weren't all lost with that student. What was his name?"

"Zach," I said quietly.

"Yeah, well, that has the whole community in an uproar. His whole family goes way back. If anyone gets a memorial out there, it's him. Who knew he was so close to Tom? The whole college is under scrutiny now."

I nodded, sensing what would come next. I didn't want to give him a chance to say what a mistake he made in hiring me, even as a low-wage adjunct. "I'll return the textbooks," I said, "and clear my stuff out by the end of the week."

He stood from his desk, and for a second, I thought he planned to lunge at me. I planted my feet in the defensive posture that my father tried to teach me a long time ago.

Fowler noticed. He held up his hands and tucked down his chin. "Hey, whoa, I was just going to say you don't need to do that."

"I don't?" I maintained the defensive posture.

"No. Jesus. What's wrong with you? That course isn't going away, and someone needs to teach it. That club too. The job's still yours. I'm certainly not doing it. Those students make me itchy. The whole lot of them."

I raised an eyebrow. "What if my terms have changed?"

"Terms? Do they listen to terms at that place that makes shells? Seriously, I don't get that. Don't people know you can find them on the beach for free?"

"They don't make . . ."

But I didn't complete the sentence. Why bother. This man never had to work a retail job in a town that catered to tourists.

He grimaced. "Look, no promises, but with Tom permanently gone, I might be able to justify a real faculty position. You'd have to apply, of course, but it's not like there wasn't an effort to make you feel like an accepted member of the staff."

I stared at him, trying to discern his meaning, and eventually, it dawned on me. "It was you who put that Slashing Sally doll in my office, wasn't it?"

"We'll see if it becomes your office, but yeah, maybe I did. Didn't you like it?"

I didn't answer. I stared at him until he began fidgeting with the papers on his desk.

"I was trying to make you feel at home, for crissakes," he said finally. "You're supposed to be into that scary shit, aren't you?"

"The knife too?" I asked, remembering when that object appeared embedded in the doll.

He looked genuinely bewildered, so I didn't press him further. I turned to leave.

"Natacha?"

The sound of my formal name made me stop. I turned to see what he wanted to say.

"It was just a joke," he said, his voice soft enough to sound almost apologetic.

"Was it also a joke to call my brother?" I described the phone call that led Erik into the woods to look for me.

Fowler's eyes shifted around the room as if in search of a logical answer. "It was probably an automated emergency call, what with everything going on. You know, you agree to receive those calls as part of your employment."

I didn't believe it, but I nodded anyway. "Good to know."

As I turned to leave, I heard his voice one more time.

"You should be thankful, Ms. Miller. People would sacrifice anything to have this kind of job."

I laughed under my breath but didn't turn this time.

"The show must go . . ."
I closed the door before he could finish.

Twenty One

The show did go on.

But not like before.

A newly dedicated space. A memorial to a student lost in the tragic events that unfolded near the campus grounds. The science faculty argued that the new pavilion's sign needed to refer to those events as a climate disaster, but the college's authorities balked at what one state official called "a controversial opinion."

After all, we can't just go around calling things what they are.

I attended the dedication ceremony, as did Erik and Isis. Halia declined the invitation, noting philosophical differences with the pavilion's designation. "They're telling the wrong story," she said, "and if I'm there, I'll just say it to someone's face. Probably get the whole library impounded. They're just itching to do that, you know."

I couldn't argue otherwise.

I also turned down the invitation to say a few words during the ceremony, a decision that drew objections from Isis.

"I would do it. If they asked me, I mean. Notice I didn't get the same offer."

Instead, Isis had to endure police questioning. On top of that, the college insisted that she consider taking a short sabbatical from classes.

"What if I don't?" she asked her advisor.

"Let's just say," the advisor said, "that we prefer it to be your decision."

"But I'm the fucking victim here!"

"The evidence doesn't bear that out—at least not conclusively. Perhaps you could clarify a lingering question: did you go into the woods voluntarily?"

"I—" Isis broke off and looked toward my place at the conference table. I appeared as a character witness, though I warned her ahead of time that I might not make much of a difference, not when I faced scrutiny of my own. The decision about Isis's future rested with three middle-aged men, and their eyes flickered in my direction.

She didn't need me, though. I silently gestured for her to continue. The only voice Isis needed was her own. But even I didn't know how she would answer the question.

"No. And yes."

All the gray, bushy eyebrows seated at the table lifted in unison.

Everyone waited for someone to fill the ensuing silence.

Finally, the man with the bushiest eyebrows of all said, "Were you under the influence of a cult?"

"A cult?" Isis couldn't help it. She laughed. "Wow."

This didn't stop the line of questioning. "And was Professor Dash the leader of said cult?"

"Maybe you're confusing cult with *occult*," said Isis.

But her quip only succeeded in fueling their speculation. The conversation turned toward the dubious nature of Professor Dash's curriculum, with its emphasis on Ouija Boards, Tarot cards, and other evidence of "devil worship." The man with the bushiest eyebrows noted student surveys that suggested a messianic streak on the part of the professor, one that would explain his unusual gift for drawing students into his sphere of influence. Such talk dominated the rest of the meeting, which ended with the recommendation that Isis consider counseling from a licensed therapist before returning to classes.

"That was a waste of time," Isis said to me as we left the building together. "They just want a narrative that will fit into their official records. Because I wouldn't give it to them, I need therapy. Which, you notice, they didn't offer to pay for."

I shrugged. "It may have worked out to your benefit, though. And frankly, I did want to hear a more detailed answer to that question."

She stopped and bore into me with dark eyes that looked so different from what I saw out there in the ruins. Her hair also bore a fresh streak of gray that stood out under the sun. No doubt the experience marked her in other ways. Ways invisible to the eye.

"Don't tell me you're taking their side?" she said.

"No, but—"

"Because I'm coming back. And when I do, I know exactly what we're going to do with the haunt. I know what story we're going to tell."

"What story is that?"

Outside, the sun felt like a relief from the room's cold air. Instead of answering, Isis crossed the walkway and approached the edge the lake. There, she stood gazing off toward the opposite shore. Perhaps she stood in the same spot when, exposed to the furies of a wild storm, she tossed a tiny carcass beneath the waves. Now, sunlight dapped the water's surface.

I sidled next to her, squinting as I gazed in the same direction. The sun and the distance made it hard to see much. Soon, bulldozers would begin clearing the land for a housing development, removing one of the few wild areas left in our vicinity. Who knew what they might unearth in the process?

Isis broke the silence, but she still didn't answer my question.

"Did you feed me paper? Like, stick it down my gullet?"

Her tone threw me off, and I wondered how I would explain myself until I saw the smile on her face.

"It's okay," she said. "I understand why you did what you did. I mean, never mind the fact that I could've choked to death. I forgive you anyway. But I know things now. I witnessed them. Things that happened a long time ago. I was there when they happened."

I wondered if that included things about me. She hosted a presence that sounded like my mother, but I go back and forth on that now. So many things about the woman who gave birth to me remained a mystery, and maybe they needed to stay that way. Maybe I needed to accept that.

Isis returned her attention to the lake. It appeared so normal now, so full of life.

"There's a spirit that lives here," she said. "When I come back, that's the story we're going to tell. You and me."

Epilogue

The haunt surpasses anything I could have imagined. And yes, it feels larger on the inside. It takes only a few sheets of painted plywood bolted to the supports of the new pavilion to create that illusion of passageways that wind endlessly. What looks so basic and simple in bright daylight transforms at night with the help of black lighting and glowing effects.

"I want to see how you brought it all together," I'd told Isis when she led a new crew of students in putting together a new haunt. After a year's hiatus, anticipation grew about what theme the students would choose and what roles they would play.

"Don't worry, Professor," Isis said, "you'll get to be the first. You'll be our dry run. If you dare go through it alone, that is. Haha."

They did a good job of keeping it under wraps. When Fowler insisted on me telling him what they planned, I honestly could provide no information. "You're a lousy spy," he said. "You're supposed to be my eyes and ears with those hooligans. What exactly are we paying you to do around here, anyway?"

I tapped the nameplate on the office door. It didn't say "Professor" by my name—not yet, anyway.

"To teach," I answered, "which I'll be doing with my own eyes and ears, thank you very much."

And which I now use as I walk into the haunt for the first time. As promised, I go into it alone, a test run of sorts. After making sure the lights and power work, the makeup is applied perfectly, the students have moved to their stations. Blindfolded so I can see none of the preparation, I can still sense them lying in wait, their mounting anticipation as they wait for me to enter and, as I round each corner, trigger the start of a new act.

I think about Professor Dash doing the same thing and getting lost inside, eventually coming out into a world that seemed wholly unfamiliar to him. He went inside a haunted house and never really came out. Instead, he learned that the whole world was haunted.

Blindfold removed, I step into the foyer, already aware of that fact.

The entryway does its job. It distorts my senses with faux spider webs and pulsing strobe lights. But I don't slow down, allowing my vision to adjust as I press forward, and soon, I find myself peering into a place called the Bloody Bucket. Music fills my ears, and wispy smoke curls in the air. I smell burning tobacco, its source a hand-rolled cigarette that dangles from the mouth of a man singing the blues. He taps his toes as he plays, and I find myself swaying with the music, the floor vibrating with the strings of his guitar.

I cannot see his face clearly, an effect of the ubiquitous strobe light. I can no longer see its source. Fog from dry ice spreads across the room, making the floor itself invisible. The music intoxicates me, makes me want to remain there and listen, but I know I'm supposed to move forward. The unspoken rule of a haunt: you don't stop, no matter how much you might want to.

But as I move, I lose sight of the walls themselves. I extend my hands, afraid of bumping into an obstacle. Instead, my hands encounter the flesh of others. I brush past their bodies as they sway and move along with the music. I want to pause and tell them what an extraordinary effect they've achieved, but I need to find my way forward, a task that the dancers make all but impossible.

Then a hand clasps mine. I cannot see who it belongs to. "This way," says the voice of a woman. I have no choice but to let her lead me out. Maybe I've failed somehow, turned the wrong way.

"I'm sorry," I say, but receive no reply.

Instead, she says, "You'll need to duck here."

I start to protest. Shouldn't the experience of a haunt come with the surprise of discovery and not someone telling how to react? I bend at the waist.

"Lower," she hisses.

I move into a crouching position, but that isn't enough for my guide, so soon, I find myself crawling on all fours. Something sticks to my fingers. Tiny legs crawl across the back of my hand. The music fades, and strobe lights diminish, rendering everything black as night. But I hear faint voices.

"Stay quiet," the woman whispers. "Keep moving, but don't let them know you're here."

On hands and knees, I crawl across a gritty floor, nothing like the concrete I expected. I hear a new voice now, intoning what sounds like scripture. As I crawl, the words grow in volume, and I can plainly hear a call to violence masqueraded as a sermon.

A wood splinter pierces the palm of my hand. I cannot suppress a sound of surprise and pain.

The woman leading me demands that I hush my mouth, and I seal my lips.

"Too late," she says. "They heard you. Hurry."

I crawl faster, ignoring the lingering pain caused by the splinter. Around us, I hear the angry voices of unseen men declaring they have an intruder in their midst.

"Tear the room apart," says the preacher, "and get a rope ready. We'll find the spy."

Not even a strobe of light to show the way. Just pitch black all around.

But I can hear the voices of the mob around me. They're tearing down the walls of the haunt, shouting orders to one another as their thirst for violence intensifies.

Spurred by genuine panic, I crawl faster, wanting more than anything to find the way outside and never go inside this thing again. Tear down its walls and disavow it forever.

"Where are you?" I whisper to the woman who led me this far.

No answer.

I reach out a hand, blindly groping in the darkness, touching nothing.

"There she is."

The words come from behind me, and I see no other option than to stand up and run. No time to choose a direction. I run harder than I have in ages.

The ground beneath my feet grows uneven, and I nearly stumble several times, but I don't stop running, not until the voices recede behind me. Only then do I slow down and eventually stop to gather my breath.

"This way."

I recognize this voice, the Creole warm and assuring.

"I can't see you," I say, once more fumbling in the darkness, my arms outstretched.

"You don't need your eyes," she says. "Use those other senses I gave you. Smell the air."

I hear her take a deep intake of breath, and I do the same. I detect notes of salty air and something sweet.

"Follow it," says my mother. "Follow it home the same way I tried to do when I became homesick. I just couldn't swim far enough."

And I do, led by the smell of ripe fruit. It permeates the air. As I do, a light appears ahead, dim and yellow, what looks like the beam of a dying flashlight signaling the direction I need to take. I wonder if I might find Erik there with his improvised headlamp.

Instead, I find a blacktop smeared with blood and oil. A figure crouches before it. Even from behind, I recognize him.

My father.

He doesn't seem aware of me at all. He keeps his flashlight focused on the human remains scattered across the road.

I touch his shoulder, and only then does he become aware of me. He looks up with a tear-streaked face.

"I'll clean this up for you, Nat," he says. "It'll all go away. I swear."

I want to cry too, but what good would more tears do? "You can't," I say. "This is my guilt, my burden."

Still, he holds a chunk of flesh in one hand. He stares at it as if wondering what he'll do with it.

I leave him. I have no other choice. The beam of his flashlight finds a face in the carnage. Taryn Hall.

Using her broken limbs, she struggles to pull herself off the road.

After years of trying to avoid her, I approach her and offer my hand. She stops struggling her way across the asphalt and accepts.

"Where do you want to go?" I ask after finding I can lift her with little effort.

Her broken jaw won't allow her to speak, but she can point with her wrist, and I understand what she wants. A place away from the road where she can rest with dignity. As I carry her, my father continues to speak under his breath: "I can put her back together."

"You can't," I say, thinking he won't listen, or maybe he can't hear me. But we arrive where Taryn wants me to stop, a place under a mango tree. When I look back toward the road, I no longer see my father. Maybe he did hear me—or maybe that part of the haunt has concluded.

I decide to sit beside her and wait to see what comes next—a violation of the rules, I know. In a haunt, the experience ends when the visitor stops moving and no longer feels afraid.

I test that theory now. Sitting beside Taryn, I peel the skin from a mango and feed pieces of it to her. Her horrific injuries make it a challenge, but she seems to savor each piece. I lose track of time. I may even doze.

Until I feel something poking me. I think Taryn wants more mango, but when I open my eyes, I find her gone. Instead, I find Milton the goat, whole and alive, butting me gently with his misshapen horn.

Time to move on, he seems to say, but I want to touch him first. He tolerates the contact, even leans into it, and I feel the contours of the skull around his horns, his rough coat.

Then he turns abruptly. He leads me away from the tree and into the deepest pool of darkness of all. I lose sight of him, finally, and only the gentle sound of the bell around his neck guides me now. All around me, I hear other inhabitants in that darkness. I recognize some of the voices, like Mr. Dennings, who calls out my name. *"Don't you want to join your mother, little Nat? I'll help you do some picking."*

And I hear a voice that sounds like Dorian, the one-eyed boy, vowing that when he finds me, he'll cut my throat next. *"Bring me that animal,"* he hisses, *"so I can condemn you both to hell."*

But these threats don't stop our progress. The gentle tinkling of the bell continues to show me the way, even as the darkness grows even thicker.

Until finally, a small light appears ahead. The bell gives way to recorded sounds of wind and howling ghosts that grow louder as I move closer to the light. "We're almost there," I say to Milton, but I can no longer hear the bell and must find my own way. The light grows brighter and brighter until it hurts my eyes. I use my arm to shield them, but I don't stop, and the haunted sounds grow louder, now the clanking of chains. My eyes burn. They water. I would open them but not with everything so bright and hot. I know I have stepped outside thanks to the smooth concrete. Still, I manage to stumble, but someone catches me.

"Turn that shit down!" shouts the person who kept me from falling. I feel myself enclosed in a hug. "She's out!"

I can open my eyes now, but I don't want to. Instead, I want to remain in this warmth forever.

"Holy shit, are you crying? Was it that scary, Professor?"

I am crying, it turns out, but I'm laughing too.

Finally, my eyelids open, and for a moment, it looks like Lenny Engel supporting my weight. No, I see Isis, her face caked with ghoulish makeup. Seeing her like that makes me laugh even more, and pretty soon, all of us are laughing madly, me, her, and the cadre of students appearing from behind the plywood walls of the haunt—they want to see what all the ruckus is about.

"Seriously," Isis says between gasps of laughter, "was it really that scary? Was it that good?"

"Oh, yeah," I say before laughing again. "It really was."

Author's Note

When I started writing *The Bloody Bucket* in 2023, I did not foresee the kind of political upheaval that would pave the way for something as horrific and ugly as concentration camps in the Florida Everglades, specifically the so-called "Alligator Alcatraz." My description of the prison in these pages and the gigantic alligator guarding its borders was intended as fantasy. The fact that it coincided with a real-life travesty was coincidental and unfortunate. In no way was it intended to mirror real life.

Speaking of real-life travesties, the history of lynching in Florida is real, profound, and still painful to many people. Nevertheless, as I write these words, Florida is experiencing a political climate which favors erasing history. I hope that my words do not add pain to the surviving descendants of these victims but instead signal a need to acknowledge that pain and the importance of historical memory. It's no accident that one of the most important characters in this book is a librarian. Libraries are under attack everywhere, it seems, while librarians increasingly find themselves at pains to preserve truth, culture, and history. I hope that librarians find their ongoing heroism celebrated in Halia, a character who previously appeared in my novel, *The Beasts of Vissaria County*.

The history of Florida is multi-faceted and made of up of diverse peoples and cultures. I hope that this book honors and celebrates this rich diversity. It is still primarily a work of supernatural fantasy, so I made up a good deal of what you have here, hopefully without making anyone's history feel distorted or excluded. If I failed in any way, I regret it deeply.

I am indebted to the love and support of my wife, Jerlin Ford, without whom none of my work would be possible. I'm also grateful for the support of my parents, Herb and Sally. Thank you also to my peers in the Florida

Chapter of the Horror Writers Association. You are truly the best people. Thank you to my fellow writers who read this novel in its infancy: Lee Murray, Jennifer McMahon, Elaine Pascale, Derik Cavignano, Robbie Dorman, Rebecca Culbert, Clay McLeod Chapman, and Mark Matthews. Thank you for your encouragement!

This book also would not be the same without Lisa Lee Tone, who brought her copy-editing skills to my work once more, and Jeff Darwin, who created the stunning cover art. Thank to you both!

And thank you, finally, to you, whoever you are, for reading this novel. I hope you enjoyed it and consider reviewing it. Please keep supporting indie horror presses like this one!

About the Author

Douglas Ford's short fiction has appeared in a variety of anthologies, magazines, and podcasts, including three collections, most recently, *Let's Cut Up Dad! and Other Stories of Transgressive Madness.* His longer works include *The Beasts of Vissaria County, Little Lugosi (A Love Story), The Trick,* and *Who Dies First.* He lives on the west coast of Florida.

You can connect with me on:

https://douglasfordwrites.com

https://www.facebook.com/profile.php?id=100064149938106